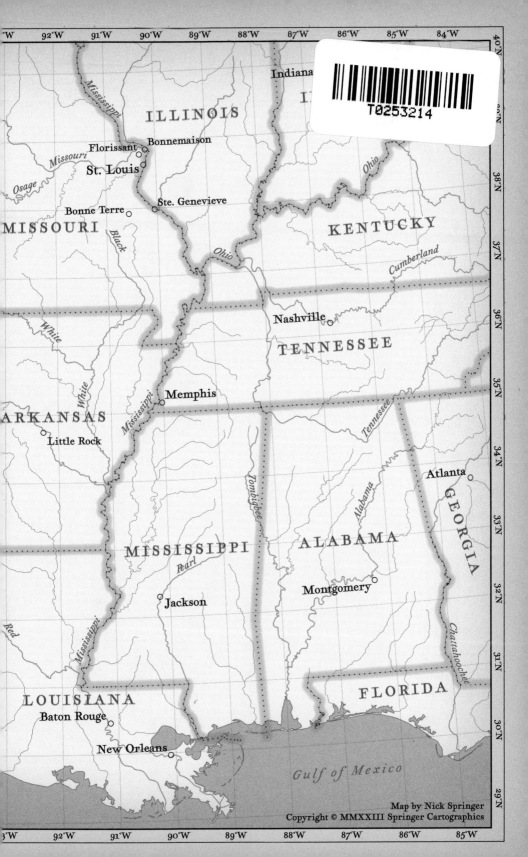

CHENNEVILLE

CHENNEVILLE

A Novel of Murder, Loss, and Vengeance

PAULETTE JILES

wm

WILLIAM MORROW
An Imprint of HarperCollinsPublishers

CHENNEVILLE. Copyright © 2023 by Paulette Jiles. All rights reserved. Printed in the United States of America. No part of this book may be used or reproduced in any manner whatsoever without written permission except in the case of brief quotations embodied in critical articles and reviews. For information, address HarperCollins Publishers, 195 Broadway, New York, NY 10007.

HarperCollins books may be purchased for educational, business, or sales promotional use. For information, please email the Special Markets Department at SPsales@harpercollins.com.

FIRST EDITION

Designed by Bonni Leon-Berman
Map by Nick Springer, copyright © 2023 Springer Cartographics LLC.

Library of Congress Cataloging-in-Publication Data has been applied for.

ISBN 978-0-06-325268-4

23 24 25 26 27 LBC 5 4 3 2 1

For Jimjr and Nadine, Faith, and Jimmy (J-III) with love

CHENNEVILLE

PART ONE

CHAPTER ONE

Late September 1865 / City Point, Virginia

DING DING DING.

He found himself lying under white sheets with very little idea of
how he had gotten there. It was the morning he woke up. A piercing,
repetitive noise broke like thin glass over his consciousness. It was the
sound of a dinner bell. He heard rolling carts, the jingle of dishes rattling against one another. His head felt tight, and he didn't know why.

He seemed to have been there for some time.

People nearby were talking. Everything was painted white: the
walls, the center posts, a wooden roof overhead. A hot breeze moved
down the aisle between rows of beds.

He looked down and saw that his coverings were neat and unblood-
ied. His hands were laid on top of the sheets as if carefully placed there
one by one. The bed was too short for him. They always were. On all
the beds were men; most of them were bandaged, some had crutches.
The low murmur of conversation went on and on. He saw that he did
not have his clothes on, but instead a sort of nightgown. He could smell
vinegar and boric acid.

A young man came walking down the aisle and stopped by the foot
of his cot. The boy's hair was as spiky as a porcupine's, and he paused
with a deep lean forward to look closely into the tall man's face. Canvas
curtains at the far end lifted and fell with the breeze.

He slowly pieced together the fragments of his present situation. He
was in a field hospital somewhere. He was still in possession of both
arms, both legs, a pair of feet, and a pair of hands. He could see out
of both eyes. His head felt as if it were encased in a bucket. He quietly

regarded the young man standing at the foot of his bed. He wondered if he were some relation to him.

After a moment he said, "Who are you?"

A pause of astonished silence and then, "Oh God, you're talking." Tears came to the boy's eyes, and the tip of his nose became bright red. He said, "I am a nurse." He came to stand at the bedside as if he could not believe his eyes. He put one hand on the tall man's shoulder. "Wait, I am going to call the doctor."

"Very well. I won't go anywhere." He drew up one leg. He couldn't understand why the nurse had tears in his eyes. He saw that the men on the beds were eating their dinner, reaching for more from the cart.

The boy hurried away. Shortly he came back with a man whose thick dark beard straggled over his collar and the lapels of a soiled corduroy coat. Both hands hung from the man's cuffs like lead weights. His nails were thick with dried blood. He had something in his fingers. A feather.

"Well, well," he said. "This is a pleasant surprise." Then he paused and looked carefully into the wounded man's light-colored eyes. He came to sit on the bed and the nurse hovered behind while the man on the bed watched carefully to see what this man with the feather was going to do.

"I'm Dr. Jameson, and I want you to look at this." The man in the corduroy coat held up a quill pen. "Watch it," he said. "Do you understand me?"

"Yes." He moved his head from one side to the other as if stretching against a collar that was too tight. The bucket on his head made scraping noises. It hurt. The doctor took hold of his chin and jaw and then let go.

"Don't move your head, just your eyes."

"All right." His eyes tracked the quill as it moved up and down and then sideways.

"Good!" the doctor said in a bright tone. "Excellent!" Then the doctor reached out carefully and put his hand over the tall man's left eye. "Now do the same."

And so he did, first one eye and then the other, watching the feather dip and wave.

He heard a pleased murmur from the nurse, and the doctor said, "Very good. Now, do you know where you are?"

"No."

"What was the last place you remember?"

"The last place I remember." He repeated this in an undertone and then turned his head with great care to look down the long center aisle; he saw men sitting up in bed to spoon food into their mouths, speaking to one another in low tones, three others who had ranged themselves around a companion's bed to play cards, men with bandages, men who slept deeply or perhaps were on the last slide down to death. One patient nudged another and nodded toward the little group at the wounded man's bed.

He reached up to touch his head bandage, but the doctor gently pressed his hand down.

A bright morning came back to him where water-light reflected from a nearby river or canal in some city and in all that reflected light he and another person were loading saddles onto a wagon. He didn't know where that was. Then a dark night in which he flew into the night sky under a great balloon and saw a fire burning in the distance. A town under his feet, far below. But maybe he shouldn't mention this.

"I'm not sure," he said. "I remember loading saddles, but I don't know where that was."

The doctor nodded as if this were to be expected. He asked, "What is your name?"

He was caught in a frozen moment of mortification and not a little fear. *Jesus God, what if I don't know my own name? I have to know my own name.* Then the word *lieutenant* came to him.

"I am a first lieutenant," he said. "Company C, Eightieth New York Infantry."

The nurse said, "Doctor, he has just now come to himself."

"Very well, Lem, we'll wait a little." The doctor let out a long breath. "Luckily Sergeant Chaney came and identified him."

The man on the bed processed this word by word. "Identified me," he repeated in a low voice. After a moment he asked, "Do I have any other wounds?" His face was a drawn architecture of cheekbones and eyes deep in his head, his skin the color of biscuit dough.

The doctor patted his forearm. "No. An older bullet wound, well healed, is all. But you know about that."

Do I? He didn't. But the doctor was talking.

"What you have here is a diastetic linear skull fracture. A fracture that passes through parietal lines. We had to stitch a V-shaped flap of your scalp back on, but it has all knitted well and you are on your way to health, I assure you."

"Good." His hand went up to the bandage and once again the doctor gently pressed it down.

"Do you know what happened?"

"I expect you should probably tell me."

He listened with a grave, intent expression as the doctor described the explosion, the great number of wounded, the dead. Five thousand pounds of gunpowder in that barge, and the rebels had hit it with hot shot. That was his entire life, those things sailing into the air. Knives and forks, blankets in streaming rags, personal diaries blasted to confetti, stables, cavalry tack and gear. Also a telegraph clearinghouse and all the telegraphy supplies—combination instruments, many miles of wire, five hundred cups of battery, all the new Clark relays blown to fragments. Men at the center of the explosion were atomized and remain forever unaccounted for. Farther from the center were those who were grievously wounded, those who died within days and those like him who lost all identity, lost their clothes, were struck by enormous boat chains and door hinges, by tools, by broken china, in an instantaneous event where anything and everything became a deadly missile.

"What did I get hit with?"

"A piece of anchor chain. It was a glancing blow, luckily."

"How did they know?"

"The piece of chain was embedded in a tree along with your cap."

"I see." A moment's reflection; then he thought about his clothes. He said, "I must have bled all over everything." He wanted to get dressed as soon as possible, but if his clothes were all stained and bloody he needed to find different ones.

"You absolutely cannot get up for another two days." The doctor rose. "Absolutely."

He lay awake all the long night as candles or lanterns passed up and down the aisle, doctors and male nurses attending to some crisis. He lay awake, and after a while he felt a great surging of happiness because it was very good to be awake and alive. To look around and see things and to know what it was he was seeing. And then it came to him that his name was Jean-Louis Chenneville. It was as if something had fallen into its proper slot with a click. *Dit* John for *les Américains*.

In the days to come, he understood that he was in the great field hospital Grant had set up just outside of City Point, Virginia, on the James River. A model of its kind. They brought him some clothes. They were stacked neatly beside his bed.

John looked at them. He realized the nurse, Lemuel, and the doctor and who knows who else had cared for him and fed him and done all that was necessary all that time of semi-coma. It was a sobering thought. Gratitude was part of that thought.

As soon as the doctor said he might get up he slowly fought his way into the clothes. He was not sure if they were his or not, and they were too loose, but they were the right length and he was hard to fit. He pulled on the uniform trousers and blouse. It took some time to do this. They were his, then, cleaned, but still with some blood specks here and there. His body was very white and thin, his hands soft, unused, and apparently his own clothes were too big for him. He found this deeply disturbing. In three years of fighting, it had been burned forever into his mind that if you were not strong and unceasingly alert you would not live. He could not shake this. Nor would he ever.

The young male nurse brought him a large pair of brogans, which fitted well enough. John braced himself on two canes and went out slowly into the hospital grounds to see the trees throwing their yellow leaves and to feel the cool nip of the wind. He fought for balance with a grim, fixed expression and managed to make it to the entrance of the hospital grounds and back again.

Last he remembered it was early spring, or late winter of some year. He had arrived, like it or not, back into this world. While he had lain for months, half-conscious and drifting, carefully fed and tended as he floated in some bright pallid neverland, Lee had surrendered, Lincoln had been assassinated, and the great Union Army had gone home. They left behind only the troops of the occupation and the wounded. The war was over.

The 80th New York had gone without him, and he alone of all his company was in this field hospital with an empty past. Speech returned to him but not coherent memory. He recalled a great deal as he lay on his bed, but he could not put things into order. He ate anything and everything they brought to him, determined to fill out his uniform and his civilian clothes again.

One day a sergeant came to him with a sheaf of discharge forms in his hand and tried to fill one out for him: his age, place of birth, height, coloring. The height and coloring were easy enough, but John's frustration was bitter and infuriating when he could not remember the rest. He could not even read it. Finally the sergeant said, "Never mind, sir, it's all right, just fill it out yourself when it comes back to you." He gave John a hearty slap on one shoulder and went on down the aisle from one patient to another, filling out the forms for them.

The doctor came down the aisle with a jaunty walk, greeting patients. "When can I leave?" John asked. "I have my discharge, and it's a long way home." He held it out, blanks and all. He lay outside his blankets in trousers and shirt; they almost fit him now.

"Yes," said Dr. Jameson. He examined the blank spaces. "Where is home?"

"It is, I now distinctly remember, someplace north of St. Louis. When can I start?"

"Soon." The doctor listened to his heart. "When you stand, lift your head; don't let it fall forward. Keep your back straight and your head level."

"Yes, I will."

"Now. Your uncle Basile from New Orleans has been sending me telegrams, letters, very concerned. Basile Chenneville. Do you remember him?"

John made a silent internal effort, called up a face much like his father's. "Yes." He ran his hands down his upper arms, feeling their slackness. He was turning into a boneless pudding. His feet were long and white and without calluses.

"And so I have emphasized to him that you are not to be troubled with anything untoward or negative, but your mind should, as it were, glide down the stream of health and healing undisturbed."

John was suddenly alert. "There is bad news. What is it? I want you to tell me." He sat on the side of the bed with his head bent down while the doctor unwound his head bandages and then unrolled fresh ones. John touched the left side of his head and felt raised scars and bristly hair.

"Indeed, there is not." The doctor was firm. He rebandaged John's head. "Now, we gathered together what of your possessions survived the explosion. Your camp box and baggage suffered water damage as well as fire, but there's a few things inside. They made you a new camp box and put into it all the, well, remnants." He tucked in the ends of the new bandages. "Are you Creole? Do you speak French?"

"Not New Orleans Creole, St. Louis," John said and paused. "St. Louis was all French, once. I'm from one of those old families. Yes, I speak French."

"Do you recall that language?"

"I do," said John, and despite this confident statement he had to sort through his head as if it were stocked with shelves and he could not find the right one. "Read something of my uncle's letter. Anything."

"Yes, well, I copied something here, mmm, luckily I read French fairly well . . ." The doctor took out a slip of paper and read, *"Bien entendu . . .* mmm *. . . ne le derange pas nullment mon neveu . . ."* Then looked up at his patient with the glaring head wound, tall and broad in the shoulders and slightly unbalanced.

"Ah oue." It seemed to supply to John a sort of spring, tripping him over into French. *"Nous sommes parents de mom pere."*

"If you'll forgive me for saying so, you don't *look* French."

"You're forgiven."

Dr. Jameson nodded with a pleasant smile. He was thinking of the report he would make on this interesting skull fracture, this surprising recovery from a semi-coma. Complete recall of two languages, speech unimpaired, balance improving daily, no outbursts of temper, etc. He would include in this report his gratitude to head volunteer nurse Mrs. Stillwell for her organization of those with nursing skills and so on. Then he went on his rounds, leaving John with the conundrum that if there was bad news, he was not to hear it.

John got dressed again in a series of careful, thought-out movements, but he did better this time. The young male attendant hovered at his back, making little anxious helping gestures in the air.

"Leave me alone," John said. He took up his two canes and kept his spine straight and his head level. He went outside thinking this over, this business of not being *dérangé*, not being upset by bad news. He concentrated on walking from one side of the hospital grounds to the other. Great chestnut trees scattered their leaves upon his wounded head; colors of citron and lemon and amber.

His other injury had never bothered him. It was a clean small-caliber hole. And then the memory came back to him; they had fished the ball out with tongs. When he tried to place the incident he remembered absolute chaos; all their artillery and provisions wagons jammed up in a muddy road and lines of march falling apart, and a Rebel sharpshooter somewhere in the woods to the left. He had been knocked down by the bullet's impact. It was a place called Todd's Tavern. That must have been before the barge blew up.

And before the barge blew up, he had gone up in a balloon somewhere. This troubled him. He wanted it to be real. Also it made him apprehensive that he might be subject to imaginings or false memories.

He asked for his possessions, and they got them out of a great tent stacked full of abandoned gear. They brought him the whole lot: a newly made camp box, greatcoat, knapsack, rifle, revolver, pommel holster, and civilian clothes. On top of his box, he saw his tall riding boots. They had both been slashed wide open from top to instep. They must have done that when they brought him in. The boots were hard to get off, and they had many wounded and little time. He knew he must have gone to some trouble and expense to have them made, but he couldn't bring the circumstances to mind and briefly regretted the ruin of a good pair of riding boots. He threw them in the trash barrel outside.

Inside the camp box he found a hard and shriveled leather folder. It was blackened on the edges from a burning, and inside were fragments and sometimes whole pages of letters.

It took a few moments for him to make sense of handwriting; handwriting itself. He finally understood that the black letters were all on one plane. On a flat surface. They came up out of a kind of obscure matrix and took form.

Finally there it was. *First Lt. Chenneville to board the* Intrepid *for limited tethered flight over Yorktown there to observe and report . . .* His relief was enormous. He sat on his cot in his drawers, holding the scorched paper in both hands. He was suspended in thought for a long time. Such pleasing fires. The swaying great hot-air sack named the *Intrepid* lifting into the dark sky on an order of physical properties heretofore unknown. All Yorktown below him and something alight on the docks.

And there too was the small portrait of his sister Lalie. It was in a folding case, framed in gilt, a daguerreotype. Daguerreotypes were going out of fashion, but the newer ambrotypes had none of their mystery nor their beauty. They were washed in a gold solution, which gave them depth and fine detail and their sitters a haunting immortality. He looked at it, searching out her voice and manner, hidden in the blacks and golds. Then he put it back in its moleskin bag. He couldn't concentrate on handwriting for more than a short space of time and closed the box. After that he slept again, for the entire day and the night afterward.

The next morning he lifted a straight razor to his jaw, and his hand shook so that the blade glittered. He tried anyway, but he cut himself, and so laid the razor down. He took up his two canes and went in search of a barber. The young male nurse finished filling pitchers of water on John's row and then hurried after him.

John sat in a chair out in the sun while an orderly shaved him and then clipped his hair down soldier-short, on doctor's orders. The clippers ran like teeth over the long scar. John shut his hands together with a tense precision as if pain were a mathematical problem, as if he had just solved it and the solution did not include making a noise if he could help it. Sweat ran down his face.

The male attendant stood at John's shoulder and watched with interest. He unfolded a shawl and tucked it around John's shoulders. It was cream-colored and in several different decorative weaves. John had no idea where it had come from. The orderly insisted on rebandaging his head, looping clean strips of linen around his skull.

The young attendant waved a hand. "Don't you worry, sir. I've had plenty of head injuries. Men hauled in here with their brains hanging out, and before you know it, they're playing the piano and reading Deuteronomy without missing a word."

"What about dancing?"

"Schottisches only. Regulations. No jigs, no high kicks."

John gave him a brief smile and remembered that the young man's name was Lemuel. He was very thin and had thick, mud-colored hair. John slowly took the mirror that the barber handed him and looked at his own face for the first time in a long time.

It was himself; eyes hollowed and deep and the light irises glittering out of two caves of shadow. His upper lip thickened and broad like a boxer's that had been hit too many times. His skin was devoid of color, and the band of his shirt collar was too large. He handed the mirror back. He was doing much better. He knew his own name now and remembered things. When they brought him in, the stretcher men didn't know who he was. He didn't know who he was either, but now he possessed, like treasures, his own name and the place where he was from.

"It will all come back," said the barber and nodded in an encouraging way.

"I intend for it to come back," John said. He lay back against the shawl, frail, transparent. "Where did this shawl come from?"

"Your uncle sent it," said Lemuel. "Sent all manner of things. Saved them for you. Wasn't easy."

"Why wasn't it easy?"

"People make off with things around this place, especially now, since about everybody's gone home. Except the bad cases like you." Then the young man caught himself and gave John a hearty slap on the shoulder. "But you ain't a bad case no more! Hey?" He poured a handful of nuts into John's palm. They were pecans and smelled of cinnamon and brown sugar. "Here, you need to eat more."

The next week, on one of his lurching walks about the grounds, John came across the boy just outside the main staff office tent. The tent was an enormous thing of billowing white canvas. Young Lemuel was being thrown about like a jointed doll by a huge corporal. There was a lot of shouting going on.

John was down to one cane now; he stalked up to the struggling figures and grabbed the young attendant by the shirt collar. He jammed his cane into the corporal's chest to shove him back. He was far taller than either of them.

"What the hell is going on here?" he said. "I can't stand yelling. Stop yelling."

"Sir!" the corporal said and came to attention. "This ratbag was caught with a box of pralines from the volunteer tent!"

Lemuel hung like a piece of washing from John's big hand as his shirt collar slowly tore loose from its band. "Well, what of it?" said John. "Let him have the Goddamned pralines, would you? Anything for some peace and quiet. We are all sick and wounded around here, in case you hadn't noticed."

The corporal bit his lip and gave one short nod. He stared hard and cold at the boy. "Keep it up," the corporal said in a low voice. "And see what happens."

John let go of the young man's collar and said, "If I were you, ratbag, I would stay out of sight for a while."

Lemuel scrambled away into the grounds, disappearing behind a patient tent as if he had evaporated.

In the ensuing days, John sat in a chair in the chill sunshine and thought through everything: his name, his rank, his family and their names. Where they all were or were not. He was not married, he was sure of that. His father was dead of a heart condition, and after that it seemed his sister had married and his mother had gone to live with the New Orleans Chennevilles for some reason. Or was she dead too? Maybe she had died and he had lost the memory.

This stopped him. It was an alarming thought. Then a young woman's face came to him, and in this recalled image she was lit by sunlight from a tall window, but he could not remember her name, only a wrenching loss that he could not put words to, and so he got to his feet and began walking again as if he could leave that loss in the chair behind him, a tall man like a dark shadow walking until evening, relentlessly moving from shadow to shadow until somebody said, "Sir, sir, it's suppertime, you should rest now."

Then came a letter from his uncle Basile Chenneville.

He spent an hour at it. It said that he, Basile, could not leave family and business in New Orleans to come to Virginia for him, but if John would hire an attendant to accompany him to St. Louis then Basile would come upriver to meet him at Temps Clair.

A view of a great river sprang up in his head; the plantation called Marais Temps Clair was their home, and it was three miles from the village of Bonnemaison. Bonnemaison itself was fifteen miles north of St. Louis in that blessed land between the rivers where it was always fair weather, where brown floods of water rushed toward those seas that lay at the bottom of the world.

Get to Harpers Ferry, Basile wrote, *and then take the Baltimore and Ohio passenger cars to Wheeling, then an Ohio River steamboat to St. Louis. Temps Clair, it is yours now—the place needs you. Have been communicating with your doctors weekly. Are you in want of funds? Tu*

a besoin de piastre? I will send all you need, dear Jean, cher neveu—how
many nights we have prayed for your very life. Your mother, I fear, is not
well; we hope for a full recovery, but she sends loving regards.

His alive and living mother sent loving regards. He dropped his
head back and watched the unmoving blue skies of Virginia, and relief
overtook him. It was a silky feeling of broad, inclusive happiness that
brought images of the rolling great Missouri River and, for some reason, three big horses named The Corbeau and Sheba and Blackjack.
He sat there in the sunlight until it faded.

John was to stay at the Robidoux House when he arrived in St.
Louis. His uncle Basile Chenneville had more money than God, but
he chose to stay in a place where he could speak French instead of at,
say, the fashionable Planter House, where he would have to deal with
English-speaking waiters, or worse, the Irish, and even worse than
that, American food. Vegetables boiled for *hours*. Flour gravy on *every-*
thing. In his dialectical French, salted with ancient words that few used
anymore except people like the Robidoux family, Basile could order
services, make demands, dine well, and bargain with far more facility.

So John hired Lemuel for thirty-five dollars a month. They were going to be among crowds, both aboard a steamboat and then in the city
of St. Louis. He needed a person wise in the ways of that semi–criminal
netherworld of riverfronts and city streets. John had never thought of
southerners as city people, but the byways of Richmond were plagued
with gangs, they said, desperate war orphans and a criminal element
one would expect only in big northern cities. Lemuel had apparently
graduated from that hard and starving school. However, John was not
interested in hearing his story. He was trying to recover his own.

He still needed the cane, and still his right hand shook when he
lifted the straight razor. He could not write well yet, but it would not be
long, because he wouldn't quit until he could.

One last visit to the doctor; the man's stethoscope lay beside him
unused, since by now he knew John's heart and lungs were in top condition, no problem there. Lemuel stood demurely behind John with
John's coat over his arm.

"You'll sign my release, then," John said.

"Of course. Remarkable recovery." The doctor signed the form. "You are a determined man. Now, are you sure about this journey?"

"Yes, my uncle has carefully written out instructions for every step of the way. He's afraid I can't tell a steamboat from a shithouse, but I appreciate his concern."

CHAPTER TWO

September 1865 / Wheeling, West Virginia, to St. Louis, Missouri

THEY MADE IT TO HARPERS Ferry in what was now West Virginia by boat up the Potomac. Then they boarded the Baltimore and Ohio passenger cars for Wheeling on the Ohio. The train was crowded with others discharged from the hospital who were also trying to make their way home. The passenger cars were torture; the train tossed from one side to another on shaky rails, and as always, the seat was too small for him, his long legs bent up and braced against the seat ahead. He was banged around like a billiard in a boxcar. He heard himself making short groans. He kept his hat on his knee because it wouldn't fit over the bandage. He distracted himself by staring at the tattoos of a navy man in the seat across the aisle; *Hibernia*, the man's forearm said. Also an anchor, an exploding ship, and *Liberty*.

The Ohio steamboat was better because the only movement was the unhinged, sliding feel of a vessel with a shallow keel as it moved across the water. The middle deck was packed with convalescent soldiers. John fell asleep frequently then to the heartbeat of the paddlewheel, lying on blankets, limp and shucked of earthly cares at least for the present. His long body seemed to gain in weight and ability even while in a deep sleep on the deck of the *St. Landry*. He kept the cane close to hand.

There were no women among the deck passengers. There were women elsewhere, but they didn't venture down here among the prone and wounded ex-soldiers who had bivouac manners and tended not only to strip down to nothing but fart at will. He peeled off his shirt to lie half-naked in the sunlight. He thought the sun might do him good.

They ran into banks of mayflies even though it was late September, masses of them hovering over the Ohio's surface.

He asked to use the purser's cabin, and there he slowly unwound the bandage from his head, wadded up the linen, and jammed it in the trash basket. He felt lighter; more exposed but better. As he walked out into the sunlight, freed at last from bandages, her face came to him again; Sebastienne. He had known her in New Orleans. For half an hour he bent over the rail and watched as the brown heart of the Ohio's current rolled under their prow, but nothing else came to him, only that unlikely name.

He discovered that Lemuel had a gift for field expedience, that is to say, an aptitude for the unofficial acquisition of any number of things. In short, an accomplished and sensible thief. Sensible because he only walked off with things of lesser value and only one thing at a time. John realized the good wool shawl had probably come from the patients' possessions tent, not from Basile, as well as the stiff and disintegrating brogans. Also the young man had stolen the stethoscope during that last doctor's visit. Now Lemuel leaned against the rails listening, with a deep intensity, to his own heart.

"Lem, you're a rogue," said John. He lay on his back and looked up at the hot, late-September sky with a half-filled canteen in his hand. "And a thief." He drank the Ohio River water in long swallows.

Lem pulled the earpieces out of his ears. "Well, sir, I wanted to listen to see if I had a good heart, and it's good." He gave John a bright smile. He had dead mayflies in his bristly hair.

"How would you know?"

"It sounds damned good, sir, just like a steam engine."

"Ah, good, well, don't be insulted, Lem, but I think I will go over every one of my possessions by the time we raise St. Louis, is that clear?"

"Yes, sir," said Lemuel. His expression changed to that of a person telling an absolute although regrettable fact. "It's about the only thing I'm good at, to tell you the truth."

"You're a pretty good nurse. But somebody's going to change your face for you one of these days if you keep lifting things. It'd be less dangerous to just learn a trade."

"Any suggestions, sir?"

"Sorry, no."

After a disappointed silence, Lem said, "You know what, you should travel, Mr. Chenneville. They say travel is good for your health. Like me, I always wanted to go to the Bahaman Islands, or I was thinking Galveston or Newport News." Lemuel got a dreamy look on his face. "Port towns."

John thought about these dubious destinations but said nothing for a moment. Finally he said, "I need to be home."

"Do you have anybody to take care of you when you get home?"

John watched a small green heron with its S-shaped neck skim low over the river surface. He knew there must be a reelfoot lake nearby; green herons did not feed in deep waters. The satiny, emerald-green bird gave out a sinister hoarse roar, oddly un-birdlike, and sailed into the forest on the other side of the river with some distant memory clutched tightly in its folded claws.

He pulled his attention away from the bird. He poured the rest of the water over his head and felt it run into his mouth and down his chest. Why did people keep asking him these questions? At length he fished the information out of some partially destroyed storage place.

He said, "No, I don't. My sister is married, and my mother has moved in with relatives."

When he got back home, would there be anybody who would remember for him? Who would do the work of dredging up events and placing them in order? And at the back of his mind the nagging thought that there was something he was not to be told.

Fermin, it would be Fermin. That's who would help him remember. And then their old house servant's face came to him, lined and somewhat aged, a bad eye and gray-streaked hair. He wondered if Fermin was dead. There was no way to know.

The next day the *St. Landry* churned past a landing on the Kentucky side where wood was stacked for the steamers. Callaway's Landing, the sign said. A man sat on top of a pile of cordwood smoking a pipe. John thought, *Wait, yes, my sister married a Confederate officer on parole, and his name was Callaway. She met him at Easterly's.* He sat on a chair that Lemuel had extracted from a first-class cabin for him; that is, he'd stolen it. John tipped it back against somebody's trunk and put one foot on the rail, watching the sign go by.

It was in a letter, in his camp box, and the recollection came back in a rush. He recalled that during the war his sister had taken employment at Easterly's daguerreotype shop in St. Louis. She was delighted with the fact that she could make her own money, she could buy her own bonnets. He had walked down Walnut to the shop in his Union blues with that clanking, bothersome officer's sword. Yes, he had been given compassionate leave from his unit because his father's heart was giving out. It was summer, but he couldn't remember the year. He came to Easterly's. A bright ringing from the bell over the door as he opened it. Then John remembered the year. It was '63.

He thought, *That's how I missed Gettysburg.*

Lalie, in her new green-and-pink-checkered dress, gave a little scream, kissed him on the cheek, anxious to show her older brother how well she was doing in this marvelous new thing, being *employed.*

He reached out his hand to Easterly, assessed him quickly; a decent man, restrained and calm. She was in good hands.

Lalie then took John by both arms and pressed him into a convoluted chair. She made him sit rigidly just so and hold his head just so. She took hold of his hair and cranked his head into the right position, and they both started laughing. She placed a potted plant to one side, and he and his sister laughed so much that she had to leave the room lest they burst out into hysterical laughter when the camera was opened.

Strange to be laughing when his father was so ill, but it was like an attack of nerves, a safety valve going off. And then somehow, into this remembered scene, William Callaway stepped in as if from offstage.

Callaway wore his gray uniform; it was an infantry officer's uniform. He bowed to Lalie and Easterly and said he would like to have his portrait taken for his mother. He was on parole. He and Callaway faced each other among the gold-framed portraits, one of them in blue and the other in gray. Lalie looked very good in that dress; why should she not be attractive to a penniless Confederate officer on parole, that *foutu berdache*, that raptor.

Then later he had come to the house to be formally introduced. Their house was built with its face toward the Missouri, where it flowed eastward and parallel with the Mississippi for five miles until the Missouri joined it at the Columbia Bottoms. There you could see its sandy waters curling into the Mississippi for miles, in cauliflower shapes, cloud shapes. For a short space, the two massive rivers ran side by side with rich bottom land between them, most of it owned by the Chennevilles.

He put the letter aside. So they had married; it was all right, people got married. Now, like the men around him, he wanted to be home, where he and they would find their hearts' desires, their souls would not be gathered with sinners nor their lives with bloody men. *Bonne chance*, he thought. He himself did not know what was awaiting him because he was not to be *dérangé*. John smoked; he was already *dérangé*, and so?

They arrived at the junction of the Ohio and the Mississippi in a rainstorm; they picked up a Mississippi River pilot and let off the Ohio pilot. They made their way the hundred miles upriver to St. Louis. They nosed into the Poplar Street landing with the *St. Landry*'s stern swept downstream. They came in at evening, and he listened to the noise of this big city. Unstructured recall tumbled into his brain.

A lot of fights here, and he couldn't exactly say what they were about. His high school; the English and Classical High School. It pleased him that he remembered it. Also he remembered elegant women and algebra and an illuminated man wearing tights and stage makeup howling for vengeance.

He said, "There's a good theater here, Lem. It's on Myrtle Street."

"We ain't going there right now, sir." Lemuel lurched down the deck carrying his camp box.

They walked down the levee with its gas lights, the traveling shadows where torches and lanterns were carried through and around and about all the stacked bales of commercial goods and in a stream among all these things swarmed workmen and passengers. Beyond, in the interior streets, were the ancient homes of the early French now overborne by new brick warehouses, hotels, saloons on every corner.

They made it to the Robidoux House at the northeast corner of Main and Elm. It was an old French-style stone house squashed in between a glassware shop and a bakery. The house looked warm and welcoming; the front windows were lit with candles on windowsills two feet thick.

In his small room, John turned out everything onto the bed. A lamplight poured onto his smooth white hands, the perfectly clean nails. It drenched the room and its mirror and basin, the counterpane. It was a place of silence and immobility. A person could think. He was at last away from crowded spaces, incessant voices. This was what he needed. He turned to Lemuel and studied him.

"Nothing's missing, Lem. You're slipping," he said. "I hope you haven't reformed. Not with that kind of talent."

Down the hall, Mrs. Robidoux was yelling for fresh sheets.

Lemuel ducked his shaggy head and lifted his thin shoulders. "You missed checking on that gold locket, sir."

John watched him a moment longer and then searched among the littered belongings and found it; a closed moleskin bag from which he shook out the small daguerreotype of his sister in a gold frame. He turned it over in his fingers and looked at her face.

"You astonish me," he said.

"Well, she is very pretty, sir; I thought she might be your intended."

Lalie's pretty, gamine face was minute and composed. She was suspended in gold and darkness inside the frame. "No, it's my sister. And she's married."

"Ah! Well, lucky man and all that. I, uh . . ."

John smiled at the boy's confusion. He thumbed off a number of bills from the packet he carried in his belt.

"Sir, I am sorry to leave you."

"I'll be all right."

"If you ever need me, well, I don't know what to tell you, as I'm not real clear on where I'm going. I was thinking Galveston, Texas, but I'm not sure where it is exactly."

"Go home?"

"Ain't got one."

"Stay here tonight if you want."

"No, sir, I wanted to go see the theater." Lem gazed at the federal bills with deep affection and then rolled them and tucked them in his waistcoat pocket.

"The world's your oyster, Lem. Take care."

He watched the young man with his porcupine-brown hair walk jauntily toward the river and probably trouble with money in his pocket. Then John retrieved his shaving gear and laid it out on the bedside table. For a moment he stood in front of the mirror. It had been hung over the basin and pitcher, and staring at himself, he tried to assess just how terrible his scar looked.

Tufts of hair stood up around the wound, and his eyes were still deep in shadow. Very well; it would get better as time went by. He soaped his face and noted that when he lifted the straight razor, his hand was steady. Good—this made him feel very good. The river journey had been good for him. The city roared by outside, he heard the distant shrieks of steam whistles from the Poplar Street landing. He shaved slowly, carefully, and without one slip of the razor. Then he slept for a day and a night entire, then rested another day and night to prepare himself for travel to Temps Clair.

He sent one of the Robidoux boys to the Iron Mountain Railroad station to send a telegram to his uncle and then onto the street to chase down a two-horse hack for the journey north to Bonnemaison. He paused over the bill; numbers still bothered him. It infuriated him that he could not make sense of the figures, but there was nothing he could do about it at the moment.

He held out a handful of coins and federal dollars to Mrs. Robidoux.

"M'sieu Chenneville, can you not count it?"

"Not at present."

"Yes, that would be ten dollars, Jean-Louis, and may God bring you good health." She chose two five-dollar bills, and her smile was disquieted and unsure.

He pulled on his big army dreadnaught against the cold and went out on the street in the old brogans. The driver hurried to take his baggage and help him in.

"I can get in by myself," John said. "Leave me alone."

"Yes sir, yes sir, I'll just give you a hand here."

When the door was shut, John collapsed in the corner now that nobody could see him. He stretched out long with his bristly, scarred head pillowed on the shawl. He laid his revolver in its pommel holster and his cane on the seat beside him and then gazed out the window as the St. Louis streets rolled by as if in an illuminated slide show; *You remember this street, you can recall this one, and this too is familiar, but you don't know why.*

They passed Biddle Street and the Kennett Shot Tower standing high against the metallic surface of the water. He was raised near rivers, enormous ones. The imperial Mississippi that came down from the north, and the Missouri, which flooded in from distant, unmapped places, rich with silt. He seemed to fall into place now, looking out the carriage windows. He was born in a big, sleepy house with the slow drone of bees and dogs and the cedars tall as houses, dark and secret. In the spring, the doors of the front entrance were thrown wide, open to the acres of apple blossoms that rained over the entire countryside like cotton scrap. In the distance, the smoking twin stacks of steamboats moved slowly.

They went north on the Bellefontaine Road. Soon they were in the countryside. The Germans and *les Américains* had moved in long ago, and any signs of the earlier French villages and their common lands were few and far between. What remained of them were only the names of towns and roads and the isolated old French families like his own.

The autumn fields were surrounded by rail fences that passing soldiers had not torn down for firewood. The harvests were unburnt, the houses had twelve-paned windows that had not been shattered by rifle fire, cattle ate their way through grassy meadows unclaimed by foraging soldiers. There were no standing lonely chimneys presiding over burnt rubble. They trotted past comfortable brick-and-log farmhouses with roses emptying their clean red petals into the lanes.

They clattered through the little town of Normandy and passed the great Lucas house, where he suddenly remembered dancing. There had been a great many pretty girls, and the furniture had all been pushed back, the gleam of the waxed floor and countless candles, the music. Perhaps they danced there still. They passed through the little village of Bonnemaison, where all was tranquil, apparently. The Sisters of Loretto were busy with their spiritual lives of canning, praying, and sewing. The church of St. Ferdinand rang out four in the afternoon.

Beyond Bonnemaison, the road stretched out those last miles to Marais Temps Clair, where at the end of September the air was saturated with straw-colored elm leaves flying and drifting. Flocks of wild geese were coming down the Missouri River valley in long, noisy arrowheads. The house was ahead. John was suddenly short of breath. His mouth was dry.

They trotted alongside a cast-iron fence. The carriage entered the gate and turned up a graveled circular driveway. The driver pulled up his horses at the steps; it was a two-story house with long verandahs. It was perched on a terrace overlooking the Missouri River floodplain. Seven immense cedars surrounded it. Its gardens were gone to jungle. A donkey drank out of a broken flowerpot. His father's house. He was home at last. Home from the war.

The driver placed his camp box and luggage on the steps. He accepted John's coins and drove away.

He had a sudden fear of entering the house. Of what he might or might not find. Something he was not to be told about. So to gather himself and his emotions he turned, briefly, to look out over the bottoms. That was all their land, down there. Seven hundred acres. Apple orchards now unpruned, the fruit probably left to rot on the ground. The tobacco leaves were yellowing and drooping. They had not been topped. Across the Missouri, between it and the Mississippi, were the Chenneville grazing lands, and the broad, flat acres of hay had been left to tangle into an uncut waste.

He made himself turn back to the house. Up the five broad steps to the double front doors. A wren's nest had been constructed over the doorway. He placed his hand on the door lever, paused, and then pressed down carefully. From a half a mile away he heard the steamboat whistles at the landing. He pushed the door open with his forefinger and stepped in.

The foyer was empty and still. A fly droned and banged its head against a mirror. His father's face beamed down at him from the familiar portrait in the hall; red-cheeked, black-haired, his high white collar stiff as pasteboard. A round, amiable countenance. The artist had pipped a white dot in each dark eye to indicate that they were "sparkling," as artists often did. His mother in her own frame beside him, blonde as a Swede. She had been two inches taller than her husband, but you'd never know it in the way she carried herself. A remote woman, cool as snow, wishing all others around her to be remote and cool as well.

Leaf shadows moved suddenly at the open door behind him, and he realized he had been staring at the portraits for some time. A cold breeze hissed through the cedars.

He turned and went through the foyer, past the stairs, into the kitchen.

Somebody had been cooking. A toasting fork and a tall blue glass jar of hominy were on the table. The kitchen fireplace still glowed with coals. The fashionable new cookstove was unlit, and the stone-flagged floor was littered with ashes. Shelves shone with bottled peaches and meat that looked years old. That was Fermin's obsession with hoarding food. John was almost relieved to see it.

The keeping-room door just off the kitchen stood open. Through it he saw Fermin in the backyard trying to drag the donkey away from the garden palings. It was after the peas. John stood still as relief washed through him in a kind of wave.

"*Eh ben*, Fermin," he called.

The old man dropped the donkey's rope and turned, his mouth open.

"*C'est toue, Jean-Louis!*" He ran toward John, throwing his arms around John's ribs, holding him tight. "*C'est toue!*" John bent and embraced him and found himself nearly speechless. As if he were a child again, this old man his loyal mentor; sarcastic, dry-witted, and loving. Fermin was, as always, very thin, and his bones were like sparrows' bones. Then Fermin collected himself and stood back and shook John's hand for a long time and would not let go, patting his wrist with the other hand. Both good eye and bad eye were full of unshed tears.

"Oh, *mon fi*, you are here!" The old man's voice quavered and broke.

"Yes," said John. His smile was slow, and his hand lay on Fermin's shoulder.

"What we heard!" Fermin said. "Monsieur Basile said you might not live. Then he said you might."

"Which was worse?"

Fermin smiled and stepped back, letting go John's hand. He wiped his eyes, quickly, on his wristbands. "More of your jokes. You've arrived! They brought a telegram and read it to me; it said you were in St. Louis already."

"I got to St. Louis two nights ago. And here I am."

"Yes, well, well, then they said"—and Fermin waved one gnarled hand in the air—"they said you were not to be excited or upset for any reason."

They went to sit in the weak sunshine, at the bench beside the garden gate. The beehives seemed unsteady on their bases, and one had fallen over. Catnip mint dried slowly in a haze of its own scent.

"Then there's something to be upset about," said John. He looked around. "Other than this place seems to be falling apart." He held both hands on his cane, one on top of the other. His palms were sweating. Everything was now so familiar, but then, not quite.

"No, no, not at all! But yes, we need you here, it has been so long— three years! Except when you came home that once. But you're home."

John nodded and felt in his coat pocket for tobacco and rolled a cigarette. *I came home on leave once.* Yes, it was that compassionate leave in '63, when his father died, and he felt relieved to have put two memories together. "Fermin, get me something to drink, would you?" He struck a phosphorus match in an extravagant gesture and lit up.

"It is terrible to get old!" cried Fermin and darted inside to the storage pantry, came back out with a bottle of red wine and drinking glasses. "Forgetting hospitality, I should kick myself. Jean, forgive me."

"You're forgiven." John tapped the thick wineglass against Fermin's and drank. It was spiced and strong, a thick carmine color.

"Do you remember everything?" Fermin searched his face anxiously. "They said you might not have memories, but look, you know me!" He slapped himself on his bony chest. "Do you remember things?"

"From time to time. Stop worrying. I'll do the worrying. I'm good at it." John blew smoke and then drank off his glass. He held it out for more.

"Yes, I know, this place looks like we were attacked by the Shawnees. No men to hire, all gone to the war. And then the blockade, where could we send the harvest? Nowhere. I kept up the stores as best I could, but now it's different! You are home."

"Where is Lalie? She married. I know she married."

A brief silence. "Yes. They left." Fermin seemed to stiffen before his eyes.

"Why can't Lalie and her husband come and help?"

"Because . . ." Fermin's eyes grew large and alarmed as if he were about to say something he should not. "Because you were hit in the head with an explosion! And Basile said that the doctor said you were like a *zonbie*. Or Monsieur Basile said that. That's what they say down there in Louisiana. But you awakened thanks to the good God, with all your mind in one piece."

John sat back and watched Fermin's face. "That doesn't make sense."

"But you have to wait for M'sieu Basile. I am old and a *zonbie* myself, ha ha."

Fermin's hair was grayer than John remembered. His face was more lined and his old homespun shirt and vest more frayed. It looked as if he had not changed clothes in three years. John got up from the bench and walked to the garden palings, looked past it to the great barn for tobacco storage, barns for hay and horses. They were empty and lifeless.

"What is it?" he said. "Something's gone wrong. What are you living on?"

"Ah, Basile has been sending me my pay; he is generous, Jean. It is so good to see your face! Let me look at you."

John stood resolutely while Fermin gazed into his face with a searching look and brushed dust from his coat. "And I am sorry that we have lost the harvest, yes, I cannot command men as you do, Jean-Louis, even if I could find any, and, so, of course you have seen the orchards down there, *un joli gâchis*, but you are to remain calm and quiet so your brains can heal."

Fermin regarded him uneasily as if John were about to burst out in unintelligible speech or fall in place upon the grass.

"I'm all right." John smiled reassuringly, and then the smile went away as if it had only been a mechanical reproduction brought up because one was required. "I'm fine. I wasn't so much before, but I am now."

"For sure?"

"Mais ya."

Fermin was shrewd in his own way; he had switched the conversation from *what is the matter?* to *are you recovered?* John knew there was nothing further to be gotten out of him in the way of information because clearly he had been told to be silent. He said, "Uncle Basile is on his way up from New Orleans, now, at this very moment, dining in first class. Loathing the food."

"Le bon Dieu soit loué," said Fermin in relief and slapped both hands on the worn knees of his trousers.

John took his knapsack and greatcoat in one hand, the cane in the other, and climbed the familiar stairs riser by riser. He looked up; how often had his mother or Lalie bent over the ornate balustrade of the landing above to call down to him? Behind him Fermin paused with John's camp box in both hands, still with an air of incipient alarm. Finally he said, "I am the only one here, M'sieu Jean."

After a moment of silence, John said, "I know."

CHAPTER THREE

October 1865 / Marais Temps Clair, St. Louis County, Missouri

IN THE NEXT FEW DAYS, John hired two girls from Bonnemaison to come and clean, wash clothes, cook something other than peas and hominy, sweep away the accumulated dust and cobwebs. He paced out the limits of the garden and tried to think who in the neighborhood understood bees. The dark brown mare in the upper pasture needed to be ridden. The annoying, importunate donkey followed at his heels everywhere.

He was born and brought up here, this seven hundred acres of bottomland, of which he knew every running stream and snye, every length of woods and the gigantic trees, the last of their kind; the beautiful plow-team horses, the floods and apples, the steamboat wrecks and the long smoky rains of Missouri.

"You are not to work," said Fermin. He stuck out one withered hand in a stopping motion. "I have been instructed."

"I'm not working," said John. He flipped over a page of the ledger that lay before him. He sat at the desk in the library. It was his father's old desk, a heavy walnut table with drawers. "I'm trying to figure out what's gone on for the last three years." He wore his civilian clothes, well fitting now; a pin-striped shirt, his old heavy tweed vest. They had all been packed away against his return.

"Your mother and I did our best," said Fermin. "But you will talk with Monsieur Basile."

John studied him for a moment. "Yes," he said and shut the ledger. "I will."

In his bedroom upstairs he unloaded the camp box. At last, he found the remains of his sister's letter. It was battered and singed from the explosion, in English by and large but occasionally falling into his sister's misspelled dialectical French. He sat on his own bed, on a bright counterpane, with a fire hot in the little bedroom fireplace and the fireplace screen with the running dogs on it forever circling in an endless pursuit. When had he received the letter? Lalie never bothered with dates, or if she did, it was the month and day and she forgot to write in the year. Neither his mother nor his sister could be bothered with the hard data of the world, like dates, times, places.

He tried to remember what he felt when he read it.

It was a puzzle, some pieces missing.

His sister was furious with him, that he should object to her marrying William Callaway, who was an officer and certainly a gentleman, could he not tell when he met him?

The war will soon be over, her letter said. *Then we will forget about all this, and he and I will have the land at Riviere aux Vases. He will sell his property in Kentucky, and Mama will give us the River aux Vases land.* (She had spelled it two different ways.) *I miss Papa every day, every night. O we long for the time when all this upset is over, cette war. I am so tired of angry people, they bore me! Et that Frances creature, pis ça faisait mal pes ça puait.*

And so on. She truly loved her dear brother and hoped this would not cause a rift between them, he would learn to love William Callaway as she did, and then a long paragraph describing Callaway's intelligence, his charm, and his gentlemanly manners, not to speak of his deep interest in the newest theories of agriculture. She closed with prayers for his safety and embraces for her dear brother, *a tué bien sincèrement, zu 'ti soeur Lalie.*

Lalie had appeared when he was, maybe, seven. She was christened Eulalie Martha Madeleine St. Gem Chenneville. Where had she come from? What cosmic stream of life? From day one she was a feminine replica of his father, with longer lashes and smaller bones, her father's darling.

Then other past scenes appeared as if they had come pell-mell down a chute. She was a lively dark-haired child; she was still very small when she tried to put on John's boots for the comic effect and had fallen down the stairs in them. He carried her and shushed her and wiped her tears, and then to make her happy he laughed, falsely, ha ha ha. It was funny, yes Lalie. She always left him between laughter and outrage. He put his large hand around the candle and blew it out. All he had at present were pieces and the remains of memory, and for now he preferred the dark. A blue-gray cold front was booming down out of the north, sending curtains of rain across the surface of the broad Missouri, and white cranes bolted from the wetlands to ride the wave of the front, their wings open to the storm.

The next morning, he lay in bed with his coffee and went on searching, obsessively, for pieces of the puzzle. He came upon a letter from his mother, two pages, half of it water-stained and one edge burned away. On it, here and there, words of peacemaking, words of praise for Major Callaway.

He stood and held it at the window for the light, and one of the girls from Bonnemaison who came to work daily looked up to see his tall, wide-shouldered figure at the window, his shirt loose and open and his head bent over a paper, and swore to her friend that Mr. Chenneville was watching her out of those whey-colored eyes and only pretending to read. He'd fallen off a railroad bridge during the war. Landed on his head. So he couldn't read. She hurried on.

The next letter was one he did remember. He had read it in his tent when it was snowing outside. An April snow in Virginia. The letter was about Lalie and Major Callaway's wedding, many of the sentences cut short by a scorched and blackened border. A cascade of recall struck him; how disappointed he was.

His mother should have stopped it. But no; she wanted to leave Temps Clair. The place was too much work for her alone without Placide; she might go to New Orleans to live with Basile and Pelagie—she could not at her age endure the St. Louis winters anymore—and when he returned, he could get the place in order, because she could not. Lalie and William were to have the land down near Ste. Genevieve at Riviere aux Vases, *He is a very fine man, I assure you*, and so on.

He recalled thinking that his mother was glad to be rid of Lalie.

Then the last one which was the top half of a charred page; Lalie and William Callaway were the happy parents of a fine, healthy boy who had been named for him. He remembered being very pleased by this. She said the planting was going well, and yet again, *The war will soon be over.* And that was all of his personal correspondence that had been saved.

He dropped the letters back into the camp box and opened his clothes press to pull out working clothes. He heard a carriage outside on the gravel. In these patched and frayed trousers and a dark blue shirt he went to the front door to welcome his uncle.

Basile held him hard in both arms with tears in his eyes. It was a long half hour before the man quieted down. Basile Chenneville with his vital, jumping energy, so unlike John's father. John heard of his travel north, his mother's state of mind, how hard it was to get a pass, and how he had to sign a loyalty oath. He handed the paper to John for him to read, and John understood that somehow his uncle was delaying, delaying.

I, Basile Adrian Chenneville, do solemnly swear that I am well acquainted with the terms of the 3rd section of the 2nd article of the Constitution of the State of Missouri adopted in the year eighteen hundred and sixty-five . . .

John skimmed it quickly.

. . . I make this oath without any mental reservations or evasion and hold it to be binding on me. Subscribed and sworn to before me on this day the 5th day of October 1865 at St. Louis, Joseph Warren (signed) W. Eager Jr., clerk, county court, St. Louis.

"Ah *nonc*, so you got a pass."

"I did," said Basile. "What does it say?" He was a head shorter than his nephew, his hair iron gray and striped with black.

"That you are loyal and true forever and ever, previous opinions notwithstanding."

"Whatever it means." Basile waved the whole thing aside. "I can't read it. English is never spelled as they say it, and anyway, it is the speech of lawyers." He folded the paper and tucked it in his waistcoat pocket.

John answered all the questions about the hospital in Virginia, about the journey home, about the state of his brain. They sat across from each another at the kitchen table. Fermin brought a plate of new hot bread and butter, poured another glass of wine with his hands oddly trembling. Then he went to stand by the fireplace to warm his thin body. A stillness fell. They could hear the distant geese. Basile placed his hands palm to palm and rubbed them back and forth.

"And so, what am I not to be upset about?" John said. He slowly tapped the end of his butter knife on the table.

A long silence. *Tap. Tap. Tap.*

Basile put his head in his hands, his jovial manner gone, and said to his plate, "Lalie is dead, *mon neveu*."

In the long moments that followed the fire crackled in the fireplace. A cold October wind made a long, descending roar in the cedars. When John could speak, he said carefully, "Dead of what?"

Basile looked up and squared his shoulders. "And also her husband William and the baby." Tears came again to Basile's dark eyes. "He was named for you. Jean-Louis."

John closed his hands hard together, attempting to perhaps complete a circuit within himself, to take this in, process it, live with it. He was taken by a serious and deep bewilderment; things suddenly seemed unreal. He thought, *Cholera, an accident, a steamboat wreck?*

Basile looked at him and then away again. "There is more," he said.

"Yes," John said, in a quiet, tight voice. "I'm waiting."

"They were murdered."

John was struck silent. And then: "Ah God! No! *Pas vrai!*"

Fermin was openly weeping. The world ground to a halt. All was suspended except the fire that turned everything to ash.

"No!" John cried again, and both hands were clutching the edge of the table so tightly it seemed he would leave marks in the wood.

"Jean, Jean."

John got to his feet, took his cane in hand and left the kitchen, walked outside. He hit himself in the forehead with his fist, twice. Then he kept walking, down the graveled driveway to the front gate, back again. The cold wind flayed his face and his bare head, and his running tears were like ice water on his cheeks. He heard himself gasping for air. He felt adrift in some kind of fix or element he couldn't describe. He thought of his sister killed. He had seen so many men killed. With one hand on top of his head and his eyes blurred he came walking back to the kitchen.

"By whom?" he said.

"No one knows."

"When?"

"May. This last May."

John suffered through the afternoon with its endless hours in a state of blank rage and anguish. He got up to walk down the corridor to the entry and back again into the kitchen with yet another question. His eyes and nose were streaming; he wiped at his face over and over. Fermin and Basile sat as if they were carved and simply waited. He paced into the foyer, where his mother and father gazed out of their frames and into some other space that was empty of people and they looked upon this non-space with sparkling eyes. Basile sat in silence, waiting for his nephew to return, tried to answer another question, waited again.

It had happened five months ago. They were found dead, their bodies thrown in a nearby spring. They had all been shot to death. The neighbors didn't know anything, the entire area down there was in chaos, and it had been chaotic for four years. The town of Bloomfield sixty miles farther south had changed hands between Confederate and Union forces fourteen times. There were locally raised troops of both sides, and then Union troops brought in from Illinois and Indiana, badly led, undisciplined, and criminals in and out of uniform, disported themselves to their heart's desire and sat, when they pleased, upon the seat of judgment. There was no front. There was no rear either. All while he was fighting a gentleman's war in Virginia.

In a tortured voice, John said, in desperation, "Maybe it wasn't them in the spring, Basile; maybe . . ." He stopped, standing halted with eyes shut and both hands on top of his head.

Basile held up his hand flat toward John. *"Mon neveu,"* he said. *"Tsois courageux."*

Then wrath came back to him full force. "Why has the killer not been caught? Why?" John heard himself shouting. He lowered his voice with an effort. "Who was he?"

Basile nodded, as if to say he had already tried, and all had been found wanting. "This would be the duty of the sheriff in Ste. Gene-vieve. They refuse to do anything. They say it is just the local French people, perhaps a boundary dispute or a matter of old loyalties."

"A murder like this?"

"It is what they said."

"They look the other way? A woman and a baby?"

"I can get nothing from them. Finally, *mon neveu*, they threatened me."

"Because Callaway was a Confederate officer?"

"Who knows?"

"But why Lalie and the baby? A baby?"

"We don't *know*, we don't *know*." Basile's voice rose and tears came into his eyes again, and he couldn't speak.

After a few moments John got up and went to the hot-water tank on the cookstove, turned the spigot with shaking hands, ran the hot water onto a towel, and bathed his face. Silence, a whisper of falling coals, a distant steamer whistle from down on the cold, gray Missouri River. Into this silence, John said in a cold, flat voice, "Somebody knows."

"Jean, I am tied by the hands. I cannot do anything from New Orleans. Your mother became afraid even though here in Bonnemaison, in St. Louis County, there is no trouble. Everybody peaceful. She had to go down there to say it was them. Father Dillon went with her. It was then she stopped speaking."

"A name," said John tenaciously. "Give me a name."

"Some said the name Dodd, a man named Dodd. He is a deputy down there, in that county."

"Ste. Genevieve County. That's a start."

"*Oue*, but no one knows for sure, and do not begin a vengeance, *fi.*

It will eat you up, and I tell you, if you take this into your own hands it will be prison for you. Fermin, please, more wood. We are perishing. The sheriffs were all appointed by Fletcher, over the entire state, and they are all afraid of another rebellion."

"What has that got to do with murdering a girl and her baby? And her husband? What?"

"Maybe the murderer has good connections." Basile's voice was low. He wrapped himself in the cream-colored shawl. The light was melting and fading back down to the world's default state of darkness. "I should not have said that, Jean. Listen, listen, those counties down there in the Ozarks—it has always been strange, a strange place—they are uncivilized. Except for the French villages, of course. Because we were always close to the river, to civilization."

"Of course," John said automatically. His mind was turning the name over and over: *Dodd. Dodd.* It was a start. "Yes, of course."

"But it did no good to press them, to ask. Nothing did any good."

John stared at the square of fading sunlight as it shrank into darkness.

Basile clasped and unclasped his hands. He said, "They are buried at St. Philip and St. James."

John said nothing. The wind had grown stronger and colder and brown leaves hard as leather rattled past the keeping-room door. Fermin came in with more wood for the fire and closed the door behind him. He lit a candle and placed it on the table.

"*Fait fret,*" said Basile, and his voice had a faint defeated tone to it. He wiped his cheeks. Like his brother he had a plump, round face with dark hair and eyes, red cheeks, small hands; hands now gripped together in a knot. "They are with God."

"*Bien maigre,*" said John. *Cold consolation.*

"I am sorry. You had to be told sometime. I had hoped . . . but then, yes, you had to be told sometime. Please don't do anything but recover. You are all your mother has left. Imagine it. First, we lost Placide. Then came word that you were seriously wounded. Then she had to go and identify the body of her daughter, her son-in-law, her grandchild. The nervous shock was more than I can say. Now she only sits and looks at *nothing.*" Basile opened his hands. "She no longer *speaks.*"

"All right," said John. "I am imagining it."

"You owe it to her to become well." Basile stood up. "Here, in my valise, I have the names of an accountant to help you with the books—he is in Ferguson—and there is a good foreman from here, from Bonnemaison. He used to work for Lucas. You must not do any of this work yourself. *Entendu?*" He placed the valise on the table.

"Yes," said John. He didn't want to hear this. Basile had been living with the knowledge of this horror for half a year. He had not.

"There is enough in the Boatmen's Bank to pay them for a year, and by that time the next harvest will pay for it all. The blockade to New Orleans has been lifted; the river trade is moving again. You will get well. The doctor said it would be very slow, a year or more. For your mother, you must recover completely." His voice was flat and dogged with this duty of saying what needed to be said, arranging what had to be arranged, despite his feelings, despite his heart, which seemed to have been taken in two demonic hands and wrung out.

John said, "Somebody knows." He leaned back in his chair, his long legs stretched out, his eyes searching the kitchen. "Somebody damn well knows."

"Give me your promise."

He did not want this place. Not now. Most men thought of the days when they looked out over their own fields and there would be all the inheritance of the years and sons and land, but he did not want it. Not his own table to put his feet under nor his own acres. He wanted nothing. Not anymore.

John rested his hands on the head of the cane, and his forehead on his hands. Finally he said, "You have it." He lifted one hand to wipe at his eyes with his shirt cuff. "For now."

CHAPTER FOUR

October 1865 / Temps Clair

JOHN THREW ASIDE THE TASK of trying to remember his childhood self, his life. He was not going to spend hours in the maddening frustration of casting about for lost and forgotten years. There was no reason to fill out the blanks on his discharge form. All was changed now. He needed to find the man who did this. He would search the world for him if he had to. The killer had had half a year to cover his tracks, and it would be more yet before John was well enough to begin the search. He must get Temps Clair in order so that he could leave. He had to regain his balance, his speed of movement, his ability with a revolver and rifle in preparation for the manhunt that was to come.

He found his old riding boots in the closet at the end of the hall, the ones he had left behind when he went to the 80th New York. He drew them on slowly, and when his heel slotted into the foot with a thump it felt right and good. Traveling boots.

Mid-November 1865 and the bells of St. Ferdinand in Bonnemaison pealed across field and river. Fermin came to the library door with the shawl, bringing him a glass of cognac, saying he needed to keep the chill off. John had the account ledger before him. He didn't look up.

He said, "Fermin?"

"*Oue.*"

"The tobacco has to be plowed under. I am entirely at a loss to know why this has not been done before now."

"We don't have teams, *mon fi.* Your mother sold the teams." Fermin set the glass of cognac down on the bedside table with a click. "I can find a plow crew in Ferguson."

"All right, then you will please do that. A foreman? Basile mentioned a foreman from Bonnemaison; he used to work for Lucas." John took up his pen.

"I didn't want to trouble you, M'sieu Jean."

"No, of course not, we should just let it all rot. Get him. It needs to be run fallow for a year. We should try to lease the Wehmeyer land for the tobacco. Is anybody leasing Soulard's?"

"I can ask."

"Yes, go as soon as possible. Tomorrow morning."

What he wanted was physical work. He slapped the ledger shut. This would keep him from the recurring anguish of his sister's death and focus his mind on what he needed to do. As he used hand and arm and the strength of his back, somehow connections would be made in the brain. That unstructured porridge that we think with. He had seen brains, unfortunately.

He left that memory behind as well. Temps Clair must become working and functional. His mother, however struck with melancholia she might be, was being taken care of by Basile and his wife, Aunt Pelagie. John leaned on his cane to walk the half mile down to the disastrous orchards. He would try to ride the dark mare soon. She was known for her independent mind. He felt that some of the grounders at least—all the fallen apples—might be salvaged for cider. The tobacco fields were a complete loss.

He told himself that as soon as he could ride the mare at speed and walk the crossbeam in the barn as he used to do as a child, he would begin looking for her killer. That as soon as he could figure and write in the ledgers in a clear hand he would lay out his routes and his plans. As soon as he could help unload supplies from the St. Louis packet that stopped every day at the Temps Clair landing, he would go. That when he could load a rifle and hit a bottle at a hundred feet he would choose his traveling gear. He walked with his cane, his head bent and his coattails flying. The neighbors came to think of him as strange, the strange man with the head wound, old Placide's boy, living alone in that big house.

• • •

THE GIRLS STOOD at the window to watch Mr. Chenneville try to get on the mare. They had been singing together, *hard times come again no more*, but then Catherine spotted this scene of trouble and excitement and threw aside the kitchen window curtains.

"Engaged for a few nights only!" cried Catherine. "With thrilling new effects!" They crowded together at the window.

They were in a litter of sieves and apple peelings and moved in an apple steam as the pieces boiled on the cookstove. They were making apple butter. They had come for daywork at Temps Clair in spite of the gossip and rumors of the injured man who had come back from the war after a year in a coma and could not count, no, not even on his fingers. Even though they were young they had knowledge of all the tools of kitchen and garden and dairy that there were. The blockade was over. There were new things to buy. They wanted the money and so came to work and ignored tales of madness and midnight wanderings.

"She's going to kill him," said Catherine.

"Who is?" Mrs. Thurman ran to open the damper and then came back to the window.

"That horse. Watch. This is going to be a train wreck."

"He fell on his head off a railroad bridge," said Mrs. Thurman. "That compacts your brains all together, and so you can't tell tomorrow from last week."

"No, no, he fell off a telegraph pole and the wire wrapped around his head and the electricity got him."

Mrs. Thurman was only nineteen years old with a big head and thick hair of a butternut color and no children as yet, and so she had come to clean and cook. Her large head made her look childlike and innocent. All day they had plied their tools and songs in the long, stone-flagged kitchen, the redbirds cried, *What cheer? What cheer?* at the back door, and the north window looked out on the tobacco-curing barn and the cedars and the broad gray sky. There Fermin held the mare's bridle and Mr. Chenneville stood with one hand on the cantle and one on the pommel.

"He used to be good-looking," said Mrs. Thurman. "But he got all banged up."

"He is yet," Catherine said, and then in a low voice, "Come on, you can do it." All of Temps Clair seemed to hold its breath: the cedars ceased their hushing, no whistle sounded down on the river, and even the boiling apple pieces seemed to simmer down and stop their blooping.

They watched as John placed his foot in the iron stirrup. He had on a worn old frock coat and a wide-brimmed hat, his high riding boots and cavalry-style spurs, his cane in his belt. As soon as the mare felt the pressure on the stirrup plate she swung away. John's foot was jerked outward as the horse swung and he fell. He managed to clear his boot and spur as he went down backward onto the stony ground. He fell heavily. Within three seconds he had raised himself to a sitting position, his knees bent. He sat still and considered the mare with a flat stare. He said something, but they could not hear it. Fermin picked up a buggy whip.

"Get up, get up," whispered Mrs. Thurman.

John turned over and steadied himself on his hands and knees, sat back on his heels, and then rose to his feet. He stood for a moment with his back straight and his head level. Then he beat the frozen grass from his trousers, retrieved his hat, and slapped it against his thigh so hard they could hear the *whap* sound in the kitchen. His hand was bleeding.

"He's going to lose his temper," said Catherine. "Look at him. He's going to knock that mare's eyeballs into one socket. Whyn't they get some *old* horse for him?"

"Something that's about a hundred years old," said Mrs. Thurman. "Half-dead. One hoof in the grave."

"That mash is burning."

"Well, go and pull it off. I'm going to watch this."

They took their aprons and wiped holes in the steamed window-panes and stood with their hands at their mouths as John tried again.

"He's *bleeding*," said Catherine. "Why don't they just shoot that witch?"

Fermin stood with his right hand clutching the bit shanks and the long buggy whip held to the mare's other side. If she swung away again, he was going to whop her a good one right down the flank. Then it would be on to Richmond and John Chenneville with a broken leg.

"Where's he bleeding?"

"He cut his hand—you can see it."

John held both reins tightly in his left hand and a good chunk of the mare's mane as well, standing steady with his hat down tight over his face and a stream of blood running from his left palm and down his wrist. John stood very still with one foot in the stirrup and one on the ground. He was tall and so he had not far to raise his weight, if only he could swing through that shift of the upper body, the right leg up and over, slot it behind pommel holster and the revolver butt.

Then he stepped up in the stirrup, threw his right leg over, and cleared the cantle with boot and spur in one smooth move, his long coattails flying. They watched him straighten his back and gather the reins in his bloodied hand. He settled himself in the saddle and braced both feet in the stirrups, a look of concentration on his face.

Fermin said something to him, but John waved him away impatiently.

"There he goes," said Catherine.

They both turned to the hallway and then ran out to the front porch. They saw him ride down the road that sloped off the high terrace and on toward the orchards, the landing, and the collapsed clutter of the tobacco fields. He held the mare to a slow trot. He rode well, as most big men do, his weight holding him deep in the saddle, but even so the mare tried a little rear and he hit her between the ears with his cane. A solid blow. She threw her head, and he jerked up sharply on the reins. In that slow trot he disappeared into the bare limbs of the orchards.

They sat down at the kitchen table, back to work at the apple butter with the last of Fermin's hoarded Arkansas Blacks.

"It's like a play," said Catherine. She laughed and then stopped herself, cleared her throat. After a pause: "They say he lost all his memory. Maybe it's better, considering."

Mrs. Thurman didn't say anything but spun a deep-red apple

between her hands and then jammed the heel of one hand into her eyes to clear them of tears.

"Well, what?" said Catherine.

"I was at her wedding. She got married before I did, about a month."

"What are they going to do?"

"I'd be fixing to kill somebody, myself," said Mrs. Thurman.

"You'd *think*." Catherine got up and found a sharper paring knife and sat back down, dramatically plunged her paring knife into the core as if it were a throat. "Whoever heard of such a thing? Innocence defiled. The stones cry out, and so on." Red peelings cascaded onto the floor. "They say he never even heard about it until just this month. Nobody told him."

"It was to keep his mind calm, what with that head wound."

They threw the peelings into the bucket for the hogs. There were only two hogs, named Bacon and Pork Chop, who lived in a rail pen, languished at their ease, and happily subsisted on leavings.

"His dad was a calm sort of man. And so then he doesn't look anything like his daddy's side." Catherine leaned down to take up the pressing boards. These were to mash the boiled apples into a sticky pomace.

"No, he looks like his mama's people. They're from New York and they're all ten feet tall, women included."

Catherine looked out the window to see what Fermin was doing, but all the panes were steamed over again. "They say he was in high cotton, down in New Orleans. Before the war. That is to say, he indulged himself in high living."

Mrs. Thurman was still trying to clear her mind of Lalie and her baby and her husband. She cleared her throat and said, "Well, woman, don't just throw that out there—give me some details."

"I would if I had any. Or I could make some up. Women and cards and duels. And some woman named Sebastienne was going to marry him and then didn't."

"You should write a play, Catherine."

"Who, me? Well."

After a while they began to put away their tools and the large kettles of apple mash for the next day and then heard the mare's hoofbeats passing by the window. Shortly after that his footsteps going up the stairs.

"Minnie, better get some vinegar and linen for that cut," said Catherine. "You go do it. If I do it, everybody, and his dog will be saying I was in his bedroom and say we were dallying. You're married."

Mrs. Thurman, named Minerva and called Minnie, stood up. "You wish," she said.

Catherine lifted both shoulders and tipped her head back and forth. "I don't know, I wouldn't have him," she said. "People with head wounds, they can come unhinged in a minute and start throwing things or choking you or something. And they're French. They just marry other French people."

"Lalie didn't." Minnie stripped off her stained cuff and sleeve covers, then her apron, and dropped them all in a chair. "Maybe she should have."

She tapped at the bedroom door and waited. "Mr. Chenneville?"

"Come in."

She opened the door carefully to see him lying back on the bed with his boots and spurs still on, his arms up and crossed over his forehead. One hand was wrapped in a towel. His eyes were closed. The old nine-patch counterpane was rucked up and stained and his hands were curled shut. His coat and hat had been dropped on the floor.

"Yes, sir, if you'd sit up, I could clean out that cut on your hand."

"Good of you," he said.

He opened his eyes and gazed at the ceiling for a moment and then swung his legs out and onto the floor and held out his left hand, palm upward. He balanced it on his knee. He'd sliced it between forefinger and thumb on the palm. She peeled off the blood-sticky towel and then soaked the cut with a cloth reeking of vinegar. She knew it must have stung, but he didn't move. She glanced at the bed and saw that there was a bloody handprint on the pillowcase and his shirt cuff was stiff with dark stains.

"What's your name?" he said. His head was bent down, and she couldn't see his face, only that white, raised scar.

"I'm Mrs. Thurman." She peered at his hand. It was a short cut, but it was deep. She wiped at it again.

"You are a very young Mrs."

"Well, we just upped and married. Hold still." She pressed hard, tapped away a few drops of blood. "There you go." With her big head, she indeed seemed very young; her frazzled hair and patched day dress made it look as if she had just come from the common school as she wrapped his hand with a linen binding.

"What was your name before you married?"

"Minerva Brady. You'd remember me. I was a friend of Lalie's, and . . ."

He held up his right hand, flat toward her. "I don't remember, and I'd rather not. I'm sorry I asked."

She wiped her hands on the waste linen. "Not remember *anything*?"

"Yes. Thank you. I don't need any further attention." His eyes closed as if he was suddenly light-headed, and he carefully put both hands on his kneecaps in a hard grip and then opened them again. He had been in a fight with that mare for two solid hours; he had had to ride her every second and never let his attention wander or he'd have been on the ground again. "I know you have a lot of work to do."

She decided to be persistent. He wasn't at all crazy, and in fact at this moment he seemed to be surprisingly reasonable. "I mean, for instance, you know what year it is."

He slowly lifted his head and at first regarded her with a questioning look. She was taken aback with both surprise and pity at the expressions that crossed his usually impassive face: confusion for a brief second, then a searching look around himself. He pressed his lips together. Mrs. Thurman was appalled at this terrible hesitation, and she was sorry she had insisted, so she began to fold up the towel for something to do. He still had dead grass leaves on his pants. He smelled of sweat and wintry toil and had not shaved. His facial bones stood out like the cornices of a building that had been through an earthquake and would never be the same again.

Finally he said, "It's November of 1865."

"That's right!" She smiled brightly. He did not smile in return. She started to say something further, but his pale eyes had a look of warning. A direct stare, cold and wintry. Her heart thumped once and then quieted. "Now, if you would give me that pillowcase, I will get you another and also your shirt."

She watched as he carefully, laboriously stripped the pillowcase from the pillow and then lay back on the bed in the dimming evening light and put one forearm across the top of his head.

"Thank you. I'll leave the shirt in the kitchen. And if you would, don't bother me again," he said, and this time his voice had a harder edge. "And I mean that."

"Yes, sir."

His eyes drifted shut. She came back later and left the clean pillowcase on the hall floor in front of his door. She had very much wanted to hear how he had messed up his head, but she tiptoed away, resolving to never gossip about the man or to cross him ever again.

Catherine came in from outside in a rush of cold air, and in her hand, she held a piece of rusty iron.

"This is what did it," she said. "He landed on this." She dropped it ringing on the table. "It's a piece of an old scythe blade."

Mrs. Thurman nodded and said, "There is just junk all *over* this place. And no, ma'am, no dallying. Ha ha."

It was late, and they had a long walk back to Bonnemaison. Pulling on their shawls and bonnets, the women slipped out the big front doors.

As they walked away, Mrs. Thurman said, "But he said he didn't want to remember nothing about Lalie."

"Or can't."

"No, Cathy, no. He just seems confused about dates. The year, maybe. And so when I said I was a friend of Lalie's he looked at me like he wished I was dead."

Catherine tied her bonnet ribbons tightly. "Instead of her."

Mrs. Thurman thought about it and then nodded. "That could be," she said.

CHAPTER FIVE

November–December 1865 / Temps Clair

CHENNEVILLE HAD TAKEN TO EATING in the kitchen like a field hand, his brogans heavy with mud, his hand bandaged, and his shirt closed tight at the neck against the cold. He finished off a plate of eggs, bacon, fried cornmeal mush with blackberry jam and butter, and a glass of clabber milk, and then took up his rifle and went out, wiping his mouth.

In a frock coat and muffler, he stood out in the November air and dropped seven prepared cartridges into the Spencer's buttstock, shoved with his thumb against the follower, and pressed it home. He swung a bottle by the neck from a great cedar in the rear of the house. He cocked the carbine, levered in a round, and took aim. Three, five, seven shots and at last he hit it in a spray of green glass that glittered in the early morning sun. He shut his hands around the barrel and the firing mechanism with his mouth set in a straight line from anger and disappointment. *Not yet.*

The leafless orchards made cranky dark scores against the sky, and a winter wind off the Missouri River cut into his eyes until they watered. He stepped up and into the saddle, held hard for a moment to the pommel gullet until the world straightened itself. Then he rolled his shoulders under the coat and turned down toward the landing. The river was late in freezing this year, and he heard the steam whistle of the St. Louis freighter coming in, two longs and three shorts. She bumped into the jetty reversing her engines while the twin stacks boiled out black smoke and muddy water bolted up in waves.

He watched as the gangplank was thrown to the shore and the new, empty barrels came rolling down one after another. There were ten of

them, and they would hold two hundred pounds each. They were for
the apples, whatever could be saved. John dismounted slowly and carefully, tied up and waited for a pause, then ran up the gangplank to help.
Alongside the deckhands, he shoved down one barrel after the other to
watch them bang together and roll down the jetty and onto the shore
with hollow wooden booms.

Sending down the last barrel, he stepped wrong, wavered, lost his
balance, and fell sideways.

"Hey, hey!" Two men grabbed him before he went over the side and
into the river. They shoved him back onto his feet and he held to the
freight-door frame for a few seconds. A big hard-faced redheaded man
handed him his hat with a look of concern.

"I'm fine," John said. "I'm fine, just let go, thank you. I'm all right."

Water-light sparkled and flashed into his eyes as he stood braced
with the invoice in his hand. He had to think for a moment before he
signed it and paid the man. He could now count out the bills and coins,
but he was slow at it. *Not yet, not yet.*

He hired two plow teams, men and horses, and walked behind
them in the new furrow to make sure the tobacco plants were turned
well under the ground. The horses bent into their collars, and the big
blades cut into the collapsed and rotten foliage, throwing it over roots
and all. The Missouri River bottomlands were phenomenally rich with
six feet of topsoil, and men said that if you struck an axe into it, the
handle would sprout. It was a joy to see the dark earth as it rode up the
plowshares and then poured away in a smooth walking wave. They had
good weather that November.

The plow crew came in at noon for a hot dinner, crowding into the
kitchen in the smell of horse and tobacco and leather to draw up around
the table, talking and joking together at first, but there was an uneasi-
ness in the conversation and in their laughter. This family had a daughter murdered, her and all her family, the old man was dead, and the
mother had turned into a speechless waxwork. The son's brains were
scrambled from some war wound. You could see the scar on his head. It
looked like the St. Louis and Iron Mountain train tracks. The laughter

and talk slowly drained away into formal silences and the *clink* of forks on plates.

He leased the Soulard land for tobacco and hired a dayman to clean water troughs and fix fence and started another crew on wagon repair, but he could not evade things the way he thought he could. His mind circled back endlessly as to who could have killed them and why.

Who was Dodd? Somebody she met when she worked for Easterly? Somebody who had walked into the daguerreotype shop? A man from former years, somebody who drove a Chenneville plow team or repaired the front steps? Who saw her, wanted her? He could not shut this off.

He stood at the old Hall square piano and tapped out a tune he could not name. It was as if Lalie were beside him, playing the chords. He was missing enormous pieces of his life, his youth, all the pleasures and disasters of his world before the war. But what good were they? He didn't need them. He slammed the piano shut and walked out of the parlor.

At night he dreamed of flying; he dreamed of a magic revolver that shot projectiles that turned into white cranes, and their voices as they fled were *dit* and *dah*. Lalie and his mother grasped burnt letters that they showed each other with expressions of horror. He dreamed that he had cornered a man named Dodd in a dark place and was approaching him slowly. He woke up in twisted coverlets with the fire nearly burnt out, the metal dogs running like elf-dogs around the fireplace screen.

In the dim morning light, Fermin brought his coffee in. They never let the girls do it because John slept without a nightshirt. He sat up to take the steaming mug, and his mind was somehow slack and confused with the intensity of his dreams.

Later in the kitchen he stood with his breakfast plate in his hand, looking out the window. It was snowing. He put the plate down and pressed his forehead against the glass and shut his eyes.

"Fermin?"

"*Oue, mon fi.*"

There followed such a long pause that Fermin placed both hands flat on the table and started to stand up. To see if John needed help. The winter sunlight came like a mist through the falling snow and picked out the lines in John's face, the slightly flattened nose and his light eyes, an oddly tender mouth, and the dense, colorless skin of somebody only now recovering from a long illness.

He said, "Fermin, I don't know how old I am."

The old man was dumbfounded. He stared at the fireplace stilled with shock. Then he slowly shook his head.

"For true?"

"Yes."

Fermin put down his coffee and was resolute all of a sudden, and he said in an irate voice, "*Esti marde!* I am not going to tell you. You must think of this for yourself."

John saw his breath clouding the cold glass. He watched snowflakes fall on the beehives.

"Nobody can not have a childhood, Jean. You will not even recall all I did for you! This is not right." Fermin clutched his coffee cup. He was working himself up into a state of indignation. "You don't even remember how I pulled you out of the river! I showed you how to make a quill pen. I took you to school in that *maudi' vieille* Estannup. Why did I bother if you were going to forget it all!"

John stood listening without turning from the window.

Fermin snorted out a long breath and took hold of himself. "Now, I tell you, you must start to get back all your memory. Ask me, I will help you." He spooned up more sugar for his coffee and John saw one of Fermin's rare moments of anger wrinkle the old man's brow. "I tell you, it's not right. *Collise*, you don't even remember that I showed you how to tie your shoes. Why did I bother?"

HE FOUND THE family Bible in the library, jammed in among the statutes of the state of Missouri, *Bleak House*, and *Medicinal Cures for the Home*. He opened the old Douay to the endpaper listing of births and deaths. He was born in 1832 to Martha Jane Chenneville, née Pryor, and Placide Étienne Marie Chenneville. He was now thirty-three years old. He placed his fingertip on the date. Soon he would be thirty-four.

He sat with his father's gold watch in his hand. It was warm and filled his palm with its patient ticking. *This is yours*, Father Dillon had said. *He felt very strongly that you should carry it.* John watched the second hand; he had improved in his comprehension of numbers and mechanisms so that he could read the face of it easily; it was seven o'clock. He got up and walked around the library trying to toss a billiard ball from one hand to the other. And now it was early December and the whistling winds seemed to say it was late in the year, late in the year, the year is going.

He had a clear recall of doctors coming to see his father when he was maybe twelve years old: Monsieur le Docteur Boisliniere, a family friend, and others. He was at the time sitting stiffly in the library with his hands clenched together until the knuckles were white. He was holding his father's heart together with his two hands. His mother kissed him on the top of his head and said, "His heart is good, Jean, it is just very *slow*."

That had to have been the year the *Columbia* blew up, 1842. He saw his father tearing open the telegram envelope. It was from the Christian Peper Tobacco Company. The entire consignment, gone. All that work, gone. She sank with their entire tobacco crop. Her boilers exploded at Chouteau Island two miles north of St. Louis in the night.

The doctors said Placide must not become exercised about anything but to take life as it came, and so he put the telegram aside and had a glass of wine. Several glasses. Lalie began to play "La Savanne" on the piano slowly and soothingly, casting covert glances at her father with big round dark eyes that said, *Don't die, don't die.*

John replaced the watch in its side-table drawer, sat down, and pulled himself out of his mental drift. The door to the library opened.

"You are writing down a list?"

John placed his feet far apart and rested his forearms on his thighs. He watched the reflections of the flames on the waxed walnut floor. He bent his head and put both long hands slanting over his eyes. Then he dropped his hands.

"No, I am remembering," he said.

"Ah." Fermin started to say something and then didn't.

"I started school at St. Ferdinand, did I not? I learned English grammar. I was six. It had to have been 1838."

"I took you to school in that old Estannup," Fermin said stubbornly, as if John did not appreciate the precarious state of that ancient carriage with its wobbling wheels and broken dashboard.

"Yes, the Stanhope. I'm going to fix it." He paused. "I can't get things straightened out. Sometimes I remember things and then I think I am re-remembering them. Like I remembered Teo down in Ste. Genevieve County: he lent me a powder measure once when pa-pere and I were hunting down there. And then, in a couple of days, I remembered it again."

Fermin's face was a blinking fixed study. "Was it the same?"

"Yes."

"Then you thought of it once and then thought of it again is all."

"Yes, yes. Very well, that's nothing to be upset about. But then I can't get things in sequence. What came before what."

"It will come, Jean."

What came to him most easily were things that happened, actions, events that did not seem to have a date. Loading, kneeling, and firing at military drill at school in St. Louis. He was good at it and accurate. He learned Morse on the third floor of the Christian Peper Tobacco Company, working late after school hours. He listened intently, sat up late in the Soulard house with a candle, going over and over the Morse alphabet. After the fire in '49, the city smelled of wet ashes and new brick. An avalanche of pumpkins and apples tumbling into the aisles of the Soulard market. They had knocked down three vegetable stands as he and his Soulard cousins got into a brawl with the Irish boys from St. Vincent de Paul. That lot had come up from First Street looking for trouble. They got it. It was probably the first time the French had won a battle in North America in a hundred years.

Again, his mind returned to Lalie. Maybe one of the hired workmen in the Temps Clair fields had seen her as a child and in him had grown a murderous lust carried in his black heart for decades. Was this even possible?

So many workmen come and gone. His father hired free workers because he refused to own slaves or use slave labor. When they married, his mother had made Placide promise to never have slaves. She could not bear it, nor could she ever confess to her people in Albany that she had been touched by the abominable practice that had so stained this country. Placide was convinced not only by his bride but by Jean-Baptiste LeConte of Ste. Genevieve, an old friend and a wealthy man, that slavery was going to tear the state apart and would bring nothing but grief.

And so it was that the work in the orchards and hayfields and tobacco fields was done by what was often very dubious white men, men who came floating down the Missouri from who knows where. They were men who showed up on flatboats, broke and hungry—riverfront trash.

How old was he when that big albino-looking *caboteur* had broken his nose? It was the first time he ever captained a haying crew. It was also the first time he had come up against a true brawler, a hardened adult with years of experience, every one of which had left some sort of mark or scar on his toughened hide.

He was home from school in St. Louis, so he must have been fifteen or so. His father had been stopped at the front doorway by his faulty heart, but the hayfields could not wait. Great towers of cloud moved across the sky, and the orchards were sticky with bees and blossoms. Mules and men sweated while in repose. The haying crew was from the Alton riverfront, and this Saturday morning most of them were hungover and out of money. The man was drinking even before the noon meal had come up. He had forearm muscles like tubers and an imbecilic, fixed stare.

John told him to put away a pint bottle, and the next thing he knew he was flat on his back. The other men glanced at one another and then drew back as young John Chenneville tried to get to his feet in the hay stubble and was knocked down again and again; he also got up again and again until other men stepped in and separated them, but the *cabo-teur* knew that the boy was not going to either quit or cry or go get his father and he would keep on getting to his feet until he was either unconscious or dead.

Now John remembered how at dinner that night he glanced up at his mother with his battered face to see her put her hand over her mouth and begin to weep. His nose was never the same again.

Had one of those men caught a glance of Lalie then, rushing down to the landing to see what was happening? Was one of them named Dodd? But this was bordering on insanity to try to search every remembered man's face for that of her killer so many years ago. John's memories were jumbled; everybody was suspect.

A memory far better: vaulting off the side rails of the ferry on a summer day, coming up foaming, others hitting the water all around him, shouts, crawling up the muddy bank and stripping his clothes to hang them over the wharf side to dry. A good thing to remember this cold night. They were all burnt brown, and the river seen at eye level was fringed on the far side by burr oaks a hundred and sixty feet tall, like the palisades of a great fortress. He floated in the milk-warm blood of a nation, of many nations.

CHRISTMAS OF 1865 arrived and ticked over without celebration of either the *réveillon* or his birthday. They were in mourning. In years past the *réveillon* had been riotous, the young people allowed to stay up all night and drink wine, sing, play piano, the girls fitted into his arms at the waltz with such a meant perfection, and then he had danced as if he weighed nothing. And the Bûche de Noël, made with whipped cream and chocolate powder, egg yolks beaten stiff as yellow damask, and sparkling sugar grains spilled all over the table, and the best wine.

But that time had passed. On New Year's Eve he wore a black band on his hat, the hard grounders had been gathered and sold for cider, and the ones that were grainy with bruising had been abandoned to the deer.

John straightened his legs and placed his feet close to the kitchen fire.

"What about yourself, Fermin?"

"*Moe?*"

"Do you remember every year?"

"Some I would rather not, me, but we are all sinners and have fallen short. Also, afflictions."

"Such as?"

Fermin turned up his glass, drank, and set it down again. "*Ben*, when I was twelve, I went up as an *engagé* with one of Chouteau's voyageur crews to the Yellowstone country. We got lost in the plains, a whole winter. Four died of hunger. I lived. When we finally found Fort Pierre, my neck was this big around." Fermin made a circle with his thumb and forefinger.

John lowered his gaze to the fire and then looked up, suspended in a quiet amazement, and lit his New Year's cigar. "I never knew this," he said. "I am astonished."

"You never asked. This is the way of children, however. So you are going to kill this man."

"Yes."

"Good. You will need all your brains. Since you were very small, you always had courage."

John gave a small laugh at this backhanded compliment. "A year is a long time to wait."

"I know. But at the end of the year, the man who did it will still be guilty." Fermin paused. "And Lalie and her family will still be dead."

CHAPTER SIX

Spring, Summer, Fall 1866 / Temps Clair

THE INTOLERABLE YEAR OF WAITING and healing gathered strength with longer days and more sun; the river ice began to change to the grainy frazil ice and disappear. John pulled on his father's old broad-brimmed hat and walked out into the blustery spring day. Things seemed to come back to him when he *did* stuff. Even if he stumbled, grabbed a fence rail for balance, he remembered things when he was moving and doing.

He practiced with his wartime Remington .44. This particular weapon had always shot high, and so he had raised the front sight, and he remembered getting the armorer to hammer it in. The muzzle bucked up in his hand and the gunpowder smoke was sieved away by the cedar's thick needles. The revolver was as familiar to his hand as his straight razor blade handle, and yet he could not keep it quite steady. He walked to the cedar and tore off the marked paper and looked at it. He wadded it up in his hand and said to himself he was getting better every time.

And so he or they thought they could just ride up to my sister's house and shoot her, and shoot her husband, and gun down a baby, and then ride away, untroubled—no Chenneville was going to do anything about it, they were all old, they were gone to the war, they were people with brain damage. Think again. It won't be long.

In the kitchen he chucked the wad into the fire.

"Miss Catherine, you look blooming today."

"Thank you, sir. You can call me Hibiscus from now on."

"I'm trying to stay with words of one syllable until I can get a brain replacement." John found his barrel snake and drew it through the barrel to clean it of gunpowder residue. "Did you ever know anybody named Dodd? Last name Dodd."

"Indeed not." Catherine had heard ladies use this expression on-stage in St. Louis. "Thinking back . . . no, sir, nobody from around here."

He did not want to go to Easter mass that April because of the kneeling and standing, but then he berated himself for being weak and he rode into Bonnemaison, first for confession and then to Easter services. He stood and knelt and stood again with the rest, smoothly and without dizziness, without a misstep. People shook his hand and looked carefully into his eyes. *Yes, I'm fine*, he said repeatedly. *Doing very well; thank you for your condolences.* He wore the black mourning band on his coat sleeve and his hat and took the long way home, past the grave-yard at old Fort Bellefontaine, to stand by his father's grave, and then returned under the April stars Sirius and Arcturus, and the smell of bergamot and bloodroot. The dogwood flowers stood out beside the dark road, white and extravagant and ghostly.

How deeply he had loved his father. It wrung the heart even to recall the good times: his father's pride in his graduation from the English and Classical High School. That was when he had the grace of being happy. Happy and careless and strong. He had lived with the Soulard family in a big stone French house on Eighth Street, spilling over with cousins, two massive chimneys and half an acre of flower garden. His first formal hat was a color called Angola drab with a six-and-a-half-inch crown. It was for him to wear when he made his visits to the Pryors who lived on Lucas Place. His father took him to Chauvin's on Fourth Street, where he reached up to set the tall hat on his son's head with a tender smile and said, "*Fi*, you are grown."

The orchards blossomed in the last of April, acres of that innocent and unclouded pink that rained all over him and his revolver in its pommel holster and his long, intractable grief, for a moment holding it in abeyance. Bobolinks rode the telegraph wires and greeted the May mornings with cascades of wild notes, but even so, even so, John found himself weighted with a deep and acid anger that Lalie was not here to see the hayfields turn a green like watered silk. He could not wait to leave. Somebody had taken her life, so she could not ride down there with him, and so he swung up on the crossbeam of the barn and proceeded for three feet and then stopped. He turned and edged his way back. *Not yet.*

Summer came. The Missouri reached flood stage and then sank back before it could damage the hay meadows. Everything had to be ordered before he left. He wrote down the names of the haying crew in the ledger in a smooth and consistent hand, with a turkey quill cut in just the manner that Fermin had taught him so long ago.

News of prices in New Orleans; their shipments at last of the late-August harvests, the apples that the southern city people relished, tobacco at last topped off and packed into barrels in the barn, the crackling of telegraph sparks telling him of prices offered. *Dit dah and Sebastienne.*

His father had sent him to New Orleans when he was twenty-four to take over the telegraph traffic for the Chennevilles as well as his uncle Basile's various concerns and those of two other steamboat companies. Good years in New Orleans. A young businessman with his hand on the latest in communications advances.

And so at last came unbidden cascades of deeply sensual and even erotic images; stylish women and voyages into the Caribbean. Down there, in those years, every day that he tied his tie and put on his Angola drab topper he knew that eventually somebody was going to have to take over at Temps Clair. That somebody would be him, the tall man who walked down St. Charles Avenue toward the house on Bourbon and St. Philip to speak with her. To ask why she had not replied to his messages.

He recalled her name, her face framed in dark hair, in uncommon detail. She returned to him entirely as if on a visit. Her square delicate shoulders and her unlikely name: Sebastienne Amable Valois dit LaFontaine. He was surprised by the quick, hot flush of desire that coursed through him and a flash image of her with her hair down her back, one long glossy fall, in the half shadows, while the streetlight

winked on a silver tray with glasses on it and her hand drawing an ear-
ring loose.

Her answer was no. She had no intention of marrying him and leaving New Orleans for some remote farm up in Missouri, the abode of
people who dressed in leather and who were unnaturally hairy, and
thus she returned to him an expensive ring. He came back from a trip to
Cuba to find in his New Orleans apartment several of her possessions
that she had forgotten and a letter from his mother. He read the letter
and began to pack for the upriver trip to St. Louis.

Then the war came. With it came the denouncing and accusations
and the endless filling out of forms, along with blood and imprison-
ment for the less fortunate.

Early on a morning in August 1861, Lieutenant Karcher and fifty men
of the 12th Missouri Volunteers came down the road from Bonnemaison. They were all singing. They sang with the strength of the Lord's
blessing as well as youth and courage and the thirty-four-star flag of
the Union. They had joined up to be soldiers in the army of the Lord
and to search out secessionists. They sought those who were said to be
disloyal by neighbors, and such was the misfortune of the state that it
was divided not on territorial lines but between one man and another,
between one neighboring family and another, a division undeclared,
unmapped, across whose lines it seemed anything was permitted.

Martial law had just been declared in the state of Missouri. The
officer's horses threw long shadows in the light of the rising sun, shadows like obscure connecting rods moving the unit forward from one re-
ported nest of disloyalty to another. Their noise scoured the bright new
day, but they had, as far as he remembered, found nothing in the way of
hidden arms caches even though they had arrested three men who were
pointed out to them by their neighbors as Secessionists, even though
they had busted up a grocery in Florissant looking for hidden rifles and
ammunition on the word of somebody who had penned a note to their
colonel and did not sign his or her name.

John had run downstairs pulling his suspenders up over his shoulders to stand with his father.

Karcher stood in his stirrups and called to John, "And then why have you not joined some unit to protect and defend the Union?"

"I don't even know who you are," he said. "I am just about to come down there and knock you off that horse."

"You'd better think that through, my man," said Karcher. And then since John did not offer any excuse or explanation, Karcher somewhat nervously filled it in for him. "I am authorized to search this house for weapons."

"Of course we have weapons," said Placide in his gasping voice. "This is a farm." He was *un homme honorable*; nobody had ever questioned his word.

"And you," Karcher addressed John again. "I suppose you're going to tell me you're the sole support of this family here." Karcher glanced up. Lalie's sweet pale shocked face would be seen in an upper window, and for a moment Karcher's gaze steadied on her. Then he looked quickly away. "Well, then you must have a certificate of exemption. And you won't get one, not from me, fellow."

"Because you're not authorized to issue one," John said. "Get the hell off of our property."

After some further bluster, Karcher turned away, trailed by his men, who were now yawning and out of step. And so the threat had passed, but in the years to come many a man lay dead in his own blood on his own doorstep for saying just those words.

His father's hands moved uncertainly on the tabletop in a wandering fashion. He said, "Under martial law they can confiscate the property of Secessionists if you get denounced as one of them." Placide blinked, choosing his English words with some difficulty. "And many of us, the French, you know, have gone for the south. That's where our markets are. That's just the truth of it."

"Confiscate Temps Clair?" John's eyes narrowed, his voice had a tinge of unbelief. The candle shone into his pale eyes. His mother had set the candlestick up on *Bleak House* to shed a better light.

"And personal possessions," said Placide. "Everything in the house. Our silver, the furniture. Yes. As I understand it."

"And give it to who?"

"Frances Grood," said Lalie with a toss of her head. *"Cette conaisse."*

"Tut," said Placide. "Lalie, *tai-tois*."

Lalie lowered her head then dramatically stared upward at them all and said in a deep, terrible stage voice, "She wants my underwear."

John burst out laughing despite himself. His mother said, "Lalie, for shame!"

His mother closed her eyes for a moment and then said, "Jean, you must go. We will be all right. I will telegraph my cousin in the Eightieth New York. You must make your plans now."

John rose from his chair. He walked over to his mother and bent down to kiss her cheek. *"Ma mère,* I love you," he said, thinking he had better say it now before whatever was going to happen, happened.

It was wrenching to have to leave them without help: his father ailing and his sentences often not quite right in either language, free labor impossible to get, these threats by that contemptible tool Karcher and the overweight, uneducated Frances Grood, the neighborhood denouncer. But there was nothing to be done about it. So he packed up, got a pass to leave the city, and took the train to the east. His mother's cousin, named Pratt, was the colonel of the 80th New York Infantry and could get him a commission as a lieutenant, and so he fought his war in Virginia, until the world exploded in his face.

THE AUTUMN DAY in mid-November 1866 had grown dark with a rain coming down in a thin, persistent weeping. John laid down his tools on the seat of the old Stanhope two-seater and walked over to the arcade post, and climbed up it to the massive crossbeam. He paused there a moment to get his balance. Then he began to walk the crossbeam. One foot directly in front of the other. He was suspended twelve feet above the barn floor. He walked with his arms out and his light eyes fixed on the corner post.

Catherine came into the front entrance with an egg basket. She looked up and clapped her hand over her mouth.

"Be quiet, *ma mie*," he said.

She watched him travel the beam like a giant from folklore come to invade the barn and take it for his own, in the cold air, in his shirt and suspenders and long unshod feet. Something from another age.

He laid his hands on the corner post. *Yet*, he thought. *Now.*

In mid-November he chose two sets of clothing with the experience of three years of soldiering and meticulously cleaned his guns. He loaded two extra cylinders for the revolver. At this time a storm swept over the bottomlands and left behind it pools of cold water. John rode out with the new foreman to meet the plow teams on the terrace road. He wanted the plowlands turned over once again and winter rye planted. He would not be here to see it grow. He ordered both of the hogs slaughtered and had half the orchard cut down and the applewood used for smoking hams.

The days of work and remembrance were done. He was not completely recovered, but he knew he never would be. He could read well, write, do his figures in the account books, and hit the bottle at one hundred feet. He strode easily down the gangplank of the daily steamer at the landing. He had walked the crossbeam in the hay barn. It was time to go.

He was going to sell the place. They had saved it, holding on even through the hard times of the blockade, but now all was changed. Men wanted to pass down great estates, family lands, but there were none to pass it down to now, except himself, and he didn't want it. Not anymore. He just wanted her murderer dead and at his own hand and soon.

The two candles at either end of the walnut table threw hard shadows and a brassy shine on the stacks of papers and account books. He sat in his vest with shirtsleeves rolled up and the library fire bright in blacks and reds. He drank off his wine and shut all the books and put them away on the shelves. Moon and shadows had journeyed through all the seasons, and once more November was draining away, this one with the number 1866. The cold and light snows had returned. Temps Clair had always been full of life and people and activity, and now it was dead. All who had enlivened it were gone, and Lalie's story would soon come to its end. Her killer would die, and it would be over. He blew her candle out. He was that one last candle in the late hours still burning.

"When will you come back, Jean-Louis?" Fermin rubbed his wrists. "Send word. Send me a telegraph letter."

John packed a satchel, placing in it his revolver in the pommel holster and ammunition for the Remington and for the Spencer. He filled a bag with the best tobacco that remained from last year's crop; the tobacco was fine and light, a blond color, aged now for more than a year. He pounded it flat and rolled the bag tight and tied it. He buckled on his cartridge belt and folded up his army greatcoat with the shoulder cape and the high tunnel neck. It was faded out of its Federal blue on the shoulders and cuffs and hem, a bit worn but serviceable.

"I will, Fermin." John's smile was slight and brief. Then it went away. He suspected that he might not see the old man again. "I will."

"Basile said you could go to prison if you kill him without a warrant. Or something like a warrant."

"Then that might happen."

Fermin bit his lower lip. He calculated the price of the Chenneville family honor, and it was high, very high. "I will come there, then," he said. He lifted one arm and drew the rough material of his canvas coat across his eyes.

John paused, not knowing what to say.

The old man reached into the pocket of his coat and said, "You must take your father's watch, *mon fi.*"

"No, keep it for me, until I return." John cleared his throat. "If anything happens to me, Fermin, you are provided for."

The old man briefly bowed his head in an acknowledgment that it was, after all, only his due.

CHAPTER SEVEN

November 1866 / Ste. Genevieve and Bonne Terre, Missouri

HE STAYED OVERNIGHT IN ST. Louis to wait for the next-day boat to Ste. Genevieve. While he waited, he arranged for bank drafts at Boatmen's Bank. Then to a realtor that the Chennevilles had dealt with for decades, one of the St. Gem brothers, where he agreed on a price for Temps Clair and arranged for a discreet sale campaign by word of mouth. He went to a boat chandler on First for rope, a folding candle lantern, a thick Hudson's Bay blanket. After that he walked to Goettlers' Hatters on Fifth Street to buy a good Hunicke beaver-felt hat with a wide brim.

Then to a harness shop; they had many more things for sale than harnesses. He bought a pair of saddlebags and then chose a stout, short cane. The one he had been using was too slim and too elegant. This one had a good heft to it, and in many ways it would be a more useful weapon than a firearm. It didn't need ammunition, and it could not go off by accident. He sat up late in an anonymous hotel room near the market and with his pocketknife jimmied off the brass endcap on the pommel holster. It was too bright; it could shine and give a man away. And with the end being open, any trash and debris that got into the holster would just fall out. He had been meaning to do that small chore for years.

The next day he caught the boat for Ste. Genevieve for the trip fifty miles south down the river to that small and pleasant town on its bluff above the Mississippi, on the Missouri side. It was full of old French houses as yet undisturbed, a village that had never given up its common lands. He walked up from the landing into the town and the small county courthouse on Third Street, an old brick building on the corner.

John did not know whether it would or would not be a wise thing to ask at the sheriff's office. He did not want to give this man Dodd a warning that somebody suspected him, but he also wanted to know if he was here, still a deputy, still wearing a star and the cloak of authority. He thought about it and then headed for the courthouse.

In the small and cluttered sheriff's office, a man with many chins sat at a desk and behind him a wall of stacked drawers. The little parlor stove puffed away hot and bright. The man's neck was the same width as his head. He looked up brightly.

"Aaaaannnd what can I assist you with, sir?" He had an open copy of the script of *The Octoroon* in front of him and hastily slapped it shut. He looked John over carefully, searching for the bulge of a holster under the greatcoat, and regarded his size with a thin smile.

"I would like to speak with the sheriff."

"Sheriff Litchfield? Gone, sir, gone into the vast interior. He is on patrol to places that have no telegraph, only those who sit and spit and relate rumors."

"Patrolling. I see."

"Yes."

"And deputies?"

"All patrolling about. Hither and yon."

"All of them?"

"Yes. Dodd, Stewart, and Maloney, out ensuring the peace and checking earmarks and one thing and another. Your name, sir?"

"Chenneville."

The man's eyebrows rose, and he opened his eyes wide, blank and shiny as eggs. "Well, I tell you what, now, you might catch them, or at least Sheriff Litchfield in Bonne Terre. There is a sort of festive event there in a couple of days, involving whiskey and perhaps bodily harm, who knows?"

"That's in St. Francois County. Next over."

"A festive event is a festive event. He should be back next two, three days." The clerk's voice changed. "You're from St. Louis and you're looking for somebody."

"No, I'm not." John turned to go. He had not taken off his hat.

"Then what is your business, sir?" The fat clerk sat up straight and radiated officialdom.

"Earmarks."

He took a room above Picot's restaurant and stowed his gear. He rented a saddle horse at the livery. He rode out westward toward French Village. It was mid-November of 1866 and more than a year since he had left the hospital in City Point, Virginia. The sweet gum trees had lost their startling colors of lemon and wine and darkest blackberry, but the great oaks still held their rust-colored leaves. Poison ivy wound around roadside trees, bright as redbirds.

It seemed peaceful enough, but people did not greet him as he rode by. In the narrow valley farmyards, silent women watched him pass. Men straightened from their work in field and woodyard to follow him with their eyes until he was out of sight down the road, among the bare trees. It was a country devastated by war and still under military rule, so life and woodcutting and everything happened on tiptoe in a tense and listening silence. Memories came back of the times he had spent in this country, hunting, camping out, mostly with his father, carrying a muzzleloader. They owned land here, much of it sold to the Desloges or the Valles. He put these memories aside. It was not the same. It would never be the same.

He came to the Aubuchon house. The man remembered him. John dismounted and walked up to the encircling verandah to hold out his hand, and the man got to his feet, smiling.

"Teo," John said formally, "*Comment allez-vous? Vous souvienez vous de moe?*"

"Yes, Jean-Louis, of course, you used to come down to hunt." The man tried to smile but could not. "Let me get you a chair."

"No, it's all right." John sat down on the steps with his boots stretched out. "You know why I have come," he said.

Aubuchon sat down again and his lips trembled and he wiped at his eyes. "Placide's daughter, oh, oh, oh."

"Take a moment."

"I am all right."

"So tell me about this man named Dodd."

The sun moved overhead in its shortened November day, and the shadow of the verandah slid out into the bare yard as Teo Aubuchon told him what he could.

"He was here, the days before. A. J. Dodd, he was with the Illinois army men that came down during the war. He was a flashy man. I never saw anything, only after. I helped pull the bodies out of the spring. Their souls are now in eternal light. It was more terrible than I have words to say."

"Was it him?" John asked. His heart was thudding. "This Dodd?"

There was a long pause as Teo Aubuchon fought with his own fear, for himself and his own family. A man tries to stay out of the clashing gears of big conflicts and warring armies because he has a wife and children, not to speak of the grains and fodder stored in the barn on which they and their animals are to live in the time to come. Madame Aubuchon came out to sit beside them with a pan full of jelled soap on her lap. John stood and touched his hat brim to her, and she motioned for him to sit again. She began to cut the soap into squares. She listened. Teo turned to her repeatedly as he spoke and waited for her to nod.

"Yes. I would say so."

"How do you know?"

"For one, as I was walking down there, he came riding along toward their house too, as if he had just happened along, but I suspected him. I always suspected him of many things. I turned to go get my shotgun and he pulled his horse around and left. For two, people saw him with their marriage picture. He showed it around; it must have been the day after he killed them. It was a little picture in a gold frame. He admired it, showed it to the blacksmith, the men who had come to sit around the blacksmith shop in Ste. Genevieve. And so everybody just shut up. *S'en turent.* Those men can tell you, it was Jacques Vivrette and Tom Mercer and Ferdinand Bouyer. Ferdinand lives still on Bouyer Creek, there—he can tell you."

"But you can tell me as much, *mon oncle*." It was a courtesy title, but not everyone could use it. John could use it.

The man looked at his wife, and she nodded. He said, "Yes. He was at the mill. I heard him say those Secessionists should be killed, nits and all. This in front of our neighbors, some *Américains*, some German. He meant her husband, the Confederate officer. And all of them."

John looked down at splintered boards of the verandah floor. At length he asked the most difficult question: "And so you went there?"

"Yes. That night I wished I didn't have eyes in my head. Their milk cow came bawling down the road to my place here, and then their dog showed up here. Then we smelled the smoke. So I knew. I knew. I went to see." His wife began to cry silently, her hands placed on the rim of the basin. Teo's eyes glittered with unshed tears. "They are at rest now."

"And no one looked into it?"

"No. The sheriff from Ste. Genevieve said it must have been the Frenchmen in a feud, fighting over property lines. We were afraid of him. Dodd was his deputy, you see. He was not elected, the sheriff; he was appointed."

"And all this time Dodd has lived near here, in Ste. Genevieve, as a sheriff's deputy, and nobody else has been killed?"

"Ah, Jean-Louis, a lot of men were killed during the war."

"But not women, not children."

"Never."

"But recently?"

"*Oue.* For three, then, on the St. Marys Road, a boy going home, and his body lay there for the crows and his horse with its throat cut. And so again, Dodd showed something, a saint's life with gold edges that was signed with the boy's mother's name. They were LaPlantes, the LaPlante people. He had taken it."

"Why would he do that?" John looked down, thinking, and then up again. "That's crazy."

Teo frowned, casting about in his mind, his eyes on a thin and inquisitive cat.

"Yes, it is. He told the coroner, who is my cousin, he wanted the book to investigate the murder. But he just showed it around. What kind of person is that?"

"When did this happen?"

"About St. John the Baptist's Day. Around then."

John nodded. St. John the Baptist's Day was June 24, but he knew he was not going to get hard dates or details from Teo Aubuchon. It was around then, at any rate, perhaps a month after his sister's murder. She and her family. So he gave it up. This was not going to be a careful police case, and he was not Inspector Bucket. He rose to his feet knowing that Dodd was in blood up to his knees and was walking free in the world unhindered.

"Thank you, Teo. God will bless you for going down there that night. And what happened to the picture he showed around?"

"I think he threw it away. Into the river. After he enjoyed looking at it. Jacques Vivrette said he had two pictures in gold frames. Maybe he kept the other one, who knows?"

"So I will ask, what for four?"

"Are we at four?"

"We're at four."

"*Ben*, he tried to drag a young girl onto one of those steamboats. She got away from him. This was last week, even. Everybody heard about it."

"I see. Well, then I need to find this girl."

"She's living with Mrs. Sanford in Ste. Genevieve. The woman who owns the laundry."

"All right. That's four. What for five?"

"He knows you are here, and he is going to run. Or worse. Take care."

John rode to Terre Bleue Creek, and in that small valley he spoke with Jacques Vivrette and Tom Mercer, who said the same things that Teo had told him. He could not locate Ferdinand Bouyer. He rode away from these talks thinking that Dodd simply liked bright things like portrait frames and gold-edged books and the souls of all who were young and had the gift of grace and laughter. As if he could take these intangibles to himself by killing those who possessed them.

He rode into Bonne Terre late in the evening. It was in the main a lead-miner's camp with a few permanent houses. The big ridgelines stood high in the west like an irregular black cutout and released the fall stars one by one into the washed and fading clarity of the day. There was Stono Mountain and Buford and Bell and farther south Taum Sauk peak and Mina Sauk. He saw fires glowing under the cowl of these mountains. He counted three or four log structures, one frame house, and the tall chimney of an ore roaster. This was a valley of small surface mines dug out by hand by local people, mostly French. Now everything was dim in the darkening hills, with the smoke of the roaster furnace threading out low to wander among the pine and oak. He heard a group singing "O Madeleine," *t'as couche dehors . . .*

John dismounted to watch and listen. What was this, this strange celebration under the shadow of the hills? Downhill from him in the blundering dark the bonfires glowed and somebody was trying to play a fiddle. A hog turned headless on a spit. Horses were tied on overhead lines. Dogs sat patiently staring at the roasting hog.

He walked down, leading his horse. He came upon a man with a shovel and a pile of entrails beside him in the grass.

"What's happening?" he said.

The man looked carefully at John's horse and his clothing, his hat. John returned the look, standing slanted and tired beside the little rented horse.

"Well, old man Desloge is trying to get the shallow miners to sign up with him," the man said. "So he's pitching a big hog dinner and whiskey party. He's got the papers there ready to sign. You can make your mark and make your fortune, he says. This here's what's left of the hog."

"Is Desloge here?"

"Nah. His foreman."

"All right, well, I'm looking for Sheriff Litchfield and one of his deputies, A. J. Dodd."

"What the hell would they be doing here?" The man tipped his head to one side.

John didn't ask the man's name, nor was he asked for his own here in this shadowy exchange, so lightly tinged with menace and confusion.

"I was told they'd be here, by the clerk in the courthouse in Ste. Genevieve."

"Yeah, but he's sheriff of Ste. Genevieve County. This is St. Francois County."

"Maybe he was coming for the celebration."

"Somebody told you wrong, is my opinion. Sheriff Litchfield's got no business here." The man shoveled the wallowing, gleaming pile of entrails into the hole and began to cover it up. All around them the little surface mines showed in a vague whiteness of spewy earth, thrown out like dirt stars. A half-moon was just rising in the east. It climbed through pine trees toward the early winter constellations. "If you ask me, he's got no business anywhere."

John stood holding the tired little gelding in silence and waited for the man to go on, but he took to banging his shovel on a rock to knock off the soil.

"Care to say more about that?"

"No. He ain't here. This ain't even his county. That clerk told you wrong." He stood back and held his shovel near the blade with the handle forward. "That man Dodd is trouble."

"Has he been through here, then?" John's eyes shifted to the scene below, where other men were riding in, probably come from the town of Summit to the north, where a spur from the St. Louis and Iron Mountain Railroad loaded lead ore and dispensed passengers. It was ten miles away by a rough road. He had traveled it, once. He caught his upper lip in his bottom teeth as he tried to sort all this out.

"Not tonight. Not that I know of. But I heard somebody was trying to locate him. That would probably be you." Then the man with the shovel leaned forward to spit.

"Who did you hear that from?"

"People coming and going."

It was late and dark and cold, and John decided to unsaddle and try to get some sleep. There would be no more information from this man, he knew. He said, "Where can I put up?"

"Try the mule barn." The man pointed with the handle. He seemed poised in a way that people are poised who expect trouble, or who have seen it on its way and don't like the look of it.

John walked the little horse down to the long mule barn through an aisle of firelight and smoke. A sense of wrongness and danger walked with him; a sense of isolation even among these wandering crowds of men. Far away in the surrounding hills a raccoon chattered and a night-hawk pelted down out of the dark and flared its wings, flashing past over and over. Kegs were open, and the fires ran high and hot. Shadows drained from the tall pines and ran black as cables into the dark.

He regretted not asking for a different horse at the livery in Ste. Genevieve. The one he rode was a light chestnut and spattered with white here and there: on two back legs, on his belly, a broad white stripe on his face. The horse was very identifiable, very visible.

He watched about himself. He did not want to get into a fight and get hurt or disabled here at the start of his search. An injury would delay him and Dodd would be on his way to somewhere else if he weren't already.

The mule barn was long and made of pine logs. There was a hayloft overhead. John found a lantern by groping down the entrance frame, took it off the nail and put a match to it, hung it up again. Many dark mule eyes lit up, and their enormous ears swiveled toward him. He saw a long center aisle and single-tie stalls on each side, almost all filled. Beside the entrance was a barrel of molasses, a pile of junk—old boots, empty cans—an anvil and shoeing tools. Harnesses in all their complex lines were arranged on pegs. He knew there was trouble coming. In this state of alertness he noticed everything; all objects were insistent and hard-edged and imbued with a fearful life of their own.

He had been sent on a wild-goose chase. He had been fool enough to fall for it, and he was furious with himself. Somewhere in these hill counties was the man who had seen his sister in her last terrified hour and he was walking free and eating and drinking and strolling at his ease. But not here, not in Bonne Terre.

There was an empty stall up front near the entrance. It had a hay hook chunked into the upright. He put his horse into it and then stepped over to a mule to look on its hip for what brand it might be carrying. Then, on the mule's broad back, he saw an odd little heap of dust and debris.

It was falling from overhead. John looked up and saw hay stems and dust cascading down in a little stream from between the planks. His shadow in the lantern light ballooned up the wall. The thin cross poles bent under somebody's weight. Another fall of dust motes shone like a sparkling rain, every grain bright in the lamplight.

A voice from overhead: "Chenneville."

He pulled his revolver from the holster, lifted it straight up, cocked it, and fired.

The explosion was earsplitting. Mules reared back against their tie-lines; his horse crashed sideways.

John reholstered, ran down the line of mules, and began to jerk the tie-lines loose out of their pull-away knots. He turned mules out into the aisle. That was his first and last shot. He didn't want any more shooting. It would bring the man's friends. Whoever was overhead wasn't going to shoot either. John knew it; the mules were valuable, they belonged to the miners, and all down the crowded aisle were kicking, blundering mules loose in the line of fire.

"Chenneville, Chenneville."

A trapdoor opened overhead, and a figure dropped down in a spray of loose hay, a bizarre figure with a harebrained tangle of frizzy blond hair and a hard leather miner's helmet. The figure sported a blond beard and round eyes. It jerked and swung a carbine one way and then another. "Oh, oh, Chenneville!" He threw one hand in the air and made odd, clawing motions.

"Shoot," said John. "Go ahead, kill a mule." The stranger ducked behind a big, excited dark mule. John darted forward and slapped it on the chest. "Back! Back!" The mule backed up into the man and, feeling something behind him he couldn't see, he kicked.

"Shit!" The man's cry was a shout of anguish.

Then the ragged figure was dodging in among the loose mules. John tried to follow him, but the figure ducked here, ducked there, scrambled and jerked through all the sharp angles of light and shadow.

Then John suddenly felt himself seized from behind, and two arms wrapped around his neck in a grip like cable wire. John tore at the arms. Fingers sank into his neck even as he ripped at them, but the man would not let go. John's shirtfront was stabbed at by some sharp object. The creature stank horribly, a strange metallic odor.

John threw his long body left and right, bent forward, back, but the thing clung to him like every bestial inhuman thought or fear one has had in a lifetime, a burden, a leech, a parasite heavy as stone. John pushed backward and slammed the thing on his back into a mule, then into a stall upright. And still, the man held fast.

"I got you, I got you. He said get you, I got you!"

John cranked one hand loose, but the wild heedless strength of whatever it was that held him was immense. The stranger's hand grabbed again, digging into John's neck with nails blackened by lead ore. John sucked at the air with a snorting noise. He was at the edge of losing coherence, fainting, being pulled into some internal whirlpool he might never emerge from.

They fought and stumbled into the front stall, where John's gelding shied and trembled. The thing on his back continued to clutch and stab until John let go the fingers and grabbed the hay hook out of the upright. He swung it behind him with all his strength and sank it into some unseen part of the man's body.

John had little strength in his backward swing, but he had hooked into something, and so he pulled and ripped and jerked and tore flesh so that the hands around John's neck loosened. The man screeched, high, thin, and demented. He fell to the ground, clutching his buttocks, blood staining his hands.

John looked at him, gasping. The man had been sent to kill him. The man's fingernails were black with lead ore and blood. He was extremely thin and his head trembled.

The barn was now in chaos. A big dark draft jack plowed through the other animals on his way to settle old scores now that he was free. John shoved aside a little red mule, grabbed an old boot, and beat the man over the head with the heel, over and over, till the leather helmet rolled away.

"Where's Albert Dodd?" John stood over the man. "Where is he?" Spurts of blood jumped from between the man's fingers where he clutched his buttock. There was a deep hoof mark on his upper thigh, delivered with such force it had torn the cloth of his trousers. He had dropped the sharp thing he'd used to stab John; it was a pritchel from among the farrier's tools.

"So you helped him kill the Callaways?" John was still gasping for air.

"No, no, you're next, you're next."

The frizzy hair was piled in layers that quivered like yellow cushion stuffing. The man seemed to jerk all over in a charge of renewed energy as he scrambled to his feet. He backed away to the harnesses and leaned against a horse collar. A red mule came tearing up, determined to get out the door and flee from the wrath of the draft jack. It ran straight over the frizzy-haired blond lunatic with his eggshell eyes, knocking him down.

"Am I?" John's pupils were dilated to the point where his light eyes looked almost black. In the lantern light, his thick upper lip glistened with sweat on a day's growth of beard.

"Well, hell, I don't know. Where are we?" The man's head swung left and right, looking at the harnesses. They seemed to alarm him. He was trying to climb out of the blows to his head.

"Where is Dodd?"

The miner shook his head and raked a hand through the lunatic, springing hair, streaking it with blood.

"Damn if I know."

John hooked the top off the molasses barrel. "I'm going to shove you in there," he said. "Headfirst."

The man tried to focus on the world. One arm wandered out and groped for support. He stared wide-eyed at John. Then he smiled, and in a gentle and quiet voice he said, "Come here, come here, look."

John dropped instantly into a squat, but the man was fast. He had a hoof rasp in both shaking fists, and he brought it down overhand. It struck John on the wrist with a slapping sound. John threw out a defensive hand, and another hard blow landed on the side of his neck. His balance suddenly began to turn like a windvane, left to right, left to right.

John's hat softened another blow of the rasp on the crown of his head. Around the fires beyond the walls of the mule barn, men were shouting to each other and calling out the names of mules that were out and running loose. *Look, there's Jerry and June Bug and Dusty and what the hell is going on up there?*

John saw the carbine where it lay in the straw, grabbed it up, and slammed the butt of the carbine into the man's forehead with all his strength. At last the man collapsed. He went down and stayed down. John stood with his feet apart, and the world stopped spinning. The miner's eyes flew open; he was alive, but John didn't care one way or another.

The miner said, "I can't see."

"Then lay there and die." John quickly jacked out the loads from the carbine, one after another, in case by some miracle the miner came to. "You *fi' de pute*." John was still breathing hard. He threw the cartridges into the molasses, where they hesitated on the sweet amber surface before beginning to sink.

Men were coming, shouting that the mules were loose. John shoved the carbine butt-first into the molasses barrel alongside the drowning cartridges. Then he kicked the man's head back and went through his pockets quickly. There was nothing to identify him, and all that he found was a fifty-dollar gold piece with a hole drilled in it, a bag of tobacco, and two human teeth.

"God," he said, and threw them all down on the man's coat, his eyes now peacefully closed. John got his horse and led him out of the barn on a path opposite the fires so that he was in shadow.

The man who had been burying the pig guts strode up out of the dark. "What's going on?"

"I have no idea," said John.

He rode east through the pines under a low dead moon of mid-November, a waning moon that seemed to be held like lead against its own rising, thin and poisoned with John's anger, the remains of anger. He rode toward the Mississippi River and food and rest and compara-tive safety. He listened to everything, and it seemed everything listened to him. Things heard his shallow intake of breath and the horse's ner-vous snorting. Faraway voices called out, and he heard a gunshot. He kept on.

The man's face and behavior came to him in discrete pictures, one by one. He had been sent to meet John and had waited God knows how long up in the loft. He knew John's name—his last name, at any rate. The man's hands had shaken ever so slightly, and he spoke like a local *Américain*, and he couldn't see that well, for John recalled him staring around wide-eyed in the dim lamplight, searching. Clearly the man had lead poisoning.

You're next. He had all but admitted something: Guilt? That he was an accomplice? But given the state of his mind, and its burden of lead toxicity, he could have been hallucinating.

John had a long night ahead of him. Twenty miles to Ste. Genevieve and in the dark. He crossed the Big River and kept moving because the crossing was wide, shallow, and open to any nighttime vagrant that might come along meaning well or ill. A mile later he turned off to the first running water he heard. He thought it might be the Terre Bleue. He crashed into it, throwing water, rinsing his hands free of molasses and lime powder. For a moment he clung to the stirrup and the fender with his head dropped. The world settled and became evenly held on all sides by the earth's blessed gravity. He listened. He couldn't hear anybody following. He led the horse out of the stream and onto the road.

He walked most of the way back to Ste. Genevieve to spare the horse, and also he didn't want to be sitting upright over those moving white markings. It was cold. At four in the morning he saw the faint lights of town. Candles in windows, woodsmoke, and the first stirring of early risers. When he had finally walked out his tension and seared nerves, he thought about the words, *You're next.* The man might have said them just to say something, anything, that sounded threatening.

The people in this county had not been like this before, if he could recall it correctly—this chaos, this land of criminals and casual murder. He felt a sense of profound loss and fell into a deep sleep with a singing noise in his head. He woke up in his room with his clothes still on. He rolled over to look out the window at Ste. Genevieve, with its solid and antique French houses, the noise of carters, the sound of steamboats at the landing. He lay in bed until late morning. He hurt here and there; nothing serious. It had been a hard ride and a hard fight. His left wrist had tiny red punctures in even rows from the rasp, and his neck was raw and probably bruised. But he had held up, he had managed himself well, with only one passing moment of light-headedness. Nothing broken, he had not got shot, his opponent on the ground and out cold.

By noon he had sponged off the rest of the molasses and the dusting of slaked lime from his clothes. He shaved and made himself presentable and went down to the restaurant. Madame Picot sat him down at a table near the window, where he went through fresh bread, butter, three eggs, coffee, and a steak, taking in everything around himself; his critical gaze followed the people in the restaurant, those working back in the kitchen, noted who it was that walked into the blacksmith shop across the street. He wondered how many people sitting at their breakfast knew him, who it was he should have known.

He bowed to Madame Picot and walked out into the day.

CHAPTER EIGHT

November 1866 / Ste. Genevieve and
Riviere aux Vases, Missouri

JOHN FOUND THE GIRL AT Mrs. Sanford's laundry.

This was a small, steamy building made of local brick, once a cottonseed oil mill but now a washhouse. An untidy girl ran here and there with buckets of water, singing. She sang, *She eats potatoes, she ain't got a penny, she eats potatoes, she ain't got a penny* . . . The woman who owned the laundry stood among the stoves and their great kettles of boiling water and the damp wash lines. She put her hands around her mouth and bellowed for Liza.

When she came pelting up, the older woman stood with her arm around the girl's shoulders as if to shield her against all the world's ills except poverty and tornadoes. Liza was frail, and her hair was unwashed, coming out of its braids in threads of streaky blonde.

"I don't know what it is you are wanting anyhow," the girl said. They sat on two upturned buckets. John was still tired, but rest would come later. Loud noises and shouting all around from other washerwomen employed there and men bringing in firewood.

"My name is John Chenneville," he said, "and I'm looking for a man. Maybe you can help me. What's your whole name?" His frock coat collar was turned up over the mark of the rasp, and as he waited he pressed his hat crown from the inside to get it back in shape.

"Elizabeth Grace MacLean, born and raised. I was married off when I was thirteen to a big fat man from Helena. I couldn't help it; they wanted to get rid of me."

John paused. Married at thirteen. *Tabernac.* He said, "Well, Elizabeth Grace, tell me how old you are now."

She scrunched her shoulders up and wobbled her head back and forth and then said, "Look at your wrist. It looks like it got run over by something."

"It's all right," he said, and gently removed her hand. "It's fine. So, I was asking how old you were."

"I guess about fourteen or so. I took my own name back. I was born with my own name and I'll be damned if I give it up for a lard bucket who ups and leaves me after three months of merrit life." And behind these words was a hard and unchildlike loathing.

John nodded. He was going to have to keep the conversation on track, and so he ignored the introduction of the lard bucket into the conversation. "Maybe you could tell me about a problem you had with a strange man last week. Somebody tried to get you on a boat. When you didn't want to go."

The girl nodded furiously. "It was a bad boat."

"Was it his boat?"

"No, *sir*, the man said it had just come up from Memphis. It was a trashy old single-boiler steamer. It wasn't unloading nothing, neither. Now that's enough to make you think right there. Wasn't nobody leaving, neither, just men going aboard. Now then, he said I could get work on the boat, you know, doing cooking."

"All right, maybe you could tell me who said this."

"The man who took aholt of me. He was talking nice, but he had aholt."

"Do you know his name?"

"Yessir, I do. He was called Dodd by a friend who was standing there next aside."

"All right. He said you could get work on the boat."

"Yessir, helping with the cooking. He spoke real nice to me, said I could make good money. He said he'd give me five dollars, he said we'd go to St. Louis and he'd get my picture taken. They can make you look like a city girl."

"But you didn't want to go."

"Well, hell no, I seen what kind of boat it was, I ain't no fool. There was a lot of those kind of women." She bit her lips together. "I seen it, I ain't no fool."

"No," said John. "You are not." He looked down into her furious and unsmiling little face. "You are not. So he wasn't alone."

"That's right, he had a sort of thick man with him. A man broke his arm."

"You mean a man with a broken arm?"

"That's right. Didn't I even say that? I wasn't afraid of him because I could sort of bust him one on that arm. But then so one of those women grabbed me to make me stay on that boat, but I was stronger than her." She drew herself together inside her ragged dress made of indestructible homespun and endless work, and her bare feet crossed one over the other. "I am not so big, but I have worked so long and so hard. I fought loose from her and run."

John felt a flush of anger like a sharp stinging in his face. He bent his head to look at his dusty boots, the nicked steel spurs. "So," he said, "you're a strong girl."

"Well, they found *that* out, didn't they? Sir, they were wicked people. Then Mrs. Sanford here took me in to work at the laundry." She lifted her chin high and then cocked her head to gaze into his face. "But you ain't one of those sorry ratbags, are you? That have fed on the powers of darkness. You're a good one."

John smiled his brief and insubstantial smile. "We've all fallen short, they say."

She patted his arm. "But *how* short, that's the question. You ought to just stay good, and you can if you try." She nodded to herself. "Yep."

"I will. Tell me what he looked like." John kept his voice level and pleasant. He again felt that need to look into the man's face, to see his eyes, to place him in the world of human beings. At present Dodd seemed dull and homicidal both, a gauche, ham-fisted fiend under imperatives beyond knowing. He said, "For instance, how tall was he?"

"Why don't you stand up?" the girl said. "Then I can tell."

John stood up and kept his hands at his sides and smiled down at her. Maybe he shouldn't smile; he didn't know. She'd had enough of strange men talking nice to her.

Elizabeth Grace stood up beside him and looked up at his face. She came to just below his shoulder. "He wasn't as tall as you, not by half. Like maybe tall as here." She leveled her hand at John's cheekbone.

"All right. And what kind of face did he have?" He sat back down, and so did she.

"Well, he had a face kind of all scrunched up in the middle, like a wad. Like God had made his face and then wadded it up out of pure D spite. You can do that with sugar cookie dough. Make a face in a ball of it and then go *rrrrt*, squash it all up."

John leaned back and put his fist to his mouth to keep from laughing. "Yes," he said. "And so you must have seen his hair and his eyes."

"Yes, sir—anyway, he had straight teeth, straight up and down, like hog teeth. He had black devil hair and eyes the color of dirty ice; you could tell he was all afire inside from the burning hell he was toting around with him in his soul. He had a big neckerchief to hide his neck— it had the mark of Satan on it." The girl nodded again, pleased with her description.

"And so what was the mark of Satan?"

"Like the great speckled bird, he had a whole rash of black specks on his neck, and thus the Lord marked him out among all mankind as a *booger*."

John looked up at Mrs. Sanford. The woman shook her head slowly, a look of commiseration on her face. Liza shrugged up her thin shoulders and spread her hands. "Well, is that about it?"

John said, "Ah, just out of pure curiosity, how did you end up here?"

"Oh, well, my ma and pa come down here out of Ripley County when I was about twelve or so, because Ripley was all burnt out in the war, including us, looking for work, and then they died of a river sickness. Both of them. They both just *died*." Liza stopped, and her expression was not one of grief or sorrow so much as wonder that these immoveable pillars of her life had simply gone. Evaporated. Did not

exist anymore. John looked into her impertinent and now absent little face, her eyes roaming from the kettles to the washing lines, not
seeking an answer but waiting for one, and John knew she would wait
forever.

"So here you are."

"Yes, and so I was orphanted, and I had to make my own way somehow. I picked cotton for Mr. Andrews just over the way . . ." She made
a waving gesture to where she thought south was. "Down in the Bois
Brule Bottom. And then they all wanted me to marry Mr. Archer. And
so I did, and then that went by the wayside and I was looking for work
to cook for somebody and that man come upon me."

John sat in silence for a moment trying to straighten it all out. "You
came from the Bottom to Ste. Genevieve looking for work. How did
you get here?"

"Well, I walked."

Mrs. Sanford looked down at Liza, and her expression was a mixture
of pride and sadness both for a girl of fourteen walking twenty miles
alone, looking for work. John stood up and thanked the girl and offered
his hand. To his great relief she smiled; it was the smile of a fourteen-
year-old girl, after all, of resilient and indestructible youth, and she
grasped his hand and gave it a hearty shake.

He wanted to give her a silver dollar, but Mrs. Sanford laid her hand
over his wrist and said, "She ain't taking no money but what she has
earned here in honest work." She let go of John's arm. "You heard what
she was offered money for."

The girl glanced hungrily at the bright coin and then dropped her
head in a fierce pout, crossed her arms, and said, "Well, ain't that a
bugger."

But he did not forget her. Who could? She had wrung his heart with
her springing courage, which even she did not know was courage. So
he went to the Sisters of St. Joseph convent, talked with the Mother
Superior, and left a hundred dollars on a bank draft with her. This
was for Mother Superior to dole out to the girl as needed. Maybe she

would stop singing her dismal and repetitive potato song. *She ain't got a penny.* Well, you do now, child, so make the best of it.

INSIDE THE BRICK county courthouse, in the narrow and confined sheriff's office, John sat with his hat on his knee and one leg crossed over the other, listening to the county sheriff tell him that yes, he knew Dodd, and yes, Dodd had been one of his deputies. He had been with the Thirty-Third Illinois Mounted Infantry during the war. The sheriff wore a bowler hat and a four-in-hand tie. The fat clerk was nowhere to be seen.

"And so where is he now?" John asked. He did not look around the office, did not read the wanted posters, had no interest in the cigar ends in a dish or the tin of Hargrave's pastilles or numbered keys hung on a board. He kept his sleeve cuff down and his neckcloth high over the bruise.

"Well, he's the wandering type." The sheriff glanced at this big man seated in his office. His Union dreadnaught overcoat made him seem even bigger. He had his thick walking cane in one hand.

"Wandered where?"

"I don't know, he just quit."

"When did he quit?"

The sheriff paused. "I don't understand why I have to answer all these questions. We already investigated that incident, and it was committed by persons unknown. Probably a feud with some other of your French compatriots. So, did you have a good time in Bonne Terre?"

John saw through the window several armed men riding by. Then he turned back to the sheriff with an expressionless face. "I had a wonderful time. When did he quit?"

"Well, a few days ago."

John's face didn't change. "And so he just left?"

The sheriff was silent and moved his logbook around on his desktop. Finally he said, "Well, like I said, he likes to go wandering."

"Where did he go?"

"He took a northbound steamer."

"Did he have somebody with him?"

"Don't know."

"Who does he run with?"

A short silence. "You're related to the Desloges, aren't you?" The sheriff was caught between a roiling interior fear and a determination to assert his authority. He was breathing heavily through his nose. He regarded the logbook again as if he had some important business there that needed pursuing. "Your old man bought up half the property in those old lead mines. But he never lived down here, stayed up north of St. Louis—they say you all have a big place up there. Now, under martial law we can still confiscate the property of those in rebellion against the United States."

"And?"

John didn't move other than to shift the heavy cane from his left hand to his right. The sheriff glanced down at it and recognized it for what it was: a weapon.

"They say your father has went to his reward, some years ago. So that's your property now."

John said nothing, but now he understood how Basile had been threatened.

"And you were injured in the war. So what I'm saying is, I can see it was a head wound and it could be you are misjudging things about how your sister died. Imagining things, maybe. Your sister and her family." He paused. "Sorry for your loss, there."

John knew there was no point in arguing anything with this man, a sheriff who would allow a boatload of prostitutes to anchor at the jetty, who would not inquire into the midnight murder of an entire family and sat safely under the umbrella of martial law, but Sheriff Litchfield now had come up against something he didn't quite grasp. Outrage and indignation would be understandable. The sheriff was expecting this, but he didn't get it and so was confused.

John said, "You threatened my uncle."

"Who?" The sheriff laughed briefly. "Your uncle?"

The tall clock beside the American flag ticked heavily through another short silence. John said, "Who is Albert Dodd's friend? The one with the broken arm."

The sheriff was still hesitant, still unsure of John's right to ask, but in the knowledge that one of these days martial law was going to come to an end, he said, "He's friends with a man called Tuesday Jones. Jones left too." Then the man seemed to draw himself up and attempt to appear to be a peace officer as in duty bound. "I can tell you that for sure."

"Good. To where?"

The sheriff, sweating into his stiff new tie on a cool day, watched John's impatient fingers drumming on his knee. He considered and then said, "St. Louis." He rolled his shoulders under his coat. "It was the first boat leaving, so he and Tuesday just up and got on it."

And so now he was sure of his man. He had never seen him or heard his voice or seen his handwriting, but he knew who his quarry was. He had nearly got himself killed in gaining this knowledge, but it left him oddly, bitterly happy.

IT WAS LATE when he rode into the little valley of the Riviere aux Vases. After four years of partisan warfare throughout the hills, what he was looking at was a broken country, a hazy and beautiful ruin. Where his sister and her family had lived there was nothing left but charred heaps. No remains to mourn. Great heavy white oaks rattled with auburn leaves. He rode to the edge of the spring. It was a round, still pool ten yards across, sprinkled with dry basswood and elm leaves. Water insects skated across the surface on tiny circles, one to a leg. The burnt timbers of what had been a large house and all the outbuildings lay in piles of black and glittery jackstraws. It was barren even of rats or snakes, who would find nothing to eat in all that sterile charcoal.

John sat his horse and looked at it awhile, but a building rage was making his palms sweat, and so he turned away.

He rode another ten miles to the church of St. Philip and St. James.

It was night when he got there. Some houses nearby had lights in their windows. He walked into the churchyard and at last found their grave. A dim winter evening still and cold. He knelt down in front of the tall limestone column and lit a match and held it before the names like an icon. The Mother of God mourned over them in her stone drapery. *Eulalie and William Callaway, baby boy Jean-Louis, May 15, 1865. Gone But Not Forgotten.* The flames picked out the sparkling limestone lettering. He shook out the match. Then all of a sudden, as the unrelieved darkness took over, he began to cry. He put one hand over his face and wept helplessly. He knew he was making a terrible hoarse noise, but he couldn't stop himself. It was grief, rage. He seemed to be down to the very paving stones of raw emotion. Then after a while it went away. He made gasping noises and wiped his face in the elbow of his greatcoat. Then he stood and made the sign of the cross. He took up the reins of the horse, stepped into the old plantation saddle, and rode throughout the night without stopping because he knew he would not sleep.

He heard the quiet, scholarly voice of Father Dillon reading the homily: *And when he had opened the fourth seal, I heard the voice of the fourth beast say, Come and see. And I looked, and behold a pale horse: and his name that sat on him was Death, and Hell followed with him.*

CHAPTER NINE

November–December 1866 / St. Louis, Missouri,
to Fort Smith, Arkansas

HE RETURNED TO ST. LOUIS on a long, unwieldy side-wheeler that battered its way up the eastern side of the river, in the slack water. He took a first-class cabin for the day trip because it would impress the purser and the steward, whichever one he could get to talk to him. And he could rest. The fight in the mule barn had taken more out of him than he wanted to admit.

The steamboat steward, when a coin was pressed into his hand, said that he had seen the deputy. Knew him from other trips. He usually just took day passage. Except now the man was claiming to be a photographer. He said Dodd had shown around a picture of a young man truer than life, set in a golden frame. He was with a man they called Tuesday Jones—a man the purser also knew, as he was often on this packet. Tuesday was a thick, squat tough who at the present time had a broken arm from some altercation in Helena. It was fixed in a rawhide cast, the kind where they wrapped your arm up in green hide and then let it dry and it became like cast iron.

"He's a friend of Dodd's?"

"I've seen them together often enough."

John said, "Thank you. Appreciate it."

St. Louis lay ahead under an atmosphere of smoke that poured from steamboat stacks, from coal fires and street dust, a place of noise he could no longer abide for long. He used to love it. He didn't love it anymore. He lay back on the bed in the cabin. It was a starboard-side cabin where he could look out at the Illinois shore and hear the endless thumping and roar of the sidewheel inside its drum. John wanted not so much to kill the man as to simply erase him from this place called the world. He thought about what came next, hour by hour.

He would find Tuesday Jones first. Dodd was likely gone to ground somewhere, smoking, looking out of a second-story window at a busy street and thinking about his next change of place because he had heard that a man named Chenneville was looking for him. Tuesday Jones, the enforcer, would be searching for a place to lay up where he could drink himself out of his pain.

As they nosed into the packed levee, the water shone in fractures and breaks and floating things unnamed. A dead dog got caught up in the sidewheel and went crashing around inside the drum. At the Poplar Street landing, they faced a solid wall of warehouses. Noise, noise, lots of noise, and crowds of passengers and workmen, loaders, and sweepers.

He got out of the disorder and racket of the waterfront and took a room at the Old National Hotel at Third and Market. He left his baggage there. He pulled on his old frock coat with the buttoned back vent. He placed his hat carefully on his head and took up the cane. Then he started walking down First Street in search of a man with a broken arm.

People got out of his way; he was a big man with a slightly unbalanced walk, maybe drunk on whiskey or laudanum. There was something dangerous about him, dangerous and faulty and out of control, and so people on the sidewalks gave him room.

He walked from one bar and one saloon to another, from the Poplar Street landing to Chouteau Avenue. He started at Reudi's Beer Garden on Second Street and then on to a saloon called La Frenchi on South Levee, up to a one-room drinking place on Elm and Third, and then a loud, crowded place at Walnut and Third and the row of gambling houses on Fourth Street.

Saloons with glass doors and waiters in black and white, others were mere cellars tucked away in alleys. Sometimes in the brick walls were the remnants of other walls of ancient stone houses. There were signs over the low doorways: No Dogs Or Irishmen. Sometimes signs in German advertising Lemp's Vienna Lager or Shwartzbier or Anheuser's

Pasteurized Beer. Men inside, heating up the room with their bodies against the chill, smoke, and talk. He kept on walking, kept on asking.

Farther into the city for The What Cheer on Seventh and Ann; he questioned bartenders and waiters about a man with a rawhide cast on his arm. He's called Tuesday, he said. Tuesday Jones. Once somebody addressed him in French, and he answered in French. How the man knew he spoke French, John didn't know, but he went on to the next place.

"Yes, Tuesday Jones that broke his arm, isn't that right?" A waiter nodded at him. "Do you reckon it was him bare-knuckle fighting?"

"I don't know," said John. "Is he a boxer?"

A man at a table behind him said, "*Ja*, if you could call an Irish stand-down a boxing fight."

"I'm looking for him," said John.

"He's had work at the glassworks on Monroe and North Broadway. I think he lives in one of those houses close by."

JOHN PUT HIS shoulder to the door and shoved it open. Tuesday Jones sat holding his arm in its rawhide cast, cherishing it as if it were a baby. His hair was dark and shiny and uncoiled in long thick strands, and John saw lines of pain in the man's face. His arm in the dirty cast rested on a pillow in his lap. The man sat on the bed. It was the only place to sit. The window was missing several panes. On the table was a brown bottle, half-full—Adams Neuralgia Mixture, which was 10 percent opium.

Tuesday Jones stared at him in alarm.

John said, "I want some information, and if I don't get it, I'll break your other arm." He put his back against the unpainted wall and rested both hands on top of the cane.

Jones sat blinking in an opium haze. "Yeah, but about what?"

"Dodd."

The man's face seemed to flatten. He stared silently and sullenly at John. John shifted the cane and grasped it at the bottom end in his right hand, like a club. From the empty panes of the window came the smell of burning coke from the glassworks chimney.

"I don't know nothing about Dodd."

John stepped forward and brought the cane down backhanded on the side of Jones's head with a loud *crack*, then stepped back again, out of reach. But Jones was a fighter; he threw the pillow at John and got to his feet, drawing back a big callused pugilistic fist. John snatched the pillow out of the air, threw it aside and moved in close, knocked the man's good arm aside and struck down with the cane sideways, hard, against the man's cast. Jones screamed and bent forward, holding the arm.

"It's going to get worse," John said.

"Oh my God, oh my God," the man said. Unnoticed tears of pain ran down his face. John took up the opium mixture and walked to the window and threw the bottle out one of the empty panes. "No!"

"So I'm waiting."

"You shouldn't have done that! Son of a bitch, son of a bitch!"

"Are you listening? You're not listening to me." John flipped the cane in the air and caught it. "I said I would break your other arm, and I meant it."

The man sat down heavily on the bed, bent over the rawhide cast. "What do you want?"

"Tell me about Dodd. You and Dodd, down in the lead mine country. Ste. Genevieve, Bonne Terre. Valle Mines, Riviere aux Vases."

"He come there with an Illinois unit during the war."

"He's from Illinois?"

"Yeah. Or I don't know. From Cairo. Then after the war he stayed on and he was a deputy down there."

"Were you?"

"No, man, listen, go get that Adams Mixture. I can't hardly think."

"In a minute." John was silent for a moment, waiting for Tuesday to focus on him. Then he said, "He killed people. I want to know who he killed."

"He was crazy. He's not a normal person." Tuesday stroked the rawhide cast as if he were comforting it.

"That aside, I'm not going to mess around with you much longer. Who?"

"I never did anything, I did not, he was just paying me to kind of assist him, he needed somebody to get horses and supplies when he was on one of his patrols. He called it 'going on patrol.' I was his assistant, he said. Me and a man had lead poisoning, one of those miners."

"I am not interested in you. I want to know about Dodd."

Jones's pain was reducing him to a humility he had probably rarely experienced. That and the shakes. "About Dodd," he repeated.

John waited. He listened to the man's short, desperate breaths.

"Well, he shot that family there at the spring on Riviere aux Vases. He said her dress made a big balloon in the water. He said the man sank like a rock. He said her dress was green and pink checkered. He said he set the house on fire. All right? You can't prove anything, can you?"

John didn't answer. His mouth was dry.

Tuesday Jones's mouth was open and sucking air. "Yeah, now will you go get that bottle?"

John was still silent. Here it was. The details, the truth, the unspeakable reality. His pretty sister. The baby. He felt his throat thicken in an odd way and a flush crawling up his face. Jones didn't notice.

Finally John said, "Anything else?"

"He said he was going out there because the woman was in love with him." Jones's eyes were glistening with tears, and snot ran from his thick flat nose.

John knew he had to say something. "Yes. Left a string of broken hearts behind him." And since Dodd had given this man a different reason for the killing than John had heard from Teo Aubuchon, he knew Dodd for what he was. One of those strange random murderers.

"He killed her and her husband and the baby." Jones nodded compulsively. "He had to have. I was sitting in Brickey's tavern, and Dodd came in. He had a picture, one of them pictures."

"A daguerreotype."

"Yeah, one of them. He said, 'They're all in the spring.' I says, 'What spring? Who?' He says, 'That woman wanted to run off with me, and

I had it out with her husband. They aren't going to cause any more trouble.' He was kind of quiet about it. But he told me that about two or three other women too—he was a liar, you know, or he made stuff up. Go get that bottle."

"Give me the date."

"Middle of May last year. Sixty-five."

"What did he do with the picture?"

"He threw one of them over the side. He gets stuff like that and throws it away after a while."

"And then?"

"A man come into town and was yelling at the sheriff about it, but the sheriff didn't do nothing. The man was yelling about how could you ignore this? How could any sane man kill a baby? And in the weeks after, people stopped talking about it because Dodd was still there. He was a deputy. He killed a boy on St. Marys Road. And maybe other people, I don't know."

John waited. The drug was wearing off, and the man began to rock back and forth.

"Just get out, would you?" Tuesday Jones pulled back his lips in a big square grimace. "Ah God. Get out."

"In a minute. He goes by other names. What are they?"

"In St. Louis here, he says his name's Charles Bain. He bought a little revolver and changed to something else. That time he said his name was Garoute."

"What did he do here in town?"

"He went and had a picture taken. Of him."

"What the hell for?"

"I don't know, I don't know. I'm about to die," Jones said. He stroked the broken arm and made a long *aaahhh* sound. "Because he thinks he's a ladies' man. Because he likes his own face."

"Where is he?"

"He got the train to Helena, said he was taking a boat to Fort Smith and going on to Texas. Said did I want to go along. But by that time,

I'd broke my arm and I said hell no. Go get that bottle, would you? I'm about to pass out."

"When?"

"When? Just about two days ago. The sheriff in Ste. Genevieve told him somebody was looking for him." Jones fell down backward on the bed and regarded the ceiling. "That's you, ain't it? Who are you?"

John thought for a moment. "He has relatives or friends down in Texas, then."

"How should I know?"

"He said something to you about it."

"Yeah, some relatives down there."

"Where?"

"Marshall—something like Marshall, anyway."

"What are their names?"

"Garoute."

"All right. Why did he come here to St. Louis, then?"

"Somebody owed him some money, he said. He needed money."

"He should rob a bank." John moved his coat aside and put the cane into his belt. He watched Jones for a moment as he rolled back and forth on the bed, regular as a metronome. Then he turned and left.

HE VISITED MONSIEUR le Docteur Boisliniere at the women's hospital. They had a long talk then, about men who murder. Those strange people who kill over and over again. He had been the St. Louis coroner for many years. At last, Jean Chenneville closed the door of Boisliniere's medical office and walked down the hall, his bootheels sounding on the tiles, carrying within himself those eternal questions, the great mysteries of homicide and memory. Of radical evil.

The policeman refused to issue a warrant on such flimsy evidence as John had. His uniform was dark blue and his hat a billed and napless wide-awake; his skills and talents lay with the criminals of the streets, and his pockets clanked with unseen metal objects. Suddenly the city that John had known all his life now appeared vexing, stifling, mindless. His sister and her family so wantonly murdered and yet the city blundered on with its horsecars and the unearthly shrieking of paddlewheelers releasing pent-up steam.

"What would it take?" John said. He was tiring, but he ignored it. His head hurt, but he ignored that too. He had taken a hired hack all the way to Thirteenth and Poplar, to the police station, and stood with one hand flat on the booking desk, his spine straight and his head level, standing six inches taller than the man he was talking to.

"To get a warrant?" The inspector shifted his paper forms. "You're John Chenneville?"

"Yes."

"You have your discharge papers?"

"Yes."

"Well, Mr. Chenneville, I don't need to see them, but you'd need the sheriff of the county in which this occurred to issue the warrant, along with various proofs and testimonies that it had actually occurred and been perpetrated by whom."

John nodded once. "I see." He spread his left hand on the counter and looked down. With the other hand he leaned on his cane. "This concerns a murder in Ste. Genevieve County. Last year."

"Last year? Down there?"

"Last year. Down there."

"Aha. Now, *you're* the kind of man that's going to be tempted to take things in his own hands, that's the kind of man *you* are. And that's just exactly the wrong kind of thing to do."

The place was deafening with cell doors being opened and shut with great clanging noises, policemen coming and going with perpetrators in hand, unintelligible shouts from somewhere.

"That aside." John's expression was flat. "I want you to take account of this. If I have to, I will file a legal complaint." He looked around the booking desk for a pen and ink. He saw an ink bottle, opened it, took up a pen.

"Well, then you just do that."

John filled out the papers and wrote in the policeman's name: Inspector Michael Bohannon. The policeman turned the form around to read it and shook his head.

"But let's consider. I know there's a lot of loose ends since the war, and we all want to see things right and proper and tied up neatly, and if it isn't, well, we just take things into our own hands. For which we are arrested and tried and we are thrown in prison."

"I see."

"However. You're not that kind of man, are you? I know people, and *you're* going to get an attorney to do this. You should have had an attorney before you came in here." He turned up a smooth, noncommittal face to John. "I observe that you have had a serious blow to the head. You have to consider that perhaps you are not thinking logically."

The policeman's hand reached out to take the paper but then paused, suspended in the dusty air of Thirteenth Street when a whistle blew for noon and a dog barked and John took this as a signal to lay the paper down and walk away. The inspector watched as John disappeared into the crowded streets.

HE STARTED ON one last search; he sought out the photograph galleries and struck it lucky at the third one. It was W.L. Troxel's Heliograph Gallery on Fifth near the courthouse. On the shop's façade a sign advertised daguerreotypes, tintypes, ambrotypes, heliographs, amazingly lifelike, all done in the best style with suitable and/or dramatic backgrounds.

There were a number of people there because it was a bright day, perfect for window-lit studio light. Around him, people sat in comfortable chairs gazing up at display portraits high up on the walls. In the back room was the studio, where a flood of sunlight came in from an enormous rear window.

John knew that daguerreotypes were expensive because they required a plate coated with a gold solution. They were taken carefully and rarely more than once. The new ambrotypes, or photographs as people called them, were also unique images but they were far less expensive and because they used glass plates they were more easily handled, so often people had two or three taken in order to choose the best portrait. John assumed that they cleaned the glass plates of the less desirable ones. Maybe they kept them for a few days. He very much needed to see what this man looked like.

An arched doorway led into the studio. John walked in quietly without being invited and stood against the back wall. He saw a spare man with loud checkered pants setting up a light-filtering device. It resembled a big square parasol made of white muslin. The ambrotype man teetered it on its long, thin stand several feet above a man's head. The man sat on a chair with one hand on some sort of book. Behind him was a painted garden. The man sat rigid in a high collar and cravat while the light from the big window flooded over him, softly, muted by the square of muslin between it and his head.

"Do not *move*," the photographer said. "Do *not*."

John watched. The photographer placed the wet plate in the large box camera, peered through the lens, cranked out the bellows of the big instrument, ran around front and opened the stops, ran back, and tripped the lens lever.

The man in the chair sat frozen and still. He was terrified of moving. Blurred images were costly. You couldn't use them, and still you paid for them. Around the room were various props: carpets, shawls, top hats, books, globes, the plaster head of a cherub, a fake Greek statue of a half-naked woman, which John glanced at and checked for veracity and found nothing to complain about.

"All done?" The man tried to speak without moving his lips.

"Yes. You may get up. We shall see."

With one gracious hand movement, the photographer invited the sitter to relax in the front reception room. John moved slightly aside as he passed. He said, "Mr. Troxel?"

"That's me." The photographer carefully drew the plate out of the large wooden box camera.

"You might have had somebody come in here in the last few days for a portrait. Medium height, gray eyes, said his name was Dodd?"

"Ah yeah." The photographer wasn't listening. "Wait, I have to set this plate." But John didn't wait. He followed him into the darkroom. It too had a window, smaller and painted in a wash of red paint. Troxel shut the door. In this deep-red glow, the photographer dropped the plate into the dipper and poured on silver nitrate.

"So, what I'm asking is if Dodd had maybe several plates taken." John would ask about the name Dodd at first, then if he wasn't found he would ask about Dodd's aliases, Bain and Garoute.

"I forget. I could look." The ambrotype man poured some other solution over the plate, tipping it back and forth, staring at the image that appeared. "Tell me about it."

After some explanations and an offer of two dollars for his time and trouble, John finally convinced Troxel to look at the glass plates from the last four days; the mistakes, the ones where a person blinked or moved slightly, where the man taking the photograph had not used the correct stop and the plate was underexposed or overexposed. John found himself growing tense; it was the bloody red light pouring over his hands, his shirtfront. He didn't like it.

"Dodd," said the ambrotype man. "Dodd, Dodd. Let's see." The door to the darkroom was closed; the room reeked of nitrocellulose and ether. Here were stacked all the background flats, various scenes where one could pretend to be where one was not: a library filled with painted books, a terrace overlooking a stormy sea. There were spilled blots of chemicals all over the floor and a dead cigar in a dish, and in the red light it all looked as if it were bathed in gore.

"You might have taken several. He has black pinpoints on his neck from some accident."

"I don't remember that, nobody like that. We generally wipe those error plates about every three days."

"He covers it with a cravat or a kerchief. He wears it high up."

"Oh. Him. Dodson?"

"Dodd."

"Medium height, grayish eyes." Troxel tipped the glass plate back and forth, catching the light just so. As John watched, the man appeared suddenly, his hand on the book, as if called up out of the otherworld. "Yes, he was particular about his scarf. Kept pulling it up around his neck."

Troxel dropped the plate into a rack to dry, and then they went carefully through the stacked error plates from the last few days searching for an image of such a man. And there he was: A. DODD scribbled on the plate at the top with a wax crayon.

Dodd sat rigidly straight. His hand was on an artfully broken plaster pillar, and his scarf or foulard was in a paisley design and choked up high around his neck. He had moved the hand, and it was blurred. A face with the features all close together in the middle with open, intent eyes. Chemical smells crowded close.

"May I pay you for that plate?" John said. He held it and searched every detail, the clothes and the eyes and the mouth.

"I cannot, sir, no, not without the man's permission."

"Not for a consideration?"

"No, sir."

John held the glass plate in two hands and gazed at Dodd's face at last, knew he would remember it always.

BEFORE HE LEFT St. Louis, he had a final task. He went to see a man in a printer's shop who did calligraphy by hand for various things such as award certificates, land titles. He was also a forger. The man sat back behind the printing floor in a tiny office, a quill pen in his hand, making circles in the air as if deciding where to begin a stroke on the paper before him. The man looked up and then dropped the quill into an inkwell.

"Aha. I remember you," he said.

"Good," said John. Then, barely heard above the rumble of the rotary presses, men hollering at one another, demands for the bindery cart, he said that he needed discharge papers for William T. Allen.

John knew he would probably be traveling into occupied territory. Texas was under martial law, and he knew well that the Union Army loved its paperwork and wanted paperwork from others. It would be convenient, perhaps, from time to time, to not be John Chenneville. The fight in the mule barn had taught him this. His name had preceded him. Dodd had writhed his way into law enforcement in Missouri, he had friends among the Illinois troops, he had relatives here and there. Dodd would have a story about being persecuted by a man named Chenneville. False papers might be useful in Texas.

The man nodded, undisturbed.

"Yes. Been getting a lot of those lately. And loyalty oath sort of things and passes. That'll be twenty dollars."

John whistled, but he brought out a gold piece.

"What unit?"

"Well, ah, make it the Ninety-Fifth Pennsylvania. Company E."

The man nodded, reached into a slot beneath his desk, brought out a sheaf of forms, and tossed them out on his desk one after another like cards. He picked up one that had a screaming Federal eagle on it, with stars and flags. *TO ALL WHOM IT MAY CONCERN*, it said in caps. Then *Know ye*, and here he wrote in *that William T. Allen*, and paused.

"Rank?"

"Ah, first lieutenant."

That William T. Allen, 1st Lt. of Company E. 95th Pennsylvania Volunteers . . . And then, as his company officer he wrote in the name of Captain William Johnson.

"People think the most common name is Smith," he said, writing in an ornate hand. "It is, but the second most common is Johnson. People think it's Jones, but it's not. It's Johnson."

He wrote on, making things up as he went; the mustering officer and *given at* and *this day of*.

John watched him blow gently on the new black ink. "Where did I muster out?"

"Well, where did you?"

"City Point, Virginia, September 23, 1865."

"Memorize this," the man said. "And get yourself a cheap watch and have it engraved with WILLIAM T. ALLEN."

"All right."

Place of residence? Alton, Illinois. Age? Thirty-four. Height? Six three. Complexion? Fair. Eyes? The forger looked up. "Ah, light," he said. "Very light. That'll have to do."

Then Chenneville carried his baggage to the train station in Carondelet, the little suburb just south of downtown. He bought a ticket, boarded the train using his cane, found his berth, and settled in.

How long do you keep it up, how far do you go to find a man like this? If it were for a debt, maybe six months; if it were for an injury, perhaps a year or so; if it were for the murder of a friend, give it several years; but for the murder of someone in your family you search until Hell freezes over and the stars wink out, until either he or you are dead. One or the other. He took the St. Louis and Iron Mountain to Little Rock and then horseback to Fort Smith, looking carefully into every face, in the beginning of a cold winter, getting colder.

In that town he asked and searched. Nothing. One saloon and one livery stable to another. Nothing. In a crowd of men unloading ties for the new railroad somebody tried to put a hand into his greatcoat pocket, but John caught him by the wrist and turned it over and bore down and the thief got away. A man in the crowd told him the pickpocket's name was Brainerd. "They don't know when to quit," he said.

At the telegraph office John watched carefully and somewhat anxiously as the telegrapher sent his message to Bonnemaison. He could hear every letter separately but would he ever be able to operate a key again? TO: MINERVA THURMAN TEMPS CLAIR BONNEMAISON MISSOURI: PLEASE READ TO FERMIN VIVRETTE ALL WELL ON MY WAY TO TEXAS PLEASE WRITE TO ME WITH ANY NEWS C/O GENERAL POST OFFICE JEFFERSON TEXAS REGARDS J CHENNEVILLE. He rented another horse for an outrageous price, had to pay for the horse's loose shoe at a blacksmith's, ate beans and corn bread in a smoky, ill-lit eating-house. A great storm was building in the northwest.

He found a hostelry that seemed fairly safe. He pulled three woolen blankets over himself. The bed was too short for him, but then they always were. He had ridden all day and eaten little, and he was very tired. Below the window of this Fort Smith hostelry, a gas streetlamp sputtered and poured its weak illumination into the night, the primitive river-night of drinking houses and bordellos and other shaky structures where animals and people slept uneasily at the edge of Indian Territory. All was splintered bright new wood, unpaved streets, a cow somewhere making a *hoo hoo* sound, the Arkansas River uncoiling past the banks with its loads of silt all the way from the gold mines of Colorado, and hand-lettered signs: Black Cat Saloon, the Half Moon, Caruther's Drugstore, Parlor Stoves and Ironware.

He listened to the deep choral sound of wind in the telegraph wires. It was comforting, hypnotic. And so he fell asleep. He dreamed of a flying cast-iron serpent or insect hurtling toward him out of a gray sky and then another webbed thing coming at him, this one glittering in copper threads like a magic, lethal web.

PART TWO

CHAPTER TEN

December 1866 / Fort Smith to Keota Indian Territory

THE STORM MOVED IN ON Keota Indian Territory behind a rolling front. With this kind of weather it had become dark by five in the evening. The front brought the night behind it and drew it over the San Bois Mountains, landscapes sank and disappeared, whitetail deer packed up together beneath the high banks of Tenkiller Creek with the wind whistling over their heads. The storm folded over upon itself and along with the heavy snow there were odd flashes of lightning that ran like incandescent marbling inside the clouds.

DECEMBER 17TH 1866 TAHLEQUAH STN: CAP MCCREA'S PATROL
EXPECTED 2NITE TAHLEQUAH FM TENKILLER. LINE MAY GO
DOWN REPORT F SEEN F LINE GOOD KN BELLE.

The storm rolled over Vinita and then Chouteau's Post and southward to Keota, and as it poured south it iced all the telegraph lines of eastern Indian Territory. In this snowed-over wilderness, a light shone out of two windows and one thread of woodsmoke streamed away in the wind. Inside this small building was a lone telegraph operator. A blizzard night and a single lamp, the rattle of passing messages. Snow pinged at the windowpanes, and the telegrapher rested from his labors in his perilous, isolated privacy with both sock feet stretched out, close to the stove. Then he heard a human voice calling out of the storm.

In a state of sudden alarm, the telegrapher bent forward with both hands lifted in the air. He sat listening, utterly still, as if he had been fired in pottery. The uproarious wind howled under the eaves and tore at the shingles.

For a moment, this voice out in the night was confused with the dispatches coming out of the sounder. News concerning Captain McCrea et al. lurching around in a foot of snow somewhere north of Tahlequah. *Dah-dit-dit dit dah-dit-dah-dit . . .*

Aubrey Robertson listened intently. Again, a shout, a voice out there, a man's voice calling from the uninhabited distances of the country some called Oklahoma.

"Hello the house!"

It came from nearby. It was very close. There was no getting around it. The telegrapher was not a particularly brave man, but life in this country interested him, especially the random surprises that were Oklahoma's gift to the universe, what with the Choctaw nearby and the summer tornadoes. He pulled his boots on, jumped up and opened the door to the wind. It hit him in the face. On second thought, he stepped behind it in case some sort of bandit was waiting out in that storm to send a bullet into him. Himself framed in the light. The telegrapher was from England and had been in this country for only six months, but he had, of necessity, learned about life in western America fairly quickly.

He peered around the edge, thin, short, his dark hair flying. Out in the blowing night stood a tall man on foot with both hands held up in the air.

"It's all right!" the man shouted. "Have to get to shelter!"

A second's astonished hesitation, and then telegrapher Aubrey Robertson called out, "Yes, yes, come in!" It was indeed a human being and not some uncoffined wandering spirit. What could he say else? *No, stay out there and die?* "Come in!"

Still the man stood there with a load of snow on his hat and shoulders with his hands raised. The lamplight reached out to him to touch his outline with gold. "I'm armed!" he shouted. "Pistol's in my holster. I'll unload the rifle if you want!"

"No, just get in here!" Robertson stood gripping the door edge. The wind was trying to flatten his entire face, and it tore through the weave of his knitted blue jumper with pinheads of snow. Out there in the storming night, the man looked big enough and strong enough to not need a firearm to commit robbery and assault. He looked big enough to break Robertson's arms and legs like twigs if he so wished and make off with all his valuables, consisting of a cheap watch, a leatherbound copy of *The Woman in White* by Wilkie Collins, fifty dollars in federal bills, and a two-shot Allen revolver hidden in an old boot.

Robertson stood out and waved him in. "Just come in, would you?"

The bulky figure waded through the drifts with long strides. A wave of subfreezing air came in through the opened door, and when it struck the warm air inside there appeared a steaming fog so that it seemed the tall man stepped into Aubrey's shack like a stage devil in a cloud of vapor. Snowflakes flew in spangles around him and then vanished. He had to duck to get in the door.

"Just you?" said Aubrey. He shoved the door to with a slam.

The man nodded. He leaned back against the wall. He was gasping like a fish. All his baggage was strung about him and coated with snow.

"Yes. Just me." He wiped his face of snow in the crook of his elbow. "Saw your light." He looked vacantly around himself and said, "God almighty." Then he put the fingertips of his gloves in his teeth and drew them off. Snow fell from him in little shelves.

Aubrey slotted the door bar quickly. "Western Union to the rescue!" he said. "Good God out in that storm! In the night. Get out of your coat. Drop your gear in the corner." He held out a hand to his favorite chair as if introducing it. "Sit in front of the stove and I'll have something hot coming up."

"Yes."

But still the man stood unmoving for a few seconds with both bare fists to his mouth, breathing on them. Then he slung his saddlebags and the blanket roll from his shoulder and onto the floor. He drew back the skirts of his heavy overcoat to unbuckle his cartridge belt. He dropped it and the revolver in its pommel holster on top of the saddlebags, and whatever was inside the saddlebags made a clanking noise. His mouth was open, and he was still drawing air like a bellows.

"Have some brandy here!" said Aubrey. "Highly recommended for perishing travelers." He wrenched at the lid of the salt keg where he hid his brandy. "You are about done in." He looked for a drinking glass, found one, shook several dead flies out of it, and wiped it with his shirt-tail. "Stating the obvious here. I'm a telegrapher. It's what we do."

"Good." The man came very near to smiling. He bent his head and with two fingers and his thumb carefully lifted his snowy hat by the crown and held it straight out and shook the snow from it. A white V-shaped scar tracked across the left side of his head. A fit of trembling overtook him. He gritted his teeth and ducked his head to try to overcome it. He dropped the hat.

"How long have you been out in that?" Aubrey poured the brandy as he watched the man go through the painful process of forcing his greatcoat buttons through the buttonholes. His hands were thick and stiff. The wind's tone shot up into a high whistle, and the window glass shook.

"Forever. Forever and a day."

"You got lost?" Aubrey stood holding out the brandy.

"No." Another button forced through. "I'm not lost." At last the tall man pulled the greatcoat from his shoulders. It was a faded Federal blue. He threw it on his pile of stuff. He moved stiffly to sit on the chair in front of the stove. He took the thick glass and poured the brandy down his throat. His short growth of beard sparkled with little steely drops of melted snow. He sat holding the glass. "God, that about set my insides on fire."

"Well, fellow, it looks like you walked all the way from the polar regions through glaciers and . . ." Robertson's voice died away as he watched the man slowly pull off his high boots in silence. He wrenched at them with hands that were now swollen with the heat. One after the other he thumped the boots down beside the stove. "Tea?"

"Anything."

"I detest tea, actually," said Robertson. He rattled nervously through his supply shelves, looking for the tea canister and the perforated metal tea egg. "Western Union supplies me with tea because I'm English, I have never been fond of it, but here it is, here it is, coming up!"

"Slow down," the man said. He dropped his hands between his thighs and stared at the round venthole of the stove with its leaping flames. They reflected in his eyes. His pupils were a thin citrus color. He was quite tall, moderately young, or at any rate not old, and heavily built. In the golden light of the single lamp Robertson saw a bullet head, a nose that came down straight off his forehead like a helmet guard and had at one time been flattened by something. A fist or a brick. "I'm not dangerous."

"Says you!" said Aubrey. He reached for the kettle on the stove and heard the man give a small laugh. The telegrapher considered that at least his weapons were not ready to hand, they were in a wet heap in the corner. "But you never know."

"True."

Robertson shoved the metal egg into the teapot and poured a high, long, hot stream of water into it. "Here, some perfectly horrible tea coming up. But it is hot. Where's your horse?"

The little shack seemed to rock with the storm's force, and all the panes of the two windows were iced up inside. Aubrey shook the teapot from side to side. He glanced at the man. The scar on his head must have taken fifty stitches to close up. He held out his hands to the heat— huge hands; they opened slowly like rusty ice tongs.

"Strayed. I camped last night by Tenkiller Creek. Woke up this morning and the son of a bitch had got out of his halter. Right in the middle of this storm." He went through another fit of trembling, crushed his hands together and bent his head until it went away. "Ah. I suppose that means I'm warming up."

"You got caught out in a once-in-a-hundred-years storm," said Aubrey. "And you lost your horse. Bad terrible luck, that."

"I am not that well acquainted with Indian Territory," the man said. "Or its weather." He looked up. "Thank you. I feel like I've been raised from the dead." He got up, dropped the boots on top of his other gear, turned slowly, and sat back down again. "You could have set me on fire, and I wouldn't have said a word of complaint." He pulled loose a red bandana that had crusted over with ice from his breath and spread it on the back of the chair, neatly, slowly. His hair was cut short, a thick brown pelt; his ice-crusted boots were the size of steamer trunks.

"Drink this," said the telegrapher. "Whether you like it or not. It's hot."

The tall man closed his hands around the hot tea mug. His heavy-lidded eyes drifted shut and then opened again as if he was still amazed at being inside someplace, out of the storm, safe inside walls.

"It's got sugar in it, hits the bloodstream, whammo, you can feel it."

The tall man tipped it up and then waited a moment. He said, "Yes. You can."

Aubrey slid out his last rasher of bacon and began sawing at it and watched him. The hot tea and brandy had settled in the man's interior, bringing to him life and fire, and so he lifted his head and looked around the shack. Aubrey saw him take note of the key and the sounder, the batteries, the pens and message blanks, all that was in this small habitation holding firm against the worst snowstorm in memory, where temperatures had poured straight down the thermometer tube as if it had no bottom and strange effervescent lightning fizzed and danced in the high atmosphere. The man then raised his head and searched the beams of the ceiling, which Aubrey had never seen anybody do before.

"Supper is bacon and cabbage, sir. I hope you have no objections." The telegrapher sawed at the cabbage head with a hand-forged sort of Bowie knife, and bits flew.

"None. But I don't want to cut into your supplies."

"Not at all. I have a dead deer hanging outside on my wall, stiff as a poker. It's supplied as Western Union provisions by a man named Cherokee Tom. A bit gruesome but edible. You've come down from Fort Smith?" Aubrey shook in pepper and salt.

"Yes. I'm hunting for a man. When I woke up and saw that horse was gone, I thought I'd follow the telegraph line south." The man paused, thinking. "I knew there had to be a relay station." He ran his hand over his scarred head. "Sometimes I couldn't even see from one pole to another."

"That's a hundred feet, give or take."

"Hundred and twenty-five."

Hunting for a man. Robertson thought, *I* knew *it would be something like that.* He opened his mouth to ask who he was hunting for, but the telegraph interrupted with its monotone chattering.

"Hold on, duty calls."

"Okay."

For some reason, perhaps because he had been a telegrapher since he was thirteen years of age, Robertson knew the man was listening to the telegraph's stuttering voice. His head had fallen back against the top rail of the chair, and his eyes were closed with weariness, but he was listening.

CPT MCCREA PATROL NORTHBOUND. HOLED UP TAHLEQUAH
ALL WELL FWD FT GIB PLS TKS BELLE.

With his eyes still closed, the man said, "Who's Belle?"

Robertson stopped dead. This large snowy man could read Morse. And he had said *okay*: telegraphers' slang. Robertson somehow thought it was best not to answer the question. He gestured with a wooden spoon.

"Ah yes, hold on a moment, I have to reply."

The telegrapher sat down at the desk to knock out a quick message to the next northerly station, which was Fort Gibson, concerning Commander McCrea going to ground somewhere around Tahlequah and all well. Then to his dearest human connection, Belle: REC'D KEOTA RS YRS FWD FT GIB. And the quick reply: OK STAY WARM UNEXPECTED STORM TKS BELLE AR 73.

Then Robertson scribbled down the exchange date. "Sorry, had to man the key, here. Duty calls with a rather dictatorial voice, does it not?"

"Yes, it does." The man smiled at the fire, and it lightened that heavy face, the big bones. Then the smile disappeared as if it had never been.

He could read Morse at speed, and he might very well be an escaped prisoner. He could be a desperado, a lunatic who had evaded his keepers. A message could very well be coming down the line full of warnings. The man would be able to read the Morse, including any outgoing call for help from himself. These fragmented thoughts briefly froze Robertson, but then he threw the frying pan on top of the stove, tossed in the bacon and half a head of sliced cabbage (his supper, now lost to a stranger in the night). The stove had grown so hot it was cherry red around the flue collar. The little shack grew warm even unto the distant corner where Robertson's favorite deer mouse sat with alarmed and trembling whiskers.

The man ate like a machine, trying not to appear ravenous, his big hands clumsily grasping the fork. "Very good," he said. Then he took another cup of hot tea, freshly made and fragrant, and sat holding it in his hands to warm them, and then poured it down. "I just ate your supper."

"Not at all!" Robertson found a ceramic insulator, stuck a candle in it and lit it to give them more light, and wondered if that was all the information he was going to get, the man's spare sentences and what he could see. He had come down from Fort Smith; he was hunting for a man. The blankets in the roll were common heavy wool; the saddlebags were new, no markings; his pommel holster was worn. The rifle looked like a Spencer carbine, and his overcoat was a Federal dreadnaught. Well-made boots. Robertson thought it best not to press questions on the man.

Then the man looked over at him. "My name's John Chenneville."

"I'm Aubrey Robertson, telegrapher." Robertson stuck out his hand, and the man shook it.

"Thank you for taking me in."

"Well, I'd be a beast to turn you aside," said Robertson.

"True. You're an Englishman."

"Right you are." And then, fishing for more information, "You abandoned your saddle?"

"I did. It's all right. The saddle was a piece of junk."

"I'll be bold here and just say I thought I heard you say you were looking for a man."

"That's very daring of you." Again a slight smile that appeared and then went away.

"Sarcasm aside." The telegrapher waved the wooden spoon. "Well, ah, what's his name?"

"He goes by different names."

A long silence. The telegrapher saw the man press one hand against his cracked lips, look at the blood on his palm. The wind died and then started shrieking once more in chaotic tonal fragments that rose and fell. The stove chuffed and back-drew for a second, then sucked air again.

Finally, in desperation, the telegrapher said, "Ah, so how was Fort Smith?"

"Pretty good." The man bent toward the stove, his hands out. They were now bright red. "I'm probably a week behind him by now." He paused. "But it could be he is behind me." The man pressed his hard knuckles against his eyes; melting snow dripped from his eyelashes. "So, that's a troublesome thought, but there it is."

"Well!" Aubrey said, bright and chipper and completely at a loss as to whether he should pursue this further or keep his mouth shut. Then again the telegraph clattered in the rattling *dit-dit-dah* language of Morse:

DEC. 11 1866 TAHLEQUAH INTEL FROM FT GIB PRISONER
BRAINERD MISSING FROM GUARDHOUSE EVE ROLL CALL.
FWD FT. SMITH AND REQUEST INSTRUCTIONS BELLE.

"That's not him." The man gazed into the round venthole as it jumped with flame.

"Ah, you mean the man you're looking for!" Robertson darted over to the table and laid his hand on the sending key.

"Right. I ran into Brainerd in Fort Smith. He's a pickpocket."

The telegrapher poised with his hand over the key. "Why, what a coincidence! Perhaps he . . ." Aubrey paused. He was clumsily grasping for information, for stories, and it was all so obvious. "Well." A brief silence, and then Aubrey bent to his work; with a rapid hand he relayed the message to Fort Smith, repeating it exactly word for word, adding, HW? and signing off, 76. He said, in an offhand tone, "And so, perhaps this Brainerd might have, as it were, relieved you of some articles—personal, ah, articles."

"He tried." The man tapped his forefinger in the skillet, took up a smear of bacon grease, and wiped it across his cracked lower lip. Then he placed one hand on his left breast pocket. "That's not who I'm looking for." His shirt was an off-white with a thin blue stripe and his thick wool vest a dark brown tweed. Shirt and vest were opened to the heat. He came out with tobacco and papers, rolled a cigarette. "I don't know why he would be in the Fort Gibson stockade." He saw a splinter on the floor, lit it at the vent, fired up the cigarette. "I lost my temper."

A short hesitation, and then; "Well, with people of that sort you never know!" and the telegrapher thought, *Jesus, maybe this man is Brainerd!* "Lost it how?"

"I broke his wrist." The man drew on the cigarette. "I hate losing my temper. Never does any good, but it had been a long day."

Robertson experienced that thin feeling when blood drains from the face. He cast about desperately for something to change the subject. "And you certainly can read Morse at speed—wonderful talent to have, employable anywhere, a portable sort of skill, isn't it?"

"Yes." Chenneville let out a long stream of smoke and closed his eyes with the pleasure of it. "It is." The fire crackled, and the stove sucked in air through the vent with a pulmonary, whistling sound. After a moment he said, "I would take another glass of that brandy. I can send you a bottle from Dallas when I get there."

So he was heading south, to the little town of Dallas.

"Of course!" Robertson jumped up and stopped. His suspicions came back full force. It occurred to him that if this man got drunk he might become one of the telegrapher's worst nightmares. He would be stuck in this little habitation in the wilderness with an inebriated lunatic the size of a clock tower.

The man glanced up at him, and then there was that quiet, amused expression. "You're afraid I'll get drunk and tear the house down." Then his hard-boned face became abstracted once again with some interior consideration unknown to Aubrey Robertson.

"No, no, not at all!" Aubrey gestured toward the telegraph key on its walnut block, screwed to the table. "I should . . ."

"Raise Fort Gibson," said John. "Do so." He blew smoke at the ceiling. "I can read, but I can't send very well anymore, for some reason. Head injury, I guess. Does strange things."

"I see." The telegrapher saw there was no help for it and once again wrenched off the lid of the ten-pound salt keg. "Not much of a drinker myself, but one appreciates a tot now and then." He dusted off the sparkling salt grains, wiped his hand on his pants.

"One does."

"And it doesn't affect your, ah, head injury?"

"Not as far as I can tell."

The wind began to die down, the glass of brandy was deep red-brown and clear in the light of the candle, and after this second glass the man's eyes closed and his head dropped back again. Robertson stood over the key and relayed the request to Fort Smith and Fort Gibson and ended, HW?

The HW? was *do you copy?*, one of the first shorthand phrases he had learned, always anxious, as a beginner, to hear if his message had gone through or not. But now there was no reply from anywhere, not Fort Gibson nor Fort Smith or Belle in Tahlequah either. It meant that out in the snowy night the line had gone down somewhere; a limb had fallen on it, or a pole had gone over and grounded the copper wire, or maybe the petty thief named Brainerd, on the run, had thrown a rope over it and jerked the wire loose. The electric voice that spanned Indian Territory was now silent. Aubrey Robertson sat quietly, silent as well at long last. His hands were flat on the table, and his blue jumper cuffs raveled thread after thread over his thin hands.

After a moment the tall man woke himself up.

"Line's dead," he said.

"Well, it is," said Robertson with some reluctance. "Just bugger all."

He didn't want Chenneville to know he was without communication. However, the stranger noticed everything, even in a doze.

John Chenneville slowly got to his feet and ran his hands through his short hair, over the scar, wiped at his face. He picked up his hat, a gray felt with a wide brim and a sugarloaf crown and laid it behind the stove upside down. He unrolled his blankets, one of which was a four-point Hudson's Bay with the familiar blue stripe. He spread it on the wooden floor, stripped off his shirt and vest, and made a neat package of them for a pillow. His movements were careful and exact. There was something machinelike about him, inflexible, something removed. He would smile and then the smile would go away completely, and his face become austere and closed.

Head injury, Robertson thought, and saw his favorite deer mouse poised hungrily in the corner. The man lay on his side, pulled his blankets over himself and then the greatcoat over that.

"I see you've got a pet," he said and then fell into a profound sleep.

Aubrey continued sitting beside the woodstove with his own glass of brandy, tapping one foot nervously. *He doesn't miss a thing, not even the deer mouse, aka Sweet Pea. Those pale eyes have inhuman powers!* But. He must stop imagining things. He must stop rereading *The Woman in White*. It was hard to make oneself leave the warm circle around the stove and get into a cold bed. His small cot was against the wall behind the telegrapher's desk. He stocked the stove with green rounds and got into bed. As he lay there, the mule burst out into a noise that sounded like a train whistle.

Then: murmuring sounds from beside the door.

It's Brainerd! No, it was the wind. No, it was the mule making noises at some deer that often came to stand in the wind shadow of the shed.

Finally the telegrapher fell asleep, clinched up against the cold with his nightcap on his head. Sweet Pea crept out on white mouse feet to lift a crumb of hardtack to her little face with many indications of joy, the stove making tinking sounds as the fire died down.

CHAPTER ELEVEN

December 1866 / Keota Indian Territory

THE TALL MAN SPENT THE next day drying out and cleaning up his gear. He split wood for the stove. He shaved outside in the cold with the telegrapher's mirror propped on the windowsill and a basin of hot water sending up clouds of steam. When he slung the foam from his blade, his gaze traveled across the tree line behind the cabin, his eyes half-shut against the glare of snow, searching out every shadow. He cleaned and oiled his boots, took an axe to the frozen deer carcass at the back of the cabin, and with a quick expert twist sectioned out the backstrap. Robertson watched him. He used the axe like a surgical instrument. Somewhat disquieting.

"So, what will you do when you find him?" Aubrey Robertson had grown braver, seeing that the man seemed so far quite sane, head injury or no. "Just curious."

"Depends on where I find him."

"Ah, then, well, you mean a public place, or perhaps he has friends . . ." Aubrey received the backstrap in his two hands. It was frozen like a stone. "Oh, very well, then. I am insatiably curious."

"You are." Chenneville seemed about to laugh. "You are indeed."

"So, this person . . ."

"You don't want to know."

Chenneville rolled up his sleeves and started a tray of bread dough, punched it down and put it behind the stove for the second rise. Then Robertson disconnected his battery bank, and he and the tall man walked out into the hills northward along the telegraph poles, to locate the downed line, carrying a coil of copper wire. Although the break could have been anywhere between this place, Keota, and Fort

Smith seventy miles to the north, they found it in the woods three miles along. A large branch from a red oak had been blown down on it and snapped it.

"Well, this is jammy!" said Robertson. "Not but three miles tramping!" He put on his climbers and shinnied up the pole. "Would you splice it, then?" His spiked climbers made a *chunk-chunk-chunk* sound as he moved upward in mechanical jerks.

Chenneville took the axe and whacked down a sapling and trimmed it to a forked stick. He spliced a section of wire and then threaded the line through the fork. All around them the newly white world wrote a brilliant calligraphy of shadow and glare.

"Excellent handling of Western Union's precious wire, there," Robertson called down.

"Yes," the man said. He stood looking up at Robertson. A slight wind, the remains of yesterday's storm, whirled up snow powder around him. Pine needle shadows moved like dashes and dots over his face, and the skirts of his greatcoat flapped gently.

"I am *nosy*," Robertson called down. "Incurable!"

Chenneville nodded. "You are. Well then, I was in military telegraphy for a while during the war. Detached service." Snow sifted down from the pine trees of the San Bois Mountains in a sparkling hush. "The Confederates tore our lines down so many times I can't tell you."

"Where?"

"Virginia. From Fort Monroe on south, through the Peninsula, Spotsylvania Courthouse, Petersburg. We usually managed to retrieve it and string it up again." Aubrey Robertson reached down for the wire. Chenneville saw that it would come short, and he expertly spliced in another length, then held the line up on the forked stick.

"Still good?" Aubrey's words were garbled as he held the copper wire in his mouth to reset the insulators. "Your wire."

"Yes, except for once. The Rebs got so damned pissed off at us they wadded up a mile of our copper wire and shoved it down a cannon and fired it back at us."

In the hush of the forest, Robertson laughed aloud and ravens answered, speaking in their sawmill voices overhead.

"It came flying through the trees, all unwinding." The man paused and moved his blunt head in a strange, searching way, his light eyes casting through the pines, left to right. "I remember it shredding into bits. Copper. Very bright. Like a web." Another pause. "Things come back to me all at once, sometimes. Like over a relay. More?"

"This is good." The telegrapher secured the wire and shinnied down and then stood with one hand on the pole to remove the climbers from his boots. His wool muffler was crusted with ice where he breathed on it, and he impatiently jerked it out loose as he tested the connection. "Live and going—we're in business again," he said.

That evening Robertson pushed the telegraph apparatus aside and drew up his two chairs, and they settled down with plates of venison backstrap roasted in the stove's little side oven, fried cabbage, and the new-baked bread. Their coats hung on nails and dripped quietly. The wind had died down to a slow, hooting sort of breeze, and the ice on the inside of the panes had melted.

GA DR YM UR RST 5NN BRAINERD LOCATED NEAR CHOUTEAU THIS NOON BY FT GIB PATROL AR BUT WD B NICE BELLE

OK BELLE WILL U CQ OR ME '76'

WILL DO BELLE

"Now then, John, my man, stay as long as you like, you know. And I say! Good of you to pile up so much wood! Really."

"I better move on. I'm eating up your supplies, here."

"Indeed not, indeed not, plenty more coming! A hundred pounds of shelled corn on its way! Western Union is very attentive to our wants, I assure you."

The big man nodded, speared up more venison with his knife. "Good. But I need to go on."

Then Robertson took in a breath, gathering his courage to ask who it was he was looking for, when the big man laid down his knife and fork and said, "I think he could be at Colbert's Ferry by now. Maybe. With this storm, I don't know."

And since the tall man had shown himself to be amiable, civilized, and helpful and had not tried to cut Robertson's throat in the night, or made off with his nickel-plated watch, Robertson asked, finally, "What for?"

John Chenneville lifted his head and for a moment regarded Robertson without expression.

"What, what for?"

"I mean, why are you looking for him?"

"He owes me money."

But the answer had come with a certain ease and quickness, even an absentmindedness that made Robertson think, *He's said that many times before.* And John Chenneville must have seen the skepticism on his face, because once again his face lightened as if he were on the edge of laughter; it softened him and made him less formidable, and then, as always, the expression completely disappeared.

So Robertson said, "It must be a great deal, to go plowing through a snowstorm like that."

"Yes, it is."

"Well then, John, tell me his name, and if he comes by here, or anywhere there's an operator, I could forward a message on to you, you see." Robertson poured out a cup of coffee for both of them. No need to inflict tea on him any longer; he had decided to share his precious store of coffee. "Modern times! Instant communication over the vast unpeopled hinterlands!"

"Western Union let you do that? Free?"

"Oh, operators do all kinds of things. I mean, outside of our official duties."

Chenneville swirled the coffee around in his cup. "Yes, they do." He drank off the hot coffee and said, "He goes by several names." Then, after a moment, "A description is better. He's about five foot nine, dark brown hair, kind of greenish-grayish eyes; he's got black specks from a powder burn under his right jaw, makes it look like his neck got dirty and he never washed it off. His face is kind of squashed up in the middle." Again, a short silence. "It's not a powder burn; it was some kind of accident."

Robertson said, "Squashed up?"

"Yes, you know some people have small features all close together in the middle of their face."

"Ah yes, I know what you mean! And the rest of their face is . . . a boundless wasteland!"

John laughed. "That's very good." Then: "Last I heard he was riding a horse with two front white socks, wears a short-brimmed hat. Maybe a derby."

"I will tell Belle in a PM, that is, a private message, and she will send it on as a PM, which is to say—"

"I know what a PM is." Chenneville's large hands rested on either side of his plate. He was very interested. He said, "Go on."

"To send news of such a man, horse and all, if seen. Is there a legal charge against him?"

"There will be when I get my hands on him."

"Yes, I see, but pardon my nosiness, with what law enforcement agency?"

The tall man hesitated and then said, "First one I come to."

Robertson had a dubious look on his face. His six months in Indian Territory had taught him about not only tornadoes and tribal feuds but the remarkable lack of law enforcement. The big American war was not long over, and people here had neither common law nor apparently US law either. Then a chilled thought appeared in his mind—*He's looking for somebody for some kind of revenge*—and whence the thought came he knew not: *The Woman in White*, plots and retaliations.

"Very well, then, I or Belle would send a message, if seen, to Colbert's Station."

"That's very kind of you."

"And so we will refer to you as 'the Snowman.'"

Robertson got up to put the plates in a bucket of water and the bucket on the stove. They moved their chairs to either side of it as the sun slid down into the forest and the hard-edged cold came back. Chenneville settled his long bulky body on the chair, and his size made it look small.

"That'll do it." The tall man gave a quick nod. "And I assume Miss Belle is permanently stationed at Tahlequah?"

"Oh no, we get moved around. She'll likely be transferred before long. But not to the west. They would not send someone like Belle, that is to say, Victoria Reavis, a most refined young lady, to some outpost west of here. No indeed. In fact, she is probably being transferred to Marshall, Texas. They say it is plantation country, more civilized—one can get imports there, ice cream, window glass, china, newest in ladies' hats, and so on."

Chenneville thought about this. He said, finally, "Not many women operators."

"No, there are not. And she can send thirty-five words a minute," Robertson said. Then he sat upright with determination in every line of his body and plunged on. "And so tell me how you learned Morse?"

"How I know Morse." Chenneville's expression showed him searching through memories, or alternative memories, or just putting things in sequence. "When I was fourteen, I learned it from some railroad telegraphers. I'm from St. Louis. So when the war came my parents wanted me to get out of Missouri, and they got me a commission in the Eightieth New York Infantry. My mother's cousin was the colonel. My mother was from New York. Then the Eightieth forwarded me to a signals unit in Virginia because I could send and they needed operators."

He took a small packet of tobacco out of his inner vest pocket and rolled a cigarette. He lit it at the stove and leaned back and blew smoke.

"Mainly because their operators kept getting shot or captured. So there I was, hammering away for two years under O'Brien. Richard O'Brien. Out of Fort Monroe and on down. Then I got sent back to the Eightieth. Back in the infantry, all the way to Richmond and the surrender." He held out his cup for more coffee.

"You were under O'Brien? Excellent! He is renowned, famed, *re-*

vered! He once sent fifty-one words a minute!" Robertson lifted a hand in amazement. "And so then, sometimes it got boring, did it not? Soldiers love to play cards and gamble. So do the brass pounders." Robertson poured the man another tot of brandy to go with the coffee.

"He doesn't owe me money because of a gambling debt," said Chenneville. "And it wasn't all that boring. They sent me up in a balloon once." He looked up with a slight smile, waiting for Robertson to be amazed.

"No!"

"Yes. I owe you a good story. You've been very kind. So here's the story. We were outside Yorktown." Long pause. "May 1862. That's right, it was May of 1862. I was sent up in a hot-air balloon to see what the Rebs were doing in Yorktown. They said there was a fire. With a wire—they sent it and me up with a wire." Another pause. "It was like flying." The man fell silent again, looking into the venthole of the Dudley parlor stove and its circle of flames, searching for words. "And I thought, *A sharpshooter could knock a great God-damned hole in this thing if he got the range*, but still it was a wonder, even if I came down a flaming wreck, hundred-foot fall, wire and all. All I sent back was *I see a fire, see smoke, something on fire*. Turned out it was a ship on fire— the Rebs had set it afire as cover; they were actually evacuating." He took a drink of the brandy and sat quietly to take a deep, appreciative breath. "Good. That was good. So, I can't think of how to say what an experience it was. Flying above everything like a hawk. God, you could see for miles." Another long silence and then a detail came to him, suddenly. "The wire came up the tether. It was a hundred feet of two-direction flexible wire coated with rubber." Several soundless seconds ticked past. "Anyway, they pulled me down fairly quickly." He glanced at the window, listened for rain for a moment, but there was none, only night and silence. "And then people usually ask, 'How did you get that scar on your head?'"

Robertson laughed and then flushed. He couldn't think of what to say.

The tall man said, "Big explosion in Petersburg, just below Richmond. It was February, I think. We were in winter quarters. A load of gunpowder had come up on the canal, it was in the turning basin, and the Rebs hit it with hot shot. It blew up and flattened everything for half a mile. I guess I got hit with a piece of anchor chain. That's what they told me. Spent a year in the hospital." A calm, blank pause while he thought about it and turned the glass in his hands. "I more or less had to relearn how to keep my balance. And had to learn to think again. Not think, just put things in sequence."

Robertson got up to shave bits of gray soap into the bucket of hot water. He said, "I'm sorry to hear it."

"I'm alive."

Chenneville put the glass on the stove's apron, picked up the coffee cup. "A lot of people aren't." He threw his cigarette butt into the stove vent and looked around the little shack and then he got up in a series of unfoldings until he was upright. He walked over to take down *The Woman in White* from the shelf of books. "Is this good? As in, keeps your interest?"

"It's very entertaining. And quite strange really, you know, it's about, ah, guilty secrets, demented people, villainous baronets, and so forth."

The man turned it over in his hands. The gold lettering on the binding glistened. He opened it to the title page, and Robertson saw his gaze slide down to the notation Robertson had made last week on the flyleaf, because he had run out of notepaper. *Burnet to ship 100 lbs. maize 4 W U. acc't.* The man said, "If I ever get someplace where books are on order I will try it." He put it back. "I started from St. Louis about a month ago, didn't carry any books with me. Too heavy." He sat down again and tilted his head and leaned back, relaxing like a long feline with his sleeves rolled up and arms that seemed to be made of cable wire. "Do you have cards? No betting."

"Ah no, but I have a chess set."

"Very good. Shall I hold the pieces?"

"If you would." Robertson placed the chess set next to the sounding key on the table.

The tall man picked up the black king and with a quick flip of his thumb tossed it up and then snatched it out of the air with his other hand.

"Trying to get my coordination back," he said. "Hand and eye."

"Very good," said Robertson and watched. Chenneville spun the white king upward, and with his left hand he tried the same thing but missed it.

"Have another go," said Robertson. He leaned forward on his elbows.

"Yes, once more."

The telegrapher watched, fascinated. This time the tall man flipped the king up and then took it out of its spin deftly with his left hand.

"Well done!"

Chenneville gave one nod in acknowledgment and held his fists behind his back to hide the pieces and then held them out hidden, one in each enormous fist. He gazed down at the narrow, spare telegrapher with something like a fond and amused smile as if at a child.

"Choose your weapon," he said.

Robertson tapped the left hand, which was black, and so they played until what seemed like late at night. Chenneville thought about each move and took his time, lapsing into long silences and then lifting his head to sounds outside. He would remain in that total silence, and then his head moved in a tilt as if stretching his neck against a tight collar, then lowered his gaze to the game again, all about him the aura of something implacable and undeviating.

In the morning the young Englishman handed him a few days' provisions wrapped in a cloth and stood waving as the man strode away south in the sticky, sun-warmed snow.

Robertson thought, *It is something more than money. A great deal more.*

CHAPTER TWELVE

December 1866 / On the Road to Edwards' Station

HE WALKED IN A SWINGING route step to the south, bent on murder. The road stayed to the valleys when it could, and when it came up over a ridge he could see the mountains pouring off southward. The Red River Valley was straight south about a hundred miles, and by that time the earth would have spilled out flat as it came to the shores of that treacherous river.

He followed the telegraph poles and the double-tracked trail, through the wet, crystallizing snow with his possessions slung about him like a tinker. His revolver was in a bulky pommel holster, Union issue, his rifle muzzle-down on his back in its scabbard. No other tracks on the road. This was the old Butterfield Overland Mail route, but so far no one had come through, after the storm. He had been told the closest stagecoach stop was twenty miles farther, at Edwards' Station. It would give him a roof for the night. He thought he might make it. He needed to buy another horse.

He stopped every half mile or so to listen. At every rise in the ground he paused to look along the horizon, looking for smoke and then searching out the forested trail behind him. Starting out this last task to be done had somehow made him different. He felt like a different man now, whatever happened. He had recovered some vital key and had opened his heart, his mind, to another and perhaps final self.

He was now in the Chickasaw Nation. It was a handsome country of one blue line of mountains after another, fading away to the south, with unnamed peaks appearing and disappearing among the spectral columns of sleet. He took off his hat to hold it against the gray, insidious light of the sky and search out the country. The trail was a double streak of white through the pine forest, rising and falling. No fresh tracks. He replaced the hat slightly off to one side of his head. It relieved the pressure of the hatband on his scar, and although it gave him a rake-hell, jaunty look, it felt better.

He followed the trail southwest into more and more difficult terrain. He came to a high ridge and looked down on the deep valley of the Little River. He had been hearing the river noise for a while. From time to time he could catch a glimpse of the water, a bright clear blue.

He sat to rest upon a convenient shelving of stone and listened. What there was to listen to was deeply interesting. The silence was thought-ful, he decided. It was punctuated like a musical score with dry leaves falling in crisp little rustles, a distant hawk calling, something stepping with great care through the snow with pinpoint hooves. The continu-ous sounds of rushing water down in the steep valley of the Little River.

He had hoped that at some time he would be able to stop thinking about how he walked, never turning too quickly, always putting one foot in advance of the other when he sat so that he might rise from his chair in a natural way, but not yet, not yet. He often stopped to look be-hind himself and then on every side, a deep examining stare that slowly took in each tree and the shadows that they cast.

I like it here. Even the words in his head made him a bit happier. *This is good. Quiet.*

He was far from his own country, his own people, and his own rais-ing, but he liked this place. He might never hear his own home lan-guage again in his lifetime. He could live with that. Yet more heavy weather and sleet broke over the ridges coming toward him. He heaved himself to his feet and started on again.

The trail ran slantwise across a steep hillside, thick with oak and pine, and there he came upon two boys walking toward him about fifty yards along. They were talking together in low tones. They carried bows.

He called out to them. "Yo!"

Instantly the two boys scattered, one to one side of the trail and one to the other. John stopped.

"Good day," he called out. "Just walking along here, on my way to the stage stop." He stood holding out both hands to the side, palms open, his innocent, ringless hands naked of weapons or harm.

After a moment's silence he heard a voice. "This is our place," called the boy on the uphill side. "You will get out of here." He shouted this from his hiding place behind a double-trunked young oak and its surrounding of buckbrush.

"No," said John. He heard the other boy on the steep downhill side making his way through the tumbling overleaved stone. He was shushing through the snow, cutting around.

The boy uphill fell silent, momentarily confused. He was waiting for John to say something more. Then, in the ensuing silence, he called out, "Well, all right to walk on, but you had best walk on fast." He spoke a regimented book-English, a language learned from print, by repetition of phrases.

"Stand out," John called. "I'm not walking past until I can see you."

The boy pushed through the buckbrush and came into sight, there to stare at John steadily and with such determination that John knew he was avoiding looking elsewhere, and at the same time noting something in the corner of his eye. The other boy. The boy he could see was Indian, but with painfully short hair and a bow in his fist. He seemed about fourteen.

John stood still with his hands out in the air. The other boy, who appeared to be about two years younger, joined the first, and now both stood at the side of the trail. They were dressed in clumsy brown suits with four brass buttons and high-top shoes. Their black hair had been recently cut short, as was obvious from the lighter glare of the backs of their necks. They both carried short powerful-looking bows, a handful of blunt arrows in the other hand threaded one by one through their fingers. If they had any baggage, it was hidden somewhere. They stared at him. John waited without saying anything to see what they would do. Seconds ticked by as the air was salted by pinhead snow.

For some reason he could not remember just now John knew holding your arrows like that was for speed shooting. The blunt arrowheads looked as if they were weighted with lead. These boys were children raised in the outdoors; they had probably held a bow in their hands as soon as they could close their fingers around the grip and now had apparently been stuffed by main force into these Indian Department suits and were escaping from a way of life they did not want. He waited.

Finally the shorter one said, "You are not to take us back, no never." The boy's face was blank and hard as a coin, and he took in John's equipment and weapons in quick darting glances.

"Of course not," said John. "Back where?"

"Burney school," said the shorter one. "Indian school."

"That's what I thought. Where is the Indian school?"

"The Red River."

The one who appeared older said, "You have come to catch us." He lifted his bow and expertly notched one of the blunt-headed arrows. The other arrows he held between each finger in the string hand. He held the bow sideways and down.

"I have not. I don't care if you're running away from school," John said. "And the less I see of both of you, the better. So I suppose I'll just go on about my business here." He stepped forward and lifted his hat, partly to salute them and also to relieve the pressure of the hat brim.

He took two strides and then was hit in the temple by something that knocked him almost out of consciousness and with a force that threw his head back. He instinctively turned to the downside of the trail, and then another blow struck him on the left side of his head, his scar a target. A fine spray of shiny blood-drops speckled his glove. He pitched forward and landed in the snow. He turned as he fell. He landed on one side with a strange crackling sensation. Even half-knocked out he scrambled on his belly toward a space under a ledge. Then he was hit in the head again before he could get there.

Everything swarmed with sparks; objects moved around in unpredictable ways. A crow screamed. He felt sick. His stuff was strung all over the downslope. His hat lay several yards away.

He lay on his back and watched the trees as they rolled from right to left, and when his eyes pulled back from following them, they all traveled right to left all over again. He tried to unholster the revolver, but the hammer caught. He jerked at it. He could feel the hammer hang up on something and cock. He was fumbling; his hand felt numb. He had to get off a warning shot before they came down here and killed him. They were capable of it.

He turned over carefully onto his stomach and laid the revolver in the grainy snow beside his head and looked at it. Yes, it was cocked. He lowered the hammer and cocked it again, bringing a charge up. He rolled onto his back, pointed the barrel into the air, and fired.

The shot echoed all up and down the canyon of the Little River, and the powder smoke drifted back into his face. His head was full of little electrical bolts of pain. Now he could feel blood running down into his ears. He tried to orient himself. They were uphill. He pointed the barrel in that general direction, cocked the hammer again, and fired another warning shot. He listened to the echoes as they fled down the bluffs.

He lay in the clotted snow in the shifting planes of gunpowder smoke for a long time as a chill worked itself into his body, down to the very heart. If only he could keep his balance. He had worked on his balance very hard over the last year, his balance and speed of movement, and here it was knocked right out of his brain by two children with blunt arrows. *Those Goddamned little shits.*

He shoved himself farther back under the shelving stone by his bootheels and lay there for a long time, listening. They weren't coming to get his stuff. *If I lie here for a while I'll be all right.* He wasn't being snowed on, and all his stuff was within sight if he could gather it. He still had the revolver. The rifle in its scabbard was uphill, near the trail. He lay collapsed in the smell of wet dirt and cold now, thinking how to get to his feet.

He rolled over onto his stomach and then raised himself on his hands and knees, hung there a moment and staggered to his feet. He was pasted all over with snow. The pain in his head was beyond belief. He knew better than to turn his back on somebody holding a weapon. But they were children. *They knew I wasn't going to shoot.* He managed

to gather his hat and the rest of his gear and made it back up to the trail.
He saw the boys' footprints where they had fled down toward the Little
River. He bent his head down and walked forward, one foot in front of
the other, a complex and difficult task, avoiding fist-sized stones, tree
roots. He picked up the rifle scabbard and straightened again carefully
and went on.

A hundred paces farther on, he saw a trail going off to the right, leading higher up. He followed it. On the other side of the spine of the ridge
were the remains of an old Choctaw house. He saw it looming, hairy-
headed among the pines. It still had a thatched roof that reached almost
to the ground. The logs were upright; *poteaux en terre*. Long unused,
abandoned for some unknown reason, but it would do; it would get him
out of the weather, out of the wind and pelting sleet that had come over
the mountains.

Inside he found a stone hearth and kindling wood laid alongside, according to that ancient custom of leaving something for whatever traveler might come next. He cut shavings, but his hands shook as he tried
to strike a light with his flint and steel, and he could not get a spark. He
fished out his block of phosphorus matches. He rebuilt the shavings
pile and cracked off a match, struck it. Between his hands the marvel of
fire in a cold world appeared as a salvation and a wonder, and it shone
up into his face as the chill set in with the sinking sun. He lay down
alongside as the flames took hold and flared high.

As soon as he had warmed a bit, he dragged his saddlebags up and
opened them. By the light of his last candle, he wet his bandana in the
melted snow that ran between the hearthstones and tried to clean his
face and ear of blood. He was all right as long as the blood was running
into his ear. Not out of it.

"*Mon Chriss*," he said, and made a short, impelled noise. He was at
the edge of weeping, and he pulled in several long breaths to stop it.

He cleaned off the leaves and dirt from his revolver, the big heavy
Remington New Model Army. He reset two charges, drank from his
canteen. His head stopped bleeding.

Chilled to the bone, to the heart. He boiled snow into water in his small mess kit pan and poured it into the canteen, steaming hot. He wrapped the canteen in his extra shirt, pulled off his clothes, and lay down, slowly, on the thick Hudson Bay. He kept his pants and drawers under the blankets next to himself and held the hot canteen to his stomach. An old campaigner's trick, a lifesaver. He pulled the other blankets and his overcoat over his head and slept heavily. In the dark and the firelight, his brain repaired of itself what it could while he drifted at the edge of sleep.

The next morning he rose up to start the fire again from the coals and slept all day in the heat of the flames. People could smell the smoke a mile away, but he didn't care. He had begun to shake with cold and the pain in his head. At last he ate some of the provisions the telegrapher had sent with him: scones with congealed butter on them and hard-fried deer meat.

Another night. This time there was no wind and he was warmer. The fire coals glowed like a living being under a blanket of ash and gave out a steady heat. He turned up his hand and regarded the revolver. Then he laid it down by his blankets again and dropped onto his cold bed, his head still seeming to move to some external tides, and sleep took him quickly.

The next morning he started south again.

The telegraph poles hummed overhead, traveling above him as he walked. They would not leave him alone but continued on with their copper messages. Maybe the messages were about him.

No, it was Belle above him in the singing wires, talking to somebody, receiving messages from somebody. The clouds were low over the mountains and heavy. Once he had been an officer and at one time he had been in a war and in that war there was an explosion where he had been struck a glancing blow in the head by a flying length of anchor chain. Then he was not the same person he had been before. All around him the uncut primeval forest was barred with tall tree trunks thin as flagpoles. Pines always made a kind of music by holding their bountiful heads up to the coming winds.

Occasionally he sat down and dropped all his stuff around him, looked at it, regarded it with new eyes, wondered why he had it. The spurs and the socks and the unspendable money. After a moment he drew the rifle out of its scabbard and threw the heavy leather scabbard into the brush. That got rid of about ten pounds. He hung the pommel holster and his handgun over one shoulder, saddlebags and blankets over the other. Then with an anxious concentration he took out a coin from the inner slot in the cartridge belt, flipped it into the air, missed, tried again, caught it. Then with the other hand. It took three tries, but then he finally caught it. This left him feeling better and lighter. Anxiety is heavy. He sighted down the rifle barrel, and the far ridgeline did not waver.

Very well. He stepped back onto the trail and went on. The day began to warm up. The San Bois Mountains were upstanding and bitter toward people on foot, but now they slid into lower, rolling ridges, and these ridges were called by the grace of God the Winding Stair Hills.

By midmorning he felt better simply from the act of walking and balancing his load on his shoulders. The headache had diminished. The Winding Stair Hills were made up of long rises that seemed to drift across the surface of the earth, drawing apart an inch a century. He walked on into the evening as it turned blue.

Finally, below him, he saw the stage stop in a clearing. He stood on a slight rise and looked down at the lamplight coming from the windows of Edwards' Station. He could smell the smoke and noted that the little dog-run cabin that served as a stage post had a sort of giant chimney on one end. It was as big as the end wall of the house itself, made out of lumps of packed mud in loaves; a clumsy thing, and it made the place look as if it were being devoured by a beehive.

As he started down the hill he went over, in his mind, in a careful and methodical way, everything he owned, that it was all in place. His revolver with five prepared charges, none under the hammer. His rifle unloaded, ammunition and spurs in the saddlebags, also his shaving gear and extra clothes, his money, and more ammunition in the cartridge belt around his waist.

On his baptismal registry in St. Boniface Church it was written

Jean. March of 1832, thereby giving him his place among the old St. Louis French, whose occupation of that great valley went back to 1720. When he returned to consciousness after the head injury he had not known how old he was. He didn't care. At that time he had no age, nor did he have a name. That had come later.

His memory had returned in fragments, unbidden and intensely real. His sister a place in his mind, kindness and laughter. Curled brown hair and a French habit of clapping her hands together when she was laughing and laughing herself into near hysteria when he held a pear out to her and said it looked like the backside of their aunt Pelagie. Ghost of a memory, impressions. His brain had gone back to the basics, remembering and re-remembering. This is truly what we are to each other: a shape, a feeling, phantoms of love or threat or laughter, those who are lucid and speak in a strange old archaic French and smell of well-worn wool, of tobacco, of apples and wine.

Somewhere ahead of him was the sort of man who would shoot a woman and her husband and their year-old baby and throw their bodies into a deep spring, to be found later by those who had loved them.

He turned his head up to the evening sky and saw Orion rising in the east, faithful and perfect in his architecture of light. He had always liked that constellation, the warrior, the belt of stars, a sword at his side.

And so he went down toward Edwards' Station, all his secrets walking along beside him like greyhounds, and the constellation seemed to walk with him as well, treading this inevitable path, the great stars with their enormous feet.

CHAPTER THIRTEEN

December 1866 / Edwards' Station, Indian Territory

CHENNEVILLE ARRIVED AT THE RAIL fence around the station and stopped. Listened. Laughter and talk from inside; maybe three or four people. There were three horses and a mule and a cow in the broad, open-faced loafing shed behind. Saddles on the racks. He thought he saw a rifle scabbard on one saddle, but it was dark and he was not sure.

Finally he called out to those inside.

A man shouted back, "Come in, come in!"

He reseated his hat to a proper angle and then walked into the dog run of the double log cabin and paused. He felt a quick flash of irrational fear because he had no idea who was in there. He knew he must have a bruise where the leaded arrow had hit him, but there was no way to hide it. He shifted the pommel holster forward on his shoulder so he would have an easy reach for the revolver. Then he opened the door into the main room.

He saw two men sitting by the fire and the owner rising with a loose, welcoming grin and a woman who was probably his wife. Didn't look like anybody was carrying arms.

"Good evening," John said. He stood with his feet slightly apart and one hand on the door frame. He searched out the room, every dark corner, noted where everybody's hands were, including those of the woman.

A chorus of "good evening" came from the others, and the man who seemed to be the proprietor called out, "Well, come in! Just get on in here!"

John Chenneville set the Spencer butt-down against the wall near the door. He did not take off his cartridge belt. He glanced at the two men sitting in front of the fire. Because of the silences that had come to inhabit his mind, he had become a watcher of men and women and their faces. He had come to read them like lines of print, like the sounder on the telegraph and its bright pinpoint vernacular. He nodded to them and touched his hat brim to the woman. They had been talking and laughing, and the laughter was still bright around their faces.

The proprietor called out in a fruity, inebriated voice, "Well, just drop your gear there, fellow, unless you're planning on sleeping with it!" Then he looked about himself and laughed.

John dropped his gear beside the Spencer and then stripped off the greatcoat. He found a chair and pulled it near the hearth and held his hands out to the fire. His hands shook ever so slightly. He stretched his legs out as well so the toes of his boots could warm before he tried to pull them off. They were wet; it was going to be a struggle. None of these men was Dodd. He had seen the man's face in a blurred photographic plate, posed with his hand on a plaster pillar with strangely wide, fixed eyes. John sat without moving, bathed in the heat.

One of the men said, "Well, sir, looks like we all got hats alike! Look here." He held up his own, a gray broad-brimmed hat with a sugarloaf crown. "Now, ain't that something?"

John nodded politely and put his hand to the crown of his hat, lifted it off and set it on his knee. He said, "Hunicke, Beaver." He felt their glances and the inevitable brand of his scar.

"You are right." A man in a tattered gray overcoat smiled and picked up his own hat from the floor and looked inside it. "Make them in St. Louis."

"They're pretty good," said John. He noted two rifles leaned against the wall in a back corner. So that's where they were. There was an old Springfield on pegs over the fireplace.

The proprietor said, "My name's Billy Edwards; this here is my wife."

"Ma'am," John said.

The two other men said their names, and John listened carefully, trying to give them some mark to keep them in his mind. One of the men wore an old Confederate-gray overcoat and was missing part of a hand. Right hand, last two fingers.

John said, "Well, looks like we're all members of the sugarloaf hat club."

"Damn right!"

John smiled, and then the smile went away. He was calculating where the other two had come from, where they were going. Finally he said, "My name's John Chenneville." He glanced around; there were companionable nods, acknowledgments that he had offered his name as part of being one of the company.

"No stage today," Edwards said. "Nope. None. Not a one."

"It's all right. Lost my horse. Just need a place to sleep."

"Make yourself to home! There's always a bed at Edwards' Station!"

Edwards, a thoroughly unlikeable man, tipped up a glass and drank. His wife was, of course, Mrs. Edwards. She was a strong and pretty woman, quite young, with thin dark hair braided in complex ways to make up for it being thin. The young woman made supper while the two other men nodded to him as he sat, tired and silent, in front of the fireplace. John thought, *This woman is cooking over a fireplace when there are stoves to be had.*

"Well, you're a long drink of water," said Edwards.

"You don't say," said John. "First time I ever heard that."

"You are just in time," Mrs. Edwards said quickly. "Before these other people eat it all up." She started handing out plates; they were of graniteware and dished up high on the sides so they could hold more.

"I'm a hog for deer meat," one of the men said. "An utter hog."

John took his plate of hominy and venison and shoveled it in. They ate without paying much attention to one another. He ate three platefuls and scraped it clean. He had eaten very little since he left Robertson at Keota. His hands were turning red again as they warmed in the heat.

When the food was gone and the woman apparently not serving out any more, John got up and went outside for more wood, which caused one of the other men to stir, get up slowly, and come out to help. They came in with two armloads, and John saw the look of gratitude on the woman's face. They scattered snow and bark everywhere as they dumped their loads in the wood box.

"You've bruised your face, Mr. Chenneville," said Mrs. Edwards. "Are you all right?"

"Yes," said John. "I slipped on the trail. I'm fine, thank you."

"No coffee, but I've got whiskey," said Edwards, oblivious to anything other than the sound of his own voice.

One of the other men called out, "It'll half kill you, but it's worth it." John reached out for the glass. "It will do."

One of the men, sitting in a rickety chair, said, "Your horse got stolen? Those young Chickasaw boys are God-awful thieves."

"No," said John. "He got out of his halter."

John drank the whiskey. It was terrible. Who knows where the man got it? He wondered how to ask about somebody on horseback who might have come here before him, on a horse with two white front socks, and which name he might have used, his appearance. Edwards was drinking heavily; the two others, more carefully.

"No. Nobody here for four, five days. We're not doing a lot of business."

"It was that snowstorm!" One of the men, a younger fellow, waved his glass toward the door. "It was snowmageddon! The storm of the century!"

John suddenly wished he could go to bed; too much talking and strange people now often left him weary, even confused. He had not been that way before the explosion.

"Hard coming through those mountains on foot," said the man with the missing fingers. Then he said he was returning to Texas, to Fort Belknap. He had been waiting patiently for the southbound stage and for the storm to pass.

After a short struggle with his boots, John unbuckled his spurs and laid them aside. They were western-style, worn low on the heel with a big rowel. He'd bought them in Fort Smith to fit into this whole new western world of clothing styles and tribal territories and Mexican saddles. He took out his penknife and began to carve the mud and stones out of the boot-sole insteps. The man's Confederate overcoat was patched in many places. He clearly hadn't the means to buy something better for the last two years. *The economic situation in Texas must be terrible,* John thought.

He said, "Yes, it's a hard walk," and scooped up the mud chunks with the ash shovel and threw them into the fireplace.

"Plenty of horses for sale at Colbert's Station on the Red," said Edwards. "That's three, four days' tramp from here."

"I know."

"Well!" The other man wore a checkered homespun shirt, and he stood to flap the tail of it in front of the fire. "Well, I, for one, am thinking about crossing at Kiamatia, and I ain't looking to buy a horse. Not until I get across. Not many of them can swim all that well, and are they to blame? No, they got better sense."

Edwards nodded and then went off on horses getting loose, their clever ways, escape artists. He was rambling, enjoying the company and the whiskey. John endured the man's attempts at conversation with short replies. They had a sleeping loft in this room, and across the dog-run was apparently where the Edwardses slept.

Edwards said, "All kinds of people come down this road, just all kinds."

"I suppose so." John stared at his hands, touched his split lip. Brainerd had gotten in one good lick before John broke his wrist. He slid away from the recollection to think about the people around him.

Edwards stood with his back to the fire. "Don't talk a lot, do you?" Then he laughed a nonsensical laugh.

John kept his eyes on the fire, but something inside him coiled itself, and it was not a thing over which he had a great deal of control. There was a slight shift of his body, an odd tilt of the head as if he were stretching his neck against a too-tight collar. Left, then right. He lifted his nearly colorless eyes to the man with an expressionless stare. *Back off,* the stare said. The man straightened a bit and laughed his silly laugh again, but now it was nervous.

"Well, just trying to have a conversation here!"

"Billy," said the young wife. "He's tired." And then: "Tired and walked a long way in the snow, but you're here now and all you need is another whiskey and then after a while we'll have some readings from the Psalms."

John nodded his thanks to her. She was becoming nervous about her husband's drinking, but still, there she was, leaping into the breach with more whiskey and a sweet voice and Bible verses. *Good luck, Madame.*

"I reckon you left your saddle, then," said the one with the checkered shirt. He was small in stature and had big round sweet eyes that he turned from one side to the other as if always looking for confirmation of his words, or approval of them. "When your horse galloped away in the dead of night."

John said, "Yes. I left it. It was an old plantation saddle, and the tree was cracked."

"They ain't no good!" cried Edwards. "Nothing to them! No cantle, no skirts! They's pieces of shit!"

The woman took a deep breath and put a kettle of water on the fireplace grill. John thought he would be happier sleeping out in the shed with the horses rather than sitting here in this flood of mindless talk and a loud drunk offering dimwitted opinions at top volume. He said, "I was coming from Little Rock and then Fort Smith. He got away from me past Fort Smith."

"Well, I come down from Fort Smith myself," said the man with the round, sweet eyes. "I thought we'd never get through those mountains. I got off that stagecoach because it was about to beat me to pieces. I said, 'I got to rest here a day or so, and then get on the next one and get beat to pieces all the way to Austin,' but in *stages*, you see. That's what I said to myself." He bit his lips together. "I mean, they ought to just take a hammer to you and charge you for it. You wouldn't even have to travel."

John looked down at his glass. He was warming up, finally. He was thinking better, and his hands were steady. He said, "I hope your stay in Fort Smith was restful, so you started off ahead of the game." He wondered how to ask the man if he had run into somebody named Charles Bain or Robert Garoute or A. J. Dodd and sat considering various approaches and fell upon a mercantile one that had to do with cattle and flour. "I was looking to hire a man for a guard," he said easily. "I'm buying provisions for a warehouse in Spanish Fort. To supply the cattle crews going north. I was told about somebody named Garoute, I think it was, or Bain. Couldn't find either one of them."

"Oh, *him!*" The small man sat up straight. "Garoute! Do not hire that man!" He subsided somewhat, nervously waving one knee from side to side. "He struck a . . ." The small man suddenly stopped, without looking at the young Mrs. Edwards. "A woman in the alleyway behind the Full Moon drinking establishment, screaming, oh Lord, he was on his way to *killing* her."

"Garoute?" said John. He kept his eyes on the bright inconstant flames, clean and red, as they ate up the split wood.

The little man tossed down the glass of whiskey. "Yes. Just about did. Then the local lawmen came and took him to jail. Oh, but they'll release him." He set his glass on the floor. "No justice in this world, least of all in Fort Smith. Might be elsewhere."

John stretched his long legs out and rolled his shoulders while the others made noises of agreement. The moment of tension with Edwards seemed to have passed. He said, "When was this?"

"Well, it would be three days ago. I mean, the night before three days go. My ticket here says 'Depart December sixteenth, 1866.' Like they think some people might not know what year it is."

"Sometimes they don't. What does he look like?"

"Who? Garoute?" Then the small man nodded with a knowing look. "Yes, so's you don't ever hire him under some other name, I bet I got that right."

"You do. What does he look like?" John felt in his shirt pocket for his tobacco and shook out a thin line of it into a square of newspaper.

"Ah, let me see. What does he look like. I would say medium-sized, and grayish eyes or blue or what some people think passes for blue, like greenish grayish? Probably dark hair. Never took his hat off—it was a saloon, you know. Kind of a look of a dandy fellow about him. Can't people fool you, though? Quiet fellow, drank like a fish and just got quieter and drunker. And then he had all these black speckles on his neck, here . . ." The small man clapped his hand alongside his neck, just under the jaw.

"A tattoo," said John. "Must be some kind of a tattoo." He spouted a thin stream of smoke into the moist and melting air of the cabin.

"No, some kind of accident with gunpowder is what I think," said the small man. "This is an exhausting world. I go in to get a drink the night before the stage leaves, and some maniac with a speckled damn neck beats up a lady of ill repute in the alley behind. Oh, they'll let him go." He sank down into his chair, abandoned to gloom and thoughts of an unjust world where jails could not confine the guilty and stage-coaches battered the innocent over roads of snowdrift and stones.

John watched the wood eaten up by flames that detached themselves and fled up the chimney. He kept a mild and vaguely interested look on his face, but the man's words struck him like a revelation. *That's why I couldn't find the son of a bitch in Fort Smith: he was in jail. He was in the damn jailhouse.* He looked up as young Mrs. Edwards came in from the door to the dog run carrying quilts. *Now what? Is he ahead of or behind me?*

The young woman had an austere expression as if she had heard nothing about prostitutes in Fort Smith. Never in her life. Edwards took another glass, tipped it up, and drank it entirely. Then he got up and carefully considered, with a blunt, determined look, exactly where it was he placed each foot as he staggered off into the room across the dog run.

Question is, what am I going to do? When he had first been told that Dodd was headed toward Texas from St. Louis, he thought it would be a straightforward pursuit, a matter of pressing forward, catching up to him someplace either public or on the road and leaving his body for the undertakers or the carrion eaters. Now it was not that simple.

"Don't hire that man."

"No. I will not, I assure you."

That night they all listened to Mrs. Edwards reading about being safe from the moon by night and the sun by day and the arrow that flieth in the darkness. John was given the loft to sleep in. He kept his revolver with him and felt relieved that he managed the steep ladder without trouble, one foot then one hand then one foot and then one hand. The other two men lay down on braided-straw pallets on the floor near the hearth. It was a crude place, but it was shelter and plenty of food and a fire in the big odd-looking mud-loaf fireplace. The loft was warm in the rising heat, and John did not so much fall asleep as pass out.

IN THE MIDDLE of the night he heard a high, thin cry. It deepened into a thick animal sound. He knew it well.

He stood up out of his bed, throwing aside the blankets, bent to the railing and swung over it. He dropped the short distance to the floor below, landing, miraculously, on both feet. The cries intensified into a shriek.

The door from the dog run came open. The young Mrs. Edwards stood in a nightgown and wrapper, a lantern in her hand, an expression of alarm, her husband drunk and dead asleep, leaving her to take care of whatever might occur in the dark night of Oklahoma.

"Just stay away from him," John said and then turned to the man lying under his Confederate overcoat on the pallet. He was still crying out, devoured by an evil dream of battle and blood. "Wake up," John said in his best officer's voice. "Wake up. It's all right. Wake up. Wake up."

The man began making muted noises. Then, finally, "What?"

John said, "You're in Edwards' Station. You're all right. Just wake up."

The other man, the young one with the sweet eyes, snored like a steam engine in undisturbed sleep. "Well, Jesus," the man said. He took deep breaths. "I couldn't get out of the way."

John turned to the woman. "Mrs. Edwards, go to bed. He's had a nightmare."

"Can I . . . ?" She hesitated, looking away from John's half-naked condition of drawers and shirtlessness.

"No, ma'am. Go to bed."

She paused, her eyes full of concern, and then turned and left.

The man sat up and John saw a glass of whiskey that had been left beside the fireplace to warm and then forgotten. He handed it to the man. "Are you awake?"

"I am." The man took the whiskey and poured it down. He closed his eyes for a moment as the liquid hit his bloodstream. "I fell in front of one of the caissons. It was running over me. The horses. Then the wheels."

John went to stand by the fire. "I keep having one about solid shot hitting a wall. With me hiding behind the wall." He wrapped his arms around himself against the chill.

The man drained the last of the drink. "That what happened to your head?"

John paused and then said, for the sake of simplicity, "Yes."

"Thank you."

John nodded.

"Where'd you fight?"

"Virginia," John said.

The man sat himself up against the wall. "Go on and go back to bed. I'll be all right. I'll just stay awake here. Afraid of it coming back."

John said good night and then made his way up the ladder.

CHAPTER FOURTEEN

December 24, 1866 / Colbert's Station, Red River

THE NEXT MORNING THE SNOW had turned to a bright, crusty substance that dragged at his boots and sent water streaming downhill from beneath the snowbanks. Green pine, white snow, hard plates of red sandstone with frosted tops and the blue distant mountain ridges rolling away. He thought it might be Wednesday. A stage might come along in a couple of days to carry him to Colbert's Station, and he thought for a moment of staying at the stage stop to wait for it, but he didn't like the Edwardses. Or, actually, he didn't like the situation at the Edwardses'. That girl doing all the heavy labor and that feckless drunk incapable most of the time, her looking for a rescuer perhaps. Perhaps him. Trouble. He had paid his bill and left early.

He thought of camping out at a good place beside the road and waiting. Dodd might come down on the stage and he might not. The stage might come, and it might not. The San Bois Mountains were difficult; they could break a wheel, lose a horse, snap one of the thoroughbraces, and now the slopes were treacherous with granular snow.

John knew that people tended to do the same things over and over. Make the same hand gestures, go to the same sorts of places, choose to be with the same kinds of people, make the same mistakes. You just had to watch them. Dodd liked city places, he was drawn to prostitutes, he always went someplace where he knew somebody beforehand, he tempted women with having their portrait taken in a studio with flattering light and backgrounds of noble broken architecture or blossoming gardens, he always took something from his victims, perhaps to relive the moment of murder when the light goes out of a human being.

If Dodd were ahead, he would be at Colbert's Station. It was a place

to stay and recuperate, buy a horse, and cross by ferry into Texas. There
was a telegraph station there. John could message Aubrey Robertson to
see what news there might be; news passed on from Belle.

At one of those odd barrens, one of those unaccountable clearings
in the mountains, halfway down a ridge, he saw a group of loose horses
running past and immediately stepped behind a barbican of red sandstone. He dropped his gear and pressed himself back into a crevice and
watched. The horses might have men chasing them. There was a splashy
red-and-white pinto and one with buckskin markings. One was a great
lumbering workhorse that seemed to have run away from the plow and
gone off to disport itself in freedom with these elven small horses. The
workhorse flung its enormous feet through the snow and called out to
the little mustangs, *Wait, wait*, and skipped and blundered after them.

John wanted him, but he didn't have any way to catch him. A horse
that size would last you forever. And he was a dark beast; big as he
was, that color would disappear in shadow and in the night.

John watched for a long time, but he did not see anybody coming
after them. Did not see or smell any smoke, did not hear a voice.

What he did hear was the rush of water. Before long, the road slanted
down into a narrow valley where a stream cascaded and leapt and
vaulted from one waterfall after another, white with its speed and volume, falling into boiling pools and then charging on.

He stopped to rest at the water's edge. It was probably the Kiamichi River. The mountainous country was smoothing out and the low
places spreading into broader and broader valleys full of good grazing
land. He tried to think as the murderer would, but who knows how a
person like that thinks? Day to day, or long-term plotting, or moving
by impulse? John reckoned that Dodd would pass through Colbert's
Station. He might have just gone straight to the ferry and crossed, but
he would likely try to buy a horse, and then he would have been noticed. There did not seem to be much about Dodd that stood out, and
as long as he kept his secrets and a cravat around his throat he could
slide anonymous and unremarkable among the crowds. He would most

likely be heading for the nearest town of any size, and that would be Paris, Texas, which was on the way to Houston and Galveston.

John made camp at a good spot higher up so he could watch the road. He found a dry rock shelter with a trickle of spring water coming down one wall, maidenhair fern like green lace. He was careful with his fire; this was Indian Territory, and there was some doubt among the people as to which laws applied, if any, and to whom. The river was noisy far below, and the forest spoke aloud as one naked branch creaked against another and small dried leaves trembled on the greenbrier vines. The new moon swam up out of the horizon and into the heavens.

Far to his right at the edge of the open valley a fox barked its miniature bark. John sat hooded with a blanket and sang part of an old French song for his heart's ease, and the melody seemed so thin and forlorn that he stopped. His thoughts went back to the times before the war. Best of all was the springtime, when their acres of apple trees made a moving sea of blossoms across the Missouri River bottoms, the Marais Temps Clair.

Then part of an old phrase came to him, out of an old story: *I will have my revenge in this life or the next.*

He turned his boots before the fire and considered the terrain, what would likely live in such geography. A mountainous world with one blue ridge outspanning another in layers falling into the remote land of Texas. He fell asleep quickly, but then deep inside his sleep he heard a repetitive noise. His mind sorted through this noise and said, *It's a horse. Get up, get up, see who it is.*

He listened; then he heard the noise of hoofbeats, a low snort. He slid into his shirt and pants, then picked up the revolver and cocked it with one hand over the works to damp the sound. He moved on sock feet to the edge of the rock shelf, looking down. The clouds had parted, the thin but brilliant moon and the reflective light of snow made of the night an undefined haze striped with leafless branches into which you could stare wide-eyed forever and not once see a clean edge or a definite shape. Through this rode a man of medium height with a short-brimmed hat on a slovenly, tired horse. The hat brim hid the traveler's face.

John could hear the clink of a curb chain and shod hooves on stone. The horse seemed to have two front white socks, high up; only the dark upper half of its front legs were visible. There was nothing he could do. He could shoot, but there was no telling if it was or was not Dodd. John knew he could not run after a man a-horseback, nor call out to him to stop for fear of spooking him altogether.

Then the rider pulled up the horse. His head turned from one side to the other. Two men paused and silent, in an utter stillness, in a forest of ice and shadow where life lay in the balance. There was no wind. Still the hat moved as the man turned his head slowly, seeking some danger he knew was there but could not see. People rarely look up; they don't think of it. John did not move, not an inch, but his sights were on the hat.

He could not shoot. It might be anybody. John breathed out between close-set lips, blowing softly, to disperse the breath clouds. He kept the barrel nosed in on what seemed to be the hatband.

And then the second hand of some remote living chronometer ticked and the moment passed, and the rider rode on.

Anonymous and solitary, John watched the rider disappear down the trail. John backed into the shelter again, keeping his gaze trained on the road below as long as possible. He sat down on his saddlebags. If the man was traveling in the dark, he was in a hurry or he wanted to stay out of sight. Then again it could have been some local person pressed for time, going to visit a sick relative, or coming home late from a gathering somewhere.

All John knew to do was to keep on until he found his man and then kill him. He had walked into a torrential wind of opposition, of mistakes, of lack of inner balance or of outer steadiness, through a mountainous country, and there was nothing to do but to keep on.

He rolled up in his blankets again and tried to sleep. He was fairly sure the man he meant to kill was now ahead of him. Maybe it was the horseman in the night. Colbert's Station was the closest telegraph station, and he needed news from Aubrey Robertson and his long-distance lover, Belle. One or the other might have news of the man, whose real name was Dodd, whose motivations were dark and obscure, whose past was filled with blood.

But Dodd was afraid now. He knew Chenneville was trotting patiently and relentlessly in his wake, like a coyote, a dire wolf. So, Dodd was caught between his desires, which were hot and fierce and knew no gainsaying, and his fear of death. All John knew to do was to keep up the pressure. Dodd would make some mistake, drunkenly confess or talk about it; he would attempt another murder, and John would be right behind him when he did.

John Chenneville walked out of the mountains of eastern Indian Territory, down onto the flatlands as the ridges became lower and lower to finally spill out onto the misted winter plains. There were small stands of trees here and there that let go their leaves into the wind as crows slid down invisible air currents and called out the names of all the things they saw. A thin wind cut through his overcoat, ran up his sleeves. The telegraph poles stalked alongside him and had done so all his journey south. Then he saw the bent and blowing woodsmoke of Colbert's Station. Beyond that, the Red River itself. It was a quarter mile across and very red. The plains rolled out like a scroll, and all was grass and grass and grass.

Now it was evening. A short distance from the station he found a good place to lay up and watch the place for a while. There was a stand of three cottonwoods footed deep in a litter of their own leaves and plum bushes grew thick around them. The crows spotted him and sailed down like a rain of polka dots to settle in the sycamore trees and caw insults at him. He dropped his baggage and sat with his legs out straight before him. The crows shut up after a while.

Colbert's Station was a remote and isolated place all by itself out on the windy plains, and everything around it was tossing and waving. The smokes rose and then leveled off in the wind, tall trees flung their branches about, lines of washing flapped in the breeze. A cable rig clacked as the ferry was winched across the river. A cable from the tall gantries whined as the pulleys rolled down. He saw a good house of some elegance plastered white with telegraph poles marching up in a soldierly array; a line ran into the house. The house had a generous front porch; to the side were a log bunkhouse of some kind, sheds, a storage barn, horse pens.

He leaned back against a cottonwood trunk and rolled his shoulders. He was not sure, but he would have bet good money that the telegraph line went on to Dallas. He thought about it for a moment, maybe Austin.

Before the night fell he had seen at least seven men coming and going, and about eight horses in the pens. The ferryman loaded and carried for two trips across the water: two freight wagons and three men on horseback. Those on horseback crossed from the southern bank and then rode off to the west. None of the men was Dodd.

In the failing light and the increasing cold, he began to stiffen up. His head didn't hurt anymore, but the bruises were tender and his hat sat on his head like a crown of fire. He took it off and wrapped his head in his kerchief. When he got down there, he would need a bath and a shave, and with luck he could get his clothes washed. He was aware that he appeared, after five days in the mountains, to be a wreck, a forsaken beggar or a wild man of the woods.

What was there, on to the west? What lay beyond? John Chenneville was in a strange land without a map, chasing down a single man in all this emptiness. He was far from his youth when he had clean linen that had always been laid out on his bed by servants. Other people had started the fires in the fireplaces and brought in wood to keep them going; others made the dinners and set them out; his clothes press was packed tight with clothing from an expensive St. Louis tailor. But the war had taught him a great deal, that things of immense value were actually small and finite: dry socks, a night's rest without danger, a tin plate full of oatmeal with currants in it, a forgotten candle stub in his pocket.

Darkness came. The windows of Colbert's Station were hazy squares of lamplight. He buttoned his vest up to his collarbone, unbuckled his cartridge belt, and laid down the Hudson's Bay blanket. He covered himself with everything else. And so he spent a cold and fireless night shut up like a shell against the night wind, buried under the load of blankets and coat.

He woke to the sound of horses behind him, coming down the Kiamichi Trail from the Winding Stair Hills. He pulled the red kerchief from his head because it would show up bright against the December foliage. He sat quietly, wadded up in his blankets in the cottonwoods and the thick plum bushes. He saw a herd of mustangs driven by two men gallop past and into the station. There was the red-and-white pinto and the buckskin and the big lumbering plow horse. They must have gotten free up in the San Bois Mountains and they were just now recaptured and being driven to Colbert's Station for sale. As far as he could see from this distance, the two men driving them seemed very young, happy, full of high spirits as they drove the horses into the pens. And neither of the men was Dodd. He saw a man come out and open the gates of the pens for them. John envied the boys' easy, unwounded strength, their impeccable balance.

He got up and took up his gear, his hat pulled down against the wind, and walked into Colbert's Station, and then on through to the ferry landing.

THE FERRY WAS tied up waiting for passengers. John raised a hand to the ferryman, watching him, calculating how much information he could get out of the man. Some people had information and would not give it, and others were merely dense and incapable of noticing things. He felt the lifting, falling surface of the deck beneath his feet and took hold of the rail. His hat strings fell down his back, and he knew he had the look of hard traveling about him, but he kept a pleasant expression on his face.

"I'm looking for a fellow," he said. "He might have crossed here."

The ferryman stood with one hand on the tiller and eyed this large man afoot and carrying all his gear. It was obvious he had lost his horse. The Red River tore past on its long journey from the known and unknown West. The tied-up ferry lopped and shifted. "Well, sir, I don't ask people's names."

"No," said John. "I expect not. But I can give you a description." John listened to the man's speech. He sounded like he was from some mid-south state.

"Yes, well, in a minute," said the ferryman. "Are you a Lighthorseman?"

John tipped his head to one side. "What's a Lighthorseman?"

"Indian tribal police. Choctaw, Chickasaw."

"Do I look like one?"

"Not in particular."

John regarded the water between this shore and the other as it curled and shone, red as rust. "All right. He's about five foot nine, gray-green eyes, dark hair, and he was riding a horse with front white socks."

The ferryman considered and then said, "Yes, I took him over." He gestured back toward the pens. "And there's your horse, right there." John saw the horse with the high white socks crowded in with the new ones. "He sold him and got another. That un's about wore out."

"All right. What did he buy?"

Another hesitation and John pulled a silver dollar from his front watch pocket and laid it on the unsteady rail. He took his hand away and waited. The ferry rocked from side to side.

The ferryman said, "That's going to end up in the river."

"Better take it, then."

The ferryman picked up the coin, studied the milling, and then put it in his own pocket. "Got himself a big tall bay with a star and a strip. Looks like a racehorse. Mr. Colbert had kept him special, but this fellow you're looking for, he offered a good deal of money, and so Colbert sold him."

"When did he cross?"

"Two days ago. Or nights, rather—he was in a hurry, wanted me to take him across at night."

John started to ask another question but stopped suddenly as a new thought occurred to him: *He travels at night, always.* "Did he say where he was going?"

"No, no further than Maupin's place there." The ferryman gestured across the water toward a group of buildings on the far side. "That's the Texas side of the river, and it's the last place you can buy liquor. Not allowed on this side; the Choctaws don't allow it."

John remembered the drinking at Edwards' Station but didn't say anything.

The ferryman said, "So he crossed into Texas and went on his way."

"Thank you." John nodded and then walked back down the ferry gangplank to the shore.

IN THE BUNKHOUSE he stood his rifle in the corner, placed his saddle-bags, blankets, and holster beside it. The saddlebags were heavy with the extra cylinders, powder and ball, but there was no way to lighten them. He stood before the fire for a moment, thinking. He stood with his feet wide apart as if to brace himself. He kept his hat on. He saw an empty bunk at the rear. He piled his gear on it to claim it.

Before he crossed the river he needed to rest, he needed a good night's sleep under a roof, he must see old man Colbert or the cowboys about buying a horse. He should take a bath, shave. It would be good to get his clothes washed, but he doubted he had time. He needed to check for messages; he needed to eat. The fire in the fireplace threw off a dry heat that felt good on his wet knees. The freighters had come in and stowed their things, and the two young cowboys were stripping themselves of coats and hats, talking loudly, laughing.

"Can you get a bath here?" John said.

"Well, hell yes," said one of the youngsters. "It's in the washhouse behind the horse sheds. It's this big old tub. You can get entirely in it, I mean your whole self."

Then John turned to see a light-haired man jump up from a bunk and stand for a moment with his forefinger upraised as if he was about to make an announcement.

John waited. He never knew what people were going to do next. When he got among too many people it seemed things speeded up and he often had trouble putting them together in sequence. He regarded the man; he was so fair his eyebrows were colorless, and he was well-dressed in a sack coat and cravat and a derby hat. John had no idea why a man dressed like that should be in a remote place like Colbert's Station.

The man approached John.

"Yes?"

"Ah, would you be John Chenneville, by any chance?"

"Yes."

The man said, "Well, there's a telegraphic message for John Chenneville there. In the house." He gestured toward the door. "Mrs. Colbert asked just this morning if a Mr. Chenneville might have arrived."

"I'm obliged," John said. Before he left the bunkhouse, he laid out everything neatly on a bed, his guns side by side.

CHAPTER FIFTEEN

December 1866 / *The Woman in White*, Colbert's Station, Red River

HE WALKED UP ON TO the porch of the Colbert house. It was impressive in this country; it had the look of a storybook about it, gleaming white. Vines tumbled down the railings, bare now in winter and penciled against the white walls in calligraphic lines. The cottonwoods bent over it with the wind in their branchy hands. John stood holding his hat. He didn't like to take it off, but this was a house, after all. He didn't want people to see the scar, but there was no help for it.

A small woman opened the door. She wore a sort of turban, and she had a long pole with a wad of wooly fluff on the end of it.

He said, "Good morning. There is a message for a John Chenneville. That's me."

"Yes!" she said in a bright tone. "There is a message for John Chenneville. We're cleaning house here for Christmas, and so pardon the wreckage if you would, Mr. Chenneville. I'm Mrs. Colbert."

"Pleased."

"It came two days ago. Our operator isn't here; he's down at Rock Bluff. The telegraph apparatus thing is back here."

John followed her through the hallway, where a young girl was scrubbing the floor, avoided the bucket, passed through a parlor where a settee had been stripped of its cushions and a whacking noise told him the cushions had been hauled outside and were being enthusiastically beaten. A heap of glass ornaments lay on the mantel. The small woman marched through the parlor bearing her dusting pole with its streaming cobwebs drifting like gossamer banners. She was very attractive and of course married, but John could not help smiling at her—at any rate, at the back of her head.

"This place is being reduced to rubble!" Mrs. Colbert stopped to pick up a can of brass polish. "The telegrapher went down to Rock Bluff to see if a herd has come up from Waco. He's supposed to report on it. Keota isn't answering, he said. He's trying to relay through Fort Gibson."

"Keota is not replying?" John was momentarily surprised, then told himself the line might be down again, Robertson might be out of battery, any number of things.

"No, sir, that's what he said."

As they passed through the parlor Mrs. Colbert heard the tall man's footsteps behind her stop suddenly. She turned to see that he had picked up a book from the end table beside the settee. He turned it over in his hands. Wilkie Collins, *The Woman in White*. The winter light shone on the gilt lettering.

"Do you enjoy reading, Mr. Chenneville?" she said.

"I do." He opened it and then said as if to himself, "'Burnet to ship one hundred pounds maize'." He closed the book and stood holding it. "Where did you get this?"

"There is something wrong," she said. "What is wrong?"

The man said nothing. A strange, cold feeling took him. A foreboding. He regarded the book and then after a short silence he raised his eyes to her.

"Mrs. Colbert?"

"Sir?" She stood with an inquiring look on her face, perhaps an anxious look because of some tone in his voice. She was young and had a round face like a Liberty Head on a gold piece. He looked down at her confusion and then gave her a reassuring smile.

"Where did you get this book?"

"A man came through here day before yesterday and left it in the bunkhouse. I guess he forgot it." She ran her hand down her smeared apron, nervously. "Is there something wrong with it?"

John bit at his bottom lip for a moment. "I don't think so. What did the man look like?"

"Oh, just kind of ordinary. Dark hair maybe, not as tall as Mr. Colbert. My husband is five foot ten."

John said, "Good. He came two days ago? So he stayed overnight."

"No, sir, he did not, he got the ferryman up out of bed and talked him into going over." She looked up at him and tipped her head to one side. "Do you know this man?"

"No," he said. "No, I don't, but I know somebody who had this book. How this man came by it is another matter." He watched her confusion and then said, "You have a message for me." With his forefinger he pressed the book back into its original spot on the end table, precise and careful.

"Yes, yes!" She turned toward the rear of the house. "They thought the line was down from Keota, but Tahlequah came through perfectly well. Our telegrapher will be back tonight."

He followed Mrs. Colbert into the small add-on room where the telegraph office had its table and sounder, the batteries and notepad. She handed him a message, and then she gripped her dusting pole, wanting to ask more, but could not decide to do so. He sensed that she was wary of him now. He took up the entire chair, and his large hands rested solidly as carvings on either side of the message form and he was still wearing the cartridge belt. He had a scrubby five-day beard and smelled of woodsmoke and sweat.

It was from Belle and dated the twenty-second. Two days ago. He held the note in one large, weathered hand. He read the note, laid it down again. He was to contact Belle immediately upon arrival at Colbert's; that was all. He felt his palms sweating. There was something wrong, terribly wrong.

Mrs. Colbert said, "The telegrapher will be back tonight to send your answer. Messages have been coming in yesterday and today, but there's nobody to read them. I wish I could. All I can do is tap out, *acknowledge, wait.*"

"It's all right. I can send it myself."

"Oh, you can? Well, it is the same price, thirteen cents a word."

"That's not a problem. And so I've taken up enough of your time."

After a hesitant little silence, she said, "Oh, are you a telegrapher too? Have you met Belle? The telegrapher in Tahlequah?"

"Unfortunately, no."

"It was the first I ever heard of a woman telegrapher, and I do so want to be one myself. They say she is very good and fast and it's all so, well, *daring.*"

John was on fire to hear from the mysterious Belle himself, but he grasped his patience in both hands and said, "I am sure you can find a way to learn Morse, and now I think I had better reply, if you don't mind."

So he found himself alone in the little telegraph office. He placed his hand on the key. If he thought about it he would fail. So he didn't think about it and began to send.

COLBERT'S STATION DECEMBER 24 66 DE SNOWMAN RE: MSG
FROM TAHLEQUAH OP. BELLE TAHLEQUAH KN

He paused, with a small feeling of celebration. If he just threw himself into it, it came back naturally, but if he stopped to work out the abbreviations, he would tangle himself up. He sat motionless over the instrument, waiting for the reply, and then added, BELLE, REPLY INTERNATIONAL.

And that he sent in the International Morse code, somewhat different from American. Western Union used American, but he hoped Belle would have been trained in the other as well.

Suddenly the sounder burst out in a flurry of International Morse.

CFM SNOWMAN OP AUBREY ROBERTSON KEOTA STN
MURDERED ALL LE TO QUESTION TRAVELERS DREADFUL
OCCURRENCE BODY FOUND FROZEN IN STN. THOUGHT LINE
WAS DOWN WHEN HE DIDN'T REPLY BUT IT IS OPEN. WHERE IS
COLBERT OP? KN COLBERTS.

"Oh my God." He sat very still. Nameless feelings broke and cascaded through his mind and he tried to stop them. He dropped his head and stared at the tabletop with its old Vail lever key bolted to the wood, and then a contained, scorching rage took over everything else. John's big raw hand closed on the knob like a vise. Robertson's life was his alone, it wasn't anybody else's to take, they were not in a war, bitterly unfair, you filthy vampire, where are you? He had to get hold of himself; a torrent of images. Aubrey Robertson and his lilting voice and cheerful ways, his laughter. He took a long breath and replied.

COLBERT OP TO RB CHECK LINE FROM KEOTA. WHEN DID THIS HAPPEN

THREE DAYS AGO WHEN NO REPLY FROM KEOTA FT. GIB SENT PATROL ALSO LIGHTHORSE THEY FOUND HIM DECEMBER 20

MURDERED HOW?

SHOT

NO SUSPECTS?

NOBODY SEEN. I WENT DOWN TO IDENTIFY TERRIBLE.

DID HE PM YOU AFTER I LEFT? I LEFT ON THE 19TH

YES, SD YOU HAD A GOOD VISIT GOOD TALK CHESS U BAKED BREAD ETC SD U WENT ON TO EDWARD'S STATION I KNOW IT WAS HIM SENDING PM I KNOW HIS HAND

DID YOU LOOK AROUND THE STATION? ANYTHING MISSING?

BOOK I GAVE HIM, THE WOMAN IN WHITE. IT WAS GONE. NOT FAMILIAR WITH THE REST OF HIS POSSESSIONS SO I DON'T KNOW.

THIS IS TERRIBLE. WORDS FAIL ME.

U.S. MARSHAL IS ON THE WAY FROM FORT SMITH W/ WARRANT.

FOR WHO?

ANYBODY. YOU MUST TAKE CARE THEY WILL TRY TO SAY IT WAS U I HAVE TO INFORM STATIONMASTER AT COLBERT'S NOW.

GONE, BACK TONIGHT. SEND AT ABOUT 5. FROM NOW ON REPLY TO ME IN INTERNATIONAL AND PIG LATIN WHEN YOU HEAR FROM ME.

13 I MAY BE TRANSFERRED TO MARSHALL

WD B BEST IF U R ALONE. MAN NAMED DODD PASSED THROUGH KEOTA STN AFTER ME AND IS SUSPECT IN OTHER MURDERS WAS ALSO HERE IN COLBERT'S BROUGHT WITH HIM BOOK WOMAN IN WHITE

WHERE IS DODD

AM LOOKING FOR HIM KN

ILLWAY OODAY AKETAY AREKAY YM SUCH DREDFL THINGS HAPPENING SHOCKED GRIEVING AR BELLE KN 73

She had not answered him as to whether she was alone or not, which meant she was. Unmarried, running a one-operator office. Maybe.

Mrs. Colbert stood in the steamy kitchen sorting out blue glass jars that rang as they touched. She looked up. "I am so glad you knew how to send, oh, lucky you!" She took a pair of tongs and lifted more jars out of a boiling kettle. "So the line isn't down? To Keota?" A great quivering plum pudding stood on the kitchen table, a Christmas dainty. It had butter icing running down its sides. She cut a large piece and wrapped the piece in brown paper.

He said, "No, the line isn't down. But for now, tell me the cost of a day and a night board and room and a bath. And then some provisions for travel, candles, Lucifer matches."

"Could you use a shelter half?"

"I could."

"It's in the washhouse, just to the right of the door. And so, yes, sir, that would be two dollars in cash, and Mr. Colbert says no bank drafts."

"That's not a problem."

"And!" She lifted a forefinger. "As it is almost Christmas, you must have this nice piece of plum pudding. It was for us and the telegrapher, and since you sent your own message, you're included."

"You are very kind." He smiled briefly; then the smile disappeared as if it had never been. He took the package in a preoccupied way, laid down the two silver dollars beside *The Woman in White*, and walked out.

CHAPTER SIXTEEN

December 24, 1866 / A Horse Named Major,
Colbert's Station, Red River

JOHN WAS PIERCED BY THE thought that he had failed Robertson somehow. He absently took up his revolver and looked at it, laid it down again. Terrible, destructive thought. It was Dodd who had passed him in the night. He straightened and made himself think of something else, quickly.

There was much to do. He found a place to spread out his overcoat to dry. He had already claimed one of the bunks and so hung up his hat on a nail and laid out the red kerchief that people in the west called a bandana on the back of a chair. He was turning this shock, this hardly credible event, over in his mind, searching for dates while the image of Robertson with the black king in his hand like a death sentence came to him in all its details.

He didn't like being inside much anymore. Certainly not with other people talking and calling out to one another and the door slamming as more people came in. The thumping sounds as tack and baggage were thrown in corners and a well-dressed man unpacked a small trunk full of shining things. Their voices seemed to cross one another; their sentences canceled one another out and left only noise. It was hard to think straight.

So he travels by night and kills by night, John thought. *That* salopard. *He crossed by night to Maupin's store on the Texas side. Why has he come south anyway? He must have people here. Find the people. He uses the name Garoute, so he knows people with that name. That's what Tuesday Jones said. If only I had been there. If only I had stayed another night.*

He calculated that Dodd was going farther east. His favorite killing ground was isolated country places that had fallen into chaos, lands of refugees and war. Then run for a city, for a riverfront town and there drift among the crowds. Dodd had killed Lalie and her family in an unsettled land where guerilla warfare had destroyed community ties. That made for hunting grounds; that made for unspoken crimes and midnight murders and a lonely young man in a telegrapher's shack who was far too welcoming.

For the noon meal, the cook brought in two Dutch ovens full of something hot. John sat stunned and unspeaking. He hardly noticed what it was other than that it was heavy on beef, but he ate two plates full and took four white-flour biscuits with butter, ate them all and tapped up the crumbs with his forefinger.

When everything had been sent back to the cookhouse, he walked to the window and looked out. He could see the horse pens. The big heavy horse stood with his head hanging over the rails and eyed the inviting world beyond. His head was enormous. Then the horse trotted to the far side of the pen and lifted his nose to the wind, scenting everything that came down on it, perhaps distant buffalo or remote felines that had cached themselves in thickets, the smell of fox, woodsmoke, other horses that were wilder and lived more inviting lives. John watched him and decided he would try to buy him if he could manage him. The horse looked as big as a locomotive. He probably took a size-six shoe. He would keep up his weight even with hard traveling.

Then he went out to see if Mr. Colbert had returned.

Colbert stood watching as John approached the pens. He was an upright, hardworking man with a small wife who wanted to be a telegrapher and likely would not ever be one. Silently, he took John's measure, his walk, his clothes.

John asked the price of the big plow horse and paid it, and also bought a bridle, halter, a good Mexican half-breed saddle.

"He'll put you on the ground," said Colbert. The man counted the money and slipped the coins and bills into his pocket. "He'll break in half, and you'll be knocked out in a plum thicket."

"That's possible." John shucked off his overcoat, even though the wind made the skin on his shoulders crawl and went into the pen. He pegged down his hat with a firm tug.

"Listen, I can tell something about you," Colbert called after him. "You are not that steady on your feet. You've fallen and bruised your face."

"I'm not going to be afoot," John called back. "Not for long."

He saddled the big horse and rode him out and around the station. The gelding was tight and humpy, but John kept the high-port bit on a close rein and the plow horse only pounced from one big hoof to another and threw his head; after twenty minutes or so, John's weight and his reach convinced the gelding that being mindful was the best course at present. John didn't think the horse would be any good at bucking, but he himself was not all that good at riding these days either. The big horse had a last go at defiance by shaking his stubby mane and then settled down.

"What do you call him?"

"Those boys called him Major."

"That'll do." John turned him out into the pen again. With his heavy-lidded eyes, he watched the horse, opening and closing his right hand. His gaze raked over the pen until he saw the horse with the white front socks. The horse stood on three feet. His offside front leg was stretched out and pointing, and he did not move even when another horse bumped into him.

"A man who came here a couple of days ago had that horse," John said.

Colbert nodded. "Yeah. He rode that horse hard until he was dead lame, and I'm probably going to have to shoot him."

John stood in the perpetual plains wind and waited.

Colbert said, "You can make time if you're willing to kill horses."

"That's true enough." John considered some other clichés and boilerplate truisms but didn't say them. Silence worked better.

"Then he turned right around and bought an Army Remount thoroughbred. He was moving fast. Now I am not sure it was the right thing to do to sell him that thoroughbred. He'll kill him sure as guns. A good

Army Remount, and I bet he don't survive more than a week. He'll get fifty, sixty miles out of him and leave him for dead. Why a man needs to travel that fast, I don't know." Colbert then considered the tall man with the still face and light eyes, the thick upper lip of a boxer; a pugilist in a dark wool coat and vest and one of the most expensive-looking cartridge belts he'd seen in a long time. Good leather and double-stitched top and bottom. It had a dull steel buckle that would not glint or shine and give a man away. Every loop filled with .44 cartridges. "Are you particularly interested in this fellow?"

John knew Colbert would soon hear from the ferryman that he'd been inquiring, but he said, "Sounds like somebody you'd want to avoid."

INSIDE THE BUNKHOUSE the others had scattered to their bunks or to the fireplace, busy with repairs. One of the young cowboys laid his revolver on the long table to draw the charges and clean the barrel, but John walked over and placed his hand over the gun.

"Son, do that outside," he said.

"Well, sir," the young man began.

"I said do it outside and keep the barrel pointed away from us old people."

The other cowboy said, in a clipped older-brother voice, "Do as he says, Shelby." He watched Shelby get up, gather the revolver and tools, and slouch outside. "I have only told him about a million times."

And now, as the sun poured itself down through lines of fast-traveling clouds toward sunset, it seemed the news had arrived. John saw a man he took for a telegrapher emerge from the main house and speak with Colbert on the porch. It would be a message about the murder of Robertson. The telegrapher had come back from Rock Bluff and gotten the news and so he would have told Mrs. Colbert. A shocked and frightened Mrs. Colbert would have told the maid that something was amiss and she would have told the cook and the cook would have said several exciting things to the young black woman who had helped carry the supper to the bunkhouse. He had to move on, and fast.

John listened as he sorted his gear and shook out his blankets. He heard somebody say, *Murdered?* in a low voice. And, *They ain't no law around here.* And behind him he heard, *Strange people just show up and you never know.* His back hair crawled as he felt them looking at him with new eyes and a growing suspicion. *Who would kill a telegraph operator? What for?* There was a strange, hostile feeling now, as the telegrapher and Mrs. Colbert stood at the windy porch rails watching the bunkhouse door.

He was a suspect and he knew it. They wouldn't bother telegraphing ahead to look for a man of Dodd's description since they had somebody to suspect, namely him. Also, this would require them to get hold of Texas law authorities, and John did not know who that would be. If any. He turned his saddlebags upside down and shook out the debris, laid them down again, and started to repack socks, money, ammunition. Dodd needed to be knocked on the head, and quickly.

The light-haired man was perusing a map. It was one of the Colton's maps, a good one. John bent over and sought out the towns to the east, those dots and printed names that he would come to one after another in an unknown geography and a country made poor by war, and through this his man would travel, appearing and disappearing.

The smaller man pushed the map forward so John could see it more easily. He said, "You see, Texas is far more populated in the eastern portion, especially toward Galveston."

John nodded and in the tormenting clashes of noise—of Shelby's complaints and the roar of kindling being dumped in the wood box while outside something was being hammered on in endless bangs—he agreed there were far more towns in the east, yes, a great many.

Then the pale-haired man stood back, clasping his hands together, observing this tall, travel-stained man going carefully over the map. After a courteous hesitation he commented that John must have come a long way, he looked worn down. John said he had indeed come a long way, from St. Louis, a month back. He turned from the map and resisted the urgent need to simply pick up and leave. He laid out his shaving gear and rolled it all in its canvas holder.

"And I have a long way to go yet," he said. He sat down in the battered kitchen chair by the fire for a moment, laid his hands in his lap, and looked at them. His knuckles and nails were filthy. Bath first, and quickly, or he would not get one at all.

"Where are you going?"

John turned to the younger man. "Why are you asking?"

"Ah, well, to tell you the truth, the Choctaw tribal police, they call them the Lighthorse, were here yesterday asking about somebody traveling through. Somebody that cut up, I suppose the word is, a young woman in Fort Smith, and now there's word this telegrapher got killed up north of here."

"That would not be me."

"No, no, well, then." A pause. "At any rate, my name is Jens Arnesen. I am a salesman, I suppose you could say—a commercial traveler."

"I see," said John. He got up with his towel and canvas holder in one hand, paused at the door. "And what are your wares?"

He watched as the man opened a suitcase full of eyeglasses, then lifted the lid of a wooden box containing a kerosene lamp, which he would soon demonstrate as the newest in lighting devices. In a hardshell case, he kept magnifying glasses and a beautiful three-draw spyglass. He said he was always at the ready to take orders if people wished to purchase any of these things for themselves. Arnesen confided that he knew he was not a good salesman. He had been born and raised in St. Cloud, Minnesota, with a piano in the house and a deep Lutheran respect for personal reticence.

John reached toward the map and asked if it too was for sale.

So he bought the Colton map and paid five dollars for it. Somewhere on that map Dodd was moving fast, away from his crimes, over the paper rivers, over the printed names of counties, farther away every minute. John folded the map and shoved it in his saddlebags.

CHAPTER SEVENTEEN

December 24, 1866 / A Federal Marshal, Colbert's Station

JOHN SANK INTO THE HOT water and closed his eyes, at a half float. The tub was almost long enough for him, and he noted various bruises on his shins and forearms. All the steam in the cold air made it look as if he were being boiled. He touched the tender place on his skull where the blunt arrows had hit. High on the left thigh was the neat round bullet hole. It had healed long ago. He always forgot about it except when he took a bath.

John thought about a night's rest in a real bed, under a roof, with a comfortable fire, before he had to go on again. He would pick up Dodd on the other side of the river, he was sure of it. Dodd had a fresh horse and was probably several days ahead of him. He would be laid up somewhere, waiting for the dark. And every mile he would watch for someplace that Dodd would be able to lay up during the day. He tried not to think about Robertson. Not in any detail.

By the dim light of a plains sundown, the US Marshal out of Fort Smith rode up to Colbert's Station, coming down the road from the north, out of the Winding Stair Hills. The man sat on his horse and looked around for a bit, then swung off. He inquired at the main house, and after a short conversation with old man Colbert he walked to the washhouse. John looked up from soaping his head to see the man standing in the doorway.

"You better get your clothes on," the man said. "I need to talk to you. I'm Giddens out of Fort Smith. US Marshal."

John regarded him out of the steam with a watchful appraising stare. His head and both hands were covered in soap foam. He noted how the man was armed, the star on display on his coat lapel. Then he poured more water over his head and said, "Well, Marshal, this is the first bath I've had in two weeks."

"I'll wait for you at the house."

"All right."

"Don't be long." The man hesitated a moment and then said, "There's only one door out of this shed, and I can see it from the porch."

"All right."

When he was gone, John stood and stepped out of the bathtub onto the canvas, spewing water and steaming all over. He drew on his dirty clothes, shaved himself in a cracked mirror, and pulled on his hat. His revolver and the rifle were in the bunkhouse, and he thought about how hard it would be to get to them. It would be hard, so he wiped and folded his straight razor and tucked it into the pocket of his overcoat.

The Marshal was waiting on the porch, sitting comfortably in a chair. He wore the star-in-a-circle badge, a short-brimmed hat, a red-patterned neckerchief, and a heavy dark overcoat. He had a revolver buckled on, and his rifle was leaning against the railings. He was trying to fit a key into a pair of manacles and not having much luck. He then abandoned the effort and raised his head to see John approaching and got to his feet. John thought the man might be a quarter Indian, maybe more.

"Let's go inside and talk," the Marshal said.

They sat in the parlor of the Colbert house. The settee's cushions had been restored, and the Marshal sat down there and stretched his knee-high boots out before him. John sat in a wing chair and leaned back, warm from a hot bath, to regard the Marshal with his colorless eyes and a noncommittal expression.

"What is your name?"

"John Chenneville. You knew that."

"Yes. So tell me where you're from."

"St. Louis."

"All right. You just come down from there now?"

"How bad do you want to know all this?"

The Marshal's boot began to tap slowly on the floor. "Pretty bad. I got a dead telegrapher on my hands. I'd appreciate some answers."

"All right." John paused, ordering his memories. "I left Missouri around mid-November. I came through Little Rock and then to Fort Smith. When I got thirty miles south of Fort Smith I stopped to camp for the night, and when I got up the next morning my horse had got loose. He was gone. So I started walking on south, and the first place I came to was Keota, the telegraph station in Keota. It was night when I got there."

"You were caught in that snowstorm."

"I was. I saw the light there. Robertson was still up."

"How long did you stay with him?"

"Two nights. Until the storm passed. Then I went on and stayed at Edwards' Station."

The man nodded and shifted around in the chair. "I know. I asked there. I was there. I talked with Mrs. Edwards. She said you were there the twenty-second."

John nodded slowly, thinking, calculating the miles. "You have been riding hard," he said. He listened carefully to the man's accent. Pure Oklahoma, slightly southern.

"Yes, I have."

"Did you ask Billy Edwards?"

"He was drunk."

John wiped both hands down his face as if to clean away all the pain of this murder, this young man, gone. He wondered if this was another reason to swear revenge. If people really did things like swearing revenge; heroic bandits onstage who swore with dagger lifted on high that they would exact payment for the outraging of mother/sister/wife/old decrepit father and so on.

"What did you do?"

John looked up. "Sorry, what?"

"So you said you were caught in that storm and came to the Keota station. What did you do that night?"

John considered the sheriff and his calm, disinterested face. Giddens was jumping back and forth in time, hoping to trip him up maybe. "Yes. It was night. Robertson offered me supper and I ate, fell asleep. The next day he found the line was down, and so I helped him look for the break and we repaired the line. I stayed one more night. We played chess. I left early the next morning."

The Marshal considered this for a moment. "All right."

John said, "And he's dead."

"Yes. Shot in the back. Yes, he was running. There was blood on the doorsill; he was shot going out the door."

John bent his head and put both thumbs against his forehead, pressed hard, looked at the floor, ran his thumbs back through his hairline, over the scar. "He was a good young man. He had nothing worth robbing. Why?"

Giddens looked at him and then fell silent for a long moment, a silence John did not interrupt.

Then Giddens said, "You told that fellow who runs the ferry that you were looking for somebody."

"I am. It's a man who killed somebody in Missouri, and now he is running; he is going on into Texas. I think he is the same man who killed Robertson."

"Do you know his name?"

"Yes, it's Dodd. Albert Dodd. A lot of the time he goes by the name of Garoute."

"Why?"

John was silent a moment and then he said, "Why what?"

"Why would he kill the telegrapher?"

"I have no idea. I think I posed that question already myself."

"You believe he came through here."

"Yes. He left this book. This book belonged to Robertson. You can check with the telegrapher in Tahlequah; she can confirm that it's his. It *was* his." John reached over to the lamp table, took up *The Woman in White*, and handed it to Giddens.

The Marshal flipped the book open and ran the edges against his thumb. He noted the inscription *Burnet to ship 100 lbs. maize 4 W U. acc't.* and for a short time seemed puzzled. "What is maize?" he asked.

"It's the word they use in England for corn."

"I see." Giddens replaced the book on the lamp stand. "And so this is definitely his book. Of course, Robertson could have given it away." He paused, thinking. "Tell me about this man you are hunting. How you know he killed somebody. And who." The Marshal shifted in the chair and said, "Tell me the whole story."

And so John told the story, as much of it as was relevant to the matter at hand, and he told it slowly, but the Marshal was patient. Finally Giddens said, "That's an unheard-of thing. Killing a woman and a baby and the husband. The husband, all right, maybe a political feud from the war. But the woman and child? I never heard of such a thing. Why hasn't anybody gone looking for the perpetrator?"

"I am."

"Yes, but you're not the law. I never heard or read about it in a newspaper. You'd think somebody would have written it up in the *St. Louis Post-Dispatch* or the *Memphis Appeal*." The Marshal looked into John's face, a direct and searching stare. Then his dark eyes flicked to the window. It had begun to rain, pinging on the glass panes. There had been no warning, neither thunder nor wind. Just the leisurely approach of a low cloud cover and now the rattle of big drops.

"If you don't believe me, say so," John said.

"You think this man killed your sister and her family a year ago, but he didn't leave Missouri until recently. Neither did you. Help me make sense out of this."

John nodded. "All right." He turned up the frayed hem of his vest, thinking. "So I've been recovering from a wound and it took a while before I could get around. I got home in September of last year, and they didn't tell me about her murder until they thought I could bear it, I suppose you could say. And then it was a while before I could walk well, or ride. And he thought he was safe there, protected."

"Home from where?"

"The war. Virginia."

"Start earlier," said Giddens, making a circle with one hand as if winding something in reverse.

John bit his lower lip briefly, thinking. He said, "I got hit with flying debris when we were at Petersburg. I spent about seven months in a field hospital in Virginia, and then made it home in September of last year." He looked up. "God let me live through the war so I could find this man. I know it. That's what I'm here for. That's why I'm alive. She and her family were shot to death, and when I learned of it, I knew there had to be an accounting."

Giddens listened carefully to John's words and the urgency of conviction that was behind them even though his voice was calm and even, listened with a still face. "Nothing was done about it?"

"That area of Missouri is under martial law and he was a deputy and the corruption is something to behold."

The Marshal nodded in a knowing way. "So it goes," he said. "Just as bad here. Indian Territory is turning into the Den of the Forty Thieves. And so go on."

"I went to where it happened and started asking questions, a lot of questions from a lot of people. He got word of me asking questions, and he ran for it. He took a boat for St. Louis. I tracked him there and got some information out of a man who had been with him quite a bit."

"So this man just told you anything you asked?"

"I didn't ask him nicely."

Giddens thought about this. "All right."

"But the man I wanted got away and I've been after him ever since."

"So how come it took you so long to get to Edwards' Station from Keota?"

John regarded the Marshal with new respect. He had never lost the trail of his thought, the paths of his inquiry; he had adeptly circled back without warning. "I was laid up a day or two on the trail. Sometimes I feel well, sometimes I don't."

"Where did you lay up?"

"There was an old house off the trail, a Chickasaw house, roof mostly fell in but it was all right." John didn't feel the need to tell the Marshal about being shot in the head with blunt arrows. By children. It was embarrassing. He patted himself for some tobacco, but his shirt pocket was empty. Giddens handed him one already rolled, and he lit it at the parlor stove vent. "It was on the ridge above the Little River."

"That would be Tenkiller's uncle's old house." Giddens thought about this and finally said, "All right. I need you to return with me to Fort Smith. We'll leave in the morning."

John said, "No."

There was a slight shift in the Marshal's body, in his shoulders, the angle of his head. "I have no idea if you are who you say you are and if this story about running down some man from Missouri is true. And it might not have anything to do with this murder. I am going to return you to Fort Smith and call a grand jury and try to get a true bill. And so, I want you to come back with me. You can clear yourself."

"Use the telegraph," said John. "It's the newest thing. Telegraph Bohannon, Michael Bohannon, inspector of police in St. Louis. You'll have to go through Jefferson Barracks. They have a dedicated line. Ask him about a civil suit I made against Dodd. Ask him for a description of me. It can be done, you know." John got up and threw the cigarette butt into the stove. "It's like magic."

"I don't appreciate the sarcasm. We can do that when we get back to Fort Smith. Or passing through Tahlequah. The lovely and talented Miss Victoria Reavis would send it on for me." Giddens tapped his boot toe impatiently on the newly clean carpet. "It's wet out there. It's going to be a long, hard ride."

John thought about the lovely and talented Miss Reavis for a moment. At any rate, anybody who could send thirty-five words a minute was talented. Then he said, "I've been after this man for a long time, and I intend to get him. I've come a long way, and I will probably go on further yet. I don't care how long it takes, how far he goes, or where, I intend to find him."

"If you do, then you will be a fugitive."

"From what?"

"Well, justice." Giddens made a vague gesture with one hand.

"There doesn't seem to be a lot of that in Indian Territory," said John. "Or anywhere else."

"I know that, but it is a task that lies before us."

"I haven't yet been served with a warrant."

"I haven't filled it in yet. I'm giving you a chance to return voluntarily and not under any charge. We are getting fed up with people carrying on in Indian Territory and the pileup of corpses down here." A short pause. "And Western Union in St. Louis is in a taking about this."

"It's not my problem. I am passing through, and I intend to keep on."

The Marshal looked out the window, gathering his words and his reasons. "I know it. But I am doing the best I can. I care about the law. To get this job I had to study six months under a Goddamned Little Rock lawyer with hay fever and a drinking habit. But here it is: You cannot decide the man is guilty and then kill him. It doesn't work that way."

"Apparently people do it all the time."

"Just be quiet and listen. You would be charged with murder. As a matter of fact, *I* would come after you and charge you with murder. You'd have to bring Dodd to a Marshal and have him charged with something so he can be held. Then he has to be extradited by Missouri authorities. That's how it works. Then he goes to trial back in Missouri, where you say the crime was committed. Where you say he killed your sister and her family. There has to be a defense and a prosecution and witnesses. Somebody has to get him back to Missouri."

"I understand that."

"Now, all that doesn't seem very likely."

"No, it doesn't."

Giddens sat for a moment and thought about it all. Then he said, "I am not convinced that it was you that killed Robertson, but you're the only man I've got. So pack up tonight. We'll leave early in the morning."

John sat in silence, tapping his foot, thinking how to reply. Clearly Western Union wanted somebody charged with Robertson's murder. Somebody, anybody.

"I don't want to have to put manacles on you," said Giddens.

"I don't think you could."

"Maybe not," said Giddens. "But I assure you I would do my damndest."

John nodded, said nothing, and then stood, picked up *The Woman in White*, and walked out of the Colbert House, knowing that he was about to become a fugitive, and before him lay another kind of life.

THE SLIGHT, BLOND man from Minnesota was a salesman, and salesmen are interested in people in general, and so he wanted to understand things like the interior engines within human beings, engines that are fired with unknown fuels and drive them one way or another, as well as to bring these human beings both light and vision. The tall man with the lightning-tracked scar on his head interested him. He watched as the man came into the bunkhouse to put his revolver in his pommel holster, take up his coat, load his saddlebags carefully. He wadded up a rope halter. He carefully loaded the Spencer, pointing the muzzle straight down, and then dropped the follower tube into the buttstock. He slung it muzzle-down on his back and to one side, the way soldiers carry their rifles. He settled his hat firmly on his head.

"It seems, sir, that you are about to leave, and in the nighttime and the rain, yet."

"I am," said John.

The blond salesman made a circular motion with one hand. "I assume there was some, ah, trouble with the Marshal."

"Not on my part."

"Have you reflected upon the dismal life of a fugitive from the law?"

"Perhaps not as often as I should have done. But we all have our regrets." John beat on the packed rations with a hard fist, forcing the bundle into the saddlebags, and then buckled them shut. "Good evening to you."

The salesman from Minnesota stood at the window and looked out into a cold rainy evening, toward the horse pens. He saw the tall man walk through the rain and out to the horse shed, where the big gelding stood eating Colbert's good, rich hay. Watched as he brought him out and tied him to the pen rails and saddled him. He used the shelter half and his blankets for a saddle pad, saving weight. He felt that he was observing some great, momentous decision that is rarely made in a lifetime. Or at least this is what had been presented to him in various modern novels; the bold Joaquin Murieta, the sneering villain St. Elmo. He stepped outside, holding his hat in front of his face against the blowing rain.

"Godspeed," he called.

The tall man glanced over at him and smiled an amused smile. Then the smile went away. "Thank you," he said.

Now the Marshal came out of the Colbert house, a man who had sat at a rainy window to watch the lights in the bunkhouse. He walked out over the muddy ground with his revolver in his hand.

"No," the Marshal said. "I told you no."

"Sorry," said John. "I'm on my way."

"I don't want to shoot you. I do not." Giddens kept walking toward him, pace after pace, in the lamplit puddles and then nearer yet.

John was taller than the Marshal, and despite his uncertain balance, still he was much faster. He quickly stepped close, grabbed the Marshal's revolver hand by the wrist and jerked hard, off to one side, and bent around and down against the hinge of Giddens's elbow and held it there in an iron grip. He buried his right hand in Gidden's lapel and twisted. The Marshal opened his hand and let go the gun rather than fire. John twisted the gun out of his hand and stepped back out of reach. He waited one second, two seconds. Giddens had made his decision and did nothing.

John raised the revolver straight up and flipped out the cylinder. He dropped all the charges in the mud. He clicked the cylinder shut again and handed the revolver back butt-first. The light from the bunkhouse window gilded them and their outlines with the glow of the new and marvelous kerosene lamp.

The Marshal took the revolver and seated it in its holster. His hat brim dripped rain. John turned and stepped up into the stirrup and turned the big horse to the east.

He rode away on the north side of the Red River, following a faint trail over the top of a rise. There, screened by small, twisted live oaks, he looked back. He saw the salesman at the window with the light of the kerosene lamp outlining him, and at the picket fence were dark shapes where several men stood to watch him go. None of them were bringing out horses. None of them were moving.

Now John Chenneville was a wanted man. A man gently reared in a pleasant old French village north of St. Louis, a person of some education, his father a gentleman farmer of many acres and a large house and great orchards stretching out over the Missouri River bottomlands. Now he was a fugitive in a strange land owning nothing but what he carried with him and the last of his family.

So he went on.

CHAPTER EIGHTEEN

Christmas Eve, 1866 / Rock Bluff on the Red River

HE DECIDED TO STAY ON the north side of the Red for now, and cross into Texas farther east at Rock Bluff. Rock Bluff was the cattle crossing, where they swam the cattle over because of the good hard banks on either side. He had heard the young cowboys talking about it. They would have stopped him if he tried to get over the river at the ferry at Colbert's Station, and then he supposed the Marshal would have dragged out the dreaded manacles, which he had most likely been issued only recently given his confusion over the locking mechanism.

And so John Chenneville continued eastward along a wooded trail that sometimes approached and sometimes drew away from the Red River. The rain had passed over. The trail wound in and out of the gallery forest that lined the river. He would have to cross over and then turn back westward again to Maupin's store and ask about Dodd: his appearance, his horse, his marred and dotted throat, his sobriety. He was close, close. He could feel it like animals can feel the approach of a lightning storm.

The big horse snorted and did a few clumsy capers several times so that John kept one hand on the saddle horn. The capering was ponderous and slow; all in all, the horse was a sensible animal. He had a long, rolling trot that was probably sixteen feet at a stride, and it was cushiony and easy on the back. The night came at John like blindness, like a dark sea. He prayed for the rising of the moon. He ducked as something tore at his hat. He grabbed it by the brim. He rode hunched over with his head down, prepared to blunder into another low-hanging branch at any second.

He was headed for Galveston. John was fairly sure of it. It was a port town, like Ste. Genevieve, Missouri, was a port town on the Mississippi nearest to the murder. Dodd had disported himself first in Ste. Gene-vieve, then run to St. Louis. *It was there where he tried to kidnap that girl, where he could ride out into the country and kill my sister, kill the whole family, then ride by night into Ste. Genevieve again. Appear the next morning at work as a deputy, shaven and tidy. Lifting his pleasant face to say,* Yes, Mrs. Picot? Somebody stole one of your chickens?

He was here, close to hand. In the unrelenting dark John felt he had descended into Hell to search out the Devil. She had so many years of life left to her. And now young Robertson. John felt he was dancing with the major and minor fiends of the otherworld, here on the Red River in pitch blackness, and this thought was reinforced by the de-mented whinnying of a screech owl somewhere ahead.

Then this darkness seemed a tone lighter and he saw that he had come to an open place and a shore of what seemed to be sand alongside the river. He had come to Rock Bluff, with the smoke-colored bulk of the great rock face showing vague on the far side, farther downstream. The river poured and murmured in a wide expanse. All its surface as well as the sky was swimming with stars. Now he must ask the big horse named Major to take to the water as if plunging into galaxies afar and yet others under the water.

John bent close to see by starlight what he was doing as he unloaded the rifle, packed his powder and caps in the oilskin packet, and wound the wrapping-strings tightly. He shucked off his coat and tied it to his blankets, then his boots, fastened by their pulls around the saddle horn. It was dangerous to swim an unknown river at night and in the cold of winter toward an unseen shore. He stared hard at the lighter patch of night, which was the loom of the bluff. He would angle down with the current and hope to strike a hard shore on the other side. Then after a moment he saw a gleam of light.

He sat very still. There was something moving across the river. He watched and soon he could see it was a dim human form, somebody carrying a light at chest height as people always did so that it shone faintly on the buttons of an overcoat and a scarf with the ends hanging down. He could see the man's clouding breath. The face was in shadow.

John sat in the saddle without moving. He wore nothing light-colored, and the big horse's dark color made him invisible. He had no white markings and was thus unseen, but John had unloaded his rifle and he was in his sock feet. Then a voice called to him over the running, liquid noise of the river.

"Cross here!" the voice said. The light wandered downshore among great sycamores whose white trunks hung spectral and disconnected in the dark. "Here!"

John ran through some quick mental calculations. If Choctaw tribal territory didn't allow alcohol, then somebody would be smuggling it across. The ferryman? Yes. And helping him was this phantom personage flitting here and there in the dark with a tempting invitation from the other side.

"Here! It's safe!"

And then, on an odd whim, an unaccountable foreknowledge, John called out, "Dodd! Is that you?"

Silence. Only the night and the river.

The light disappeared. John instantly kicked Major forward and struck him on the flanks with the rein ends and they plunged into the water. The plow horse proved to be a powerful swimmer; his big feet were like paddlewheels and his body fat kept him safely afloat, and so they churned like a steamboat across the swift currents of the Red. John slid off to one side and he hung on to the saddle horn with his right elbow and the revolver held over his head as they roared noisily out and onto the far side, throwing off sheets of river water. John sat to jerk on his boots and then ran up the slope. He heard the roar and rattle of the big horse shaking himself. The stirrups flapped and banged, and then the hush of the night closed in again.

He stood still for a long time in the total darkness. He was soaked and cold, but he watched intently for any sign of light. Carefully, slowly, he unwrapped his revolver, making as little noise as possible. The big handgun was reasonably dry, and so he cocked it; *click-click*.

There: a tiny glimmer bobbed and then steadied. Without hesitation he lifted the revolver and fired. A spanging noise as the bullet struck stone and ricocheted with a wowing sound, off into infinity. Powder smoke drifted past his face. Then the light was gone.

No cry or shout. He hadn't hit anybody. Whoever held the light was already gone into the gallery forest and disappeared. By the light of the lantern the man had held up in the dark forest, John had seen that the man wore a scarf. The ends of the scarf were brightly patterned in red and gold. The coat was black or brown, he could not tell which.

Now the only noise was the river, a slight wind in the sycamores. After a while he perceived a faint red light floating in a square. It was a cabin, the door open, with a dying fire inside. He walked up to it, stumbling on empty beef tins, and stood to one side of the door. He did not hear anyone inside. He tied Major and then went in.

By the light of the dying fire he could dimly see the stub of a candle standing in its own congealed tallow on a shingle. He searched out every corner. This was clearly a place for whoever helped drive the cattle across, and their tatters and ends were everywhere. He lit the candle at the remains of the fire. He went through a heap of blankets, a box containing four bottles of some kind of whiskey, some torn and discarded clothes. He pulled out one of the bottles and looked at the label. Johnson's Imported. Probably a fake label. So this was how he had made the money to go on, to buy a fast horse and other horses to come. Disposable horses.

The case of whiskey had been abandoned. They probably got two or three cases across, but John had surprised him. Dodd didn't think he would come on when it was night. He tried to calculate the markup but, lacking any knowledge of prices on one side of the Red or the other, all he knew was that he must have had a shot of this sort of spirits at Edward's Station, and it was a perfidious drink that tasted like old grease and coal oil. He put the bottle back with the others.

He stopped his search frequently to listen. Nothing but the noise of the river and the night wind shaking drops from limbs overhead that drummed on the roof.

He came upon a pamphlet of some sort. He held it up and ran the candle down the pages. It was a crew change booklet from the *Hermi-*

one. That was the steamboat that traveled from Helena to Fort Smith. John looked at the list of names, the notations of who of the crew had shown up and who hadn't, changes of stewards, pursers, and engine-room men on the layover at Little Rock.

Dodd had left one thing of himself, that crew change booklet, and so he must have left others. John walked squelching in his wet boots from the doorway to the fireplace, shaking with cold, looking into cor-ners. He found an empty tin that had Hargrave's Pastilles written on it and a playbill for the Little Rock Show Time Theater.

TWO NIGHTS ONLY!

Don Cezar de Bazam; or, The Gambler's Fate!

New musical arrangements
With new mechanical effects Never Before Attempted!
To conclude with the farce of DR. GRIMMENHOFF, Horse Doctor

He sat down by the fire. He was soaked and frozen. *I nearly had him.* He knew he had to have a few hours' rest. He went out and unsaddled the big horse, turned him into a pen where there was a water trough full of rainwater and brought the saddle and shelter half and blankets in-side. He found a stack of kindling that somebody had placed there for the morning and threw the sticks on the coals. When they flamed up, he threw on more wood until he had a roaring fire, and then he stripped down to nothing, pulled a blanket over his shoulders, and stood close to the fire. The relief of warmth from the fire was enormous.

He faced the flames and held the blankets out to catch the heat; his body hair stood up all over like thin fur. He drove his fingertips through his hair to press down on the scar, a gesture that had become recurrent, automatic, as if somehow he could make it go away and make all that had occurred go away. The flames were hypnotic.

John thought back to what Monsieur le Docteur Boisliniere had told him: *You can never understand people like that, do not waste your time or your thought on this.* They had spoken in English because John did not want to use his country French, the driving accent and the lilt of it. Boisliniere spoke like a Parisian. He was an old friend of John's father, and if John remembered anything about the big St. Louis fire of '49, it was that Boisliniere and his family had taken refuge with them at Temps Clair until the flames died down.

John had sat with his hands on his knees in the medical office and said: *I'm listening.*

In my years as coroner here in St. Louis, Jean-Louis, I came across so many terrible things, things I will not bother to describe, and some were inexplicable. This is why the law requires no explanation, only the application of the law. There are some murderers to whom we attempt to ascribe human motivations or reasons; that they kill for money or jealousy or to inherit the old man's property, but, you see, they don't have any. I have perhaps seen two or three men like this in my time. They are not human. So all we can do is apply the law if we can.

We always want to give them human motivations but they don't have any. So they are always one up on us.

He laid everything out before the fire to dry. He rolled up naked and warm inside the blankets to get a few hours' rest. Maybe Dodd had a deeply abnormal brain, maybe he was possessed by a demon, but he still had to eat and sleep and rest and find allies somewhere.

John went over the towns ahead in his mind and then the particulars of his present circumstances. His breath clouded, and the clouds became pink and red in the firelight. Sleep welled up from inside him. Thoughts drifted and parted like mist. He was in Texas. It was occupied. He wore a Union Army greatcoat. Faded but recognizable. We want to give things human motivations. The river said *going, going, gone* and the big horse exhaled into the wet night air. He fell into sleep and dreamed of a flying cast-iron chain hurtling toward him out of a bright, soundless detonation.

CHAPTER NINETEEN

December 25, 1866 / On the Road to Paris, Texas

JOHN STRUCK OUT AT MIDNIGHT along the telegraph road on the Texas side of the Red River. *What a country, what a country*, he said to himself, a land with unknown animals, volatile weather, unmapped roads, and people with alien motives as yet hidden in their homes if they had any. A people defeated and their crops unharvested. As far as he knew it was Christmas Day. As he rode along, he leaned back to grope in his saddlebag and came out with the slice of plum pudding from Mrs. Colbert. "Merry Christmas, Chenneville," he said. As he licked his fingers for the last of the butter icing, he wondered how the big horse would be with gunfire.

He wadded up the brown paper, put it in his pocket, and then unholstered the revolver and cocked it. Major heard it; *click-click*. His ears flicked back and he tensed up. John fired into the air, and the big horse jumped slightly but held firm and kept walking. John fired twice more, once to each side, and each time the plow horse gave a small sort of jerk all over his body but kept on.

Good. John reloaded two chambers, put the revolver away, and considered his options. Dodd was traveling by night. He would be a bat under the constellations and a lightly flitting creature pressing on toward someplace less open, more chaotic, more populated. Dodd would be in a hurry if he was heading toward Marshall, as John had been told, and not Dallas. Dodd was a city creature with urban tastes and urban fears.

Once in a while John got off and walked. He rolled a cigarette and lit it by lifting his coat front to guard against the wind and snapping a match to it, and so he strode along the eastbound road on the south side of the Red River. He watched as best he could all the dark movements of tree limbs or grass heads, the swoop of a night bird. Jupiter moved like a blue-white diamond through the crowded stars overhead, but then as the night went on these stars dimmed as clouds moved in and the wind increased. It made strange sounds. Once he almost thought he heard Lalie's voice calling his name, but then he knew that was not possible, but it pierced his heart. He made himself think about something else.

How empty was this country? No house lights, no clearings, no smell of manure or woodsmoke. He saw no campfires of night travelers. He was leaving tracks of a large-sized boot straight down the damp road, and he was tiring with every step.

When daylight came, he looked for a place to lay up. He had slept very little in the past twenty-four hours. The wind was becoming sharp and hard; it bit at his lips and ears, his hands. It was bringing rain. To the south of the road he saw a motte of post oaks, great thick-trunked trees, and what looked like a declination of the earth toward a streambed. On that side he could build a fire and the smoke would blow away south and not alert any traveler coming down the road.

In the stand of post oaks he found a hunter's lean-to thrown together with mill sidings. It was a bit of luck. He started a fire in front of it, using the brown paper from the plum pudding, and there he warmed himself, his coat held open. He turned Major out with a halter and his rope trailing to let him graze on the winter grass, free of a saddle. John filled his canteen at the small stream, standing blown and dripping in its rocky bed, and then ate nearly everything in his saddlebags.

He stripped himself of everything except his long drawers. Long ago during the Peninsular Campaign an older sergeant had told him that in the winter cold he should sleep with as few clothes as possible and as many blankets as he could get. Naked if convenient, and keep your shirt and pants inside the blankets with you, to keep them warm. The sergeant was from Maine and knew what he was talking about. John pulled his saddlebags and saddle under the shelter, leaned back into his blankets, breathing wet clouds.

For a few moments he felt again that suspended, almost magical feeling of being out in the wilderness and the weather and yet safe against it. Here was rest and a respite against bereavement because the world was going on without him in its deep rhythms, deeper than he could see. And then he wondered where Dodd was in this weather, where he found shelter, but then he had been with the 33rd in all weathers in Missouri as mounted infantry, so he must have learned something. After a while John crashed into a sleep like a coma.

When they started out that evening, both John and Major had eaten well and were rested. The light faded imperceptibly around them, and the wind was clearing the air. He found himself thinking about Dallas, and if Dodd had gone that way, John would be far behind him. If he had to turn around and backtrack, he would lose precious weeks. All he knew to do was ask people along the way, if he could find any people.

Then he started thinking about Belle. Because she was a mystery and her face unknown.

John had the gift of not thinking about things if he chose not to, and thus he could pay deep attention to the night and all that occurred in it. But he had to admit that it was true, once in a while he let his mind drift to think about women, but this was Adam's curse and Adam's joy and he was in no way immune to it and had nothing personal against Adam.

He passed a crudely lettered sign on a white board: Paris 40 Miles.

He might make Paris in two days traveling. Then to Mount Pleasant, then Jefferson and finally Marshall. Despite himself he was taken by a running stream of thought. It was about the existence as yet unproved of the woman named Victoria Reavis, telegrapher. *Dit dit dit dit dit-dah dit dit dit dah-dit dit dit.* She would of course be all robin's-egg blue and ash blonde with bright notes of Morse sparking around her head.

Come along with me, darling, lay your body alongside mine, surrender yourself unto my capable hands, and for what? You shall have the delights of the cold road and a grimy Hudson's Bay blanket, hardtack and wartime canned beef. Think of the entertaining nights upon the glebe! Stars innumerable will not be visible because it will rain upon our luckless heads.

Major lifted his head, pointed his ears, and stared intently down the dim road.

No? Wise girl. And, I forgot, I might soon be on wanted posters. A description: six foot three and slightly unbalanced, medium brown hair, armed to the teeth, and of interest to the Federals. A likeness: include the broken nose and the cane. Avoid people like me, Miss Reavis, unburdened by trivial concerns about property. I just sold it all at a loss or soon will have done.

He had gone without a permanent companion in life so far, despite his best efforts, and so should continue in the same vein. When you are a wanted man it ruins your social life and it makes you unwelcome at cotillions. Consider: Belle had lost her one love to murder in Keota, the remarkable and cheerful Aubrey Robertson, and she would be in mourning. So keep your hands to yourself, Chenneville, and your intentions honorable.

But his thoughts kept circling back. He knew she had to be at least moderately young or Aubrey Robertson would not have referred to her as a most refined young lady, would he? As John walked along mulling this over he felt the repetitious pain of a stone in his boot.

Major was still staring, and John was still thinking about the mysterious Belle as he sat down in the middle of the muddy road, cross-legged like a Hindu swami. He pulled off his boot. Then his sock. Shook both of them out and heard the tiny pebble hit the road surface. Then he heard a low *huh-huh-huh* sound.

Major called out in a long shaky whinny. John jumped to his feet to draw the revolver out of the pommel holster. He stepped behind Major, looking for a target. He watched before and behind himself with one bare foot and his abandoned boot standing in the middle of the road.

More *huh-huh* sounds. It sounded like a feral hog, maybe an idiot human being loose on the nighttime roads.

There was the deep golden glow of a half-moon rising out of the trees like a house afire. By this illumination he saw the thoroughbred. The dark form came limping out of a stand of twisted trees and calling out to John's big horse. A call of complaint and loneliness and desperation.

John put up the gun, snatched his sock on, and then lay flat on his back in the middle of the road with his leg upright and both hands jerking on the pulls until his foot slammed firmly into the boot. Then he got to his feet and took the lead rope from his saddle.

He went up to the gelding, looking at him closely. It was Colbert's Army Remount thoroughbred, sure enough. He led both horses off the road, shared out what feed he had between them. He smiled, he slapped Major with hearty affection. He was close behind him, then, and Dodd was on foot. Good. He dallied the lead rope onto the saddle horn and kept on into the night, more slowly than he wanted, but the thoroughbred was limping on his left front leg, and he was done in. He watched as best he could the dark road ahead, for a walking form, the glimmer of a campfire. It would be splendid good luck to come upon Dodd here in the dark, on a lonely road. Shoot, shovel a grave, turn around, and go home.

At first light that morning he came upon an elderly man walking down the road ahead of him. The man carried a cane and apparently did not hear John approaching.

John stepped down from the saddle. He called out a "Good morning."

"What?" The old man turned around quickly.

"Good morning!" John said, more loudly.

"Yes, yes. To you as well. I'm in search of my hoass."

"Yes, sir, he got away from you?"

"'Tis an old hoass, but 'tis mine, and I don't care for him being taken against my wishes." The old man wore a tall bell-crowned hat, the kind that had been fashionable in the 1830s, and spoke in the language and accents of that time.

John said, in a rather strident voice, "Somebody has stolen your horse?"

"Well, sir, I was taking him to his new pascha thar in the ley and I was a-walking alongside him and this fellow come along and insisted he take and borrow the old fellow."

"Somebody on foot?"

"Indeed. He said he was just borrowing him but 'tis *my* hoass. 'Taint his. And what could I do?"

John walked slowly to stay even with the old man, leading the big plow horse with the thoroughbred limping along, pulling up on his left front.

"When was this?"

"Day before yisty. And since then I've been walking and looking for him."

"What did he look like?"

"My hoass?"

"No, sir, the man who took him."

"Taller than me, and his boots had too much heel to them for walking. A wide face. A fancy red neckcloth and a disreputable hat of wool felt and carrying a bridle over his shoulder." The old man's hand wobbled on the top of the cane; it was a silver knob with some intricate design. "You can tell a wool-felt hat, you know. They are shoddy, and they don't stand up. He was going in the same direction as me, and he just took him. Said he was borrowing him. I asked his name, and he wouldn't say. Now, that's not right. That theya is theft."

The road was an aisle leading on into the rising sun. Thin clouds in lengthy chalk-marks scored the red eastern sky.

"Yes, sir, it is. What did your horse look like?"

"*Does*," said the old man. "He ain't dead yet. Neither am I. I have hopes of recovering him because he is of my own raising. He was an orphan colt, and we've been together for twenty-three year." John was silent, waiting. "He is the color of eggshell, and here and there he's gone freckled as a guinea egg, as they do when they get old. A white hoass gets old and they get freckled upon they heads and they backs."

"Yes, sir, it is theft," said John. And then, "I have this horse here, if you want to take him." John turned and indicated the thoroughbred on his lead line. "He's lamed up but I think it'll pass."

"No, sir, I want my own back."

"Well, sir, if I come upon the man or the horse, either one, tell me your name so I can return him to you."

"Watson. Granby Charles Watson. I'm a hermit." John heard *hoimit*, and it took a moment to figure it out. "I live by myself back there, and I don't care for company other than my old white fellow and various other critters. I don't care for company. People have forgot about me during this waw." The elderly man looked up at John with his leaking, red-rimmed eyes and fumbled in the pocket of his wide-skirted frock coat. He drew out a pair of spectacles and put them on slowly and then looked at John again. "You're a great tall fellow," he said.

"Yes. Well, I'm going to go on. I wish I could help."

"It'll be a long time before you see that fellow, I warrant, and that hoass of mine, his name is Tiffin, he rode off on him bareback and going hahd. He's too old for hahd going." The elderly man's voice broke slighty, and he walked along wiping at his eyes and stabbing the cane into the red dirt of the road. Then he said reflectively, "I should keh a weapon, I suppose, but I never thought I would have anything woith robbin'."

John rode on into the early light. It illuminated the very tips of his big horse's ears, every standing hair, and shone straight down his eastbound road. Dodd was two days ahead of him on a weak, old horse. He watched for the blur of an elderly white horse, either standing or down, but saw nothing.

He passed small abandoned cottonfields of three or four acres here and there, hoarding their unharvested bolls behind rail fences. These fields had been cut out of the forest and prairie land in isolated squares, and now nobody to tend them, and so the wads of rain-soaked fibers had rotted and fallen like dead hair into the blackland earth.

After another five miles or so he felt the weariness of a long night's travel, the tiring, constant pull of the lead rope in his right hand, and then from a distance he heard a dog barking. He stopped and listened.

Then he smelled smoke. He pulled off to the north of the road and into the hardwoods to ride parallel to the road, wondering who might have lit a supper fire and in what sort of habitation. Major lifted his head and called out in a long whinny.

By the time he came to a little entry track leading north off the main road, the smoke was gone. Somebody had put the fire out. Somebody had heard him coming, had heard Major's call. He turned up the entry road.

He rode through a post-oak grove and then stopped within its protection. He saw a two-story house of sawn lumber. The white paint was fading. He still smelled the smoke but saw none rising from the stone chimney. A long verandah and no dogs. No horses. No chickens. No wash lines. He saw a well with a boxed-in cover and a little roof over it all. A bucket and a loose rope lay to one side. The rope had come off the windlass barrel, and nobody had fixed it.

Water was splashed around on the well box. He had surprised somebody drawing the evening water.

There was a long building attached to one side of the house that had no windows that he could see. It was also made of sawn lumber. A storage building of some kind. He thought about riding on, but he didn't. He very much wanted to sleep under a roof and rest his horses. He wasn't as strong as he had hoped he was. Not on a grind like this.

He got down and tied up. Best thing to do was take a chance and walk straight up to the house innocent of all subterfuge and ill intentions. So he did; he left the revolver in the pommel holster and the Spencer between a double-trunked post oak. With both hands lifted slightly out to the side and his hat pushed back to show his face he walked up the few steps onto the verandah. If somebody was looking at him from hiding, they could see his faded blue greatcoat, by design and pattern clearly Union Army, but he wore no military insignia nor any star, and he was unarmed, which he was now beginning to regret. He called out and got no answer.

He opened the door. The small narrow entryway led back through the house to a kitchen, and to each side there were other rooms. He had to duck to get in the door. Not much but a little. Mud on the floor; still wet. He called again. He looked into both small rooms and saw there one bedroom and on the other side a kind of parlor. The bed was unmade. He didn't see any clothes. The parlor was a workroom, with spinning wheel and a loom and a piece of work on the loom in that old Whig Rose pattern. He stepped over and looked at the low window. If there were dogs here, there would be dog-nose smears on the bottom of the windowpanes, and sure enough there were.

So somebody had tied the dogs and shut them up. So nearby a person watched and hid and was afraid. The hair on his neck seemed to crawl.

He called out, "Hello," again. He thought momentarily about his horses unguarded and his revolver in the holster. He walked back into the kitchen. Two tall windows lit the room and the shelves. Only a few dishes and tools, a kettle. There was a back entrance. Somebody had thrown water on a small fire in the fireplace to put it out, and ashy liquid ran in small streams onto the hearth. He didn't see any food. There was a square of cardboard on the kitchen table: "Ladies' Pocket Calendar 1866 Clark's Quality Cotton Thread."

He sat down at the table on a rush-bottomed chair and picked it up. He was very tired. He held it to the light; there were checks here and there on the days of the month, made with a graphite pencil. He observed it more closely. Then he lifted his head at a noise at the rear entrance.

In a second he was on his feet. He had the pistol that was pointing at him firmly gripped in his left hand, jerked it hard toward himself, and pulled her off her feet. She fought with him. He twisted her wrist upward and shook her hand savagely until she let go and the revolver dropped onto the kitchen floor. By the grace of God it did not go off. She twisted and hit him with her other fist and yelled at him to let go, let go!

"I will in a minute," he said in a reasonable voice. "Do you have any other weapons?"

She pulled away against his grip. "Would I tell you? Would I?"

"If I let go, you'll fall, so stop pulling back. And I will."

Still she pulled back with a fierce strength, her body aslant.

"Ready?" He opened his hand and the force of her resistance made her stumble backward against a shelf and a saucepan came ringing down to the floor, and as she grasped the shelf for balance a pierced dipper joined it with a noisy rattle.

He stepped between her and the rear entrance, glanced out, then down the entryway. Nobody else, apparently. He repeated carefully, "Do you have any other weapons?"

She grasped her wrist where he had twisted it. "Go away," she said. "Leave. There's nothing here for you." Her dark eyes were sparkling with fury and fear both, and with these things also a clear determination to fight him to the last extreme.

"Yes, I will," he said. "No, you don't have any other weapons." Keeping his eyes on her, he bent and picked up the gun. It was an old Whitney pocket percussion revolver, fully loaded. The hammer was cocked. He shook his head and uncocked it by pulling carefully on the trigger and slowly lowering the hammer with his thumb. She was backing toward the hallway door.

"You should have fired," he said. "From a distance. You should have fired through the window." He moved a step at a time to lay the revolver on the kitchen table. "And so before you go running off into the woods without your breakfast, you see I am unarmed, myself." He opened his greatcoat so that she could see his cartridge belt without a holster, and then held his hands out to the sides.

She swiftly grabbed up the Whitney from the kitchen table and started to cock it once more, so he took her by both upper arms and whirled her around against him so they were facing the same direction. He held her firmly.

"Unload that Goddamned thing," he said, and his voice, this time, was hard. "Point it away. Do what I tell you or I will take that gun and drop it down your well."

She held it pointing straight up between her hands at chest level. She was held tight in an unbreakable grip in both of his big hands.

He said, "I am not going to cause you any trouble. But I am not going to leave until I am sure I am not going to be shot in the back."

"All right, I will," she said. He saw that her hands were shaking.

"Do it."

He was actually curious to see if she knew how to unload it. If she didn't, that meant somebody had loaded it for her and she was not alone here. She wore a wedding ring, a thin sparkling thing with a gold band no bigger than a kite string, and her workaday dress was a fine dark green. She had dark hair and stained hands. So she had no blacks to do the hard work and probably a dead husband. He watched as she shakily opened the gate on the cylinder and shook it out, then pushed out the loads one by one. There were only three of them. They fell on the floor. They were paper cartridges. He let her go and stepped away.

"Now go away," she said. "Just get *out*. I don't have anything." She dropped her hand with the empty pistol still in it and half-hidden in her skirts.

He backed to the window and glanced out over his shoulder. He picked up the three cartridges from the floor, spilling powder from between his fingers, and looked around for someplace to put them. On a shelf was a small coffee mill. He pulled out the drawer where the coffee would fall when ground and dropped the cartridges in the drawer and shut it again. He leaned against the door frame.

"I've been traveling a night and a day," he said. "I need to rest. I'm not going to hurt you or steal anything from you. Why are you here by yourself?"

"I'm not by myself," she said. "Neighbors come every day. You can't stay here. They will make you leave." She had drawn herself up to appear taller or more fierce or perhaps commanding.

He thought about it. He thought about the loose well rope and the marks on the calendar and somewhere a silent, frightened dog. In the few seconds of silence he listened to the day. Birds sailed from one tree limb to another to take up the warmth of the late December sun. In the distance crows called out, but not nearby. There wasn't anybody to disturb them. Nobody was coming.

CHAPTER TWENTY

December 25, 1866 / The Parker Plantation

"DID YOU LOSE YOUR HUSBAND in the war?"

"No, he's on his way home." The tip of her nose was red, suddenly.

"It's been a year and a half," he said. She opened her mouth and shut it again. She could not think of what to say. She stood in her silence in a kind of hauteur that was likely her interior armor and the only armor remaining to her.

"All right," he said. "Here's what I'm going to do. I've got my horse and a led horse. I'm going to build myself a fire out there in the post oaks and make myself something to eat. If you want to follow me out there I will unload my rifle and my revolver where you can see me do it."

She turned her head to one side with her eyes on the kitchen floor as she listened. She raised her eyes to him. "You wouldn't need a gun. To take whatever you liked."

"I know that. But as a gesture." He ran his hand down the front of his greatcoat to rid his thumb and forefinger of the black powder. "And then I'm going to make camp and sleep by the roadside. I have a shelter half. Then tomorrow I'll be on my way."

She glanced over at the coffee grinder.

"I'll reload for you before I go." John felt suddenly very tired. "Now I'm going to do as I said. Come with me."

She hesitated and then followed him out to the woods that lay between the house and the road where his horses were tied. They raised their heads and murmured at him hopefully. She looked at them and stood well back. She had picked up a shawl as they passed out the front door and stood wrapped in it, shivering, as he took up the Spencer and pulled the follower and dropped all seven rounds into his hand. He put them in his pocket.

From a distance she watched his efficient and practiced movements, the quick slide that brought the revolver out of the pommel holster, watched as he flipped the cylinder out and clicked out the cartridges and put those in his greatcoat pocket along with the rest. He put the revolver back in the holster. The horses murmured again to him and the big horse nudged him. They were hungry and thirsty and tired. She saw the poor condition of the thoroughbred.

"They are very tired," she said in a loud voice. She was a good ways away from him.

"Yes, they are." He threw up the near-side fender and stirrup and laid his large hand on the latigo.

"Well, wait," she said.

"For what?" He pulled the latigo and ran it in loops into the D-ring.

"Come and put them in the barn. So they don't have to stand tied."

He stopped. He turned to look over his shoulder at the house and the long storage house and then, just overtopping it, a barn roof.

He thought about it. "All right. I'll follow you."

She hurried well ahead of him, her hems flying out with every step and one hand nervously caught up in her skirts. She went around the storage building and into a barn lot, holding the gate open for him. He led them into the fairway of the barn and dropped his saddle over a stall rail and led the two horses out again. There was very little water in the horse trough. He remembered the well rope lying loose and the heavy oak bucket. They drank up all the water in the trough and then made sucking sounds.

"Not much water," she said and there was a note of apology in her voice.

There was a white horse standing out in the pasture. It stood very still. John stood without speaking with the bridle in his hand and watched it. As it tried to graze, it stepped once forward and the back end dropped, wobbled, one hind foot crossed over another, and then it managed to stand upright and fell into immobility again.

"He's injured, isn't he?"

John said, "That's bad."

"Well, he just wandered up here."

"Yes, ma'am. When?"

"Two days ago. I don't know what to do with it."

Still she stood with the fence between them and was prepared to flee, it seemed.

The horse was an elderly white gelding with old-age freckles on his head and chest. It was, of course, the old man's horse. John said *Damn*, privately and to himself. He felt a great sorrow for old Granby Charles Watson. He walked out to look at its front hooves, speaking soothingly to it. The horse was not shod and one front hoof was cracked and split all the way to the hairline and something had gone very wrong with his spine. He must have had a bad fall. He would have to be shot. Dodd had ridden the old fellow half to death, and when it took a fall hard enough to fracture its spine he walked away from it. He must have made some miles.

The old white horse stood without grazing. John turned out both his own horses and they began to tear up grass hungrily within three or four steps.

"Rain is coming, I'm afraid," she said.

He leaned on the rail of the barn lot fence. His back hurt. "I have a shelter half. Would you like to keep the ammunition until I leave?" He put both hands on the buckle of his cartridge belt, prepared to take it off and hand it to her. Anything for a good night's sleep.

She glanced down at her hands wrapped in the ends of the shawl. "No. You may sleep in the storage house, if you would like."

He said, gently and with a slight smile, "And what if some evil desperados came down the road?"

She turned out one hand, palm up. "Then perhaps you would shoot them."

"More than happy to."

"And I will barricade myself in my room with Zoe."

"I don't believe I've been introduced to Zoe."

"She's a miniature Scottie. She'll bark if I allow her to."

He said, "When did your husband die?"

She glanced at his face, startled. She laced her fingers together and said, "Just before Thanksgiving. His lungs had been weakened some-how, and they simply got worse and worse . . ." She paused. "Perhaps consumption, perhaps his heart. He got it fighting people like you."

"Yes," said John. "People like me." He shoved off from the rail and shifted the halter from one hand to the other. "I would appreciate sleep-ing in the storage room. Thank you."

She nodded once. She hesitated a few seconds, perhaps regretting her offer, and then stood erect with her skirts moving in the slight evening breeze, as if she were a person of the nobility giving gracious permission, with her gray shawl wadded up around her neck and her hands buried in it. She had a still, wide face and a thin neck, young and light-boned altogether even though her waist had thickened so that the cloth where she had let out the seams of her dress was not faded and it was more brightly colored. "Follow me, please."

She had made her decision in an irrevocable and regal way, and so she walked ahead of him and her skirts swung and belled with her long steps. She led him to the storage building beside the house and opened the door. John ducked in after her.

In the light of a small window set in the back wall he gazed over shelf after shelf of goods. Dust motes drifted down. As he turned from one side to the other he saw stack after stack of gray wool uniforms. There were trousers and shell jackets, gray forage caps, brogans, haversacks, gray overcoats, Confederate officers' frock coats of all ranks with the gold braid up the sleeves, shelter halves, and knitted goods—socks, mufflers, blankets, undervests, and woolen drawers.

"*Tabernac,*" he said.

"It was entrusted to our care," she said. "And it is in my care yet. So you may sleep in here and build a fire in the fireplace there."

John looked from shelf to shelf, at the kegs of nails and shoes packed between the stanchions. The building was about sixty feet by forty, and every inch was taken up. He said, "Why is this here?"

"The town of Bonham was the distribution for the Army of the West." She paused. "Confederate. Under General McCullough. Bonham is five miles on to the east of here. But then it was impossible to distribute it, you see. Everything broke down, roads, railroads, boats with no fuel. There was no way to get it anywhere. And then of course the surrender. We were not sure what to do with it. And Mr. Parker did not indicate what I should do with it."

"You're Mrs. Parker."

"Yes."

At last John swung off his hat. "John Chenneville," he said.

She bowed her head in acknowledgment. "I am sorry we've met under such uncivilized circumstances, but so it is. I will leave you to your rest. I'm sorry I tried to shoot you, but there was no way to know. You were sitting there in my kitchen."

"Understandable."

Then she went out and into the house. He heard the door slam and the noise of a lock snicking into place.

He went out to find wood, built a good fire in the fireplace, and was very glad for the warmth. He stood before it for a long time, growing sleepy. After a while he shook out his blankets to see if anything had gotten in them in the way of small life, such as mice or centipedes. Then he heard a light knock at the door.

He opened it. He saw only her disappearing dark green skirts, but at his feet was a Dutch oven full of hot biscuits and bacon and hominy. He ate everything and wiped up the grease with half a biscuit. He found a candle in a brass holder, lit it at the fire, and walked up and down the shelves. As he remembered, toward the end the Confederates were lucky to have any clothes at all, much less uniforms. Once he saw a prisoner brought in in the cold of winter wearing a woman's bodice, barefoot.

At the end of one shelf he came upon a pile of flags. He shook one out: a strange banner he had never seen before.

It was the reverse of the Virginia battle flag, a blue field with a red St. Andrew's Cross. It made his eyes jump. He refolded it in the regulation manner of triangles and then put it back. He put one foot behind himself for balance and looked up to the ceiling. Across the rafters were long poles with elaborate caps at one end—guidons for company banners.

He then pulled down three blankets from the shelves and laid them down in front of the fire. He slowly stripped off his clothes and dropped onto the blankets, covered up, and slept away the evening and then all through the night till nearly dawn. He slept among the gray remains of an army he had fought; three years of bitter and desperate fighting. Empty sleeves, forage caps devoid of heads, outlandish enemy flags in an unaccountable reversal.

He woke up in the night. He had been ambushed by a dream of Sebastienne, lifting a lace shawl, *blanche comme la neige*, which was then confused with the fake Greek statue at Troxel's photography shop in St. Louis. For a while he watched the taffeta waves of fire moving through the coals, then pulled a blanket over his shoulders and got up to go out and look at the stars. The Big Dipper said it was three or four in the morning, and it was bitter cold, so he went back in and slept again.

The next day he dressed and drank hot water from his mess kit pan. He was short on coffee. He had to get more water to the horses, and so he went out and went to work on the well windlass. The boxed-in opening of the well had a roof over it about eight by eight. He found a good set of tools in the barn: hammer, various sizes of nails, a handsaw, and a crowbar. They were lined up on the wall on pegs just as Mr. Parker had left them in his journey out of this world and into the next. The feel of his hand was still on them. A shaft of gray rainy light poured into the entrance, dim watery daylight on steel and cast iron. Another front had closed in.

The well had a differential windlass with two different circumferences in the barrel, and since this would be too complicated for her to repair if it were ever to come loose again he took an hour to pull the crank loose and then reset the cylinders. Just one simple rope to wind.

A distant voice spoke to him: "I hope you have had a good sleep."

He looked up. She had come to sit at the back verandah steps and call out to him. She was bundled in the gray shawl, and a very tiny dog sat at her skirt hem.

"I did." He pulled the main bolt and laid it and the washer aside. "I must have slept twenty hours altogether."

She didn't say anything but sat and began to shell peanuts in her skirt.

He said, in a loud voice, "Do you have a saddle?"

"Yes. I have a ladies' saddle."

"Do you have a riding horse?"

"They took it. Of course they had no need of the saddle."

"Who did?"

"Some people last week." She stood up with her skirt bunched and then shook it to toss away the shells. She hesitated and then came closer, carrying the chair by the back rungs and the sack of peanuts in the other hand, and the little dog scurried along behind her.

She sat the chair and herself down at the edge of the uncut grass of the back lawn, to one side of the well path. She looked up at the sky and then began shelling peanuts again. In a more conversational voice with less volume she said, "They said they were patrolling and needed horses. It was the Sanderson boy, and the other one was related to the Inglish family. They have become feral, I'm afraid. But then that loose horse showed up here."

"Ma'am, that horse belongs to an old fellow named Watson. He might come looking for him. He's a pet horse and the old fellow will be very distressed by his condition."

"Yes. He's very lame."

John put his hand on the well casing and shoved at it. He found it strong and solid. "You should not be here by yourself. Do you not have people you could go to?"

"Yes. But it's a long way. And this was our home. I have duties. I can't desert this place. I have obligations."

Then a wind came, splattering big drops, and she at last moved her chair under the well roof not seven feet from him and still regarding

him carefully as if he were an oversized demon only temporarily do-
mesticated. John listened to the rain. He took the windlass cylinder of
two different sizes and hammered them together, the smaller inside the
larger.

He said, "That pistol only had three shots in it."

"Correct," she said. "I shot off the other three at a man who rode
up here in the dark a week ago. He was shouting for somebody to
come out. He sounded drunk. I more or less aimed in his general
direction."

"I see." He hammered in a ringbolt, slipped the rope through it, and
tied it in a Turk's head. "Do you have more ammunition for it?"

"It's in a box in the storage house."

"Can you reload?"

A hesitation. "I hope so."

John reminded himself that southerners often said "hope" for "believe." "I'll look at them," he said. "Those are paper cartridges, and
they split."

She finished with her chore and shook her skirts out once again
and stood up. "When are you leaving out?"

"At dark."

"Why are you traveling at night?" She stood with a questioning and
even accusatory look. The wind took her tight-braided hair and made
the stray ends stand up and her shawl corners lift and wave.

John gave her his best smile. "Don't ask," he said.

She gave him a gracious nod and went into the house with her chair
and her sack of groundnuts and Zoe.

John thought to test the rope itself, doubling it and jerking it open
again. It held. She had been throwing the bucket straight down the
well and hauling it up probably a third full, which would be all she
could lift given the weight of the wooden bucket.

He cranked the windlass and brought up a bucketful to take to his
grateful horses, then another and another. He walked through the barn
to see what she had to take care of a horse—what feed, shoes, tack.

He checked the cinch on the sidesaddle and found the latigo was dangerously weak with dry rot. He found a set of harness, cut a new latigo length from the breeching, and punched holes to secure it with a thong. The D-rings were secure and the leaping horn as well. The velvet-quilted seat was worn down to nothing, but there was aught he could do about that. He went back to pack up. He put a kettle on the fire and then shaved, since hot water was easy to come by.

She tapped carefully at the door and stood there like Penelope with a loom shuttle in her hand. Her face was not so severe as before.

"You have worked hard, Mr. Chenneville, and I would like for you to have a substantial supper before you go."

"That's very kind of you," he said.

"Then in about an hour? Do you have a watch?"

"No. But I will be there in an hour."

Just to sit and talk with a woman, to hear her light voice, her considered reply, the tilt of her head. In a house, under a roof, with good china patterned in hazy willows and Chinese people wandering around. The cup felt very small and breakable in his hand.

Click of their silver utensils, another candle lit to open up the dark shadows as if they were small intimate doors into the unknown. Her apologies once again. He waved this aside. He said he had had firearms pointed at him many times but by none so gracious and well-spoken as herself.

He thought of the calendar and the month of October, when the checkmarks—twenty-eight days apart—had stopped. He regarded her with a sort of hesitant compassion and a knowledge there was nothing he could do to help and despite himself remembering how he had held her close against his body and the smell of her, which at that time was of homemade soap and fear and ashes.

He told her he was from St. Louis and had come down to see about cotton. Then a discussion of cotton in general, and the Freedmen's Bureau, which was hiring out the newly freed slaves like an employment agency but perhaps not so fair.

He said, "I am going to leave that bay horse with you. The one I'm leading. I found him on the road. He's an Army Remount thoroughbred, and with a little rest he'll do you very well. I have no need for him, and I can't feed him."

He told her that he had a long road ahead of him and must saddle now and load his gear. She said that of course he would not want to spend another night among the uniforms of his enemies and he could not tell her that it was not so. That in fact there was a man of incomprehensible drives and desires loose upon the roads and his business was with him.

But Dodd must have long passed by, and John wondered how the man had missed this house and its lone woman. Because she was careful with her fire, because she had remained hidden and asked no one for help so as not to advertise her presence and her storehouse of the goods of a defeated army to anyone. John wondered how far ahead Dodd was. Whether he was afoot or no. Given the lamed horse in the pasture, he was probably afoot. He was traveling very fast and killing horses. John was not willing to kill horses and so was falling behind.

She picked up a roll of something and walked out with him to his horse. The thoroughbred was calling frantically from the pasture in great distress over being left behind. The other horse, the lame one, had lain down in the grass. He would likely not get up.

He stepped up on his big plow horse. "You can't stay on here," he said. "You must move in with other people. Your family or friends. You know this."

"I know." She grew red in the face and looked down at the ground.

He didn't know what else to say.

"Take these," she said. She handed up a roll of cream-colored blankets. "Leave me your old ones. They're dirty. These are clean. They're not marked." He hesitated. "They do not have CSA on them."

He dismounted, unsaddled, stripped off his blankets, and then took the ones she handed him. "What are you going to do with all that in the storehouse?" he asked as he replaced the saddle on Major's broad back and swung up.

"Somebody will come and decide. Not me, but somebody. And here." She handed him a small packet that smelled of coffee.

"Thank you. Much appreciated. Is there some message or request you want me to carry to Bonham?"

"None." She reached her hand up to him. He bent down to grasp it. "Thank you," she said. "You are a gentleman."

He lifted his hat briefly and gave one quick nod and turned away to the main road.

A few hours' travel in the cold, familiar dark led him through Bonham, which was not a town so much as it was a depot, a collection of mercantile establishments supplying the countryside and had at one time supplied McCullough's Confederate Army of the West, which, like all armies, had fallen into its separate parts: human beings, men, walking slowly home.

CHAPTER TWENTY-ONE

January 1867 / The Road to Paris, Texas

SOMETIME AROUND FOUR IN THE morning, with scattered stars emerging now and then from the clouds, he came to the town of Paris. In the sudden drop of temperature that had come in with the rainy front a few wisps of smoke from chimneys bloomed heavy and gray. Stores with long glass windows lined up on three sides of a big town square. Darkness made the town austere, artless. Only roofs and angles like a watercolor without detail. He stopped in front of a barn that said Livery. From inside came the smell of horses and manure and a voice that called, "Who's there?"

"A customer. Come get this horse."

John stepped down stiffly, bent over briefly to relieve his aching back, and then stood and waited. The world was lightly frosted. At this hour, everybody's fire was nearly out. A man came shivering out of a small door beside the big carriage doors of the livery stable. He was hatless and armed. "State your business, sir," he said, and his breath bloomed out in a cold fog.

"I am on my way to Marshall. Couldn't find anyplace to stay, and so I kept on traveling. I need to put my horse up and get him fed."

The man nodded. "Wait here."

Ten minutes later he was back with a Union officer. The officer was buttoning up his coat; he carried an Army Colt in a holster and in one hand a bull's-eye oil lantern.

"We've been told to watch for somebody like you," the officer said. "I'm not too sure why."

"I hope you find him," said John. He listened to the man's accent. It sounded big-city, northern Midwestern. Probably Chicago. "So what do you want, Captain?"

"Well, let's just talk here a minute, and you tell me who you are and where you're from."

"Are you checking everybody who comes through?"

"Regulations."

"I see." John thought about it; there might be a record of Dodd passing through this town in the reports. He wondered where their logbook was and how he could get his hands on it.

"Is there a tavern or a hotel here?"

The officer glanced at John's greatcoat. The shoulder cape and upright collar with its three standing seams and five General Service buttons down the front was something the officer knew well. He said, "That's all right. You don't need to wake anybody up. Just bring your gear and you can doss down in the orderly room."

John looked back at the hunched-up livery stableman, who was blowing on his hands, and to make sure he asked again, "So you're stopping every traveler that comes through?"

"Yes. So I am not singling you out in any way. Unless your name is Chenneville."

"It's Allen. William Allen."

"Got your discharge papers?"

"I do." He pulled his packet of papers out of his saddlebags and handed them to the officer.

The man blinked, held the papers close to the lantern and read the discharge. "Ninety-Fifth Pennsylvania. You were at Spotsylvania."

"I was. Do you keep a record of them? The people you stop."

"Regulations."

"I suppose I am the only one tonight."

"So far, but the day is to come. Very well, sir, let's not stand out here anymore. Just follow me."

John pulled his saddle, removed his blankets, and then handed the bridle reins to the livery man.

After the officer had returned to his sleep, John made his bed on the floor of the orderly room. It was the sheriff's office. He stood listening for a moment. Heard nothing; nobody up, nobody walking except the man on guard duty out in the street. So he took up the candle and stepped over to the long table, which served as a desk. He reached for a fabric-covered volume that said *Record Book*. He searched through the entries, and his breath bloomed in a wet mist as he carefully turned the pages, his light eyes intent and glittering in the candlelight.

He saw that the unit stationed here in Paris was the 46th Illinois. Chicago, or Springfield, just as he had thought. Crisp sounds as the cold paper turned over leaf after leaf of names and dates. Daily reports, but Dodd would have come through in the night, walking quietly, and he might not have been seen, especially if the man on guard duty had perfected the wartime skill of falling asleep standing up without dropping his piece.

And there was his name. John gave a low laugh in surprise and delight. "Shit fire and save the matches, here he is."

4 a.m. Dec. 30 single traveler on foot claims foundered horse, going to jefferson to seek medical help for relative. Name garoute. 5 9 gray eyes dark hair, low-crown tan hat. Seeking medical aid in jefferson. Bought a horse of j. Harner, livery.

He's calling himself Garoute. Gone back to using that name. He must have gotten a horse from the livery and was now several days ahead. John stood up, shut the logbook, blew out the candle, and lay down to sleep in his malodorous and increasingly ragged clothes.

The next morning he rode out of Paris, Texas, without breakfast, with a lifted hand to the officer of the day. He had had five hours of sleep, which he figured was enough to keep him going for a while.

He didn't know how long it would take to make that eighty miles to Jefferson and then on to Marshall. He was guessing. He was guessing that Dodd had relatives there, that he would rest up under their protection and silence then head for Houston or Galveston. He had to lay hands on the man before he got on a boat and sailed away into the infinity of the bright blue sea, the Gulf of Mexico and destinations unknown. An image came to him unbidden, that of a year-old child who bore his name shot in the face, and he knew he could keep up this pursuit forever.

Long morning shadows streamed away behind him. He passed more and more fields laid waste by neglect and lack of slave labor. A flock of turkeys burst up under Major's nose with their mechanical clatter, flapping and then sailing, flapping and sailing, coasting straight down the tunnel of the road ahead, then melting into the browns and golds of the winter forest.

He rode through a country with empty houses and fields choked with dried weeds. They had thrown everything they had into the war, cotton and grains and men and animals, and here was the aftermath. *We beat the hell out of them*, John thought. Once or twice he passed other travelers with a nod and a lifted hand, and once or twice he heard distant gunfire.

Every day a winter sun arose and blessed the world with its thin rays leaf by leaf and a promise that spring would surely come, if you would abide, if you would survive, if you would do what you set out to do. He almost felt it was the price of being alive. He sat in a schoolhouse before the fireplace, where he had built a good fire, holding out his hands to the flames. The schoolhouse had long been empty. Where were the children that should have been here? A fallen blackboard said:

SEE THAT POOR MAN. HE HAS NO HAT ON HIS HEAD.
WILLIAM, WILL YOU GIVE HIM YOUR OLD HAT?
YES, YOU WILL.
YOU WILL BE GLAD TO HELP HIM.

While Major wandered a rail-fenced cornfield nearby, finding here and there grains and even whole cobs of field corn. John turned a piece of chalk in his hand and wondered if he would ever have children, which now was not very likely, and the process of getting them, which was somewhat likelier but not just at present.

She said she was going to be sent to Marshall. He should stop thinking about her, but the simple rustling silence of the vacant school building led his thoughts on and away. On the other hand, she was something to think about other than killing Dodd. And staying out of the way of Giddens. Something warm, something lovely, something of life in abundance.

At evening he came to a sign that pointed onward toward the Sulphur Fork of the Red River. It was a white-painted board with the black words telling of the river next to come printed in a neat hand, and it was all shot up. This was the hour of the day when the whitetail deer would be getting up from their day's bedding, going to water.

He tied Major to a post oak's twisted limbs and carried the Spencer into the woods south of the road. After an hour's hunt, he came close to the river; he could hear it. There he saw one. He cocked slowly and carefully with one hand over the works to damp down the noise and then levered up a round, aimed carefully in the late, level sunlight, and brought down a whitetail doe. He hit her behind the left front leg; she bounded into the air in a wild, galvanized leap and then fell on her belly with her front limbs cranked up in unnatural angles, and then as he watched she fell over on her side and the light went out of her and she died.

The *crack* of the carbine echoed for miles. He sat on his heels for a long time and listened. While he waited he looked for the cartridge shell casing, found it, and put it in his pocket.

It took him most of an hour to get the doe skinned out and the head, legs, and entrails buried. The river had carved itself a deep bed in the thick layer of soil, and in this soil he slid down the banks among sumac and grapevine to wash the bloody hams and backstrap. The water was red as well as the earth.

In the dimming nightfall he knew he had to rest himself and rest his horse. He saw a house, off the road to the north. It was not the sort of glamorous plantation house as he had seen in *Harper's Weekly*, but it was substantial. There were no lights anywhere. It was two-story, maybe fifty feet by thirty, with long columns, stained by leaking drainpipes, holding up the porch roof. The house seemed to glow, surrounded by immense, dark pines.

He stood and listened a long time. He had pushed Dodd hard enough that he had overridden the thoroughbred, then another, pushed him hard enough that he was not stopping anywhere that John could see. If he could just keep it up, if he could only stay on his feet and not tire, he would have him. Dodd was a younger man, a stronger man, one that had no head wound, but simple, dogged persistence should do it.

Probably Giddens was thinking the same thing.

He walked slowly up the steps to the porch. It had twelve-paned windows, and each pane reflected his dark figure in succession. He stood and listened. Nothing. No noise. Something creaking in the wind, a shutter perhaps. His horse had not called out to any other horse.

He tried the door handle lever. It was locked. The door had many small panes in it; some of them seemed to be colored but he couldn't really tell. He unholstered his revolver from the cavalry pommel holster, and with the butt he tapped out the lower left-hand pane. It broke with a tinkle of falling glass. He tugged out the shards and then carefully reached in and around and grasped the inside lever, but it wouldn't secure to the spindle. He withdrew his hand, took out his sheath knife, and levered the tongue back by inches, then shoved the door open inch by inch.

Nobody, nothing. A dead and empty house. But then he heard something. A little cry. He went back to his saddlebags and brought out the folding candle lantern, unfolded it and fixed it, then placed a candle in it and, after striking three different phosphorous matches broken off the block, he got it lit and went back.

He stepped inside. He hoped there would not be trouble. He needed sleep and rest, and it would be good to be under a roof.

As he walked down the wide entryway he heard the yip sound again, and then back in the kitchen a pair of eyes glowed at him in the candlelight, small snarling noises, tiny ones, and a kind of low growl that slid off into an ingratiating whine.

He stood in his heavy boots, tall in the doorway, the caped greatcoat making him appear enormous.

"It's all right, Mama," he said.

A redbone hound lay in a heap of rags and blankets beside the kitchen fireplace with three squirming puppies. She drew back her lips and showed her teeth in warning, but at the same time she beat her tail on the floor. She was cadaverous; every rib showed; her eyes were sunken.

"Well, they went off and left you. You and the pups."

Her tail beat on the dusty rags in a frantic drumming, and in the light of the candle and his looming presence, the puppies fell silent.

John went back out with the candle lantern. He saw a carriage house, outbuildings, and the dark entrance of a barn. His horse would be good for the night in the carriage house. There were no carriages. It was an open space that could be closed off, and it looked like there were no farm implements the big horse could fall afoul of. John unsaddled, dragged the baggage off, let him loose inside, and found a wash pot in which to bring him water.

He brought the deer meat inside and gave the hound one of the hams. He watched as she fell upon it in a display of appetite that astonished him. She chopped wildly at the meat with her fore-teeth, swallowing great chunks, gulping, tearing.

He managed to make a fire from loose siding boards that had fallen from the gable end of the house. It was beautifully fine-grained cypress lumber. As he tore off several more, he could see underneath that the core of the house had been a log cabin. They had built over it, sided it, made a second story, added columns in front. Whatever family it was, they had come here a long time ago. They had probably arrived here when Texas was a nation.

The fire in the kitchen fireplace lit up the room, and at last the red-bone hound lay back down on the blankets with a heavy thump. Her belly was round as a pumpkin, and the puppies crawled all over her and then began nursing. Their tails waved happily. They were all a deep chestnut red.

He laid the rest of the deer meat high up on the mantelpiece, cut filets out of the backstrap, and made himself supper, thinking about bread, freshly baked bread with a good crust, butter spread over it and maybe jam of some kind. He thought about those French loaves called *miches* made from whole wheat flour that Fermin baked, making the oven temperature so hot he drove everybody out of the kitchen, including the cook, to make the crust very crisp, and then Fermin would bang down a pot of honey before young Jean-Louis with a fond smile. Then John pulled himself back to the present, told himself to stop allowing these memories to take hold of him. Temps Clair was gone, or soon would be, and this life was a changed life that might not last much longer.

He decided he would explore the place tomorrow; no matter if Dodd got another day on him; he had to rest and recoup. He stood the carbine in the chimney corner, laid the revolver on the mantelpiece, and sat on a rush-bottomed chair to spend a moment watching the puppies with his boots off and his legs stretched out and his shirt and vest open to the heat.

It had been forever, it seemed, that he simply watched young things playing and tussling with one another. Enjoying them, enjoying anything at all. Taking pleasure in anything at all. Just sitting peacefully and laughing, watching the smallest one toddle over to his sock foot and attack it, throwing its head side to side as if to rip his sock off. The mother hound was sleeping so deeply that she was twitching with dreams.

He lifted the puppy away. "Go to sleep," he said. "Go to your mother."

He woke in the morning covered with puppies. One of them was sleeping curled around the top of his head. He stood up in sections, his spine straight and his head lifted to the new day, and he did not waver. Balance; it was coming back to him despite the hard road and the exertion of traveling.

That day he discovered a kitchen garden behind the house. It was unharvested and still had cobs of corn dried on the stalks for Major, and in the dark recesses of the barn he found a saddle tree hung up high on one wall. Looped to the crudely carved saddle horn was a glossy fan of animal hair, perhaps from a horse's mane. He found a pole and knocked the saddle tree down. When he picked it up he saw that the hair was a scalp. A human scalp.

Thick black hair, now dusty and full of some kind of insect shells. The skin it was attached to had been cured. He dropped it on the dirt floor.

"Jesus Christ," he said.

Who knew the story behind it? There was some memory or tale caught up in that hank of hair, but he would never learn what it was. It was closed to him, a story transparent as rain and invisible. He hung the whole thing back up on the wall and wiped his hands on his pants.

The redbone hound came out and sat watching him.

"Think you'll live?" he said.

She beat her tail in the dirt, raising dust.

Now the day was waning and the light was that color of a winter afternoon, with short, deep-gold sun rays that turned all shadows a rich black. It was still very cold. He listened. A distant crow gave one call. Nobody nearby. Back in the pines he saw four tiny cabins all in a row. Slave cabins. He had seen them often enough in Missouri, and now they seemed like the inert, dead evidence of an ancient human injustice or quarrel like the rows upon rows of graves outside the hospital at City Point, full of dead men. Nobody wants to be on the front lines. But many people found themselves there whether they wanted to be or not.

Despite a night and a day's rest, he felt tired. He hurt. No place specific, just throughout his body. Even though he was wearing thin and in need of rest he felt uneasy in this place with its scattered signs of archaic violence, which would return, he knew, like the full moon returns.

His mind turned again to the past, remembering his little sister, Lalie, trying hard to be firm with the dressmaker and not succeeding. She was too charming. She had never learned how to not be charming. There was a saying: *Those who are wise take care of their own.* But he had not, had he? He had not been there to tell her, *No, don't marry that man, don't go to Riviere aux Vases.* To say, *No, don't begin this chain of events that will put me on a hard road to find a wandering murderer.*

He shook himself, willing away these thoughts of the past. He had to find something else to occupy his mind, quickly. So he gathered up his blankets, packed hurriedly, and fed the mother hound again. She was not so greedy this time but allowed her young ones to worry the stringy tissues of the deer meat and growl at one another with tiny savage sounds. One ran away with a particularly appetizing scrap, followed frantically by the other two.

He was ready by sundown. He had more than enough food to get him to the town of Jefferson. He should pass by Mount Pleasant in the night and reach Jefferson by dawn. His big horse was rested and well-fed.

He started out at a good clip but slowed down when he realized that the mother redbone was hurrying after him, with three pups trailing behind. Their little tongues were hanging out, and she trotted in a head-down, determined way right at Major's heels. Even after a quarter of a mile they had not given up.

"Well, shit," he said.

The pups were falling out. One had stopped about fifty feet behind, and it was howling in a heartbroken way, while the mother darted back to it, ran back to John, ran back to the pup again, and the other two in the middle of all this sat down exhausted.

"I'll be damned," he said. "What next?"

He stepped down off the big horse and picked up one puppy after another, stuffed them into the saddlebags, and swore a blue streak, cursing the day he had ever fed her.

"You should all be drowned," he said. "I wouldn't waste any ammunition on you."

The pups hung out of the saddlebags and yipped. Noisy little devils. What the hell was he going to do with them? It sounded like a traveling circus. Major shook himself energetically, and the pups shrieked. The wind whipped leaves from the trees and hurled them down the road.

He laughed despite himself. "It's like the Ti-Jean story," he said aloud. "Where he ends up being followed by all the animals. *Viens, si tu veux, mais marche derrière*." His father's face came to him in a firelit image, spinning out the story. It was all so logical, it had a neatly tied-up ending, it was for heartening a person. That's what they were for, those tales, because their small heroes never died at the end, but they did not live either except in the telling of the tales. And so they must be retold without end, the gift of the grateful dead.

CHAPTER TWENTY-TWO

January 4–5, 1867 / From Paris to Marshall, Texas

JOHN RODE ON FOR A few miles until he saw back in the pines a tiny gleam of firelight. A well-beaten path led in that direction, and so he took it. He needed help—dog help. He dismounted and made sure his revolver was loose in the holster as he led Major by the reins. As he came nearer, he stood and watched. No barking dogs. Good. They needed some dogs, obviously.

He saw a longhouse in a small clearing. It was capped by a thatched roof that hung down in a fringe. The longhouse was made of upright posts with a blanket-hung opening for a door where firelight streamed out through the overhanging thatch in stripes of shadow and flame. He heard people talking and smelled coffee and some kind of bread baking.

These people were either Caddo or perhaps Choctaw, maybe Chickasaw. The longhouse was like the one he had stayed in in the San Bois. John speculated that they had slipped away from the arbitrary boundaries of their appointed reservation in Indian Territory to return to these piney woods, this increasingly swampy country, which was, he had been told, their ancestral homeland. He called out.

"Hello the house!"

A man came to the door, astonished, alarmed, carrying a rifle across his body. The man slipped out and stood to one side, out of the light. The door-blanket beside him glowed orange and was banded with moving shadows.

"Who are you?"

John held up both hands, palms out, and walked a few steps nearer. In the light from the door, he could see that the man beside the doorway was dressed in a calico blouse, canvas pants, and an old Confederate infantry jacket. He was barefoot. Tattoos ran down his chin in blue dotted stripes.

"A traveler," John said. "I got a lot of dogs with me." The big horse sighed heavily with a bellows-like expansion of his ribs, and the pups yipped. "Maybe you could take them. You don't have a dog. People need a dog. Or several."

A woman and a small girl shoved the blanket aside. They stood regarding him in his big caped overcoat, his horse, his boots and hat and the rifle on his back. They stood astonished and dubious and perfectly silent. John held up a hand as an indication for them to wait and reached back and got hold of a pup. When he held it out, the girl lifted her hands, crying out in another language. He knew perfectly well what she was saying. *Oh, can we keep it? Oh, please let us keep it!*

He told the man how he had found them and how they had followed him. By this time the girl had two pups. Then she darted off into the interior, where another, older girl lay on a bed with bright flushed cheeks. The wife sat down beside the bed and handed her the third writhing puppy with a smile. The older girl was clearly sick with a fever, but she sat up and grasped the wobbling small creature, crying out in delight and surprise.

The man shook his head and said something to the little girls in a resigned voice. Then he nodded toward the mother hound. "Now, what do you expect to do with her?" He spoke English with a strong southern accent.

"I don't know."

"Shoot her. She'll come back here for the pups."

John thought about it. He couldn't do it. "I'll carry her," he said. "Until we're a ways away." Then he said he was looking for someone, a man alone, a man probably on foot, and he described him.

"Yes. Him. I sold him my wife's horse. I ain't never heard the end of it. I figure if the girls could have the pups it would kind of make up for it."

"What kind of horse?"

"Just a little tacky. *Mesteño*. Mustang. Roany, kind of."

"Red or blue?"

"Red roan."

John heard this with relief; it lightened his heart. He had not lost the man. "When?"

The man tipped his head back and forth, thinking, and then turned and called out something to his wife. She sat beside the sickbed on an upturned bucket, watching the girls and their pups. John saw the central fire light up her elaborate twist of glossy black hair and a string of large orange and silver beads. She said something to her husband.

"She said it was a week ago or maybe more."

He was losing ground. He was losing it more quickly than he had thought.

They offered him a drink of hot coffee from a gourd, which he poured down gratefully, thanked them, and left, and in general felt a great deal better about the world.

And so he rode on toward Mount Pleasant in the night with the mother hound across his lap in front of the saddle. He knew if he let her go she would return to the Caddos' house, and that was a death sentence. So he kept hold of the loose skin on her neck, and they trotted on, eating up the miles, with Major pushing ahead strongly with long strides.

AT DAWN HE came to Mount Pleasant and tied up in front of the telegraph office. It was too early; there was nobody there, and so he sat down on the steps and waited. Before too long the operator came ambling down the street in a hat with earflaps and a thick homespun coat.

"I can send myself," John said. He stood back as the operator fired up the little parlor stove, opened the shutters to the weak early sunlight, and hooked up his local batteries. From the side of his eyes the telegrapher assessed John's clothes; his coat, his hat, as well as his horse and dog outside.

"You can, can you?"

"Yes. I'll pay by the word, same as if you sent it."

The operator listened with squinted eyes as John took the key and sent in International Morse and pig latin.

PM BELLE MARSHALL OP FM SNOWMAN MT. PLEASANT KN

"What the hell is that?" the operator said.

John held up one hand for silence and listened to the reply:

BELLE AK CFM R U WELL

He recognized her hand now, that manner of sending particular to each operator, as distinct as handwriting and unmistakable. Hers was a precise hand and quick but not so fast as to be careless. The operator smoked his pipe and listened, now wide-eyed and confused.

YES AM OK SEARCHING 4 ALBERT DODD AND AVOIDING
GIDDENS US MARSHAL. ROBERTSON NOT HIS ONLY VICTIM
DODD KILLED ONE OF MY FAMILY AS WELL.

Then John sent a description of Dodd, once again drawing from the St. Louis photograph, the man in black and white with his hand on a broken pillar.

SORRY TERRIBLE CNFM DESCRIPTION. WHERE IS HE?

NEAR MARSHALL I THINK TAKE CARE AM EN ROUTE C

NIL GIDDENS R 73

73

The operator stood at the door to watch John Chenneville ride out of town southward on the Jefferson Road and was still trying to sort out the confusing jumble of International Morse and what was an apparently simple code he could not make head nor tail of. He stood chilled and puzzling over it all as the tall man on a big horse, the red-bone hound trotting behind, all somewhat the worse for wear, disappeared into the pines.

After Mount Pleasant the pine forest became absolute dark and chill. Late that night he lay with his back to an oak in the cold, rested with his face to the moon, where clean fairy things lived in a bloodless, candied light. They did not sing but expressed themselves in thin howls and spoke in tongues. He realized he was dreaming. The wind told him that there was a sudden storm on the way. He sat up, strung up the shelter half securely, lit the candle lantern, and tried to read *The Woman in White*, but the winter woods in a sleety storm are not a place for reading, and so he gave it up. The hound lay against his legs. She was warm.

"You need a name," he said. "How about Dixie?"

She lay curled in a mist of smoking dog breath, and the freezing rain pittered down on the shelter half. He might have a letter in Jefferson. The thought kept him awake, this turning of his mind to yet other memories, recently acquired. If Fermin were well, if the place had been sold.

After these few hours of fitful sleep, he rode into Jefferson on the Old Colony Road, and he was weary and not shaking exactly, but he felt a kind of thin vibration throughout his chest and back and arms. At the Jefferson post office he spelled out his name in pencil for the postmaster, a letter was handed to him, and he sat down on the front step to read it. He cleared his throat several times when tearing open the envelope and took a deep breath. *Temps Clair December 17 Dar Mr. Chenneville I am glad to report as of this writing we are all well her and Fermin says if I understand him correctly that he would like to hear from you more often . . .* That was all he wanted to know for now. He glanced through the rest of it. There was news of the donkey and Lucas's foreman *and he is a 'something' Fermin says but does not dain to tell me what it is in English however I supoze it is not a compliment as he uses too much firewood says Fermin . . .* John folded it and put it away for later. All well. Like a bell the phrase rang and eased his mind.

He got on Major and rode down Dallas Street to the steamboat landing. A dissolving tissue of steam from a cottonseed oil mill drifted through the streets. The landing was on a body of water called Big Cypress Bayou, its surface a glassy jade color. There black men sat on top of cotton bales and waited for work, but none of the paddle-wheelers had a head of steam up, and so they seemed to be poised, stilled, waiting for something. A Union officer rode by on a red horse with his hat turned down against the wind.

John was drained and in need of comforts: whiskey, a bath, clean clothes, a meal served on a plate. Bread.

He turned up the next street and saw the Excelsior Hotel. The two-story building poured out cheerful woodsmoke from enormous chimneys at both ends. He pulled up there and tied up.

The frontage of the hotel lay flat to the ground and was paved in limestones, shaded by a lengthy verandah. The second-story windows had cast-iron balconies in fancywork, and this gave the place a New Orleans look to it which drew him immediately. It looked like a place where he could get the horse taken care of, maybe convince the stable hands to take the dog, get a bath, sleep in a warm room.

He ducked under the verandah roof and then opened the right-hand side of a double entrance door. The upper parts of both doors were glass. He looked through as the door came open in his hand and saw Giddens standing at the registry desk.

He immediately stepped backward, shut the door again. Turned and untied his horse and took him around to the back of the hotel. There was a livery stable there. He led his horse into the big entrance. A man came out of a stall and lifted his head to John in an inquiring way.

"Where's the Marshal's horse?" John said.

"That Marshal from Indian Territory?"

"Yes, Giddens."

"Over here."

John followed him down the fairway and the stableman pointed out Giddens's horse: a dark bay. It was in an end stall, and John noted there was a rear exit just after the stall. This rear door opened onto a street dominated by a roaring millhouse of some kind that filled the air with a lot of sawing noises. Giddens's horse was a stout animal in good condition. His tack and equipment were piled against the wall.

He asked the stable hand, "There's a telegraph office here, is there not?"

"Yes, sir, but there's a note on the window. Says the line's down."

John stood and looked at the Marshal's gear. He was not carrying very much. There was a scabbard for a rifle, which meant he was probably carrying a Henry. It would protect the exterior magazine tube with its openings from being fouled. There was a slicker, and a kind of three-pack saddlebag, one pack to a side and a third in the middle that would rest on the horse's back, on the saddle skirts.

He said, "Got any use for a dog?"

"No, sir, we got plenty."

He took a currycomb from a nail and said, "I'll look after him."

When the man had gone, he laid down the currycomb and quickly went through Giddens's saddlebags, but before he opened them he unholstered his revolver and laid it beside him as he squatted down. There was a good chance that Giddens would return, and John did not mean to be taken away in manacles, if that was what Giddens was planning on.

The hound laid herself down beside him as if guarding him, alert, her head raised, looking down the fairway.

John found a leather folder with a packet of official papers. In it were a pocket map of Texas like his, made by J. H. Colton, 86 Cedar Street, New York; an identifying letter from a judge in Fort Smith stating that Giddens was on official business; a pocketbook with notes; and a warrant for the arrest of himself, John Chenneville, alias William T. Allen, with a description of said fugitive, and the reason: suspicion of murder of Aubrey Robertson, telegrapher, employed by Western Union Keota I.T.

I didn't kill him, you stubborn son of a bitch, he thought. He flipped quickly through the notebook. He probably had very little time. As soon as Giddens got a room, he would be back here for his gear. Unless he decided to eat first. Shooting Giddens was not an option, but a presented revolver would stop him long enough for John to beat the man into unconsciousness. That would be another charge, but John was not looking much into the future. He had no future and he knew it. After Dodd was dead, he didn't care much what happened to himself; it was a task he must finish, and whatever came after didn't concern him.

He heard the dog give one subdued yip, and the stableman called out, "Morning, Marshal." John quickly jammed everything back into Gidden's saddlebag and took up the reins of his own horse, went out the rear door without looking behind himself, passed the big mill, and headed for the ferry landing.

A ferryman took him across Big Cypress for twenty-five cents, and he and Major and Dixie drummed off the plank deck and onto the red-dirt road to the south. The pine forest of East Texas was thick all around him.

He had slept three or four hours in the last twenty-four, and he had not caught up with Dodd, but now evading Giddens seemed to be the first priority. When he heard voices ahead he pulled off into the forest and stood down.

It was a light one-horse celerity wagon driving past in the sleety weather, and in it were people talking and laughing. Women, an old man driving. Dixie said *wuff*.

"Hush," John said, and ran his hand over her head. He listened to the women's voices, laughing and chatting. She would be in Marshall, with a voice perhaps as light, perhaps as cheerful. He listened until the little carriage was beyond hearing and the horse's clopping had died away. It was good to hear women's voices. Light, chatty, sewing the world together with minutiae, with tiny stitches. They were talking about beehives. About bees and their attitudes, their riches of stored honey.

As he stepped up into the stirrup, it occurred to him that someday he would remember this ramble through East Texas and the long road through the San Bois with longing. He would remember it with an ache for lost freedoms. He had never had a traveling year or years as did most young men. Some he knew had gone to Europe, others to New York or up the Missouri to the Yellowstone country. But the responsibility of the Chenneville acres had always been on his shoulders, even in New Orleans. Then the war. He thought about this as he watered his horse at a nearby stream, then fed Dixie once again. Now she was his for life. However long that might last.

He came into Marshall, Texas, later in the day. It was a good-sized town. This was the populated eastern part of Texas, near the Sabine River, near the Louisiana border. The weather had settled into a fine drizzle. The first houses he came to were cabins off the main road. The road had become busy with people on foot, horseback, and various sorts of wagons and carriages. The cabins were shoddy, one-room places, occupied by pigs as well as people. These were refugees, or people displaced by want, people who had abandoned failing farms, a cashless people hard as cartilage and bent on survival.

He stepped off the big horse and walked up to a doorway. It was wide open.

"Hello!" he shouted.

A man came out of the kitchen in the rear of the house, carrying a bloody butcher knife. His head was done up in a cone-shaped checkered cloth. He was barefoot.

"Yes, sir?"

"Good morning. I'm looking for some people named Garoute."

"Yes, there's some Garoutes around here."

John stood with his hat in his hand. "Could you direct me there?"

He looked John up and down and thought about it. Finally: "You come past their road already. You passed it a mile back. They live north toward Big Cypress. Go back north and that road goes off to the east; there's a stand of fireweed in an old burn there where you turn. They're back in there about a quarter mile." He paused and said, "They ain't from here." What he meant was, *We're not that kind of people.*

"Where are they from?"

"Damned if I know."

John turned around and found the old burn and a shallow sandy road going off the main road and into the pine forest. Major's hoofbeats made little noise, and the red hound trotted tirelessly beside him. He passed other cabins back among the pines, and several of them looked like army structures, thrown up as a temporary camp with horse pens alongside. In these, black folk were living, smoke from their fires going up into the longleaf pines. He lifted a hand to them and they nodded back and watched him silently as he passed.

THE CABIN WAS in an open space littered with stumps. He pulled up while he was yet in the cover of the pines to sit and watch the place. *He could be here*, he thought. *Come back to family of some kind, laying low.* There were wads of torn newspapers all around him in the underbrush.

Quilts were strung on a rope between pines, and junk seemed to take up most of the area around the house. He saw a broken-down buckboard wagon lacking a wheel, empty kegs, three US Cavalry saddles piled one on top of the other over an enormous pine log. He saw a very large gray hog staring at him from under a collapsed structure of some kind, probably an outhouse. If they had horses or cows, they were letting them forage on their own. There was a man up on the roof.

Dixie growled, low and insistent.

"Shut up," he said. She shut up.

Some dogs started barking. A cow was bawling somewhere. It was cold and a gray cold sky showed through the forest crown. Then he saw the dead horse. A long tail and mane. Mustang. A red roan. Large birds erupted from its carcass at John's appearance, and their wings made a rattle like wet sheets as they caught the air with their wings and fought up a ladder toward Heaven.

Finally he shouted, "Hello the house!"

A short silence and then, "Who's hollering? Where are you?"

The man sat astraddle of the roof spine, his shirttails hiked up and tied in a knot around his waist. He was old—seamed, worn, and barefoot. As John watched he stood up with some kind of tool in one hand.

"Here," John called and rode out into the clearing, and at that moment three dogs burst out of the front door of the cabin and came for Dixie. The man yelled at them and they slunk back. Dixie stayed close to Major's back hooves.

The man was thin and hawklike as he poised on the roof spine. He had a long gray pigtail hanging down his back. John didn't see anybody else. No women, no children.

"Is this Garoutes'?"

"Yeah."

"Are you Mr. Garoute?"

"Near enough."

He listened to his manner of speech. It was not East Texas. It was flatter, thinner, the vowels were wrong. It was more northern. Not Yankee but north of Texas, that was for sure.

"I'm looking for somebody. He goes by the name of Dodd, sometimes Garoute, Robert Garoute."

The man bent down and with the tool wrenched up a cypress shingle and flung it down. Then another. This one he spun sideways and it sailed toward John like a bat.

"He's no good," he said. "Can't do nothing."

John sat still. He didn't say anything for a moment. He thought maybe he'd outwait him.

He was right. Into his silence the man started talking again.

"He goes to chop wood and he cuts himself. He picks up a jug and he drops it on his foot. Picks up a screwdriver and stabs himself. He's my nephew, and I flat-out despise him, but he's family."

"Was he here?"

"What you looking for him for?"

John said, "I need him to do something for me."

"Ha ha," the man said. "Ha ha. He sits there and never says a cryin' word. Do something for you. You're a fool."

He flung a cypress shingle at John and disappeared to the far side of the roof. He was still talking, but John couldn't hear what he was saying.

He spurred Major into the clearing, rode around to the far side amidst the accumulated trash, and called up. "Where is he?"

"Try and find out," Garoute said and this time aimed a shingle that John managed to catch in midair at the cost of a hard rap on his fingers.

"Stop that or I am going to come up there," John said. "When was he here?"

"Oh, big fellow, going to abuse a old man, well, that's what kind *you* are."

"Listen to me, Mr. Garoute. I will come up there, and you're not going to like it."

"New Year's. He brought a bottle and drank up his tot and took my horse. Gone again. I have no idea where he was going."

"Which direction? Tell me now."

John sat easily in the saddle and watched him. His hands were wiry. He was about sixty or so. His long pigtail flopped about and the hair behind his ears was loose as gray snakes. He tossed the crooked nail bar from one hand to the other. Finally he decided John was serious. He said reluctantly, "Well probably south on the Tenaha. He could have took Trammel's Trace, but his partiality in getting to one place or another is what you might call the creepingest way. That good enough for you? He took fifty cents of my money and my dead wife's serving spoon. That there was the only silver we had. He ate up everything and wouldn't even boil water for the dishes. Afraid he'd fall in it maybe."

John bent forward, crossed his forearms over the saddle horn, and sat listening without saying anything.

The old man kept talking. "He got all showy. He was showing out. Trying to make things like a stage play. He says, 'They're after me, Abel.' I said, 'Who is after you?' He says, 'People who have vengeance on their mind.' I said, 'That'd be about half the population of several states.'"

He nodded as if he had delivered the information and had nothing else to say, turned and made his way along the roof spine, and put one hand on the chimney to gaze off into the pines and trash as if he were posing for a picture, as if it were a plaster pillar in a heliograph studio. John trotted his horse over to the front of the house, crashing through broken kegs and pieces of machinery, a pile of rags and a dead cat, circling him. He was crazy, but he had more information if John could just get it out of him.

"Why did he come to Marshall?"

"Money. He's got ways to get money from people. He knows things about people here. And he said he wanted to stay out of sight in a general way until things settled down. What things was he talking about? Who knows. You got vengeance on your mind?" The old man bent in his narrowly wired armature of spine and arm and pried up more shingles and stacked them as if gathering ammunition.

"Why did he leave?"

"He says, 'They're after me, Abel.' All I know is he's bound for glory somewhere. He'll go for the fleshpots. That's what he is living for, fleshpots, whatever they are."

Old man Garoute turned one way and then another, kicking at the loose shingles. "So he probably took off for anywhere there's Illinois troops that's occupying. He was with the Illinois, the Thirty-Third, and he can always claim some kind of kin with them. He said he liked ships. So I expect he's gone to Galveston. It's occupied. Probably Illinois troops. He don't talk much. Never did."

John got off the big horse and went into the house. It was chaos. The three dogs fled as he kicked through piles of bedding on the floor, pulled dishes out of the shelves, threw everything from a trunk, took up a shotgun from the corner and breached it, saw that it was unloaded, put it back. He lifted a bottle from a shelf and looked at the label: Johnson's Imported. Same as Rock Bluff, with a badly printed fake label.

John flipped through a stack of old newspapers and then found a handful of shells inside a pillow. It stank of dirty hair. He picked it up and crushed it between his two hands and felt the hard objects inside and then cut it open. There was no revolver anywhere that he could see. He spilled out the feathers and the cartridges; .52 caliber, probably for a Sharps carbine. As far as he could see there wasn't a Sharps carbine anywhere around.

Outside he heard a thump and a crash as the man dropped from the roof.

"That's what he was carrying." He stood in the doorway. "A gun that took those shells."

"Rifle or pistol?"

"A long gun." Outside, the bawling of unfed animals grew louder; the hog, a cow. "I hid it. Now he ain't carrying nothing."

"You hid the ammunition from him."

"Yah, and the carbine too. Do you know what fleshpots are?"

"I have no idea." John walked over to the greasy kitchen table and dropped the ammunition on it in dull thuds of lead and brass. Hen feathers stirred slightly on the floor as he walked past.

"He killed some people up north. He got drunk and said so."

John turned to the man slowly. He stared down at him with his pallid eyes, his hands hanging loose by his sides. "Who did he kill?"

John didn't move, and his taut, immobile body seemed to frighten the man. Feathers drifted around his boots.

"He was laughing. He said her skirts floated like balloons. Some woman that was crazy for him. Said her husband attacked him. Up in Missouri."

John was silent.

"You need a drink," Garoute said. He came upon the bottle and turned it up into a mug, lifted the mug to John, but John shook his head. So the old man shrugged and then drank it himself. "There's more in here if you want it." He looked around at the mess John had made, which was not that much different from the mess it was in originally. "He took my horse, one of them piney-woods Caddo horses, and he went off."

"After he rode that one out there to death."

"Them tackies ain't no good. Just as well."

John walked outside and stepped up into the stirrup and rode away, down the small sandy path, out onto the main road and into Marshall. He bent his head against a slight rising breeze and felt it skim off the sense of waste and garbage, the decomposing cat, the dead horse, the feeling of low-grade minds and ignorance and random clumsy violence. Life as a slovenly enterprise in which nobody rose out of the trash except at a dead run, toward the light, abandoning all who dwelt there.

CHAPTER TWENTY-THREE

January 5, 1867 / The Capitol Hotel, Marshall, Texas

JOHN RODE INTO THE TOWN of Marshall down the northern road. He pulled Major up and then swung down to walk for a while to relieve his knees and back. He fell into a rhythmical route step to shake off the wastage of the Garoutes' sordid life. He had other things to think about. A lady telegrapher, for instance.

"Well, here we are," he said. Dixie looked up at him and Major's ears flicked back as if to catch his words. The January temperatures hovered at freezing in the winter chill, and the wet air dripped off everything. Dead leaves chased one another down the road, which had now become a street, and John wondered what turn of the wind might bring him good fortune now. He was on Dodd's track; the man had not been able to shake him, close but falling behind. *Keep moving,* he told himself, *keep asking, don't be detained by the company of a lovely and talented lady telegrapher whether she is in fact talented or even lovely.* He took off his hat briefly; he felt overly warm, walking on the broad red-dirt street.

He passed large and wealthy houses, or formerly wealthy perhaps, with cast-iron fencing and brick walks and long verandahs. He had no doubt they were all built with slave labor. Great leafless chestnut trees and alders made moving shadow lines across his face. He was joined on the street by wagons carrying pumpkins and onions, by sulkies and people on foot. It was probably market day. It had occurred to him many times in his life that slave labor was a thing of utter insanity and never more so than now. To ship uncounted thousands of human beings over an ocean, all the way from a remote continent, just to do agricultural labor, was an extraordinarily stupid thing to do, not to speak of the cruelty of it, and here was the result: a four-year war and seven hundred thousand dead and a countryside brought to ruin.

But that was over and done with, and so he walked on. He touched each fingertip in turn to his thumb in a nervous, apprehensive gesture. Over and done with, and so he assumed it would all shake itself out. He had done his part and now had other things to think about. No matter what the lady telegrapher looked like, he had to ask her to help him with information and then go on. She would have handled messages from Giddens. She would tell him what was in those messages. John had no hesitation in asking her to breach confidence because Aubrey had been her friend, if not more than a friend. Explaining his sister's murder, her and her family, would be painful as it always was. It made his stomach twist to think of talking about it again.

He felt strangely hot all of a sudden and opened his coat to the winter air, but then after a moment a chill struck him and it struck deep. A shivering traveled all through his body. *What?* he thought. *What was that?* He buttoned his coat again and pulled the standing collar on his greatcoat up high and tight and thought about locating the Marshall telegraph office.

Now the houses were close together. People seemed given to standing and staring at him in their yards as he walked by as if it were important to examine his every detail and come to a conclusion as to whether he was or was not a threat. Soon he found himself on Washington Street, according to a street sign, and this street led to the courthouse. It stood in the middle of the town square.

He halted and got back up in the saddle. He knew he looked worn and so did all his clothes and equipage. His boots were so beat-up that most of the brown color was gone from the toes and all his seams were frayed. He had come nearly four hundred miles and had been on the road a month since Fort Smith, much of it on foot, and he had slept under a roof only five times.

In the square, low runnels of stove smoke drifted from the chimneys of the stores and depots. Union troops walked by in groups of two or three. *Patrols,* John thought. *There's not enough of them. They are stretched thin.* A feeling of caution grew in him with Major's every footfall, but here somewhere would be the telegraph office, and in the office would be Belle, Miss Victoria Reavis, with her hand on the key.

A church bell tolled twelve times and from some industrial place out of sight the noon whistle sounded. The whistle seemed to drill right through his skull. He rode on through market wagons and women shopping.

He pulled up in front of the main hotel, the Capitol: square, un-adorned, and brick. It had tall windows on which were imprinted passing winter clouds and curtain lace. Next to the Capitol Hotel was Sattler, Crosby, and Hanlin's Stage Service. Always On Time, the sign said. Mail Delivery Guaranteed.

He turned Major toward the hitching rails. It was a damned ugly building, but he might get lucky and actually get a room this time. Before he went to find this unknown woman he should do something about the rip in the knee of his trousers, about his mud-rimmed cuffs, about his unshaven face. Then he saw the notice on the outside wall of the hotel: "Telegraph Service: New Orleans, Nacogdoches, Galveston, Austin, San Antonio."

So the telegraph office was in the hotel. All right. He took a deep, jerky breath. He swung off slowly, throwing his leg over the high can-tle. When he stood on the ground, he held to the saddle horn for a few moments to wait for the world to right itself. This had not happened in a while. He was tired; his mouth felt hot. His hair was damp under the hat. He bent down to touch Dixie on the head as she lay down beside Major's great round hooves.

He walked inside with careful steps among a crowd of men and some women. He heard his spurs make ringing noises on the tiles. It was still an elegant hotel despite the loss of a long war, despite the crash of their Confederate money. There was a wide carpeted staircase and chande-liers, and throughout the lobby people came and went, one of them a man with two hunting dogs on leashes.

In the rear of the lobby, behind an elegant glass-and-wood screen that partitioned off the telegraph office, he saw a young woman sitting behind the desk. He stopped and stood very still. His heart seized up momentarily. He had to take a short breath through his nose as if the air had temporarily escaped him. He stood watching her.

She was slim and upright, intent on her work. Her eyes seemed dark, but that was because her face was as fair as new linen. A pretty face, bent to her work. In front of her were the sounder and a brass camelback key.

"Sir?"

"Yes, excuse me."

John moved out of the way of a man with a heavy carpetbag and turned toward the glass screen again. On her head she wore a little Glengarry hat tipped forward over her brow with a dashing guinea feather in its fold. She spiked a message and went on to the next. Through the glass panes he could see that she had a boyish hand with very short nails and thick fingertips, caught up in a flurry of incoming messages.

That's who he had been talking to, all this time, all these miles.

He stood as the hotel guests came and went around him. Her hair was a rich brown and rolled up in thick braids. There was a lot of it. With a sinking heart he saw how attractive she was. How appalling this could all become. But she seemed to him a lamp in a dark place and a saving grace from the cesspit of human waste from which he had just come. He felt an uncoiling inside himself, an unbending perhaps. He realized, finally, how much he had had riding on this. How deeply he had wished her to look exactly like this. He stood suspended in these conflicting thoughts as some tall clock ticked quietly behind him telling out his heartbeats.

Then he made himself stop staring and turned to the registry desk in the rear. Behind the counter a young man with a clean-shaven face and a checkered waistcoat said, "Yes, sir?"

"May I see your registry book?"

The clerk looked up at him and hesitated, unsure about this tall man in worn and splashed clothing looming at him on the other side of the counter, regarding him with unusually light eyes. The man's hat was finger-marked around the rim and on the crown, and he had several days' growth of light-colored flinty beard. The clerk took a breath and drew himself up. He placed one hand against the cash drawer.

"Registry book?" he said mindlessly.

"Registry book. I want to see if a friend has arrived. And I need a room, bath, and laundry services, and also I have a dog."

The young man squared his shoulders. "We are required to see your discharge papers."

"I see," said John. "In a minute. Let me look at the registry." The young man thumped the registry on the counter and John flipped through the pages. Neither Giddens nor Bain nor Garoute nor Dodd. He was good so far. He shoved the folded discharge across the counter. He waited for the young man to read it; William T. Allen of Alton, Illinois, with his age and description written out in a fair hand. He noticed the clerk's hesitation and so reached into the inner pocket of the cartridge belt and took out a two-and-a-half-dollar gold coin and laid it on the counter.

The clerk glanced down at John's battered hand resting beside the coin. "Yes, sir, indeed, we do have one room left. Actually, it's a suite, and I can give it to you at the price of a single room, which would be two-fifty." The clerk calculated there might be a tip awaiting him and smiled brightly, hopefully, and then nodded as John shoved not only the gold coin but a silver quarter forward to him, took the key, and walked away.

The lobby was crowded. John walked over to the far wall to choose a place where he could see her. He found a small settee near some potted palms and sat down there and peeled off his tattered gloves. He watched her and her charmingly severe expression. She was far too pretty to be severe, but she was trying. The glass panels on the upper half of the screen were beveled, and it made human figures on the other side waver and suddenly jump. People came and went, in and out of the office, in and out of the bevels, men in Union uniforms and men in civilian dress.

Despite the general noise he could hear the rattle of the sounder and key as she sent with great rapidity, at least thirty words a minute and maybe more. He listened as she signed off to Shreveport. Then he looked somewhere else and down at his boots and then back to her again. He couldn't stop looking at her. He ought to, but he didn't want to. He saw a young woman who would marry well someday to a man who would appreciate her, and it would be a kind and steady man who was not a wanted fugitive, who was not him, John Chenneville, homeless, somewhat feverish, and, as soon as he killed his man, traveling straight into a destiny of prison or flight.

He sat with his left side toward the potted palms so as not to draw any attention to the scar on his head. He crossed his legs, removed his hat, and put it on his knee. He put his arm along the back of the settee, lifted his forearm, and rested the side of his face on his knuckles to sit and watch her through the glass. The girl was all business. She had one pretty ring, and it was on her little finger, right hand. She was sending right-handed and he saw the flash of a red gem. She was good to look at, like a daguerreotype portrait, like something encased in a gold frame that you could hold in your palm.

He was going to fall in love with her. Probably within the next half hour. He should not do this. He should not greet her or introduce himself. He should not even tell her he was staying in this hotel, and certainly not his room number.

He sat with an infinite patience; the patience of people who are very tired and also find themselves in a safe, warm place. He liked everything he saw. He liked the way she had arranged her little office, the minute Glengarry hat, a wicker screen in the rear, which was where she probably kept her coat and muffler and reticule, her small private things. It would be a place to go and be out of the public eye for a few moments.

He watched her rise from her chair, glance left and right, and then lace her fingers together, turn them palms out, and stretch her arms out as straight as she could. She dipped her head to stretch her neck muscles, and he saw she was of average height, and she wore no hoops—

smart girl; he liked her even better for it. He listened to an incoming
message as it rattled in the sounder box.

ATTN COL. BRASHEAR CMDR 46TH ILL. MRSHAL TX CFM
SVP FROM FORT SMITH FEDERAL WARRANT ISSUED JOHN
CHENNEVILLE SIX FOOT THREE 180 LBS +OR- HAIR LIGHT
EYES LIGHT SCAR LEFT SIDE OF HEAD WANTED ST. LOUIS MO.
CHARGE ASSAULT ON B. THOMPSON JONES ALSO SUSPICION
OF MURDER INDIAN TERRITORY. LAST SEEN COLBERT'S
STATION PER REPORT OF U.S. MARSHAL GIDDENS FWD
HOUSTON RSVP FM BRASHEAR.

Her quick reply: CFM MARSHALL. Which meant the Western Union
operator at Marshall Texas acknowledges. The warrant would go to the
colonel as soon as the messenger boy returned. She began to write on
a message form.

John said quietly, "Well, damn."

He realized that the warrant was now upon the telegraph wires and
rocketing everywhere. It was no longer a single writ carried by a single
man. This made things a bit different. He had been singled out; the
mark of the beast was upon him. A federal warrant out on the wire . . .
just damn. So now he had to walk carefully and stay out of trouble and
probably get out of Marshall as soon as he could. Of course he would
have to speak with Miss Reavis before he left, but must remain formal
and remote. Calm and composed. Like a sort of distant relative.

He would do that as soon as he managed to clean up.

As he stood up he saw an officious and bustling sort of man walk
into the telegraph office. He had a sheaf of papers in his hand. The
man began to speak to Miss Reavis in a stern, rather loud voice. John
paused and watched the man wave the papers around, pressing close to
the desk. Miss Reavis sat bolt upright and placed both hands flat on the
desk on either side of her key with an alarmed expression. John heard,
If you don't mind, sir! and *You cannot speak to me like that!*

John stood without moving to see what was going to happen. The man's bearing and expression were hostile in a flaunting kind of way. These displays involved expressive tossings of the head and spasmodic gestures. Belle had now gotten to her feet behind the desk. Her cheeks were turning bright pink.

"Complaints to Mr. Upshaw!" the man was saying. "Abusing privileges, fired, private messages!"

From the men in the lobby around him John heard, "Again?" Another man standing in a group glanced into the telegraph office and said, "That man could start an argument in an empty house." John turned to look at the men who spoke to search for a clue as to what was going on. They laughed quietly and nudged one another. One was the fellow with the dogs on leashes.

"Excuse me, who is that man?" John said.

A thin gentleman with a lit cigar between his fingers said, "This is affection spurned and unrequited desire, sir." He drew on the cigar and blew out smoke. "Western Union took away most of the business from Sattler, Crosby, and Hanlin's stagecoach mail service. By a mere girl. Also it is said she refused to take tea with him."

"Tea." John considered this. "What's his name?" He wiped his hand across his mouth and his unshaven chin and turned back to watch the man, looking for weak points. There were plenty of them. He was still carrying on at a great rate of speed. He was shaking the sheaf of papers almost in her face.

"Sattler, son of."

"I see." John looked from the cigar man to the one with the dogs. "You aren't going to do anything about this, are you?"

"No." They looked at him with a cool indifference as they sat, smoking, and the dog man regarded John's overcoat and smiled a thin half smile.

John was furious. He knew he was not to bring attention to himself; he was to slide into Marshall silently, without being noticed. Maybe he could just put the man in an armlock and march him out the door without a lot of fuss. He gave the men one nod and then walked toward the office. His entire body had changed; his head turned left and then right as if he had a too-tight collar, and his weight had shifted in some subtle way. Behind him he heard somebody say, "Go get 'em, bluebelly."

John threw open the telegraph office door with a glassy crash. This was to be noisy and threatening and make the man turn to him. As soon as the man did, John took his Hunicke beaver hat, hardened by rain and campfire smokes, by the brim, and with a hard backhand he hit the man in the face with it. He hit him as hard as he could.

"What!? You, you!!" The man's voice was a thin scream. He fell back, his hand to his astonished face. He looked up at John with eyes as wide as eggs.

John said, "I just wanted to be sure I had your attention." He grasped the man by his lapels and swung him around so his back was to the door.

"You struck me!" The man pawed at John's hands. His mouth hung open like a mail slot.

"Yes, I did," said John in a reasonable voice. "Now get the hell out of this office." He let go the man's coat. In his second-best officer's voice, he said, "You should never speak to a young lady like that." He watched the man's hands to see if he might reach for a hidden revolver.

"Sir! I don't know who you are! This is none of your business!"

"Wait till you see what's coming next," John said. He shot his fist forward and gave the man a good rap on the shoulder with his knuckles, knocking him off balance. "Get out of here now, before I really hurt you."

He wanted this to be over quickly, because this sweaty tedious dunce was completely botching up his first meeting with the lovely and talented Victoria Reavis. Would he not just go? He didn't have a chance in hell in a fight with John Chenneville, but John had been forced to come in here in his grubby traveling clothes, unshaven, clanking with spurs and making a spectacle of himself.

The man was gasping, and the mark of the hat crown was red on his face. "This is . . . ." He thrashed around and then at last gathered his wits. "Actionable!" Pointing with the sheaf of papers, he cried out, "Sir! I can see to it that . . ."

John snatched the papers out of his hand and ripped them all in half. Then with the smile of a sort of courteous predator he threw them in the man's face.

"I am on official business!" the man cried, holding his face, backing away into the lobby. Men stood frozen, watching. "I have received complaints from Western Union customers about this young woman . . ."

"You're a liar."

Miss Reavis squinched her eyes shut for a few bare seconds at those words, knowing what it meant for one man to call another a liar. With both hands on her cheeks she shouted, "Stop!"

The man's nostrils flared. "Sir, I will meet you at any time . . ."

John realized this had to be ended quickly. He took hold of the man's cravat, pulled him close, drew back his right fist, and punched the man directly in the nose. He watched as the man dropped to the floor of the lobby in a heap. He didn't hit him as hard as he could have. He wanted this Sattler person to get up and walk out of the place on his own. John looked up at the crowd.

"Anybody else?" he said. There were no takers. John rubbed his right fist. The cigar man drew slowly on his cigar and expelled smoke in a lazy, unwinding stream.

He glanced quickly back inside the office door at Miss Reavis. She was bright red and her mouth had dropped open. He looked into her eyes; they were shining with tears of humiliation and anger. He bowed briefly and turned back to the loud person, evidently named Sattler.

"Get up, you *teteux, fi' de pute*, get on your feet or I'll kick your head in."

Sattler struggled to his feet. His nose poured bright splatters of blood down his shirtfront. In a low threatening voice, he said, "I will speak to somebody in authority about this!" He kept on backing up through a flutter of torn paper, backing, backing, and finally hurried out the front doors of the hotel with his cravat to his nose.

Voices from the far side of the lobby: "Actionable!" and then laughter and someone else said, "He deserved everything he got."

John knew nobody was going to do anything about this fight,

including any authority. There probably wasn't any authority. There was only the frosty cynicism of embittered men as they lounged about the potted palms, watching and laughing.

John came back into the little office and shut the door behind himself firmly. Then he turned slowly to the telegrapher. He stood back against the wall to be less of a threat in case she thought him threatening. He dropped both hands to his sides.

"Miss Reavis?" John's heavy greatcoat was open and the cartridge belt visible, full of ammunition. Pointy brass things. He drew it shut in an embarrassed gesture. "Belle?"

She drew a breath and held it, then said, "Snowman." She clasped her shaking fingers together.

"Yes."

"It's you." She said it in a quavering voice. "You've just come."

"I have." Then he nodded once. His silence said, *Your move.*

"Oh, I had so hoped to meet you, and that dismal man . . ." She looked anxiously out the glass panes into the lobby. "Is he gone?" The guinea feather in her little Glengarry hat shook in a minute vibration.

"He'd better be."

She shut her hands into fists. "I . . . This is awful. I just got a warrant for you. It's been sent by Giddens to the colonel of troops . . ."

"I heard it."

"Oh yes, of course. That man . . ."

"I don't think he's going to be any more trouble."

"He has been a constant trial since I got here." She took up a message form and laid it down again. "Thank you."

"You're perfectly welcome." And again he said nothing more, and again the message was, *I'm waiting.*

"The warrant is unfair."

"I know."

"You didn't have anything to do with Aubrey's death. Giddens is so stubborn, he is a bulldog, and it had your description, which is just like you here now, I can't believe it, that vile Sattler person, everything at once, I mean . . ."

"Calm down." John saw that her hand was not near the key and she was not sending a message anywhere, for instance to Fort Smith. He did not know what he would do if she did. "It's all right. We're good. The door is shut."

"Your real name is Chenneville?" Her dark eyes were wide. "Not William Allen?"

"Yes," he said. "But before anything else, tell me about that man. Or let me guess. You didn't welcome his attentions, and so he's trying to get you fired."

"That's right, yes," she said. "Among other things." She took up her account book. Her hands were still shaking. "I'm *glad* you smacked him. I wanted to smack him myself but then Western Union *would* fire me. But he's not worth thinking about, not right now." She grasped the account book to herself as if a minor panic had taken hold of her. "But you. You're now a fugitive because of this warrant. It just came in!"

"Yes, you said that." He could understand her alarm. He was a man on the edge of lawlessness, but so was the entire country, and she had no idea of his present circumstances. Also he had just beaten the stuffing out of a man right in front of her lovely eyes. "I know. It's all right. Everything's all right." He let out a short breath. He glanced out the glass panels of the door and then back to her as if searching for a place of quiet and reason and found it there in her face.

She dipped her head down and raised it again and looked into his face. "Let me get hold of myself, Snowman. I'm a bit shaken."

"Take your time."

She glanced down at the written-out message for the colonel. It had to be delivered, like it or not. But it did not have to be delivered today. She could write any date she wanted on it. She slipped it under a stack of message forms and lifted her head and smiled in return and said, finally, "We have a great deal to talk about, Snowman. And I am very, very glad to see you." She came around the desk to reach out and lay her hand lightly on his coat sleeve. He was edgy and trying to be calm; his shadowless eyes had a light glitter. She said carefully, "You rescued me. I don't know what I would have done."

He stood very still so she wouldn't take that small and boyish hand away and then gave one nod as a kind of formal bow. "For months I've been looking for a fair damsel to rescue," he said. "From an evildoer. Today was my lucky day."

She smiled, holding on to his coat sleeve. It was as if he had stepped into the parameters of his description: a tall man of about one eighty pounds, light hair, light eyes, scar left side of head, and the weight of a great many miles wearing him down.

"This warrant was the first description of you I've had," she said. "The mysterious Snowman, and you've shown up right behind it."

He didn't say she herself had been mysterious until now but instead offered his large and grimy hand, and she shook it in a light clasp.

"Happy to meet you, Mr. Chenneville."

"As well. Charmed."

Then she took a quick breath and looked around her. It was as if she had come to life and the demanding present. "Wait one moment, Mr. Chenneville, just wait." She quickly drew off the canvas sleeve guards that protected her cuffs from the pencil graphite, threw the circuit lever on the key, and snatched up her reticule. "I'll just be a moment. I have to close down."

She ducked behind the screen and came out with a short coat, a small feminine version of a shell jacket. She wiped at her face with fierce, angry wipes of a wet handkerchief, upset that she had nearly cried in front of that cretin Sattler. John opened the door for her and stood out of the way as she came through in a rustle of full and hoopless skirts, struggling into her wraps, shut the door, and hung up a sign: Closed.

"We have so much to discuss," she said. She turned and lifted her head to examine his face carefully, eyes narrowed. "Snowman, you are not well."

"No. I'm not."

"You have a fever. Do you feel hot?"

"I do, but I'm hoping it will pass."

"Where is your room?"

Now a crowd was coming in and out of the lobby talking loudly;

there seemed to be some disturbance going on outside in the square. He could hear it. It was a noisy disturbance but so far no gunfire. Some of the people in the lobby glanced at Miss Reavis and John speaking together and after the ejection of Sattler, son of; the glances were polite and respectful. A tall heavy man touched his hat brim to John.

John nodded to him in return and then turned back to Miss Reavis. Belle, she of the copper-wire messages and the light angelic hand on the key. He said, "I don't want you to come to my room."

"Why not?"

He should be firm and stop this onrush of an irresponsible gladness; at any rate, he tried. He looked down at her scrubbed face and her pretty mouth. "Miss Reavis, I am just arrived. I'm not presentable. Everything I own smells like dog. Like horse."

She shook her head. "I am going to get my maid to accompany me, and I will *certainly* come there. We have much to talk about." She placed her wet handkerchief in the palm of his hand. "Wipe your face." He did. He was sweating with fever and the exertion of knocking somebody down. She wrapped her wooly muffler around her neck and a distressed look came to her face. "The warrant is unfair. It is just unfair. I know you didn't kill Aubrey. But you know who did, don't you?"

"I believe I do."

"This man Dodd."

"Yes. Don't come to my room."

"Don't be silly," she said and straightened her small hat with a quick, efficient gesture. "You saved me."

"I will feel better by tomorrow, and then we can discuss this at the hotel restaurant. I am firm about this."

"Don't be silly," she said again. "Give me thirty minutes."

A wavering pause. "Make it an hour and a half."

"Certainly. What is the number?"

He told her.

He stood outside the hotel for a moment to calm himself. His skin seemed to crawl with the light, persistent thrill of fever. He told himself it would pass. There was some kind of confrontation going on in front of the Freedmen's Bureau office between the local occupation troops and a crowd of white men, and a loose, uneasy crowd of freed slaves. Good; the colonel would not be preoccupied with locating a man named Chenneville with all that going on.

He had meant to stay quiet and unnoticed in this town and also to present himself to Miss Reavis in a scrubbed and well-dressed condition, and both those things had gone right up the spout.

He settled his hat on his head and put up Major at the hotel livery stable. He crossed the main square to a butcher's shop and bought a half a cow's liver for Dixie and left both the dog and the horse to their dinner and their rest.

And then with a bullheaded determination, putting one foot in front of the other, he found a dry goods store. As he walked toward it he thought of the feverish girl at the Caddo longhouse, himself drinking coffee from a gourd the woman had handed him. *That's what happened*, he thought. *That's why.*

He bought a ready-made shirt with a French yoke, wool trousers of riding length, drawers, socks, and a new neckcloth. He bought a pair of gloves made of a light calfskin that had inset thumbs. With this bundle he went on to Sander's Drugstore down the block. He was so hot he felt as if he were glowing. There amidst placards urging him to purchase Van Deusen's worm cure (Death to Worms!) and baldness ointments, he bought powdered quinine bark and a bottle of whiskey.

At last, with fading strength, he walked into a hardware store and there he found, among other handguns, a Smith & Wesson Model Number One revolver. It was one of those with the tip-up barrel and a seven-shot cylinder. He bought a box of the .22 rimfire cartridges for it. Excellent. She wouldn't do well with cap-and-ball. Then he stood out in front of the hardware store between the barrels of tools and took in long breaths. After a moment he made his way back across the square to the hotel.

He climbed up the stairs with one big raw red hand gripping the banister. He needed to make it through another hour without collapsing and still make sense.

He opened the door to his suite. He stood for a moment looking at everything, every detail, where the exits were, how high the windows. Then he relaxed a little and thought, *A suite. This is high living. Two rooms, all mine.* He had a small front room stuffed with mismatched furniture and faded green velvet drapes to draw against the cold. The bedroom had a cast-iron fireplace set into the wall. Both rooms had windows looking out on the square. That was good. He pressed a drape aside with a forefinger. If there were to be riots, he would see them coming.

A boy followed with his gear. John dropped his hat and overcoat on the floor of the bedroom and clawed his fingertips through his hair to relieve the pressure of the hatband. He sent the boy down with orders for a bath and then firewood or coal or whatever they burned in that thing and then slammed and locked the door behind himself.

That felt good: being able to lock a door. There was a wavery mirror between the windows, and he saw himself in it. His face was cross-hatched with a four-day beard as well as flushed; his pants sagged at the knees, and one of the knees was torn. He clumsily pulled off the red bandana and his big greatcoat and then struggled with the cartridge belt.

The bath was on the first floor behind the kitchens. There was a long tub with claw feet. He did not linger in it for long. He was already hot, and the hot water made him feel as if he were being seethed. He scrubbed himself of dirt and odors and sloshed out. He was bright red all over. He toweled himself dry. He was determined to remain cool and distant and formal with her. But there was nothing wrong with being presentable, was there? He shaved meticulously, slowly, all the way down his neck and under his nose, carefully, not missing a spot.

In the hotel room he struggled into the new clothes. He tied the new neckcloth in a barrel knot and wiped the soap out of his ears. He would take the quinine and whiskey later.

He thought to rest a few moments on the bed. He lay against the pillows in his clothes and his boots. He had tried sitting up in one of the little chairs in the front room, but that didn't work out. He managed to drag his spurs off. He threw them across the room. What had possessed him to give her the room number? Old Adam, that's who. He poured aspirin powder into a glass of water but forewent the whiskey. Also he put aside the quinine for now; it gave him the shakes, as he well knew, and he did not want to be shaking when he talked to her.

He had sense enough to raise himself on his elbows and look around the bedroom to see if it was neat. It was not. His saddlebags were heaped in a corner, and the Spencer lay carelessly on top, his blankets in a folded roll, his old muddy clothes wadded in a ball, and the cartridge belt looking like some sinister jointed creature piled on top of the clothes. Beside the blankets Dixie lay curled up and asleep. He had no idea how she had gotten there.

A knock on the outer door. He called out for her to come in. She carefully walked into the little parlor and then peeked into the bedroom, regarding him with a serious expression. He swung his legs over the side of the bed and sat up.

"You're still alive," she said.

He held himself straight with an effort. "So far. I had good intentions of sitting up in a chair in there, but that went by the wayside."

"The road to Hell," she said. She looked at him in his entirety, the new clothes and hard-shaven face and his boots braced on the floor. "You've got worse," she said and dropped a rattling market basket at her feet. "And you've certainly cleaned up."

"I hope you're impressed."

"I am!" She glanced around the room in search of medicines, bottles, powders. "What are you taking?"

"Water." He managed to smile at her and for once the slow, warm expression on his face did not go away but lingered there and softened the hard angles of his face. "Quinine. Sorry to sit here like a lump, but right now I really don't think I could stand up."

"Ah, I'm safe, then," she said and wrestled a chair into the bedroom and sat at a small distance, leaving the door open. Outside, in the entry room, sat a young girl with dull brown hair and a dress that was far too large for her, stitching madly at a drumhead hoop of stretched muslin.

He said without preamble, "Where is Giddens?"

She looked down at her hands, hesitated, and then made a decision. "He telegraphed the Colonel here that he was going to Houston."

"Does he know I'm here?"

"No." Victoria Reavis, telegrapher, pulled off her gloves and said, "Not yet."

"All right. I've been seen down in the hotel lobby, but people forget." He was trying to think and keep himself upright at the same time. He was hauling air into his lungs, it seemed, hand over hand. "You handle traffic from Louisiana, Galveston . . ."

"Houston, San Antonio," she said, hesitated, and then: "What Giddens has done is unfair."

"He's a lawman."

"And I'm a telegrapher, and I've breached confidence."

John looked at her—her honest, candid face and the poised way she held herself. He regretted asking this of her, but there was only one thing in his life now: finding Dodd. Or that ought to be the only thing. Other than this graceful young woman with the Glengarry hat. He felt light-headed and thirsty and on fire.

"Breaching confidence is a bad thing," he said. "Except when it's a good thing. Like now." He paused to draw in several rattling, hot breaths and to think. "I need you to tell me of troop movements as well. I am interested in the Thirty-Third Illinois Mounted Infantry, and in any reports of homicide from locals." He meant to say *local law enforcement*, but there were too many syllables. "He's moving, moving fast, farther away every minute. I have to get on my feet."

"Yes, Snowman. But you must get well first. Whatever happens, you have to get well first." She checked the pitcher for water and took up the poker to tip over a log. "And I am here to help you," she said, "for Aubrey's sake." She bent down to the basket and brought out a stone bottle wrapped in a cloth. She poured a steaming tea into a mug. She placed it in his hand and closed his other hand around it as well, as if he was too done in to know how to hold a cup. "Sheriff Giddens is stubborn. He will not listen to reason. This is a restorative tea. All. All of it."

He drank it all. It tasted like old, decayed straw. "That's absolutely vile." He pressed his new white sleeve cuff against his mouth. "And he's a US Marshal, not a sheriff."

"Yes, yes, Marshal. But the tea is *good* for you."

"He's determined to get me to Fort Smith."

"I wish . . ." She paused and looked down briefly and then lifted what John saw as that admirable little head of hers with the brown braids shining now in the firelight. She seemed to have almost no eyelashes. It made her dark eyes stand out. *I am besotted*, he thought. *Felled. This is disastrous.*

"Sorry, what? You wish . . . ?"

She shook her head. "Oh, just . . . Aubrey was very happy with your company, you know." She tucked her gloves into her pockets and then sat and clasped her hands in her lap. "You played chess; he said you could bake bread. Any man who can bake bread is all right in my book. But now you must lie back down again. I insist." She regarded him with an open, frank gaze. "You are very tall," she said. "And Aubrey never said anything about the scar on your head."

"I was scalped by Eskimos when I was five."

"Not Turks?"

A short shake of the head—short because he felt a great headache creeping up the back of his skull. "Eskimos." He looked down for a moment as if his head were too heavy to hold up and then slowly swung his feet up and onto the bed. He shoved himself backward with his bootheels to get more or less in a sitting position against the pillows. The sun came in a bar between the bedroom curtains and laid a luminous stripe across her blue skirt and one shoe. His throat felt tight and sticky. He said in a hoarse, low voice, "There's water in that pitcher."

"No, there's one cup left in here." She tipped up the stone bottle and decanted the rest of the vile restorative herbal tea. "I have three younger brothers, and it's always hard to get medicines down them. Finish the tea. After that there's more things in the basket, but let's get the worst down first." She looked up with a concerned expression and said, "It might make you throw up. I'll close my eyes and put my fingers in my ears."

"I refuse to throw up. Puking not allowed in polite company."

He poured down the second cup and handed it back again and felt the touch of her fingers. He lay very still. The window backlit him and the gleam of sweat on his cheekbones, his light brown hair shiny as quartz. Outside the roofs grew dark with evening and released the town from its daily tensions into supper and homegoing birds that skimmed into the thick southern forest all about. Finally he said, "I'm good."

"Excellent. It will do you good, you'll see. And you weren't really scalped by Eskimos?"

"No. It was much less amusing than that."

He felt the fever running through him and did not trust himself to say the right things. He turned his head on the pillow and looked at her and thought, *Darling girl*. She was a bird in the hand, one come lightly sailing into his life, but he must not pursue this, and so he simply put out one hand with an open palm and continued to look into her face as if at a portrait. She laid her left hand in his, and then tears came to her eyes.

"Aubrey was such a good man, Mr. Chenneville," she said. "So solitary, and you and I were his friends. And him so far from home. From England."

"Were you engaged?" He closed his fingers under her hand and with his knuckles lifted her hand up so that the ring with the red gem was uppermost.

"Oh, well, I knew he was going to ask me." She drew her hand away and wiped at her eyes. "And yes, he gave me the ring."

"I'm very sorry. I liked him very much. Tell me how you went to Keota. Tell me about Giddens."

Close to an hour passed as they spoke of these things, talk that brought up dates and times and names; where Aubrey found his final resting place in the Tahlequah graveyard, where Giddens might be at present, pressure from Western Union to solve this murder. And so they talked for as long as he could make sense, about his journey from

Colbert's Station to here, about the man he was hunting and why. A death in his own family. Things done, things left undone. He did not go into detail. Details were escaping him at the moment but he was pretty good with broad outlines. She told him that Giddens had ridden up to Tahlequah to talk to her, that he wanted information about John's stay with Aubrey Robertson in Keota.

Dixie made a gappy yawning noise, and a wave of faintness blew through him so that he wadded the edge of the coverlet in his hand and it felt rough and starchy. She laid her hand over his and he released it slowly, finger by finger.

"Are you well enough for this?" she asked. "All this talking?"

"Yes. Go on, if you would."

Yes, all right, she had very carefully explained to Marshal Giddens that John could not *possibly* be a suspect because Aubrey had PM'd her the evening after John left. Aubrey *said* he had left and had said many approving things about him. But then Giddens's fertile mind cast about among the probabilities and said that John was known to be an excellent telegrapher, so he thinks John sent it himself. It would be diabolically clever, wouldn't it?

His head pressed back against the pillow. He closed his eyes and then opened them again. Images of cold water came to him; a glass of cold water, clear and sparkling. Then there was a rustle of skirts, a pouring sound, and a glass in his hand. He drank all of it and handed the glass back to her.

"Yes. Clever." He tried to keep his train of thought lined out and logical. "Diabolical." Mrs. Colbert would have told Giddens that he knew Morse. "But my hand would be different from Aubrey's."

Exactly. She had explained to Giddens *very carefully* that telegraphers all have a distinct way of sending, that it is like handwriting and very recognizable. It would be a dramatic courtroom scene where she would be out in the hall—the halls of justice, as it were—with a jury-rigged line and John and some other person would send her a message, and she could tell which one was John. *Irrefutable proof!* But the obstinate Giddens had said it wouldn't stand up before a judge. But it *would* stand up before a judge. She banged her small boyish hand on her knee. Of *course* it would.

He lay, loose, feeling like some jointless water plant. "I have no intention of going back to Fort Smith," he said. He saw that she wore tiny drop earrings that moved and sparkled as she spoke. Hypnotic small flashes of light. Another pause. "I will be more coherent tomorrow, probably."

She leaned forward to place her hand on his forehead and said, "Lord." Then she sat back to regard this tall man collapsed on the bed with his painfully new clothes and a face provisionally handsome were it not for a thick upper lip and a flattened nose bridge. He was mild-mannered in this illness but apparently of substantial determination that might preclude drawing-room manners, but this was, to her, of little importance. He was on the wandering track of a murderer. Whenever he could get on his feet.

Don't get sicker and die, she thought and in a careful voice said, "Snowman, I am going to send for a doctor."

"Yes, if you would. In a moment."

His eyes drifted shut, and then he opened them and asked her to look in his saddlebags for a book. He apologized for the condition of the baggage. He had not had time to shake it all out and clean up his various belongings, but she said it was not in the least a matter for concern. He listened to her make thumping noises with one or another of his possessions. Then she was sitting beside him again, and he carefully took *The Lady in White* with the gilt lettering from her. The book seemed to have become heavier since he'd opened it last.

He said he had come across it at Colbert's Station and told her what Mrs. Colbert had said about the man who had left the book and who had taken the ferry in the night. A man who had been described to him as having Albert Dodd's face and height. And there on the title page was the notation about the maize to be delivered, in Robertson's handwriting.

She put her hand to her mouth, and her nose grew red. She looked at the handwriting for a long time. Then she closed the book. Who is the man, she wanted to know, who would shoot an inoffensive and, well, *merry* person like Aubrey? And apparently also a relative of John's, and how had he evaded the world, the law, the retribution of men?

"The sons of bitches do it all the time. God, excuse my language." He wiped down his face with both hands. He had suddenly grown tired of all the facts and the telegraph messages and the when and the where of it all, had forgotten himself and used swear words, but at least he hadn't thrown up. There was that. It was her he wanted, and all her details, this bird in the hand that he mustn't lay a hand to.

He said, "Tell me how and why you're here."

She gestured out to the girl in the parlor; her escort. "Because I went to school here in Marshall at the Masonic Female boarding school. She's a first-year student. We treat them abominably as a sort of school custom. So when Aubrey was, well, killed, Western Union wanted me to leave Indian Territory; they said it was too dangerous for a woman. They said the Marshall office was safer and they needed somebody, and I have friends here from school days."

"Good." He was being reduced to single words. "Friends. A female boarding school." It had grown dark in the room. John groped in his coat pocket and came out with a block of Lucifers. "You could light the lamp." He ran his fingertips across his sweating upper lip and saw the sudden flash of the match, then the warm light of the lamp flame as it underlit her face and her fine skin. "And you were taught . . . ?"

"Pig latin!" She smiled and went to the window to pull the curtains against the bald light of the moon, waning full. She sat down again, and now they two were alone in a lamplit room and their faces and hands outlined in gold light. "And French and music and all the usual things. My father sent me here before the war. It was such a long way away from home."

"And home is . . . ?"

"Louisville." She took out a length of muslin from the basket and began to fold it into a neat packet.

"You're a child of the war."

"Oh, not really. We were occupied by the Northern Army from the very first, you know, and it wasn't so bad. My brothers were all too young to fight. The twins were only ten." She looked up. "But we've gotten off the subject. I intend to stay on it. Don't try to stop me."

"What subject?"

She tilted her head and searched his face and said quietly, "I forget, Snowman. We've talked for too long."

She ran the edge of her hand over his forehead to wipe away the sweat. With three little brothers, he considered that she had probably helped see them all through fevers, chills, and diapers, and so she had a brisk, experienced touch as well as what was probably a rather clinical knowledge of male anatomy. *But let us put this out of our mind, Chenneville.* Her touch felt very good to him, and he wished she would not take her hand away again.

She said, "Your face is so hot."

"I know."

"I have also brought delicacies and whiskey."

"I already have whiskey."

"I should have known." She unpacked her market basket. "I will be back tomorrow and you'll tell me all your stories. Where you are from, what happened to your head, and where you got that lovely dog." She placed a jar of jam and a packet of small toasted things beside the pitcher and then poured water on the muslin.

He lifted one arm and laid it over the top of his head. "Where I got the dog," he said. He was infuriatingly weak. He had expended all his strength in beating up on that weedy villain who had been shouting at her, whereas in ages past he would have been able to beat up three weedy villains without raising a sweat. He felt a light touch on his arm.

"Snowman," she said in a soft voice. "Drink this."

He sat forward with an effort, using his elbows, lifted the glass and poured down a stiff whiskey embittered with quinine. He paused, tilting the glass to see the gritty residue.

"All," she said, and saw there were sweat drops on his eyelashes.

"Urg."

"More whiskey." She tilted in another tot and that went down too.

He slowly lay back on the pillows, and he could feel every separate drop of the whiskey decanting into his bloodstream. He hoped she had been in love with Robertson, that she might consider herself a sort of widow. That would solve everything. Then Victoria Reavis leaned forward with the wet muslin to wipe down his whole hard clean-shaven face.

"I first knew your name a month ago," he said.

"Yes. When I sent the message to Aubrey. You were there." She opened her eyes very wide to avoid any tears spilling over. "Warm and safe."

John thought, *He had twenty-four hours to live*. "Belle," he said. "Belle. I wondered about the woman sending." And then, "Dixie and Major. Need to see that they're fed, somebody look after them, brushing, Major's shoes."

"It's okay. I will see that they look after Dixie and your horse."

Telegraphers. They said *okay*. "I'm thirsty. God, when will this end? Did I tell you about them?" Unguarded words then arrived unbidden, and he didn't care. He closed his hand around her wrist and laid her imprisoned hand on his shirtfront. "You're lovely. I knew you would be. And brothers." He moved in a sort of random way. "Can you shoot?"

"No. I couldn't talk them into teaching me. Don't get any sicker. I will have a doctor here soon." She drew her wrist out of his grasp and put another glass of water in his hand. He drank it all.

"And would you have said yes?"

A pause. She got up and poured more water over the muslin. "Oh. To Aubrey. Well, no, but . . . it's a hard question." She took his big heavy arm and pressed it to his side so she could lay the cool packet on the crown of his head, and then she stood up and called out the doorway, "Beulah?"

The girl looked up, startled, and so did Dixie. Both the girl and the dog had been fast asleep. Dixie said *wuff*, and the girl said, "It's not Beulah, it's Bronaugh."

"Oh. Yes." Belle went out to her and bent over the girl. Bronaugh with her thick Irish name was wiping the sleep from her eyes. "Are you ready to go home?"

"Yes, ma'am. It's time for supper."

Belle came back to the bedside and untied John's neckcloth from its barrel knot, drew it off, and folded into a neat square. She took the wet muslin and wiped down his face once more, stroking away the sweat from his eyes and forehead and mouth. "I will send a doctor. What can I do in the meantime?"

He thought, *You can just show up in my room again.* But he said, "Not a great deal. I am reluctant to ask you about any further communication from Giddens."

"Well, swallow your reluctance, along with another glass of quinine and whiskey. I know you were gone when he was killed. I *know* it." Her eyes filled with tears again, and she made a quick wiping motion. "Whoever did it, I want them to burn in Hell."

"Strong language, Miss Reavis."

"For *eternity.*"

"We'll have to arrange it." He held out his hand. This was to say good night and to remember her own strong hand in his dreams as a guard against the old familiar horrors that came to him sometimes in his sleep. And inevitably to remember her sweet mouth and what were apparently small and perfect breasts beneath that body armor of blue twill. Old Adam.

CHAPTER TWENTY-FOUR

January 1867 / A Ride along the Sabine River

THE NEXT FEW DAYS WERE timeless, in that he was never quite sure of the time. All he knew was that it was passing. He couldn't mark the hours, even with the steam whistle and the stage arriving and departing beneath his window, couldn't get to his feet and begin the search again. He had brief images in his mind of ships sailing away from Galveston, ships sailing to rich port towns where chaos and Freedmen's Bureaus reigned as well as anonymity and danger into which Dodd could disappear. A man came in and helped him get out of his clothes, into a nightshirt and then under the covers. The man left a brown bottle on the bedside table, which he ignored.

Then she was there again. He pushed himself upright. She arranged his pillows for him and then, whether it was the quinine or the fever he didn't know, but he reached out to place his hand carefully on the side of her face. He felt the fine skin and the delicate bones of her jaw.

Then she was lifting his travel-stained clothes from the floor, shaking everything out, folding everything neatly.

"What?" he said. He sank back down in the pillows. "Girl. Those are filthy. Don't even touch them."

"They are going to the laundress. She can do wonders with wool." He smelled woodsmoke from the fireplace, heard the jingle of the cartridge belt buckle. It had been a long time since he had been in a place where the whole room was warm. Then he became suddenly restless and shoved the covers away from himself.

She said, holding his enormous boots with both hands, "I'll see that the boots are cleaned and restitched and, you know, Dixie has become a favorite with the kitchen staff." She gave him a fond smile, as if he were one of her three younger brothers. "They are saving scraps for her." Dixie heard her name and began to beat on the floor with her tail. "Now, what else is there to be repaired, cleaned, or replaced?" She brought the sheets and coverlet up to his chest again. "The bed isn't long enough for you."

"They never are." John lifted his hand to his mouth and wiped away sweat from that thickened upper lip. "The greatcoat. Horse gear. My horse. Needs re-shod."

"I'll tell the man he needs new shoes."

Just watching her move made him feel good. He struggled with a drifting feeling. "Don't do anything with the pistols," he said. His breathing sounded ragged, and he couldn't seem to get enough air. "Or the rifle. They're loaded. I don't want to unload them."

"Not for the world."

She sat beside him, facing him. They regarded each other silently. Something had happened, something he had not wanted to happen. Death and illness had brought them together as if these things were orbits and they heavenly bodies flung into certain trajectories to accompany each other through trials, troubles, and perhaps even times of happiness. Her hair was slipping out of its braid and down around her collar. She unpinned her small hat and dropped it and her hands in her lap.

"I have to be at work in a few minutes."

"Your hair is coming down."

"I know." She reached behind her head, separated her hair into two thick strands, and began to twist them together. He thought of her doing that in a nightgown, after they had been in bed together all night, her waking up and doing that with her hair. He raised one knee to make a tent of the covers and took a long breath, his eyes closed, and when he forced them open again with a shake of his head she was gone.

IT WAS A day of storm. He said to her that they should go out for a ride together in two days if she could get somebody to take over the key for her. That he was going to be on his feet in two days.

"I can," she said. "Tell me about the person in your family who was killed."

"Starting where?"

She knew it was hard for him but did not know exactly why and did not guess that it was only because of the simple, ordinary event of a man and a woman sitting and talking together, the unquenched decency of this slow, cloudy day pouring slate-colored light through the curtains and how reluctant he was to break it. Because so much worse was to come. He did not want to interrupt this wonderful ordinariness with his story. But it was the only one he had.

She turned a sober, attentive face to him, sitting in the chair by his bed again, stitching. "I know it must be hard to talk about."

"No, it's just that everything is so quiet." She didn't say anything. "Yes," he said. "Get my cartridge belt if you would."

On the inside there was a compartment that he opened and brought out the daguerreotype of his sister. She took it, gazing into that gold-and-shadowed interior beyond the frame.

"She's very pretty," she said, and then looked up with a question in her face.

"Yes. My sister. He killed her and her family."

It took him a long time to tell her where he was from, and about the explosion, his time in the hospital, Temps Clair, the murders, his mother gone into an unspeakable melancholia, and his journey. Even then he was sparse with words. His cheekbones were high-colored, his skin still hot. He bent his gaze on her as if she might be wavering in and out of his vision, but he answered her questions with long pauses in his attempt to tell her about Lalie, her brightness, as one might describe a shattered lamp. And Temps Clair, and his father's people. Their love of gardens and rich soil, turning plowlands, rivers, and good wine. Of the war he had less to tell her because his memory of more recent years was spotty and still fractured. Nor did he want to recall it.

He wanted her and quiet, long days and even months of tranquility, and he was not going to get either one. Except now, in these instants ticking away and gone so quickly.

Victoria Reavis, telegrapher, had learned that her younger brothers never talked about scrapes, bruises, wounds, or fights with other boys, and she knew better than to ask. If she waited long enough they would tell her, if only in some sideways manner that did not bear questions, and one must never appear upset. She had not even appeared upset when Ryan happened to mention that Cullen had fallen into the Ohio River between the paddlewheel of the *Malta* and the Louisville docks and it had taken three men to fish him out. But the brief recounting of the afternoon when Basile had told him of the murder of his sister and her family was more than she could bear with a calm face, and so she put both hands over her face and wept.

He sat resolute and dry-eyed until she stopped. "I already did that, my dear," he said. And then: "I'm sorry, I don't have a handkerchief. I forgot to buy one." He stroked one large, callused thumb across her cheek and then held out his neck scarf, the old red bandana, newly washed.

"Look here, I've cried all over my face." She took hold of his hand and wiped her tears from it. "So what are you going to do when you find him?"

"I'm going to kill him."

"Giddens will take you in."

"I know."

She did not know what to say, and so they sat in silence together for a long time, listening to the light soprano notes of the storm whistling at the window, the cadence of raindrops on the panes.

MAYBE IT WAS the third day. He said, "I only have a little while with you, *ma belle*. Just this short time. So brief. Every minute counts."

And the minutes fled like minnows swimming way into deep and unseen currents, bright, silver, flickering.

"But you will come back."

"No. Giddens is, as you said, stubborn."

"But nobody has to know," she said, and then realized that she, Victoria Reavis, telegrapher, was suggesting clandestine murder.

They were speaking quietly into the warm nighttime air of his room with only the sound of the fire burning crisply through the oak rounds. His fever was nearly gone on this third day, and he had dressed himself in shirt and trousers, the better to lean upright against the headboard and look at her. He wanted her very badly, but this was not something that was going to happen.

"I want people to know," he said. His hands were on top of each other, strictly clean and trimmed and lying lax on his stomach. "I want them to know. That he's dead. That nobody can do this to my family and live. And so we only have this short time, you see. Look, it's nine o'clock already." He reached for her hand and laced her small fingers between his own.

"Yes," she said. "Already." She was stricken with ambiguous and undefined feelings and did not know how to name them or even speak of them. He saw the confusion on that open and candid face, her large brown eyes and nearly colorless eyebrows, her eyelids bluish and deep. She looked so good in candlelight, he thought. Or in daylight, or in the light from the hall as she walked into his room. "Another day," he said. "Maybe two. But we're going for a ride together before I go. Don't be sad."

"But there has to be some other way." Her voice quavered, and she quickly cleared her throat, looked down and then up again.

"There isn't." He touched her mouth with his forefinger. "It will be short, crude, and public."

He turned up his palm, and she placed her hand against his, flat and, in a way, promissory. She felt held there by his large presence and his proximity and the smell of laundered shirt and himself, also recently laundered, old scents of leather and horse and the uncommon stillness of the hour as it shut up around them.

FOUR DAYS LATER, the twelfth of January of 1867, they rode out together toward the Sabine River. She had come to his room carrying his old, repaired trousers from the tailor and sat on his bed while he shaved in front of the mirror over the washstand. Steam drifted up from the basin of hot water, and they spoke together easily now, familiar and comfortable with each other. There were no more stories to tell. They had recounted all their pasts as well as they might and had arrived at the current day. He felt her presence there behind him as he rinsed the blade and wiped it on a towel, shut it and slid it into the case.

"Is the world still out there?" he asked, smiling. "I will have to leave tomorrow."

She nodded. Somehow she could not speak. She wore a little derby and a neat riding habit with quite a lot of skirt to be gathered in the left hand. He buckled on his cartridge belt, pulled on the big overcoat, took up his pommel holster and revolver, and put on his hat. Then he tucked the smaller pistol into the overcoat pocket.

"I'll teach you how to shoot," he said. "Then you can make your brothers jealous."

Long sandbanks were being flayed by the wind. The layers of fine red sand were being redistributed in long waves downriver. Dixie trotted relentlessly behind. It was a foggy, cold day; mist crawled over the river's surface, and long-legged birds flew ahead of them with cries of warning. She had a fine bay horse and her dark blue skirts poured down the horse's left side. She was happy and laughing, and she and the horse seemed to make up a procession announcing something. She should have been carrying a flag.

When they came to the deep sand, they got off to walk. He stood by her horse's side and reached up both arms to take her light-boned body between his two hands and lifted her down, out of the confining sidesaddle and away from the horses' side so that her skirts swung out. For a moment, a brief, quick, guilty flash, she thought about how good it would be to be lifted out of her life of endless concern for others. She had long been a parent to her giddy mother and a mother to her brothers. To be lifted out and away. To be a telegrapher forever and sometimes, surprisingly, find a person like this person by chance or by grace. In these conflicting thoughts she took up her front hems and struck out ankle-deep into the sand.

They held the reins and walked side by side. After a moment he took her hand and tucked her arm into his elbow. Dry January basswood leaves curled like shellfish, brown and hard, where the wind had blown them into every dip of the broad sandbank. On the other shore the leafless hardwoods made a gray haze. He stopped to run his gaze over the tree line on the far side of the Sabine to check it tree by tree, but of course there were no hidden Confederate sharpshooters or pickets. He made himself stop and then saw a giant cypress log carried down at some remote time by a flood.

"That's a good place to sit." He was still slightly weak, but good hotel food delivered three times a day, plus whiskey and quinine, had done wonders.

"Look at it—it's a giant!" she said in a delighted voice and trudged through the deep sand toward it.

He felt she wanted to say something; he didn't know what. He waited, watching the tree line on the opposite shore, and told himself he was looking for deer or perhaps otters. He heard her clear her throat and turn to face him. He lifted his large hand with its rein calluses and thick, muscled wrist to run his palm down her cheek to rest on her neck, his thumb under her jaw. The feel of her fine skin made him draw breath.

"Let's be quiet," he said. "Let's not talk." They went on a few steps. "I have something more to say, but I am thinking of how to say it."

When they sat down, Dixie bumped Victoria's hand until she was petted and then lay down to sleep. It occurred to him that this was what normal people did. That this was ordinary and common and that these ordinary, common things were attained at great cost; they were actually fragile and could be destroyed even in a matter of days by artillery, by riots, by hatred. A man and a woman met and spent calm, unruffled hours in each other's company, they rode out together on peaceful small journeys to talk and laugh together, and nothing was on fire, people did not shoot at one another, nothing blew up. Nobody's family was murdered. It was all very usual. He knew he would think about this day in the times to come.

He laid the little Smith & Wesson on the broad back of the log and showed her how the barrel disengaged, how to take out the cylinder, and how to load it with the prepared cartridges. He took hold of her derby by the brim and lifted it off, laid it on the log, and then stood behind her, directing her in aiming the little .22 revolver, how to hold it steady in both hands. She raised it and fired and did a credible job of hitting an upstanding piece of driftwood fifty yards away. She neither screamed nor flinched.

Then the Remington .44. He warned her it was quite powerful and would kick, and he stood with her between his arms, looking over her head. Her skirts drifted over his boots. He felt her light body against his chest where the big overcoat had opened. The gun bucked up into the air, and she nearly dropped it, and so he told her to stay with the Smith & Wesson. The reports of the gunfire rattled through the bare trees and cracked up off the water.

He looked in his saddlebags and took out the box of loads for her, and he placed the box on the broad back of the great cypress log. He told her she must never get within reaching distance of a threat; she was not strong enough to hold her own. Stay far back and be patient and calm and fire carefully. He wanted to see how fast she could reload. Not good, but he said she must practice. If the threat was serious, fire all seven, reload, and keep shooting. They would think there were two of her.

He said, "I have another cylinder for it."

She paused. "What would I do with it?"

He smiled. "You can switch out cylinders, and then you have fourteen shots altogether. You must practice doing that." He replaced the revolver in the pommel holster and made sure the hammer was sitting on an empty chamber.

"You think I might need it."

"Anything is possible."

"You think Dodd might be in the area."

"And that's possible too."

"Where do you think he's going?"

"Galveston. He's going to take ship as soon as he can get the money." And as he said it a sort of despair came to him like a sudden chemical reaction. It was not overwhelming despair, just a touch of a nonliving hand or breath for which there was no gainsaying, no answer.

"That means going through ships' manifests, asking everywhere."

"Yes."

"But Giddens would have a clear case with you, if you killed Dodd." She was relentless. A sweet and solitary telegrapher with worlds of information flowing through her hands, arranging it, sending it all to the right person or persons, and coming to her own conclusions. They sat down together.

"Yes, he would."

He looked down at her with that slight, fond smile that came so rarely. She was good to look at, unmarked by war or losses, life at her fingertips. He put his arm around her shoulders and tucked her up against his long body and outstretched legs in a way that was anything but brotherly. "I hope you're hungry. We can get dinner at the hotel. I need to sit upright at a table. Rejoin the human race."

He took off his hat and ran his two fingers around the inside band. They rested on the great cypress log and its colors of smoke and steel where it lay in isolation. It seemed they were on a ship moored in an ocean of sand. The flat olive-colored river made small sounds, and somewhere a fish jumped. A slight breeze lifted strands of her hair under the jaunty little derby. The dog and the two horses dozed as if in an enchantment in a fairy tale where the entire world except they two fell asleep, and danger was held back by a hedge of magic thorn, but after all they were on the shore of the Sabine River here on this earth, within this time and Texas. He caught his lower lip in his teeth and stood up. So did she.

Then he took her in both arms and kissed her, long and slow. The flesh is weak. The flesh is intemperate. It is wordless and treacherous. He felt her response and at last merely stood without speaking, one arm holding her against him, his hat in the other hand, his face pressed into her fine brown hair. Then he stood back and held out his hand to her and they walked on down the long sandbar. He bent down to hear her against the small harsh sound of the January wind that had started up.

"I will lose you, John," she said. "And you have lost everybody."

"But I have you. As a friend." He cleared his throat nervously, trying to order his words and thoughts, the most important one being that she was a sanctuary in herself: sane, lovely, and at the moment occupied with blurred eyes and Dixie treading on her skirt hems. "We could actually plight troth. Have you ever plighted a troth?"

"Not to any great extent. There was Miley Epworth in fourth grade."

"Doesn't count. But actually, I thought a plight was when you were in a fix."

"Apparently not. I could plight you something or other if I could think of one."

There was a long, contented silence as they walked back to the horses, side by side. Why had he kissed her, then, if he did not want them to be tied together and himself so soon to be brought before a broken justice system? If he could even find Dodd. Because he not only wanted to kiss her but also to do other things. He wanted to start unbuttoning those small pearl buttons on her collar. The top one was already undone.

As they walked on, he tried to recover lost ground. He said, "If we become very much attached it would be misery all around and enough to spare, Miss Victoria. I apologize for the kiss. I could possibly end up in the big house in Huntsville, clanking with chains, eating boiled cotton stalks and dead rats. And then it would be all wretchedness and despair. All our affections shattered and brought to naught." He threw up her horse's reins and held out his hand for her foot.

She stared at him with squinted eyes, suspicious. She had her riding skirts gathered up over her right arm. He could see her slim ankles and the clocked stockings, the silver spur on her left boot.

She said, "You've been reading some novel."

"Yes, that *foutu* Wilkie Collins book. Up you go."

"What does *foutu* mean?"

"Did I say that? Good God, don't use that word. Not ever."

She was laughing as she settled herself. And then, "But of course I am attached to you. It has already happened. And you're bent on your plans and I'll help you any way I can."

"You probably should not. Not any longer." He stood with one hand on her knee and felt the bones of it beneath his spread-open hand, the warmth of her flesh, a kind of taking possession. He watched as a pinkness poured up her neck and into her cheeks so that he took his hand away and stepped back, standing in the bright winter sun with the water reflections from the Sabine running across his hardened face, which now had a look of regret.

But she was not to be flustered and so placed her reins and the crop carefully and just so in her fingers and the flush faded. John swung up and into the saddle and turned to see that she was following just to look again into her face, to see that Dixie and her horse were making it through the deep sand, that the tree line across the river was clear of people or the glint of long-barreled Springfields.

AT DINNER HE sat back in his chair and said very little but took in her every movement, her gestures, her laughter. It was evening, so she could dispense with the hat, and her face was outlined in a smooth backsweep of hair. Without looking he could tell every man in the dining room had glanced at them and their glances lingered on her. John finally turned and raked the room with a precise, assessing stare and they hastily went back to discussions with others at the table.

The waiter said they had very little wheat flour and so no dinner rolls, but the corn bread was superb. Also they had Country Captain chicken and smothered steak. They watched these two dishes sail toward them in his hands, through the crowded restaurant, and realized how hungry they were.

After a while he saw that his answers were short and not conversational, and so he gathered his wits and made himself entertaining. He told funny stories about finding Dixie and her pups, the leaden personality of his big plow horse, all the while wanting to be alone with her and say things and do things of far greater consequence. He kept thinking of her in a low-cut dress at a ball or a dance, whatever they had here, of them riding out again together, just the two of them, of the rigors of clothing and clothing's impenetrable nature, of fig leaves and lace.

But what he had meant to say as they walked in the sands of the Sabine River and had been unable to was that she deserved a man who was studious, stable, somebody of consequence, somebody with family. Somebody who had a house and lived in a town. That would probably be a person back in Louisville. He had no intention of ruining those chances.

He decided to try again. He began in a firm tone. "I can't thank you enough for your care for me, for which you have my eternal gratitude." She ducked her head and looked upward at him with a suspicious glance. "And I don't want to be one of those sorts who take advantage of a girl for, well, a passing sort of adventure or . . . That's not the word. Wait. Wait." He leaned back and looked around, seeking the right phrase. "Your help and kindness, among other things. Information. You've done a great deal for me, which is enormously appreciated." He lifted a hand to stop her answer. "I'm sounding like an after-dinner speaker, I know."

"It's like an award presentation," she said. "Most appreciated member of the church landscaping committee."

"Yes, hush, listen. I'm trying." He cleared his throat and continued in a formal tone. "I expect you have a friend back home. You are beautiful and charming, and any grown man who hasn't paid attention to you ought to be abandoned on a desert island somewhere." He paused. "Again, I apologize for kissing you." Another pause. "It was uncalled-for."

She turned up her face to him, unsmiling and serious. "I *like* you. You're *brave*."

"Victoria," he started.

"Vicky."

"Miss Reavis, you have to understand I have no future. Or if there is, you don't want to be part of it. I don't want you to be part of it. It will not be pleasant. Do you understand this?"

"Of course." She had a blank look, between puzzled and suspicious. "Of course I understand it. We have to do our best to avoid it." She paused with a bite of chicken, dripping garlic and tomatoes, on her fork.

"There's nothing more I can ask of you. And I've asked for a lot."

"I see. You mean you'll be gone looking for Dodd and then you'll do him in and then it's prison or flight."

"Yes."

"Because Giddens is a hound dog."

"That's about it." He wanted to reach across and take her hand and didn't. "Why are we going through this? I'll reach Galveston in a few days, and it's possible I'll take ship."

She tipped her head to one side. "Alone."

"Yes, of course."

"No female companionship?"

"In Galveston? Depends on what you mean by companionship."

"Never mind, I have three . . ."

"Three brothers, I know. Let us hope they continue in Christian charity and purity of soul according to the Lord's commandments and don't wear themselves out with untoward experiments on riverboats."

He said this in a quiet voice while around them the hotel restaurant was full of loud-talking people, families, men in counsel with each other, absorbed in serious matters. The tall windows were steamed, and waiters hurried here and there with little china pitchers of gravy.

He said carefully, "There is no good outcome here. There is no happy ending to this."

"No." She put one hand to her eyes, then laid it in her lap again. "No, there's not."

"But I will always love thinking about this time, and maybe even thinking of you with somebody who'll be amazed and delighted by your sending thirty words a minute. Somebody who'll love that beautiful hair and your eyes, maybe even your brothers."

"You're going to make me cry."

"Don't do it."

"All right." She was tempted to wipe her eyes on her napkin, he could tell, but refrained. He smiled, watching her. She said, "Tell me what you would have done if all this had not happened?"

He thought, *I would fall on one knee and offer you all my lands and chattels as well as my entire anatomy, scarred up as it is, which I hope you would not find displeasing as I have not had any complaints on that score.* He said, "We would spend hours and days together. And then at some point we would have dinner at the Capitol Hotel. We would be joyous and disreputable. I would finish an entire plate of smothered steak and corn bread. On one side of us would be a man in a tailcoat eating corned beef and cabbage and on the other hand would be . . ."

She leaned forward and whispered, "A table full of people where the men are all drinking too much. And you've changed the subject."

"Of course I have. The other subject was likely to get seductive." He saw the color rise in her face. "And I have a great many words for that. Far too many, Miss Reavis. To wit: *Entice. Allure. Debauch.*"

"And it's an enjoyable sort of thing? Debauching?" She couldn't meet his eyes.

He watched her face for a moment. "The fun never ends." He moved his head from one side to the other as if stretching against a too-tight collar. "Victoria, I don't have to explain why I can't ask anything of you. Nothing. Nothing."

"Why did I say that?" she said. She fanned her hot face.

"Because you're thinking of how good it would be to have Aubrey in the world again and alive."

"And you. Free of all the trouble."

He hesitated and then said, "Perhaps."

"Your face is very serious."

A creeping, diffuse sadness had come upon him. It was like a change in temperature, a change in the light.

"I'm sorry. This was a great day. A long, great, beautiful day."

"I can help." She leaned forward, appealing, squashing her napkin in her hand.

"But of course you understand what I just said." A wordless silence fell between them. "I have no future."

"But that's terrible, not having a future!"

"I can't stand this," he said and reached across the table and pressed his large hand on her wrist, pressed hard. "Stop."

"Let me come with you. I can go through ships' passenger lists with the best of them."

"Girl," he said.

"What?"

He rolled his head back and looked up at the pressed-tin ceiling all full of curlicues. "Let's have the meringue."

He walked with her to the Masonic Female academy. He wanted to put both arms around her and hold her very closely this one last time, but if he did he would never let her go. Instead he took her hand in a formal way. His whole body seemed to withdraw inside his greatcoat as something cool, remote, disengaged. Somebody else would do the taking care, another man would join her in that daunting enterprise of plighting troth, not him. With a sudden flash of anger at himself he felt his eyes burning and damp. He touched his hat brim to her and turned away quickly without speaking. He returned to his hotel room and began to pack.

John threw his shirts and gloves onto the bed and started stuffing things into his saddlebags without thinking of her. It took some rather painful and grim determination, but he did it. He kept his thoughts on the road ahead. He knew his calculations as to Dodd's behavior were tentative at best, but they were all he had to go on. He was counting on the probability that Dodd would take ship and then John would be able to find his name on a ship's record as enrolled. It would be a gift from God to be on the same ship with him. It would take care of the awkwardness of disposing of the body. And after that was emptiness.

•••

THE NEXT MORNING on the main street he pulled off his glove and bent down to take her hand. They were in front of the Capitol, and John didn't care who saw them or who remarked on them. She was going to tell him to be careful. He didn't know what he would say in reply. Being careful was not in his plans. He looked long and intently at her open, honest face.

To his relief she said nothing about taking care. "I hope you find him," she said fervently. "And kill him graveyard dead."

"I am going to do my best," he said with a slight smile. "I may not see you again."

"Oh yes, you will."

She turned to see the drab Irish child called Bronaugh wanting her attention by pulling on her skirt. When she turned back again he was riding away into the crowded street, sitting his saddle easily, his rifle on his back, the buttstock standing up between his broad shoulders.

CHAPTER TWENTY-FIVE

Late January 1867 / South toward Galveston

THE ROAD TO GALVESTON WENT south from the courthouse square and past many a grand house on the way out, houses of brick with double chimneys and Pride of India trees now bare as broomstraws. This all soon gave way to the forests.

The first town of any size he would come to would be Nacogdoches. There were small places in between. The road was cut through heavy timber, and there was very little undergrowth. The pines were enormous. He rode through that pine forest that stretches from southeastern Missouri through western Arkansas and Louisiana and East Texas, a primeval and uncut dark fabric grown up untouched since God made the hills. Beneath these giant trees were darknesses without end as well as ginseng and the clear poisons of a great variety of snakes hunting slowly as they unwound themselves toward their prey. No other travelers on the road as yet, but the day was young.

He hadn't the slightest doubt that Dodd would circle back and waylay him if he could, if he knew where John was. He watched the road ahead and searched the passing giant boles to either side, depending on Dixie to give him a warning of anybody approaching from behind. The roadway was of a sandy soil, and so Major made little noise as he paced southward.

John tried to shut down his recent images of her, but his mind revolved back and back again despite him. How she and Lalie would have liked each other. The girl was rich in family, wealthy in brothers, and for herself she had a future, a homely and untroubled warmth waiting for her somewhere, and that somewhere would not include him.

Winter shadows ran in long lines from the trunks. They dwarfed him on his big horse. Thin shelves of snow lay unmelted. He could see his breath. It rained off and on and made bright red puddles in the iron-saturated dirt. The trees were so tall they met overhead and the road was a tunnel between them. He heard the double note of a Carolina wren, piercing and insistent. Far above the canopy sailed a red-tailed hawk. Once he heard the call of a wolf. He liked hearing it. He pulled up and listened. He was riding along with both anger and sorrow in the back of his mind like some equipage he could not rid himself of, and so he liked the sound of that singular cry of wildness and life unhindered.

He made camp at Ramsdale's Ferry and then the next day he was on Trammel's Trace, which was in places worn down into the earth like a tube. He made camp well off the road and sat up late to listen. The waning moon came and went behind blind traveling cloud masses. His fire was small and hot with pine branches. The sparks shone in Dixie's eyes.

So he came to Nacogdoches. It was an old town of stone buildings, on a slight rise where it stood in the smoky air of a Spanish trading town from the last century. The trees came directly up to the town's boundaries. Somewhere a steeple with a bell in it sounded out the round and resinous hours of the piney woods and noon.

John splashed across a shallow bayou that rose to his stirrups, then up the hill. There was a small collection of steep-roofed houses and, as always, a town square of beaten earth. He heard a great deal of noise from that direction. He stopped to listen.

There was a kind of torrent of sound, a tinny sort of gibberish at high volume. This meant an excited crowd. It also meant somebody was addressing the crowd. A leader, an inciter.

They were gathered in front of an old stone building. Loud, angry voices, and through this he heard a plaintive sort of running talk in a high tone, which was the sound of somebody trying to explain themselves and not succeeding. Laughter and then shouts and insults.

"What's happening?" He rode into the fringes of the crowd and then stood in his stirrups in an attempt to see what was going on. A man on foot beside him stood with both fists on his hips and his coat open to the wind.

"We've had enough lawbreaking around here," the man said to him. "Military rule, what good is it? They don't do anything, and men shooting one another and thieves making off with anything they can lay their hands on. The innocent laid low and the common man without remedy."

Another man hurried alongside them and cried out, "Oh yes, yes, certainly, they're fed up with crime running rampant! Then they're going to commit a crime themselves! Does that make any sense?" The two started arguing, and so John pressed on until he came into the square. It was packed with horses and men. Chickens and dogs ran pell-mell between people's legs. He was half expecting what it was when he was finally able to see over the heads of the crowd. Yes, there he was, it was Lemuel indeed, hoisted by the suspenders by a man much taller than he was, and the boy's hands were waving, making circles. *I had one like it! I thought it was mine!* John could see that his face was cut up and one eye was swollen shut.

"Excuse me, excuse me, coming through." John pressed his horse forward. The crowd was thickest in front of the old stone building. Before this building the man stood on the running gear of a freight wagon and he had jerked Lemuel up onto the reachers. He was holding something in the air.

"And what have we here?" he shouted. "Hey?"

At the far ends of the crowd men and a few women stood in wagon beds to see. Some boys were up on a roof gawking with their hands shading their eyes. The pines out in the uncut forest were taller than the buildings and looked over the heads of the boys, and the wind was bringing up big sodden gray clouds that sagged at the bottoms with their loads of rain.

"I'll be damned," said John. He got off the big horse, tied him to the nearest thing he could find, which was the handle on a large clay flowerpot with some sort of straggling plant in it. He made a quick decision about his revolver, shucked the rifle and jammed it into the straps of his saddlebags, and then unbuckled his belt and drew it off. Then he rolled it around his right hand with the buckle uppermost. He elbowed his way through the crowd. The town square was small and easily filled, so the crowd looked bigger than it was. Some few black people had formed a fringe on the eastern edge of the square, but it seemed most had decided to stay far away from irate white men in crowds.

The man who had Lemuel by the suspenders was holding up a gold watch with a chain, and the golden chain slithered glittering through his fingers.

"He had one like it!" he bellowed to the crowd. "He thought it was his!"

A roar of laughter. Then the man jammed his fist into Lemuel's back, shoved him forward, and then jerked him back again. The suspenders stretched out and slackened. The man kept doing this. John was appalled to see two or three soldiers in Union blue watching and laughing at the natives and their peculiar customs.

John shoved people aside to get to the front. Several men turned angrily and then saw how big he was and the look on his face, so they fell into indistinguishable noises of affront and let him pass.

"What are we going to do with him?" the speaker called out to the crowd. He was having fun, being up front, all eyes on himself. His hat was on the back of his head, and he was the King of Nacogdoches and the Prince of Glee, at least as long as he could hold everybody's attention. Lemuel's hands flew out, trying to balance himself. "What'll we do with him?" The boy's mouth was bleeding.

"Hang him!"

"Drag him behind a horse!"

"Headfirst down Menchaca's well!"

John walked through the crowd using his elbows. A man said, "Hold on there, fellow," and John gave him a good rap on the sternum with the belt buckle and passed on. A circle had gathered there in the front, packed tight, and as always with a street speaker they left an empty space inviolate in front of and around the speaker into which no one ever ventured. John did not know why this was, but it was. He walked straight into that space, stepped up on the wagon bed, and broke the man's hold on Lemuel's suspenders by crashing the belt buckle down on his knuckles. The boy was the color of limestone, and his head was shaking. He looked up and cried out, "Oh my God, Mr. Chenneville! Mr. Chenneville!"

"Sir!" The speaker stood back with his back extremely straight and the watch in one hand. The watch shone in the sunlight, and his mouth was open in astonishment. John jammed the belt into his pocket.

"Give me that Goddamned thing," he said and wrenched the watch and chain out of the man's hand. "If you mess with me I'll knock you flat on your back." The man began to bluster, which meant he was not going to do anything, and John turned to Lemuel. The boy shook like a leaf; he was shaking all over, including his knees. He was about to sink into a faint.

John held up the watch and called out to the crowd, "Whose is this?"

A tall thin man in the very back of the crowd called out, "Mine!"

John stood back on his right foot and launched the shining watch with its chain like a flying kite tail into the crowd. Best thing to do was to get rid of the point of contention. A man caught it, and it was handed back from person to person until it reached the hand of the thin man. Then John grabbed Lemuel's shirtfront, jumped down to the dirt street, swung Lemuel down after him, and backed the boy up against one of the stone building's verandah posts. He stood in front of him.

"If you lay hands on him, you are going to have to get past me," he called out. "I know him. I'm standing up for him, and I won't move, I won't give in. So come on." He made a come-hither gesture with one hand. "Come on."

His words were repeated one to another back and back like an echo. Nobody moved. He was a head taller than any other man in the crowd. His eyes were alarmingly pale, and his huge overcoat was so weather-beaten that it looked like it had become bulletproof, and so everybody thought twice about responding to the invitation.

All that could be seen of Lemuel, behind John's broad body, were his feet and white shirt elbows, so the object of their rage was now out of sight. The noise began to settle and slow. Instead of a crowded, packed roar of broken phrases, people began to speak in complete sentences. They were not shouting. There was nothing to shout at. The boys on the roofs of the wooden shops and stores stood up and watched intently.

Lemuel had hold of the back of John's jacket and was mashed up against the big square post. He started to say something, to move out to the side, but John brought his fist up to his chin and then drove his elbow backward into Lemuel's chest in a powerful blow. The boy said, "Ooof!" and hunched up still.

Somebody laughed. A gray-headed man with a high silk hat in one hand called out, "Do you testify for him, then? Do you stand security?"

"Yes." John was shouting, his words repeated. "I was in a field hospital for a year in City Point, Virginia. He was an attendant there." The crowd became silent. Texans like a good story, and this sounded like it might go somewhere. "He was a nurse. He saved my life. If it weren't for his care, I wouldn't be alive. I don't give a damn what he did. You all have got no courts, no judges, and no sheriffs worth a shit. That man got his watch and chain back, and so I'm leaving Nacogdoches now. He's riding behind me. I'm carrying my revolver in front of me, cocked and loaded."

"He's a thief!" somebody shouted.

John shouted back, "I know it!"

He walked through the thickly packed men and their astonished faces, dragging Lemuel behind him. The crowd had separated now, like clabber from whey. People had started to talk among themselves, one man to another, one woman to another, and so the cohesion of the mob was broken up and the flash point of rage and indignation, Lemuel and the gold watch, were separated and rendered harmless. John had hold of the boy's suspenders. He located Major, who was wandering toward the grass on the little courthouse lawn, pulling the remains of the clay flowerpot with him.

John knew the crowd wanted more, more of the story, but he was not going to give it to them. It would involve questions and arguing. John didn't like to argue. There was never any point to it. He untied the big horse from the dragging crockery handle, stepped into the stirrup, and swung up.

"Get up, asshole," he said to Lemuel and threw his leg forward of the stirrup so Lem could get his foot into it. The boy clambered up as John loosed his revolver from the pommel holster and pulled the hammer back two clicks. Everybody heard it. *Click-click.*

"My stuff!" said Lemuel.

"Too bad," said John. "We're not going to go hunt it up."

The man with the gray hair and the silk topper came beside them and said, "I will walk alongside you out of town."

"If you wish," said John. The man was going to stand security for them, as he himself had done for Lemuel. "Much appreciated."

"Here is your coat, young thief." The man handed up a thick brown wool sack coat. Lemuel snatched at it with quivering hands. At a slow pace they went down the main street toward the south, and Major, utterly unexcited, plodded along with his great feet and looked longingly at the winter grass on lawn after lawn.

"When is this all going to stop?" the man said.

"Beats me," said John and lifted his hat briefly to the man as they parted at the edge of town, and so he and Lemuel went on.

A mile into the forest John made Lemuel get down and walk. Dixie came running up to them with her ears flying. She'd become separated in the excitement and by the exhilarating smells of the crowd, delayed by other dogs, distracted by a pile of chicken guts, but at last she had caught up and took her rightful place at Major's heels. John lowered the hammer of the revolver slowly and carefully and reholstered it and bent forward to feed his belt back into its loops. Here was something else to foul up and complicate his search for Dodd. What next? It was discouraging. He hated to admit it, but it was discouraging.

Lemuel walked alongside with his head drooping. He was now bereft of everything: whatever baggage he had, probably some money, certainly a few other things he'd stolen. He was still shaking, and he pawed tears out of his eyes. He was careful with the swollen left eye. It would soon be blackened and baggy. The cuts on his face were from blows, probably a whipstock.

"They were going to kill me."

"Looked like it," said John. He buckled the belt. "I want you to swear you'll never steal another thing in this life, for all the good it will do. The thing is, it would involve me, and then there would be shooting. So consider reforming. Permanently, or maybe just until you've gone your way."

Lemuel walked on, close to Major's side. "I swear to God, never again. I mean, it was just laying there anyhow." His coat was suspiciously new, while his boots were breaking out at the toes.

"Things usually do just lay there."

"I swear right here and now, forever from this here place I am standing on, never to take anything that's not mine. Even if it is just laying there in the middle of the woods. As God is my witness. May He strike me dead."

"That's very convincing," said John. "We'll see what happens when there's nobody threatening to hang you."

Lemuel held himself with both arms. He had probably also been kicked in the ribs. "Where are we going?"

"Galveston. You can come or not."

"I think Galveston sounds good." Lemuel bit his lower lip to stop it from trembling.

"Where were you going in the first place?"

"Galveston."

John considered that sometimes fairy tales become true, at least in certain details. The detail being that Ti-Jean gathered all sort of animals in his wake, all of them asking to join him for no reason John could ever figure out, but they were on their way to the Giant's House, and in his case it was the Giant part of your mind that deals in such things as murder, revenge, trickery, and fighting. And also this persistent sorrow that was growing on him and that he could not shake.

"I need to get to a telegraph," John said. Lemuel didn't answer; he was out of breath.

ON THE WAY south of Nacogdoches, through the great forest, they passed a white family afoot and packing everything they owned, including three hounds that got in a fight with Dixie until the man took his walking staff and beat enthusiastically on his own dogs and John took Dixie up on the saddle. They passed by black people walking who said nothing but gave a quick nod when they saw John's Union greatcoat. People were draining south like wintertime migratory birds. On the way he gave Lemuel a brief account of where he was going and why. That it mainly concerned a man named A. J. Dodd who had killed a member of John's family and the situation needed resolving.

John was tired of telling this story. It was a terrible tale, and it left him bereft every time and a man apart from others and weak, somehow. Someone whose family could be killed and he could do nothing about it. An unlucky man following the telegraph poles. Voices he could not hear.

Lemuel listened and fell silent.

John tried to call a halt to that kind of thinking, to think ahead. Consider the next step. For instance, Galveston. This was going to take a great deal of time, and now he was weeks behind Dodd at the outside. The idea of living in a coastal city while grinding through books of enrollment in shipping offices, walking here and there to ask about the man, describing him, tracking him down through boardinghouses and bars, asking the local provost marshal about murders, deaths, and missing persons, was disheartening. John was sure the man was going to kill again, and a chaotic, occupied city would be fertile ground for him.

After a while he pulled up Major to wait for the boy. He wondered if perhaps his search had come to an end. If there was no further place to go. This was a foreign country to him. His demons were now interior ones: discouragement, bafflement, weariness. A flush of anger came to him. It was unfair, unfair. He stopped this internal monologue by looking up quickly, seeing the forest around him and the deep red soil in the road leaching into the puddles as if in remembrance of some ancient crime. The woodland seemed bitter and disordered, and he remembered a better way of life with great imperishable rivers and silky hayfields in windblown waves and apple blossom petals cascading like snow. They were a great possession, those memories.

But still he was, he had to admit, at his wits' end. How much strength did he have left? Was it a certain quantity, like the ten gallons in a keg, the sixty-two gallons in a hogshead, so many feet in a *toise*, acres in an arpent? And once it was gone, it was gone.

Lemuel was talking at him. ". . . and so I came down with the freighter hauling the millstones."

"I see." John dug out the Colton map. Next town of any significance was Livingston. It was a small archipelago of log houses and waist-high stumps in the surrounding great woods with a thin copper line coming down from Nacogdoches.

When they got there he gave Lem a dollar in silver and told him to get as much corn as fifty cents would buy and something for Dixie and whatever supplies he could find for themselves.

At the log-built post office John tied up and walked in, while a man sat outside on the steps and watched him.

"Is there a telegraph connection?"

"Operator's gone to Marshall to do the books with the lady operator up there. She knows how. He don't. The military's been by. They's been a boy killed."

"When?"

"Been more than three weeks. Military's always late to the party." The man wore a narrow-brimmed hat and two different shoes. "Now, I don't care for electricity myself. I wouldn't touch it with a ten-foot pole. There are things about it we don't know."

"That's probably true. But for now, is it working?"

"Yes, it is. He left the circuit open."

"I can send myself." And without asking permission he walked into the little office where dead flies dotted the windowsill like raisins and a five-foot rattlesnake skin had been stretched onto the wall with carpet tacks. He saw that everything had been disconnected and so set about reconnecting it all. He attached the local battery, the ground wire and relay battery. He rapped the key, and it sparked.

OP MARSHALL TX PM TO BELLE. This was to tell other operators to stay off the line.

Within a minute the reply came in.

134?

SNOWMAN

Then the reply came in International Morse and pig latin.

REC'D. NEWS OF YOU WELCOME. MRSHL. G. DELAYED ON
ANOTHER CASE BOY KILLED ON TENAHA TRACE AFTER
NYEAR'S. SZ HE HAS INFO ON YOUR MAN BCAUSE VISITED
GAROUTE AND NOW MRSHL G DROPPED OUT OF SIGHT SO NO
NEWS G. R YOU WELL? KN

He smiled in spite of all his anxious thoughts. There she was in a shower of sparks. He didn't reply for a moment. His big, callused hand paused above the key, and he wondered if she had her hair securely pinned, if she had left that one pearl button undone, the one at the top of her ruffled collar.

NEVER BETTER. ANY INFO ON DODD KN

TRYING. SFR NEGATIVE. G FEARS DODD HAS KILLED BOY SO IS
PROBABLY ON THE TENAHA.

AM EN ROUTE TO GALVESTON 88

88

John asked about the location of the Tenaha Trace. It passed to the south nearby, the man said. It hits the Camino Real going west to San Antonio. John knew that if this was Dodd, seized again by a hunger for slaughter, then he would have killed and be moving on, and quickly.

Then they went on through the woods. The giant trees reached up to one hundred and eighty feet, trees that were ten feet around and made reedy, hushing noises in the evening wind. The trees seemed to possess a huge indifferent intelligence that lay just beyond the reach of human knowledge. The trunks drove toward the sky in towers. He watered Major at a crossing called Dog Pond Creek, and there he saw that the red sandy soil had been churned up by a great many horses and the bootprints of men on foot. Lemuel drank extravagantly of the reddish water, lifting handfuls to his swollen mouth.

They then came upon a patrol that was dismounting and preparing to camp. Given the nature of the country and the loose characters wandering the roads, John sought out the captain of the patrol and asked to camp with them. All of the men's trousers were plastered with red dirt up to their shins.

The captain stared at John's greatcoat and his horse and especially the pommel holster. He questioned John closely, asked for his discharge papers, and said a boy had been murdered on the other southern trace, Tenaha, and they were looking for who might have done it. Then he nodded and handed John's discharge papers back to him. "As you like, sir."

Lemuel went out to collect firewood and observe the troops unloading in the shade of the winter pines. John thought about rescuing him a second time if he lifted something and decided he would not. He was still in a black mood. He unsaddled and fed Major, gave Dixie her ration of dried beef, and spread out his blankets. Lemuel came back and flopped down, exhausted from the long day's walk, with one arm around Dixie. The time of day gave out that evening settling feeling in the resinous smell of the pines and the tarnishing damp that rises from a winter woods.

"I'll cook," Lemuel said.

"Glad to hear it," said John. "Honest work builds character." He unbuckled his cartridge belt and drew off his spurs, laid them on his bedroll.

"I got some pigs' feet and hominy."

"God."

John listened to the soldiers around him. Every word seemed some strange phrase of dejection and unhappiness. Their voices were rough and flat, and their speech composed of short sentences. There was no laughter here. He leaned back. He was hungry, but the thought of food repelled him. He tried to comfort himself with images of the San Bois Mountains, the Winding Stair Hills, their isolation and cleanliness. In the snow they had been so beautiful and silent. About Belle, finally and inevitably. Lifting her up to the saddle. She couldn't have weighed a hundred and ten pounds. His hand on her knee. That sweet electric flush. But at present let us consider other things more seemly, like pigs' feet and hominy.

"Hell no, we're just wanting to go home," said a soldier by a campfire next over. "This is *not* what I signed up for."

He was talking to another soldier beside him. They were both enlisted and their uniforms were faded and their shoes were sodden with red mud, but the man's voice was precise and educated, a Midwestern accent. He turned to John sitting in the smoke of Lemuel's sooty campfire. He was sawing at his rifle barrel with the ramrod and dislodging grains of unfired powder. He stood and gazed down at John, at his horse and his gear.

"Who are you?"

"Just traveling," said John. "Got any books?"

"Oh, at one time I had several." He glanced over at John with interest. "This was when we were among the civilized." He extracted the ramrod from the barrel and clicked it into its holder. "And people say, *Do you read books?* As if I would read, I don't know, playbills or accounting ledgers." He came to sit nearby. He took off his forage cap and vigorously scratched his head. He was a bearded man with a cap mark in his hair and a private's insignia. He leaned back against a pine he had chosen for his own for the night and dragged out a pipe. He lit it. It was bad tobacco; John could smell it. Barrel leavings. "So tell me your favorite, then."

John said, "That's poor tobacco. Here." He pulled his own tobacco bag out of his saddlebag. It was the last of the Chenneville crop, fair and blond, aged to perfection. He handed a pinch of it to the soldier. The man put it in the pipe bowl and lit it and nodded. Dark crawled out of the earth and seeped up into the overstory. Major ate his shelled corn with great crushing noises.

"That's excellent. That's top-rail stuff. And so you read books?" He sounded almost hopeful.

John smiled briefly, and then the smile went away. "Yes. I've been stuck with *The Woman in White* for months."

"Oh, that. A mystery, involving a city police detective, I believe. I never liked Wilkie Collins. Now, there's something new I managed to buy when we were in Natchez. It's called *Alice's Adventures in Wonderland*. It's extremely odd."

"Odd how?"

The soldier waved this away. "Hard to explain. Other than that, I had a copy of *Barry Lyndon*, but I misplaced it in St. Louis on the way down. Or it was stolen. Maybe on the steamer. The Mississippi is a thousand-mile sewer, and I defy anybody to tell me otherwise."

John listened to the tones of disdain, which came so easily as to seem habitual with the man. Along with his own personal sense of discouragement this was not doing him any good. He said, "What's this unit? Where are you all from?"

"Me? I'm Thirty-Third Illinois. Fifty-seven of us got transferred from the Thirty-Third to this outfit, Forty-Sixth Illinois. We had orders to go home, but here we are, in darkest Texas. The Forty-Sixth is a wicked, depraved, iniquitous outfit of farm laborers and Germans."

"Thirty-Third Illinois?"

"Yes. Perhaps you've heard of our deeds of valor. Our fame has spread far and wide." Then he laughed and puffed out clouds of pipe smoke that slid in planes between the boles of the immense cathedral pines where they shone red in all the campfires. John sat quietly as if this small hope, this narrow chance, were a bird within reach of his hand and about to fly.

"You all were in Missouri," he said.

The man turned to him and regarded him silently, John's length and his greatcoat. John's accent was slightly southern.

The soldier said, "You-*all*? I thought you read books."

"Yes. I do."

There was a short silence. "Our men have been getting ambushed by people around here." He stared at John and closed and then opened his eyes slowly. "We were ambushed in Missouri as well." And so the air of evening soured into a thin hostility between them, between John and every other soldier in the camp.

John said nothing. He placed each thing in his mind; his revolver was in the pommel holster buckled to his saddle, close to hand, and the carbine was on its buttstock and leaning against the tree. It had perhaps four or five rounds in it and more in the cartridge belt. Things you always want to keep in mind. The soldier said, "That's an old army greatcoat you got there."

"It is. I was with a New York State outfit. We were sent to Virginia. I'm from Missouri."

"How come you joined a New York State outfit?"

"Relatives. My mother's relatives. Did you ever know anybody named Albert Dodd?"

"Yes. I do."

John lay back on his elbows, suspended and stilled. He crossed his long, booted legs at the ankle and said, "Seen much of him?"

Lemuel sat up with his eyes pegged wide open and startled but then instantly, and wisely, yawned a great wide yawn. He lay back on one of John's blankets and started petting Dixie.

The man was still suspicious. "Here and there," he said. "He's a peculiar sort. How do you know him?"

"I don't. I know his brother. His brother has died, and they need help back home in Illinois. I said I'd try to find word of him."

Lemuel sat and listened to this outrageous lie and put all the tips of his fingers together with an air of puzzlement, gazing at John and the soldier out of his blackened eye. John hoped he would not open his mouth and reveal his thick southern Richmond accent.

"I didn't know he had a brother," the soldier said. "He isn't from Illinois, anyway. He was just living in Cairo when the war came and he joined up with us. Why would you think he's from Illinois?"

"Where is he?" said John. "Do you have any idea?"

The soldier gave him a squinted and suspicious look and got to his feet slowly. John, with a dropping interior feeling, knew that the bird had flown.

"No, I do not." The soldier settled into a blank, neutral expression. He closed his coat against the winter evening. He had the air of a man who had not fought a normal war, a man whose friends had been shot from ambush in a hostile country and who had learned the hard way that you gave no information to strangers who had a tinge of a southern accent and had appeared upon a lonely road out of nowhere with a boy who had clearly received a serious beating.

"Well, he needs to get this message."

The soldier smiled. "Not a hope in hell," he said. "You have something else going on here. You've been reading too many of those sensationalist novels, I warrant. *Ivanhoe*?" The man's laugh was unpleasant, and it seemed a bit triumphant because he had something that somebody else wanted and he could refuse. "You should give up reading things like *Ivanhoe*."

John was not good at appealing to people. He didn't know how. He was never very convincing, and he had told few lies in his life because he could not make people believe him and wasn't interested in doing so. Deception was for the weak, and direct action was always better. He sat and pondered how to handle this, what to do. He thought it might be possible to follow this troupe in their patrolling, this group of reluctant men sent to pacify an unpacifiable people. The man had seen bitter and angry country people in Missouri and Arkansas and Louisiana. John didn't want to be considered one of them.

He tried one last time. "He ought to have this news. If you would tell me where I can find him."

"No, sir," the soldier said. "Don't think I will."

"Well, maybe you can get the news to him."

"I might."

The only thing to do was to stay with this patrol and dog the book-ish soldier until he revealed something, sent a telegram to Dodd and was posted a reply. It was the only lead he had now. If he could get the information it would save him a month of fruitless work in Galveston or Houston. John lay back and watched the man walk away. He walked stiffly as if indignant, as if caught at something.

Old man Garoute had said that Dodd stuck close to the Illinois troops on duty in Texas, and he was right, but it had come to a dead end. Where were other Illinois troops? He could ask the captain in charge. But he was tired. Tired to the very bone. For the first time he felt truly defeated. The murder of his sister and her family was some-thing ordained. Ordained and final and a thing that would never be solved or made right.

John put both hands over his eyes to ease the pain, and this made him realize his head hurt. A few pine needles drifted down and spat-tered on his coat, and the sounds of the camp around him seemed surly and tedious with poor jokes and neither songs nor laughter. Everything had a strange, tinny sound.

"Sir?"

John kept his hands over his eyes. "What?"

"That fellow knows where he is. The man you're looking for. He knows."

"He might."

"What are you going to do?"

"I'd like to get drunk, actually."

"Can't help you there." Lemuel handed him a plate of pigs' feet and hominy, and John took it and looked at it. He set it down in the needles and duff. It was night now, and their faces were defined by the flame-light. Around them the camp of soldiers made cooking noises, kettles banging and calls for more firewood, men were told off for guard duty, and the officer's horses ground up corn in their big square teeth. "Well, I was thinking, since you saved my life back there in Nacogdoches and everything, that I would help you go through the ships' manifests and lists and stuff. The enrolled passengers."

"Deck class isn't ever written down."

"I could try."

"You want to see Galveston. You want to see the ocean."

"Not all that much. I seen the Atlantic in Virginia and it was agreeable, but I ain't wild to see a lot of gulf water. I could help."

"All right. I suppose that's next."

"You sound very discouraged."

"I am."

CHAPTER TWENTY-SIX

February 1867 / The Road to San Antonio

HE SLEPT AND WHEN HE woke he did not want to remember any dreams. They would be the old ones of the anchor chain that had destroyed his life and his joy in life, they would be the one where he sought some faceless being in a dark place of contaminating evil. He would wander in a great storehouse trying to sort out the shelves, and the shelves were a mass of confusion and trash.

He was silent as he fed Major, saddled and mounted up. He tried to get a grip on himself. This was no way to live, in this messy chaos of despair. He didn't see Lemuel and wondered if the boy had gone on by himself, and he couldn't make himself care. Dixie was nowhere to be seen. Well, if she wanted to come with him she could make up her own mind. He rode out of the camp of the 46th Illinois and onto the road south. He had been close, but he had been close before, up at Rock Bluff on the Red River, and it had come to nothing. The eye of the spring had swallowed his sister and all her fetching ways into a clear and eternal midnight, and there was no help for it. He pressed his cold hands against his eye sockets and said in a low voice, "Stop, stop."

He paused at a bend of the road and listened. He could hear them moving out. He supposed he missed army life—at least you were given a purpose, a goal, a task, as well as horses and decent rations. As long as you weren't in a hot fight or under bombardment, it was not bad.

So it was Galveston now. He didn't know if he had the will to sustain a long search there, flipping page after page looking for a name, scouring the saloons, but it was the sort of thing that got it done. Slow and steady and unremarkable. Not a fight in a mule barn, not a struggle to get information out of somebody with a broken arm, an old drunk man on a rooftop, or a beautiful telegrapher who deserved somebody better than a man with a head wound and a devastated family.

As he rode through the pines he heard somebody behind him, running. He heard Dixie barking. He pulled up.

"Sir! Sir!"

It was Lemuel. John sat in the saddle and watched as the boy pelted up with his spiky hair and broken shoes and Dixie galloping alongside him. Like all hounds she had a loose skin and it was shining in this sunny morning, her ears flying and jowls flapping as if she were about to fly apart.

"What?" John crossed his hands on the saddle horn.

"I got it." Lemuel was fighting for breath in the chilled and humid air. He stopped, both arms hanging down.

"You got what?"

"I got his letter."

John was silent. Finally he said, "What letter?"

"A letter from A. J. Dodd."

John's heart stopped. Crashed, thudded, and started up again. He said, "A letter. From that Illinois soldier?"

"Yes, sir, I got it. Middle of the night. Went through his saddlebag. And here it is. I guess God is going to strike me dead, but you know you have to trade off one thing for another."

The boy was panting as he grasped the bridle reins. With the other hand he pulled a folded envelope from inside his shirt and held it up. For a moment John was frozen. He was deeply afraid of another disappointment, another dead end. He was afraid not of other men but of despair.

He reached down and took it.

"I'll be Goddamned."

"Read it, sir, read it, it'll tell you where he is."

"Maybe." John looked first at the postmark. It was stamped San Antonio. "It's sent from San Antonio."

"Well, what's the date?"

John glanced at him. The boy already knew. He was now smiling and happy and young and had all his bodily parts and was wiry and his wounds and bruises seemed to count for little. For a moment he wished the boy wasn't a thief, but on the other hand he had gone through a man's possessions in the middle of the night and had gotten away undetected. He hoped.

"January twelfth, 1867," John said. "San Antonio, Texas. Addressed to Private Sidney Anselm from A. J. Dodd." Then, "That's where he is." Lemuel said nothing but stood with his hand on Major's reins. "What's today?"

"Well, I think it's the end of January anyway," said Lemuel.

"Yes."

"Well, read it."

John turned back to the letter. This was him. This was his very handwriting.

Well Sid I got $225 for that nigger gal from the old man in Marshall and right south of here is Mexico and if I get a few more dollars I might go.

No, he won't, thought John. *If he's in San Antonio he is going to stay there some time, it's a big town, there are crowds, he can blend in.*

I spent $105 on horses to get here because I traveled pretty fast and wore them out and so there went most of it. You had better come here to San Antonio there's not much reading to be done as nobody has many books and I know you always liked books but there's plenty of other things and a river to dispose of your mistakes in ha ha I am well set up here you will never guess the goodlooking ladies that are after me come help me fight them off I don't think I'll ever go back to Ste. Genevieve or St. Louis too many saints for my taste, I remain yours ever Dodd

Life seemed to come back to John. He wanted just to savor this moment. Everything that had seemed dark flew away in the chill air like buzzards rising up off a carcass when you passed by, everything grimy and terrible flying away in a heavy clatter, beating upward.

John said, "Well, then, are you coming with me?"

"What are you going to do?"

"I'm going to kill him." There was a long silence. "No, you had better not. Come as far as Houston and I will get you a horse and supplies. I owe you a great deal for this."

Lemuel slowly shook his head. "We're even, sir." He lifted a hand. "God knows we're even."

"Nevertheless. Let's move; that soldier is going to see that his letter is missing before long." Then a sudden, alarming thought struck him. "Did you steal anything else?"

"No, *sir*! That was an honest theft."

John laughed. "All right."

"So do you think God's going to strike me dead?"

John saw that the boy was serious. "I haven't heard from Him lately. But if a lightning storm came up, if I were you I would get under a roof." And his heart perceptibly lightened. The darkness had not gone, nor would it ever, but life was not so heavy now. The sun was brighter.

As they went on Lemuel told John his plans: that he was going to Galveston to ask for employment as a nurse in the hospital. It was work that he'd always liked, and he wanted to work with the Sisters of Charity there because then he wouldn't be tempted by people's possessions lying around loose, mainly because the sisters didn't have any, isn't that right? Vows of poverty and everything, and if you were steady and honest then you could work your way up to doctor. He'd always wanted to be a doctor. And with his deft hands he could learn to sew people up and give enemas painlessly. He writhed his fingers in the air as if to demonstrate his gentle touch with the enema tube.

"Very good," said John absentmindedly.

He folded the letter tightly and shoved it into one of the pockets of his cartridge belt. The man was within reach. The ignorant, shabby killer, the man who thought other people's lives were his to take.

Their progress toward Houston was slow with the boy on foot. John often got down and walked with him to spare Major his weight, for they had had a long hard journey from Colbert's Station, even with the rest in Marshall. Sometimes John felt the faint remains of the fever and at other times almost like his old prewar self. He was going to need all his strength to meet the coming years, and so he hoped the bad moments would fade away eventually. Lemuel chattered on by the hour as they walked and took turns riding, asking John's opinion on all his plans for the future. John understood that the boy regarded him with great deference; after all, he had seen John get up and walk away from a serious head wound, and John had then rescued him from a mob bent on murder in Nacogdoches. He probably saw John Chenneville as invincible.

If only, thought John.

At the edge of the town of Houston they came upon sawmills that had begun to eat their way into the stands of massive pines with the villainous, aggressive noises of circle saws to reduce them to planks, siding, and railroad ties. The air was filled with drifting sawdust that caught the long bars of sunlight. A drover stood by a pen of horses to lean on the rails, smoking a pipe, and called out to them, gesturing toward his horses for sale.

John walked among the horses and waved a hand at their eyes to check for blindness or dim vision and ran his hands down their legs. At length he bought a solid brown gelding for Lemuel and the equipment he needed. Then farther on their way they came to a little supplies store made of sidings and pine shingles. There John found Lemuel a decent pair of trousers, a shirt, coat, and boots. He also bought a bone-handled knife and an enamel cup that held two quarts so that Lemuel could either drink from it or cook in it.

Lemuel sat stiffly on his own horse, in his new clothes, with one hand raised in farewell.

"Will I see you again, sir?"

"Probably not," said John. "You could look me up in Huntsville and send me a pie. I prefer peach."

"What's in Huntsville?"

"State prison. For murder."

"Don't do it, Mr. Chenneville," said Lemuel in a thin voice. "Just don't. Let him answer to God."

"I want you to take Dixie, would you? Take care of her."

John dismounted and sat on his heels, holding out his hands to the redbone. She came and put a paw on his knee and looked anxiously into his eyes. He stroked back her ears and then held her head in both hands. The boy couldn't find words for a moment, and his distress showed on his face with its cuts and bruises and the lonely droop of his blackened eye. Then he finally managed, "I will."

John stood and remounted Major.

"And so then, goodbye." And John rode away to the west.

IT WAS A long stretch to San Antonio. With the rains it was going to be a journey of two weeks or so. He cut west on the old Galveston-to-San Antonio Road. It was a road that came out slowly from the eastern piney woods and decanted itself westward. On this road he caught up with and passed a freight convoy drawn by oxen and all the people said good day to him as he passed and asked him where he was bound and he said only, "To the west." When he came by the lead wagon the man tried to press some San Antonio mail on him, as he was moving faster than the freight, but John refused. He had other things to do, he said.

The lead teamster leaned out of his high seat behind the oxen and held out something to him. It was an orange. "Here you go," he said. "Godspeed."

And they watched him ride on in his faded Union greatcoat and dusty boots, a large man on a big horse, and everything about him seemed worn to the very warp and weft of all of his life's fabric.

The pines fell away into isolated clumps, and then the grass took over the world. John rode easily, but still the incessant movement took its toll. One of these days his knees were going to give out, but not now. Not just yet. His thoughts and his soul were weightless now that he knew the man would come to justice and that it was worth time in prison. Everything has a price. He tied the reins together and dropped them on Major's neck, peeled the orange, and ate it slowly, segment by segment.

He didn't much care about what would happen afterward. But his thoughts went back to Victoria because she was good to think about—

her radiant and fragile skin and that bright hair and her quick mind, all held as warranty against the darkness that had come upon him in the last while. Since that fever in Marshall, since he had said goodbye to her. He thought of the San Bois Mountains. He knew the chances of seeing them again were small.

Big clouds with incandescent edges stood up in the northwest. They seemed solid as marble, and they were uncommonly beautiful. They bore down on him and their insides crackled with unseen lightning in all their hallways and their enormous interior ballrooms, where dissolving specters led the dance and then poured away in long, draining columns.

At San Felipe he bought supplies and crossed the Brazos on a shaky little ferry and a man there told him he would have the wind in his face all the way to San Antonio and that there seemed to be no end of rain this year.

He was held up three days at Columbus because the ferry cable had broken, and so he watched from under a verandah roof at Beason's Landing while shivering men fought with the soaked hemp rope over the Colorado. All the surface of that widening river was torn with raindrops as big as field peas. He listened to the talk of others also waiting. They spoke of little things, things that mattered. The death of a baby from fever, that Jameson's mare had come home herself after being stolen, that a man had come who read aloud from newspapers gathered from the entire world over, including stories of polar explorers and sinking ships in the Atlantic Ocean, that there was coffee and sugar for sale in San Felipe.

He asked about a man of Dodd's appearance, but people were busy with the cable and cold and half-drowned and were not inclined to reflect back over two weeks or more for every lone traveler who had crossed the Colorado.

After Columbus he saw droves of wild horses that were not afraid of a lone rider, whose manes ran in the grassy yellow wind like lost and ragged banners. Each town was now an isolated island in the winter plains, as that place called the West began to take over the world, a world beyond cities that held to its own doings, its own grass and wild horses and kept its own people to itself in an indifferent secrecy.

HE KEPT HIS nighttime campfire well away from the San Antonio Road, built it in some slight hollow, and it lit up his studious face as he watched it burn like an alphabet of light where a man could read the future and know what lay ahead. At evening now Orion the Hunter was far to the west, and so all the great winter stars had begun to leave the sky for some other journey. He wished he could join them. He leaned back and sent up a spout of tobacco smoke into the darkening sky, his restitched boots close to the fire.

At Gonzales he came in on St. Louis Street. Somebody had hung a flag out of the county courthouse that said Come and Take It, but he didn't know what that signified. Trouble of some kind, probably.

There on the broad town square he found Brighton's Livery and put up Major for a rest and a day of good feed. The rain came, and he sat on his saddlebags and watched it drive through the streets beyond the open fairway door.

The liveryman asked, "Sir, was you wanting a hotel room? Also there's a boardinghouse, cheap."

John didn't want to sign his name to any registry or have to present his discharge papers to anyone. He wanted to not be present to the world of people, of Texas or this grassy rolling geology of plains. He said no, he was fine where he was, he would just wait out the rain. It came down in curtains from the roof, and the horses inside lifted their heads to greet the big plow horse and all of them watched it pour. John wadded up the brown paper from the bacon and then fell back onto his baggage and slept with his greatcoat as a cover and his hands knotted together under his chin for warmth.

He woke up in the middle of the night. All was freshened and wet outside. There was a half-moon. It was on the wane. He was within sixty miles of San Antonio, a bit less than three days' travel. He struck a match and found a lantern and lit it. He spit on the glowing head of the match to make sure it was out. By the lantern's light he went over his map and then carefully cleaned his old Army Remington and then the Spencer and reloaded them both. They felt good in his hand, weighty and judicial. He would not try to get away afterward. He would not be a fugitive.

He blew out the lantern, watched till the wick stopped glowing before he replaced it on its nail. He sat back on the piled stooks of grass hay and tracked the moon's shadows that slid across Gonzales's town square. When he saw candles being lit in windows he re-saddled and made sure Major had had all he wanted to drink and then went on west.

He came through Seguin and stayed the night in the liveryman's extra room. He cleaned up and shaved. The next day he crossed Martinez Creek and Woman Hollering Creek and then was among the traffic heading for San Antonio with produce and small herds of cattle and sheep, donkeys pulling the big-wheeled carretas loaded with early melons. He bought enough to make a breakfast and kept going. He carved the seeds out of the center of a half melon and ate it leaning over to the side, dribbling melon seeds and juice. Dodd might be in a hotel, or he might have managed to find a welcome with the army, wherever they were bivouacked. He would have to find out. It might take a few days of asking and searching.

As he approached the city he fell in with local traffic. The other travelers glanced at him with his light eyes beneath the hat brim and his size and the Spencer down his back and then away again.

By evening he had come to the crossing of Salado Creek. This was a sparkling clear stream that circled San Antonio on the eastern side. It was about seven o'clock and still light. He heard the distant church bells of the old Spanish city ringing out the hour. There was heavy timber all around in this creek bottom, great thick trees with limbs that bent down to the earth and up again. He thought they might be live oaks. He was calmed by the running sound of the Salado. Somebody was building a house up on a hillside among the live oaks, and he heard people talking and saw a candle in a window.

Next to the road ahead of him he saw a campfire and pulled up. He watched for shadows coming out of the timber. Then by the red fire-light he saw a man rise up and take a rifle in hand by the barrel, toss it up and into the crook of his elbow. John pulled the revolver out of its pommel holster and laid it across his lap. He did not want to ride on and turn his back to this person. The thought of getting killed before he could find and kill Dodd was unbearable.

The man stepped out into the road with the barrel of his rifle point-ing down and one hand raised. He called out, "Chenneville?"

John saw the man's hat and his shape, his manner of movement. He said, "Yes. Hello, Giddens." He raised the revolver barrel.

"I've been waiting here three days. I figured you'd come in this way." Marshal Giddens bent and laid the rifle down in the dust of the road. He straightened and held out both hands to the side and the firelight lit up his left side, his frayed coat, and his empty hands. He said, "You're looking for Dodd."

"That's right. You're looking for him too. I want you to get out of my way." John didn't care that Giddens had laid down his rifle, was standing with both hands out and harmless. He cocked the revolver and brought up a load under the hammer. *Click. Click.*

"He's dead."

John sat without speaking for a long space. In this silence the night birds began their calling. The fire crackled.

Finally he said, "You'd better tell me more."

"You don't believe me," said Giddens.

"I'm waiting."

"He was killed in a bar fight a week ago. He was stabbed to death by a fiddler. I tell you the absolute truth, the fiddler killed him with his fiddlestick."

John was perfectly silent, and Giddens just stood and waited. After what seemed like a long time of stunned wordlessness John said, "*Mon Chriss.* No."

"It happened."

John put his elbow on his saddle horn and his face in one hand, covering his eyes. At length he slid his hand down his face and stared at the lawman. The look on his face was fixed and cold. "Say that again."

"I'm telling you, he's dead. He was killed in the Plaza House saloon by a fiddler."

John said in a low voice, "No. No. Only God knows how I wanted to kill that man."

"I understand."

"I don't think you can."

"Well. I don't know."

"I want to see his body."

"You'll have to dig him up."

They stood in the road facing each other, John on his big, tired horse and Giddens on foot. The world had changed completely, in a heartbeat. John's lips parted as if to speak, but he didn't; he felt rage, a kind of cheated fury. It swept over him in a cascade of anger. If he had not been held up in Columbus, if he had not come down with a fever, he would have had his heart's desire: the face of that man at the end of his gun barrel.

In an unbelieving tone he said, "With a *fiddle bow*?"

"Yes."

"How can you kill a man with a fiddle bow?"

Giddens nodded and reached down for a stick; it was cedar. He broke it with a slight twist, and the stick separated with one very sharp end. He held it up. "A fiddle bow is rosewood. Pretty hard. He hit him with it, and it broke. That's how. He stuck the sharpened end right into his heart."

John sat without saying anything.

"He went by the name of Pruitt when he got to San Antonio. He could play a banjo, more or less, did you know that?"

"No, I didn't."

"He was here a while and was nothing but trouble from the day he arrived. This is what they told me. I asked for a description of Pruitt, and the coroner described the specks on his neck from the gunpowder accident—general description checks out. I telegraphed here and there and traced him. I talked with a man named Garoute, outside of Marshall. I arrested him. Garoute. I put him in a cell and it was not a mild or considerate sort of conversation. He said Dodd left Marshall about the first of January."

John said, "I got there a week behind him."

"Yes. There was a young boy killed on the second or third just south of Tenaha. I got a description of him from one of the Tenaha men. I figured he was coming down the old Camino Real to San Antonio, and sure enough, he bought a horse of Micah Preciado in San Felipe and came on to here."

"I tried to get information out of Garoute as well."

"I know. He said that. But you're not a US Marshal. Uncock that thing."

John pulled slowly on the trigger, and with the heel of his hand he carefully lowered the hammer. "What took you so long, Giddens? What took you so Goddamned long?"

"I was also hunting for you." Giddens bent down to pick up his rifle. "You're a determined sort, Chenneville. But the country's in chaos, I mean Texas is, and it's easy for people to disappear, be who they are not, cover their tracks." He tipped his head toward his camp. "Tie up. Come to the fire."

They sat across from one another, a private inquiry of two. It was full dark now, and the only thing that had occupied John's mind for the last year and a half had evaporated. The fire was well made with a big section of live oak for a backlog. Sparks streamed upward and all the bare white bodies and limbs of the sycamores were lit red on their undersides, and at a little distance they could hear the running of Salado Creek. The bells of San Antonio rang out eight. They heard somebody pass by on the road, pause, and then hurry on.

John sat on his upturned saddle. Major and Giddens's mare had become companionable. Their uncurried sides shone in the firelight with sweat marks where the saddle skirts and cinches had been. He was hungry. He was free. He was drained.

Giddens tossed the stick up and caught it, tossed it up again.

John said, "I can't leave this unfinished. I don't know if it was Dodd."

"I understand that," said Giddens. "He was supposed to be from Illinois, but he wasn't. He crossed the river from Arkansas and joined up with an Illinois regiment in Cairo is all. He was from Arkansas. Couldn't you tell from his talk?" Giddens watched John's face.

"I never met him. I never heard him speak." John looked down at his boots and then up again. "I was looking forward to hearing him beg for his life. I thought about it a lot." Giddens was silent. "I could feel myself jamming the muzzle between his eyes and firing."

Giddens considered this. "I have had those thoughts myself," he said. He moved the glowing, square coals with a stick. "We have all fallen short." And after a moment he reached into his small vest pocket and held something out to John. "I want to give this to you. This was in his effects."

He held out a glittering object, and John reached for it. It was a daguerreotype in a gilt frame. He turned it to the light of the fire. It was marked on the back with Easterly's stamp, and it was himself, John Chenneville, in his Union lieutenant's uniform, with a face of suppressed laughter in the rich gold and sepia tones of times gone, of an afternoon when his little sister, Lalie, had sat him down in an ornate chair with velvet cushions, both of them on the edge of uncontrollable laughter.

When she was so alive. Before she married, before, before. Before he had been hit with the anchor chain, before the light had faded from his family and his life. Dodd had to have stolen it from the house after he murdered them, before he set the house on fire. John looked down at his own face washed in sepia and gold.

He didn't know what to say. There wasn't anything to say. He wasn't going to go to prison after all. The future came back to him, like it or not. He lifted his head.

"You're good," he said to Giddens. "You're a good lawman."

Giddens bent his head in a modest, acknowledging bow. "Thank you. There's the law and then there's justice," he said. "Sometimes the two overlap."

"What about Robertson?"

"It's moot, at this point. But you have *The Woman in White*?"

"I have carried that damned boring book across half of Texas, because it had his handwriting in it. And you have the word of Miss Reavis, that it was him sending on the night of the twelfth, after I left."

Giddens gave a short nod. "That's enough for me," he said. "That's enough for me."

March 12, 1867
Indian Territory

He paused at the edge of the tumbling, white-stoned Kiamichi River and searched the mountains to the north. First there were the Winding Stair Hills, and then he would come to the San Bois. The air was very fresh and throughout the forest the dogwood was blooming on its slender trunks, the dark understory spangled everywhere, with white blossoms as big as your hand. They were wild and native trees, and yet they were as extravagantly showy as if they were from a private garden. Here was solace for a time.

He put his hands on either side of Major's neck to warm them, to make a gesture of affection. "There's good grass up there by now, *mon homme*," he said. "In that clearing where I first saw you running after those mustangs. It's not that far."

Right now he had nothing to offer anybody. He might later. Overhead the telegraph wires whistled in the mild spring wind like flutes, and he wondered if she was speaking on them with her small boyish hand, crackling with sparks. He would find a station somewhere and send her a message to ask if she would wait for him. If she would be patient. He knew she would; his confidence in her was deep, but his losses were heavy and he needed to unburden somehow, he was not quite sure how. So he went on toward the old Choctaw house that he knew far up in the San Bois and thought no further than the day ahead and then the day after that.

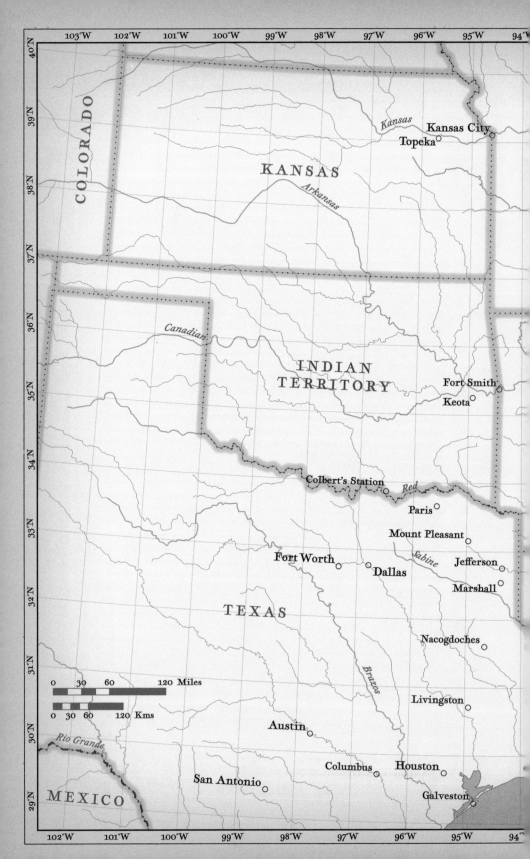